Tree Rings

Tree Rings

RICHARD MEIBERS

MARTIN AND LAWRENCE PRESS
GROTON, MASSACHUSETTS
2005

Tree Rings

Published by:
Martin and Lawrence Press
37 Nod Road
P.O.Box 682
Groton, MA 01450

ISBN 13: 978 0-9773898-3-4

Tree Rings
by Richard Meibers 1st edition

Cover design by Gwen Snider

May, 2007

To Lou

Acknowledgements

I would like to thank so many people for helping me with this story: David Brody, Kim Scott, Katherine Liebowitz, Gena Corea, Jeremy Townsend, Dwight Harshbarger, Ann Levison, Taeve Neese, Alice Rennie, Lynne Lawrence, and Paul Eisenberg. For help publishing, I would like to thank Sally Reed and Jenni Alden.

Chapter 1

FATHER AND SON, AND HOLY SPIRIT.

What does it profit a man if he gains the whole world but still hears the voice of his ex-wife carping inside his head, telling him what he should be doing? Scheutz came awake in the darkness with that question posing itself—a life of its own. Pointless to bother tracing the origin of thoughts like that. But, still. No danger of him gaining the whole world, or even a tiny part of it. But his ex-wife, Gerry, did carry on in his head, cajoling, suggesting, mentioning, in that ever so slightly mocking way she had always had.

Did the question wake him, or was it the small noise downstairs in the kitchen? Gerry's voice could be so vivid, he sometimes expected her to be actually there in the house again. He listened. His brain came awake. Footsteps moved up the stairs. It couldn't be her; the step was too heavy.

"Marty, is that you?" he asked as steps moved past his bedroom door.

"Yeah."

"Time is it?"

"Two, maybe." The bedroom door opened and his son's silhouette came into view, backlit by a dim glow coming from Marty's room across the hall. "Hey, Big Daddy. What're you doing awake?" Big Daddy. Marty still called him that even though, at six-three, the boy had him dwarfed by two inches, with probably another inch to go by the time he hit age twenty, if his older brother's last growth spurt was any indication.

"I don't know what woke me. It wasn't your car this time. Thanks for that." Marty's restored '67 Belvedere had mufflers that were recognizable a mile away in this quiet countryside. Scheutz had asked him so many times to stop roaring up their long dirt driveway at two or three o'clock in the morning, slamming on the brakes just inches away from smashing the barn door. Kids.

"Come on in." Scheutz rolled over onto his back. "Sit and talk to me. I don't get to see you much lately."

Marty left the door open and slid his silhouette, thinner than Scheutz's even though it was taller, to sit heavily on the edge of Scheutz's bed. The smell of beer and cigarettes on Marty's clothes signified yet another party in the long string of parties occurring in these last two weeks between the senior prom and graduation. Maybe too much beer was being consumed. But Marty didn't seem at all tipsy. That wasn't the kid's style. Nor were the cigarettes. Unlike most of the other kids he hung out with. According to him, both he and his girlfriend Regina might have two beers, three tops, at any given party. This did not stop him, according to what some of his friends had told Scheutz, from being the life and core of any party he went to, entertaining a crowd, as he was want to do, with his teenage-witty, always vaguely smart-assed, running monologue on just about anything or anybody that might cross his purview.

"So, tomorrow's the big day, huh?" Scheutz said, needing to say something to hold his son there, to hold off the shift to his own room, the one more small move helping to make up the large move coming all too soon when Marty walked out of his life.

"You mean today's the big day," Marty said. A long pause as Marty leaned with his elbows on his knees. "Yeah…red letter day in the life of Martin Scheutz." He was, he had told Scheutz, so happy to be out of school. In the fall he planned to head off to an art school in New York. For now, though, he sat patiently doing his filial duty, waiting to see what his father wanted.

"Big day for me, too," Scheutz said. June 16th, 1979. Marty's graduation from high school. Scheutz's own graduation day as well. His older son Dan had graduated four years ago, and now with Marty's official ascendance into adulthood, Scheutz's child-raising days were over. He had often looked forward to the day when he could start, maybe, doing what he wanted to without having to think first of what his duty was to the kids. But with the day finally looming, it seemed a little daunting. His life from here on, with his beautiful child anxious to get out the door, looked like one long empty tunnel.

"How's it a big day for you?" Marty said, turning his head without lifting it.

"Well…" Scheutz had never actually formulated the thought into words. It wasn't like he'd see his son any less. This whole last year in high school, Marty spent either in school, working at his after school job, or out with his friends. Or else heading down to New York on weekends to visit his mother. Scheutz missed the bantering conversations he and Marty had carried on since the kid was four years old. Marty's first complaint that Scheutz could remember had something to do with the fact that Scheutz had no right to tell him to clean up his room. The banter progressed from there, in a convoluted arc they called a learning curve as the boy's mental capacity increased. "Well… let's see," Scheutz said. "It's a big day because…maybe after today I'll be able to get some sleep."

"Hey, don't put that on me." Marty snorted. "You go to bed at eight o'clock, what do you expect? Isn't three o'clock when you usually wake up, anyhow?" Marty sat up and leaned back against the one knee Scheutz had cocked in the air. "You know, you should get yourself a normal girlfriend, go out and party once in a while like a normal person. You wouldn't have any trouble getting to sleep this time of night. I don't have any problems sleeping at two o'clock."

"I know. You don't seem to have much problem sleeping till two in the afternoon either. Besides, I already have a girl friend."

"I think the operative word here is 'normal', Dad." This kid, who never seemed to have a problem engaging anyone in conversation, clammed up around Nanda. Not that she had a lot to say to Marty. She didn't take to either of his sons.

His relationship with Nanda had twisted into a knot that needed to be unraveled. That knot, though, bothered him not nearly as much as the one that tied him into the push-me-pull-you with the boys' mother. That gnarled hank of need and anger had hung him in suspension for all his adult life, or at least for the entire life of his children. And today, with Marty's graduation, he could unloosen it to finally see the end of it. Raising the two boys had almost become his raison d'etre over the last ten years since she'd gone, and the ache of missing them would come, was already here. But the release of the infinitely gnarled knot that linked him to their mother could more than offset the hole in his life.

Marty leaned forward again, now with his head in his hands, a study in patience, waiting for a sign from Scheutz that would allow him to toddle off to bed.

"So, what is this, twelve parties in a row since your last day of classes?" Scheutz asked.

"No. Don't be silly. Twelve parties in a row; nobody can do that. We all took a sleep break a few days ago. Let's see… it's only four parties in a row."

"And six parties in a row before the sleep break."

"Dad, come on. You got nothing better to do than sit around counting parties?"

"Don't you all run out of things to talk about? What can you possibly find to do at that many parties?"

"Hang out. Listen to music. You know. Tell me you didn't do the same thing."

"I was in the army at your age."

"Yeah, so? And what did you do when you weren't crawling around in mud holes?"

"Hang out. Listen to music." They both laughed. "But, what else? Come on, I'm sure you and your friends can think of a lot more things to do than we could."

"Nothing else. What do you think? Look, I'm just trying to spare you from the shock of hearing all the lurid details about, you know...about our punch and cookies. And pin-the-tail-on-the-donkey, and all those crazy colored little party hats. And kazoos. One night we even got blasted on ice cream and cake and everybody ran around in the yard waving lit sparklers."

Scheutz extricated a foot from under the sheet and jabbed Marty's upper arm. Marty, who would normally have risen to such provocation by grabbing Scheutz's toe or something similar, merely allowed his body to give with the jab and wagged his head like a tired old dog. "I gotta go to bed, Dad."

"And Regina? Where is she tonight?"

"Took her home like I always do."

"Really? Always? You mean except for the nights you sneak her in here and then out again in the morning after I go to work."

Marty lifted his head and opened his mouth in mock horror. Then smiled and patted Scheutz's leg under the sheet. "Goodnight, Daddy-O."

"Goodnight, Marty." The door closed behind him with a click. One more small step down that dark tunnel.

Gerry's voice broke in on him. *Your son—our son—from what I can tell, is a little stoned, or a little drunk. I don't know which is worse.* Her voice sounded loud and clear in his head. *It's two in the morning and he's been out driving the back roads in that damned hot rod you helped him rebuild, and which is now threatening to take his life. You know, all it takes is one slow reflex on a sharp curve and...*

Yes, Gerry. I know. I know.

Well, why don't you do something about it?

And what should I be doing? What do you want from me? You want me to install a set of chains and manacles in the basement? Keep the kids till they're forty, till they wise up like you and I like to think we've done?

Gerry's voice in his head made today a red-letter day. Maybe she would finally shut up. The kids were both grown now, so let her carp to them awhile. Raising the two boys had seemed like not too much more than an exercise in channeling their mother's voice. This voice of hers in his head all started over the boys in the first place. After she sent them back from New York to live with him. He had missed her so much when she left two years before that, but he had missed them more. And having them back with him had been more than he had ever hoped to ask for. But he had been so unsure of what to do with the kids in those early years that he tried to imagine what she might say or do in a difficult situation with them.

At first he imagined the voice answering his questions, picturing her sitting across the table from him at night, after the kids were in bed. And then one day when Dan was fourteen, she just began talking to him as if she really was there in the room with him. He no longer had to ask questions. She knew. Just as if she was there with him. Like the guardian angels the nuns talked about in grade school, watching to correct his mistakes, keeping him from doing harm to her precious children. Not on purpose, but from not knowing what he should be doing. He constant questions, like, what time should a ten-year-old be in bed on a school night? Is it okay to let a fourteen-year-old use the hydraulic wood-splitter? How in God's name do you cook for teenagers who dislike everything but pizza? Just what do you do about catching your fourteen-year-old son having sex in the attic with the fourteen-year-old girl from down the road? By this time Gerry's voice was no longer a pretense. He actually heard it. Softly at first, then louder and more persistent, until he could hear it as loud as a person's voice standing in front of him. And, by this time, he found he could not shut it off.

The tone her arguments took were not too much different from the real ones they had had when they were still together, never rancorous, always practical, more like discussions on how to get through life. Now that she was just a voice, the tone was more cajoling, and less gentle than she had been in real life. And often counter to whatever mood he was in. While they were still together, he had felt as if they were a matched pair, always in sync with each other, their opinions different only in content.

After Dan graduated from high school, four years ago, Gerry's voice began handing him opinions on things in his life that had nothing directly to do with the kids. She commented on his dealings with old man Brockton, his boss at the lumber mill. She had something to say about his logging partner, Pelletier, and about his sons' friends. She put her two cents in like a nosy neighbor, except that he couldn't just shut the door in her face. She even went so far as to give commentary on his interactions with the real Gerry, whenever the two of them talked about the kids in person.

The bedroom door opened again and Marty stuck his head back in. "By the way, I almost forgot to tell you. When I left here this afternoon I saw that lady that's a friend of your girl friend. She was parked out on the road near our driveway."

"Who? Goncharov?"

"Is that her name?"

"Really? I wonder what she wants."

"I hope we don't have to go that shit again." Nanda and her friend had had a huge, screaming fight in the driveway of Scheutz's house a few months back.

"Don't worry about it. We won't."

"I thought you told me that woman moved away."

"She did."

"Oh, well. 'Night, Daddy-O. See you in the morning."

"Morning? When was the last time you got up before noon?"

"So I'll see you in the evening."

Marty's door closed, smothering the glow of light and putting the house back into pitch darkness. Scheutz lay on his back and pulled the sheet and light blanket up to his chin, waiting for more of Gerry's comments. Nothing. These days, she mostly talked either when he was at work in the woods, or when he was driving his pick-up truck. Three months earlier he and Pelletier had done a logging job up on the border not far from the Canadian town of Notre Dame des Bois. Our Lady of the Woods. That was how he had come to think of Gerry's voice. Also Notre Dame des Camions. In the woods with his saw running, and in the truck alone, he had fallen into the habit of talking aloud to the voice.

On the Christmas Eve just past, he had picked Gerry up at the Amtrak station in Bellows Falls and driven home to Acworth so she could spend a few days with the boys. They had only just crossed the river when the voice started in about being careful on the icy roads. The voice said, *Put the truck into four-wheel drive.*

"No, it's okay," he said aloud.

"What?" Gerry said—the real Gerry—sitting in the truck's cab, scrunching herself down inside her city-stylish leather coat while the truck's heater fought a losing battle against the cold.

"Oh, nothing. Nothing," Scheutz said to her. "Just thinking out loud."

You better watch yourself. People might start thinking you're nuts.

Well, if I am nuts, it's your voice that is driving me there.

That's not a drive. That's a short putt.

He and the voice carried on this way almost through the town of Alstead. Just at the Acworth town line, Gerry's voice said, *Don't you think after all these years, you ought to tell your ex-wife you've been carrying on a conversation with her that she never knew about?*

What do you mean, she? I thought she was you.

She is. I mean, I am.

So, if she is you, she'd know about these conversations, right?

Well, we are the same, but we're not, if you know what I mean.

What do you mean, like the Holy Trinity they have in the Catholic church?

Yeah, sort of. I'm like the Holy Spirit.

You think you're like the Holy Spirit? You must have an ego the size of Spain.

Yeah, big enough for both of us. So, go ahead, tell her about the conversations we have.

And what good would that do?

On the one hand, she might be flattered that you think so much of her opinion.

And on the other, she might think I really am nuts. Is that what you're saying?

She probably already knows she's been talking to you all these years. Why else would she trust you to raise her children? I mean, considering what a dope you are.

He glanced sideways at Gerry sitting across the cab seat from him shivering and staring out the windshield as if she would allow herself only so much endurance and no more. Actually, she might be flattered if he told her about her voice in his head. Or she might be impressed by how he had solved the problem all these years of not really ever being sure how to raise their children. One of the strands of the tightly woven knot tying the two of them together was his never-fulfilled need for her approval. "You know," he said. "For the last twenty minutes, I've been carrying on a conversation with you in my head, and here you are, sitting right on the other side of the truck." He waited, glancing back and forth between her and the winding road in his headlights.

She pulled her chin out of her wool turtle neck sweater and, without looking at him, said, "Well speak up, boy. Don't be shy."

What was it that put him off? Was it her calling him 'boy'? She had often called him that over the years. He had learned to tell her emotional state by what she called him. If she was angry about something, she called him 'boy'. Like "Let me tell you something, boy." If she was being cool and jazzy she called him 'man'. "Hey, man, what's going on." Friendly, it was always 'Clem'. Distressed, it was 'Clement'. Lovey and sexy, she picked up Dan's expression of 'Big Daddy'. So what was she pissed off about now? The cold? Being alone in the truck with him? Having to leave the city in the first place? He didn't mind her being angry, but what really put him off was that off-handed, almost dismissive tone that she used with him ever since they'd split up.

And why was he thinking about this lying awake at two o'clock in the morning. Anxiety, as always at this time of night, floated free, attaching itself to anything handy.

Chapter 2

TANTRA

He had to be up at four o'clock to go to work, and he was damned if he'd get up now. He tried doing a yoga exercise that Nanda had taught him, but found himself anxiously trying to force himself to relax. Why did he bother; it never worked. He'd not been sleeping well for the past few months. This graduation day had floated before him like the two-faced Janus, smiling serenely with the promise of release on one side and frowning forlornly on the empty world beyond on the other.

Until tonight, he had always been able to push the knowledge of this day's advent out of his mind. But now it was upon him. An old guy, a lumber handler at the mill, who had been in prison for almost fifteen years, saw the date of his release coming up, he had told Scheutz, and it both elated him and filled him with horror. The stricture and violence of prison was a kindergarten compared to the unseen snake pits awaiting him on the outside.

A headlight played across the ceiling as a car hurried up the long driveway. That would be Nanda's Volvo with its one headlight—the other one mushed into a crinkled fender. It stopped behind Marty's car, then backed up and pulled to the left off the driveway and around to the back of the barn. Well, no chance of any more sleep tonight.

Now be nice. Gerry chiding again. *Maybe it's an emergency. Maybe she needs your help with something.*

Maybe she's horny.

You know, if I was a real person, I'd slap you.

If you were a real person, you could find someone else to haunt.

He clicked on the small bed lamp. Outside, from behind the barn, the muffled sound of a car door slamming. A few minutes later, the door to the mud room off the kitchen slammed. Then the kitchen door slammed. Nanda's high heels clonked across the floor boards and up the back stairs from the kitchen. He lay with his hands behind his head. Nanda seldom came at night. Usually, it was in the late afternoon after work. Maybe something was wrong. Maybe he should get up and get dressed.

If she does need help with something, it might be better to have your pants on.

For close to four years now, he and Nanda had carried on an almost purely sexual affair. Two, three times a week was all he needed, which may not have been so with her. Nanda's appetite seemed to increase the longer he knew her. And not just for him. Her girl friend, Goncharov, or Goncharova as she should have been called if she had not insisted on masculinizing—was that a word?—her name, was only the latest in what seemed like a steady but ever-churning stream of lesbian lovers.

He'd met Nanda at the Hitchcock Health Center in Hanover. She taught a course at Dartmouth in Comparative Religion and moonlighted at the local Hanover health center, teaching yoga in the evening. She wasn't really Indian as her name would imply. Years before Scheutz met her, she had changed her name from something more prosaic, like Rita Shapiro, or...no, he couldn't remember what she'd told him. The name Nanda had apparently been that of the Buddha Gautama's half sister, now revered by some neo-buddhists as the true prophet.

Though she had helped him when it seemed that nothing could, her sword had a double edge. She had taught him the yoga techniques he still used to dampen the explosive sensations in his chest, the rage that felt like hot lava about to erupt. Before Nanda, his image of himself—embellished by Gerry's voice—had been that of a stone gargoyle on the corner eave of some cathedral, spewing vituperation like rain-water. Since the rage did not focus on anything, it needed to be dissipated rather than spewed, she said, like excess heat from a truck engine, heat that could not be used for anything, and that would destroy the engine if let alone.

But with all that help, she showed another side. She helped her students open their chakras and then pounced on them to satiate the intense appetite of her own.

Just after Dan graduated from high school, Gerry's voice had intensified to the point where he feared he had become crazy. Hearing the voice was crazy in itself, but it had reached a point where it seemed to take over his entire mind. A counselor at the health center had recommended he sign up for yoga classes to try to ease his torment. It was Nanda who made him see that the voice was a by-product of his rage.

It took a while in the beginning for him to catch on. Not until the third weekly yoga class did he have any inkling what Nanda was teaching. When he finally talked with her about it, they both realized he'd signed up for the wrong class. This one was kundalini yoga, focusing, as Nanda pointed out, on releasing the female energy from the base of the spine. The only reason Scheutz had stuck out as many classes as he did was that he actually didn't mind being in a room full of women in leotards. He didn't meet a lot of women in the logging business, and the companionship of Gerry's voice alone left something to be desired. The vision of Nanda herself distracted him from listening to what she had to say in class. She was thin like Gerry, with long muscles, but not as tall. Her mass of black curls framed a somewhat angular face, and her dark eyes widened whenever she stressed a point.

His conversation with Nanda about what he was doing in her class brought from her a fit of laughter that sounded like she'd been bottling it up since the first night. She had wondered, she said, what this ham-handed hulk was doing in such a setting. To cover his embarrassment, he laughed along with her, which, she mentioned later, she found utterly charming. She invited him to brunch the next Sunday at her farm in Claremont. Dan and Marty were in New York visiting with their mother for a few weeks during summer vacation, and so he drove to Claremont.

He'd never been to a brunch, and had no idea what to expect when he got there. He wore clean chinos and a light blue Mexican guayabera packed away in the attic from twenty years before that still fit him but was tight in the chest and shoulders. There must have been other guests because four vehicles were parked in the farmyard. No one answered his knock on the front screen door, so he followed the sounds of music coming from behind the barn. There he discovered Nanda and, as he learned later, her live-in lesbian lover plus two other lesbian couples, all skinny-dipping in a pond that reflected the summer sky. Nanda stood before him, dripping and beautifully nude, explaining the situation to him and apologizing for having forgotten she had invited him. Then he had to put up with Gerry laughing inside his head.

In the darkness of his bedroom, he could just barely make out Nanda's form as she opened the door and walked straight to him. "Hold me," she said into his neck.

He put his arms around her. "What's wrong?" Her body shook inside her mini-skirted, flower-print, summer dress. There had been a chill in the air outside. Her body smelled of sweat and fresh air, with a taint of fear. "What's the matter?"

"Goncharov," she said in the same tone someone might say 'Armageddon'. "Turn off the light so she doesn't stop here again." Goncharov, the latest lover, was a frightening bruiser of a woman, a professional mud wrestler. For almost a year, Scheutz had been listening to the serialized drama of these two women as their battle of intimacy waxed and waned. He had hinted once last fall that it seemed to him the tears and screaming always seemed to coincide with their shared menstrual cycle. Nanda, not taking well to his murmured suggestion, turned on him then, and their argument ended up with her not talking to him until the next time the mad Russian erupted. The last time this happened, in March, Nanda came to Scheutz's house in the afternoon, followed by Goncharov who stood outside under the window wailing about how she was going to do herself harm if Nanda didn't love her. Nanda opened the window and yelled down that the woman was crunching her soul. The next day, after assuring himself that Marty would be okay by himself for a few weeks, Scheutz volunteered to go with Pelletier up to the Canadian border to help out with cutting an enormous amount of lumber the mill was buying from some Quebecois logging company.

"I thought Goncharov moved away," Scheutz said, holding Nanda's quivering body. "You know, I don't think I can hold up under much more of the sturm und drang between you two."

What do you mean, hold up under it? Are you that frail?

"I broke it off with her." Nanda's said, her voice soft in his ear. "She said she was moving down to Massachusetts. To Northhampton. I don't know if she did or not; this is the first time I've seen her in over a month."

"So what's this all about? It's two o'clock in the morning."

"She's back. She's stalking me. I'm scared. I can't go home. She showed up at the health center this evening, crying and carrying on." Nanda pushed herself into Scheutz's chest.

This is not what he wanted to be doing this time of night. Or any time, for that matter. Arguments between couples seemed like such a private thing. Listening to lovers, or ex-lovers, scream at each other was a little like watching people go to the bathroom.

Nanda pitied the big woman who was nowhere near as intelligent as herself. Tres déclassé. Or was he merely projecting onto them because that had been how he perceived Gerry's feeling about him, a prole lost among the bourgeoisie. Though he'd never really liked Goncharov, at this moment he could feel an empathy for her, and getting a little pissed off at Nanda, hanging onto him for comfort and safety from the wounded Russian bear.

Come on, Clem, give the lady a break. How do you know what went on between them. Nanda just might have a legitimate gripe against the Russian.

You mean like she's had with the other two long-term lovers she's had since I've known her?

Yes. Just because you still sulk around like the jilted lover after all these years. She's your friend. Give her some solace.

But I don't even know what to say to her.

Bullshit. You know what to say. Tell her you know how hard it is for her, even if you don't know.

"I know how hard it is for you," he said to Nanda.

"Oh, it was awful. I felt so sorry for her," Nanda said into his chest hairs. "She really is in pain. But I can't take it anymore. I love her, but she's cuckoo bunnies. What do I do? I asked one of the other yoga teachers if I could follow her home. She lives in Lebanon. Goncharov called up there looking for me. Aaagh. I had to get out of there, so I came down here."

Scheutz had to smile. These little speed-raps of Nanda's when she got anxious reminded him of some cartoon character, but he could never remember who. Maybe Olive Oyl. He could feel himself getting an erection.

Aren't you the compassionate one. The woman's pouring her heart out and all you can think about is getting laid.

Oh, yeah? Well, just wait.

"Mmm. That's nice," Nanda placed her hand on his cock and murmured into his neck. "The quivering damsel in distress thing turns you on, huh?" She moved away from him and he heard her shoes drop one by one in the darkness.

On the bed Nanda straddled him. Her clothes had dropped silently behind the shoes. She perched there quietly above as he felt himself slip slowly into a kind of tantric state, as Nanda had taught him. This is really why she had come here tonight.

Now isn't that nicer than being all pissed off.

Yes. Now mind giving me a little privacy here?

Chapter 3

Losing Time

The windows showed the grayish light that came before the sun. The bureau with his folded pile of clean clothes had taken shape, as did the subtle mound of Nanda's body beside him. She lay on her back with arms flopped to each side, the knuckles of her left hand resting against his arm. The sheet covered to her navel, her small beasts flattened, leaving only the nipples protruding up from her chest. Her face in sleep was no different from when she meditated, soft, serene.

What was he doing lying here like this? From the light it must be at least five. He'd overslept. He never did that. His body normally woke him at four, or whatever time he needed to get up. It had been doing that for as long as he could remember. He'd fallen asleep with Nanda on top of him only a short while ago. He put his hand on Nanda's stomach and leaned in to smell her hair.

He pushed himself up and out from under the sheet. Like the dawn, his mind glimmered at half light as he propelled himself slowly around the room, putting on work clothes from the folded piles—flannel shirt, brown canvas pants with bright red suspenders. Then he pointed himself down the hall. The overly large bathroom, converted from a small bedroom at the back of the house, had been his and Gerry's first project when they bought the house. It retained the flavor of a room in an old house, but with modern bathroom fixtures providing a nice contrast to the pine plank floors, horse-hair plaster on the walls, a free-standing linen closet that dated back two hundred years. How many years ago had he and Gerry plumbed this room? Dan was eight at the time. Fourteen years ago, in early spring. He looked in the mirror and spoke to Gerry. *You never want to talk about those days, do you?*

Life is in the present. Get on with it.

You're right. Today's the day. After today, that's it. I'm just going to get on with it.

And the rest of your life will be cakes and ale.

What's that mean?

Something I read somewhere. But, for right now...

For right now I better get a move on.

Downstairs, the big kitchen always reminded him of her.

But then what doesn't?

He retrieved his boots from behind the wood stove and, moving aside the book he'd been reading the night before, sat down to lace them up. This had been her favorite room, naturally. It throbbed as the heart of the house, where the kids had done their homework, where people sat and visited in the evening in chairs around the wood stove, where Scheutz relaxed for a half hour each day after work in an old Morris chair, and then often, on a chilly night, sat reading. He and Gerry had installed counters all along the two outer walls, removed the plaster from the brick chimney and discovered a warming oven built into the chimney's structure. They lightened the room by removing the two six-over-six windows and installing a row of smaller windows along the entire south wall above the counter. During the day, light poured into the room giving the feel of being on a sun porch.

He opened the door of the wood stove and squatted to look at the few embers still glowing in the back. The coals from the fire he'd made the night before to take the unseasonable chill from the house still held warmth. The wood stove extended out into the room. In winter, cranked way up, it comfortably heated one whole half of the house. After Dan had graduated from high school and left, Scheutz and Marty closed up the other half, the eastern half of the house, in winter. Six rooms were enough for them. The closed-up half of the house pretty much fell into disuse.

The dark hole inside the stove, dimly lit by the embers, mesmerized him. *There's my life in the present, Gerry. A black hole with a few lingering embers.*

Where does this self-pity come from? A new low for you, Clem.

Self-pity? Is that what he felt? Aww, poor widdle Clement Scheutz. Got no honey to call his own. All that was left was her voice, nagging, harassing him day and night. For how long? Ten years now. Most people get over it by this time, and go on, find somebody else. And what has he found? Nanda, the lesbian kook who didn't even like men, that he let treat him like a dildo. He was like the house he lived in, half empty. Even on his good days, he was only half full. Kind of like the embers burning in this stove. He still gave off a little warmth, but he certainly wasn't setting the world on fire. But whose fault was that? Victims and self-pity go together. Isn't that how you get to be a dildo?

No need to put more wood in the stove. Marty wouldn't be up till noon at the earliest, and by then the outside temperature would be warm. He straightened, closed the stove door, and picked up his book to put back on the Morris chair. It was a book Nanda had given him about the Zoroastrian religion. That was her new kick, the Avestas of ancient Persia. And he had found it interesting, the early myths of Gilgamesh and Mithra, and stories of the beginning of the world, that were later copied to make up the book of Genesis for the Bible. There was nothing new, was there, once the sun came up?

Which is what it was now doing, touching its first rays to the peak of the barn outside the windows. He picked up his spiked logging boots that sat next to the chimney and set them by the outside door. At the counter he made himself two olive loaf and cheese sandwiches and bagged them along with a handful of Fritos. Outside, at his Chevy pick-up which sat in front of the barn, he tossed the sandwiches onto the dash and the spiked boots on the passenger seat next to his work gloves.

As he descended the long drive with sun now directly in his eyes, a red fox scampered in front of the truck. At the lower edge of the south field, which he let his neighbor use for haying, the sun cut through the low-lying fog to show the ruins of an old paper mill on the river next to his property. Burnt mostly to the ground in the 1920s, one of the two-story brick walls still stood next to the old stone dam like some valiant old soldier who'd seen his share of action in the industrial revolution.

Only a few houses lined the paved road heading down the hill to where the main road ran along the river. Behind the houses stretched either second growth forest or else hay fields, still in use by the few dairy farms. The town of Acworth, with only seven hundred or so residents and no actual center, had only one place to eat, and not any other commercial establishment except a small grocery store in South Acworth across from the Congregational Church. The town did have a numbered road, Route 123A, that wound through it along the river, but never, at any time of day did the road have so much traffic that a dog could not lie asleep on the center line. Gerry had once referred to the town as a Brigadoon, a town you can't get to from wherever you are.

He'd grown to love the town in the fourteen years they'd lived there. But it was a trap. He turned east on the highway and the first tip of the sun, still reddish, shone directly into his eyes. What he loved about the town most was the same thing he still loved about working in the woods all these years, the Eden that allowed him to disconnect from the rest of the world. It really was a Brigadoon, enchanted and out of time, and the longer he'd allowed himself the complacency of its seasonal, its daily routines, the harder it had become to so much as walk down the street in a small city like Keene. This was the trap. He could live out the rest of his life in this place, listening to his ex-wife's voice in his head, moving eventually from the hard physical labor of cutting trees to something less strenuous like marking them with orange paint for the younger loggers to cut. He had already ascended, as Nanda would say, bodily into Nirvana. So now what? So he'd achieved Satori, so what does one do once he goes to heaven?

I know we've talked about this before. That's why I had to leave.

Why, because it's heavenly?

No, because you can't go to heaven without dying first. I was dying here. And so were you.

His first stop, just like every other morning, was Georgina's Kitchen out on Route 10 that skirted the town line. The dirt lot in front of Georgina's held three pick-up trucks, a white Toyota, and a brown and green state police cruiser. The diner had once been someone's private home, and the eight tables for customers filled what had been the living room and foyer of the old nineteenth-century farmhouse. Black and white photographs of various sizes, mounted without frames and fronted with clear panes of glass adorned the walls. Georgina, before opening the restaurant in her house, had been a professional photographer whose work had been seen in several national magazines, but more recently, could mostly be found in New England periodicals. Her subjects were always people, single or in pairs, ordinary people caught in the background of their everyday lives, much like the portraits of the turn-of-the-century German photographer, August Sander. Several Acworth townspeople who frequented the restaurant for breakfast and lunch did so under the gaze of their own portrait on the wall. Georgina and her daughter lived in the upper rooms of the house.

Three old, gnarled farmers in their clean bib overalls sat at their usual table where they carried on lively conversations each morning about the 'weathah', the cows, the 'bahns', God, and other local 'fahmahs'. Being retired couldn't shake their habit of getting up early. At another table, Sally Ann, a nurse who worked the night shift at the hospital up in Hanover, waved at Scheutz and smiled around a mouthful of muffin. Johnstone, the state trooper, stood at the coffee pot on the sideboard, filling a styrofoam cup. "Morning, Mister Scheutz." He nodded.

"Morning." Scheutz nodded in return. He and the trooper had treated each other with nothing but aloof courtesy since they met four years earlier on the night Dan graduated from high school. Dan had thrown a graduation party in their barn. Well after midnight, Johnstone had showed up, in response to a complaint, he'd said, to break up the party. Apparently, Dan mouthed off to him and, by the time Scheutz got out to the barn, the trooper had Dan by the back of the neck. Scheutz removed the policeman's hand, bending his fingers back, and locking Johnstone's eyes with his own. They stood that way for a few moments while the party seemed to go on unconcerned around them, Scheutz knowing he could be charged with assaulting a police officer, but also knowing he would never allow anyone to put a hand on his son in that way. Dan apologized to the trooper for wising off, Johnstone left, and the party eventually wound down to a few couples necking in the vacant horse stalls.

Scheutz filled his own Styrofoam cup, added cream, and then picked a Boston Globe off the pile at the end of the sideboard.

"Maybe I'll see you tonight at the graduation party," Johnstone said.

Scheutz slid his eyes over to meet the trooper's gaze. *Careful,* Gerry's voice warned. His hand that held the coffee cup tingled. Johnstone's face was almost a parody of friendliness, but Scheutz could sense the smirk just behind it. He wanted to slap the man, knock that silly Smoky Bear hat off his head. *You caused him to lose face, Clem, and he never forgot it.* But it was more than that. Or other than that. Johnstone's presence, and the unspoken challenge he felt whenever they met belonged to that half of Scheutz fallen into disuse since the day he'd made the promise to Gerry eighteen years ago in Mexico to not give in to it. Not that slapping a state trooper as large as himself and a few years younger would be an intelligent way of opening that door again, but the temptation on this last day of his child-care obligation felt like a boil straining to burst. "Yeah." Scheutz smiled at the trooper. "Maybe I'll buy you a beer." He turned his back and took his usual table next to the old farmers.

"I don't know how those fellahs in Israel tell each other apart," one farmer was saying. "I can't tell the difference between a Jew and an Arab."

"Well, they go to different churches," another said.

"I don't have no trouble," the third one said. "The Jews all have a mustache and the Arabs wear those little hats."

"It's the other way 'round."

"It is? You sure? Well, whichever, it don't make any sense what they're doing. Like those Irish up there in Belfast, blowing each other up just because one likes the pope and the other don't. Don't make sense."

"Oh, I don't know. You ever try having a conversation with one of those Evangelical Christians? That'll make you want to blow somebody up."

Georgina's daughter, Sharna, popped through the kitchen door with breakfast plates for the three farmers. "Yours'll be right out," she said to Scheutz as she passed his table.

A moment later, Georgina herself came out. "Sharna, Clem's is on the stove shelf. Put some butter on the toast when it comes up and get him fed." She poured a cup of coffee from the urn and sat down across from Scheutz. "Clem, how the hell are you?" she brayed cheerfully. She said the exact same thing every morning, ever since the day a few years earlier when he'd accused her of being a sour puss. She was heavyset but not very tall with gray-streaked hair, a rosacea complexion and a penetrating voice. "So what's up with you this today?" she said. "You don't look so good."

"Not enough sleep."

"Out alley-catting with your girl friend again?"

He shook his head. The question was hardly worth a response. Anyone who knew him knew he did not go out at night. Sally Ann, at her table, caught his eye and winked at him. His relationship with Nanda and Nanda's relationships with the mud wrestler,

Goncharov, and other women before her, had passed for the past few years as fodder for a continual round of jokes and gossip among Georgina's patrons. On the one hand it irked him and on the other he kind of enjoyed the attention. He winked back at Sally Ann. A group cackle emanated from the three farmers. He looked back to see Georgina smirking at him over her coffee cup.

"Gerry coming up for the graduation?" Georgina asked. She had been Gerry's friend since before they moved to Acworth years before. Her daughter was the same age as Dan. For Gerry, Georgina was the introduction she needed to whatever resources were available in the area for mothers and small children. For Georgina, Gerry sparkled as an exotic, a representative of the world outside her small town. The two women had met at an art camp workshop in Taos, New Mexico years earlier and had maintained a friendship. It was through Georgina that Gerry and Scheutz found the old farmhouse in Acworth, and through her also that Gerry had met people in the local art world. That was before Georgina's restaurant, and before Gerry's attention drifted elsewhere. Before Gerry herself began drifting off to Hanover or Brattleboro, and then Boston and New York on weekends. In the months before Gerry left for good, Scheutz and Georgina had many a Sunday morning coffee together while their respective families slept in. Whatever bond existed between them since was based on not much more than their both missing Gerry.

"Yeah, she's coming up. Wouldn't miss it. Dan's coming, too."

Georgina opened her mouth to say something but stopped as her daughter came out with Scheutz's breakfast plate of eggs, sausage, home fries and toast. When Sharna returned to the kitchen, Georgina said, "I'm sure Sharna will be glad to see him." She gave Scheutz a hard look bordering on disgust. Sharna had been one of Dan's more unchivalrous conquests in high school. As a shy, skinny freshman, her headlong pitch into the tar pit of adoration had left her a weeping mess when he ended all contact with her after a week. She stayed home from school for a month after that, and only seemed to come back to herself the next school year. These days she helped her mother run the restaurant and dated a nice boy from Keene State College.

Scheutz dug into his breakfast. Gerry's voice interrupted. *I can't believe she's still bent out of shape about her daughter's high school crush after all these year. Can't you find something to say to her to ease her off of this?* Scheutz shook his head as he speared a piece of sausage with his fork and dipped it into the runny egg yolk.

"Be nice to have your family all together again, won't it?" Georgina said.

"You going to the graduation?" he asked her

"I hadn't planned on it. Gotta get ready for the party after."

"Be nice to have someone to talk to."

"Where's your girl friend?"

"Not her cup of tea."

"Why not talk to your wife?"

"That gets complicated." Time spent with Gerry—the real Gerry, not the voice in his head—always found him floundering in a fog of surface ambiguity produced by dual underlying urges, to either hug her or strangle her. Whatever she said or did was always very clear, direct, simple, and dismissive. He, more often than not, ended such encounters disgusted with himself. He hung himself on her nuances, looking for any little opening in her demeanor that might allow him to touch her. Not physically touch, but touch her in the old way, in the way she touched him still, where a word or even an inflection could produce a momentary emotional spike, a softening. At least the voice in his head displayed a seasoning of vulnerability with all its advising and carping. They could engage in a bantering repartee that with the real Gerry would be taken, on both sides, as insult.

He folded his newspaper and finished the cup of coffee. "Got to go." He stood, leaving her with a questioning look on her face. He always paid Georgina for a week's worth of breakfasts at the end of the week, which was today, in fact. But he could pay her on Monday; he just wanted to be out of there, to get in the woods by himself.

Chapter 4

The Chainsaw Dance

Like every other workday morning, he stopped to pick up Pelletier. He turned off the highway onto the deeply rutted dirt road leading to the clearing with Pelletier's double-wide trailer. In the ten years he'd known Pelletier, the man had never held a valid driver's license. He relied on people like Scheutz to get to work, and on his girl friend, Nicole, to get to the store or wherever else he needed to go. All Scheutz knew about his background was that he was some mixture of Micmac Indian and Quebequois, and was illegal in the United States. He'd grown up on the Mastigauche reservation in Quebec and left because the Royal Canadian Mounted Police needed him to cooperate with them on some investigation, the details of which Pelletier would never divulge.

He parked in the debris-strewn clearing and tapped his horn. Nicole's car was not in sight. Pelletier's dog, an over-sized German shepherd, raised his head and went stone still, watching the truck.

Scheutz opened the lid on one of the two styrofoam coffee cups on the dash. He sipped the steaming liquid and watched the dog. Every day it was the same thing. No matter how long he waited, the dog never moved until he either rolled down the window or opened the truck door. Some days he had to wait a good fifteen or twenty minutes for Pelletier to get himself out of bed and out the door. Scheutz himself had never been able to wait that long before giving in to the temptation of setting off the dog's fury. He'd often wondered what would happen if he ever did, say, come here when Pelletier was not home and just sit there in the truck for an hour without either rolling down the window or opening the door. Would the dog remain in that alert position until he keeled over from fatigue?

He had no patience for the dog this morning and opened the car door just slightly. Only then did the dog leap, growling and running to the length of its leash chain, where it alternated barking and bearing its teeth. Once set in motion, no matter what a person did after that, the dog thrashed in its frenzy. In order for anyone other than Pelletier or Nicole to enter the trailer, the dog had to be led to its cage. Scheutz sipped his coffee and watched the dog threaten to strangle itself on its own leash. The dog's viciousness gave him a familiar tingle in his chest. He hated the dog. He wouldn't want to kill him, or maybe the tingle was just the animal urge in him to fight the dog. He could picture himself flying out of the truck door, jamming a stick into the dog's mouth, or sinking his own teeth into the dog's neck.

Jesus, Clem. That's even sillier than slapping a state trooper.

What the hell was Pelletier doing with a dog like that anyhow? Probably a lot of paranoia connected with his days of avoiding the Canadian police. Pelletier probably had good reason to be paranoid, but that never bothered Scheutz. He and the Canadian worked well together without having to waste a lot of talk. Each one, instinctively it seemed, knew what the other would do in the woods. A little like the way he and Nanda made love.

Yes, but you don't love Pelletier the same way you love Nanda.

It's got nothing to do with love.

Hmph. So, is she sexier than I was?

No.

Then why didn't we have that kind of sex?

Aren't you violating your principles here? You're not supposed to ask about the past. Life is in present, remember?

I want to know.

You and I couldn't get that just because we did love each other. That's what Nanda would say, anyhow. She'd say you don't get love without pain. If you love somebody, after a while you can't see beyond the pain.

Nepenthe.

What's that?

You know, the drug in the Odyssey, that liberates the mind from grief. That's what you and Nanda are doing with your tantric sex.

See, you are jealous. That sounds like a put-down. You don't approve.

It's not my place to approve or disapprove. I just think you ought to be aware of what you two are doing. She's got you believing it's some kind of religious ritual you're indulging in. What you're really doing is the same thing you're doing hiding out in this tiny town and working in the woods. Self-indulgence. You two fucking without loving each other is nothing more than shutting yourselves out from what really goes on in the world.

What is that, some kind of New York psycho-babble. No wonder Marty spends so much time looking up at the ceiling when you're talking. Besides, Nanda doesn't need to do that, she takes the world as it is. She's pretty tough, you know.

Hah! She's just like you. Inside that cool, lesbian demeanor is a quivering mass of insecurity.

Scheutz tossed his empty coffee cup out the window. The dog lunged so hard against the leash, it flipped his hind end around. Scheutz kept himself from rolling the window back up, giving himself a little extra adrenalin rush with the thought that the dog just might someday drag the whole trailer off its base of cinder blocks and fill his open truck window with whopper-sized teeth.

Where the hell was Pelletier? He needed that calming affect Pelletier always seemed to have on him. The day hadn't even started and he was as taut as a guitar string. What he and Pelletier did when they worked together in the woods should be called tantric logging. They were extensions of each other out there, tuned to a rhythm that produced the greatest amount of work for the least amount of effort. In old-country style German weddings he'd been to as a child, the new bride and groom performed an ancient Teutonic ceremony of sawing a log with each one holding the opposite handle of a cross-cut saw. The Teuts believed the cutting of a log released the spirit of the tree. In more recent times, the ceremony came to symbolize the cooperation needed for the husband and wife to work together and the reminder that they should revel in a life of hard work. He and Gerry had been like that once. And he and Pelletier were like that now.

You ought to adopt him as a pet. That's why people have pets, you know. It works on horses, too. You put another animal, like a goat maybe, in the next stall and it calms the horse right down.

Why should I think of him as a pet. He's my friend.

Bullshit. You don't have friends.

I don't have pets, either.

Except for maybe the old tomcat that lived in the barn. God only knew how that cat got through the winter each year. He wasn't the kind of animal anyone would spend time with, but Scheutz had a grudging respect for him.

Pelletier stepped out onto the packed dirt in front of the trailer door and patted the dog's head as it took a break from barking at Scheutz and nuzzled his master's hand. Pelletier gave it some morsel of food and, walking past a pile of rusted water pipes, a smashed hot water heater, two-by-four boards with nails still in them, an outboard motor, and three empty fifty-five gallon drums, opened the passenger door of the pickup. He already wore his spiked boots, which would add yet another pattern of holes to the floor mat on that side of the cab. Scheutz had asked him so many times over the years not to put his boots on till he got out at the cutting site, but he might as well not waste his breath on it.

Once a year he put a new rubber mat over the old one. Pelletier took the other coffee cup off the dash and opened the lid. Scheutz rolled down his window and waved bye-bye to the dog, setting off another leash-yanking explosion.

How would you like it if someone tormented you like that?

You mean the way the dog torments me with his threat of horrible death every time I come into this yard?

That's different and you know it.

No, I don't know it. The dog and I are on the same wave length. I hate him and he hates me. Isn't that what you'd call the balance of nature?

But the dog is just an animal.

So, who isn't?

Pelletier wrinkled his nose in disgust after the first sip of coffee, put the lid back on and set the cup back on the dash. He sat for a moment in his usual early-morning stupor, gazing out the windshield and then curled himself into his corner of cab and was soon mumbling in his sleep. The drive to the cutting site took a half hour. Pelletier made as good company asleep as he did awake. He in fact talked more in his sleep than he did awake. Scheutz headed north on Route 10. If Pelletier didn't want the coffee, he could use it himself. He punched a hole in the lid and sipped, driving with one hand. A string of unintelligible words came from Pelletier's side of the cab. They sounded French. Most of Pelletier's sleep-talk came out in guttural French. He imagined his cohort entering some kind of wormhole when he slept and coming out into a totally different reality. Like the time they'd gone up to the Quebec border together, the night of the chain saw dance.

Three months before, in the beginning of March he'd volunteered to go north to get away from Nanda's last blow-up with Goncharov. Pelletier, on the other hand had been ordered up there by old man Brockton because he was the only one at the mill who spoke fluent Quebecois. They had crossed the border into Canada about four o'clock in the morning. Pelletier slept while Scheutz told the guard at the border station that they were both born in New Hampshire just to save any further questions the man might have for Pelletier. They met the foreman of the other logging crew in the little town of Notre Dame des Bois. "J'sus l'bucheur, la," Pelletier said in his Canuck vernacular in answer to the man's question. Scheutz followed the man's truck to the cutting site that straddled the border of New Hampshire, Maine and Quebec. They were to be at the site for three weeks, and Gerry's voice kept bugging him about leaving Marty, still in high school, at home to care for himself.

He's eighteen years old and he's got a lot more sense than I did at that age. I was younger than that when I went into the army.

He's still my baby.

For Chrissake.

In the morning's first light, the camp in Quebec, tucked in a narrow valley between two hills, resembled an old sepia-toned photo from the last century, with smoke drifting up from a stove pipe in the middle of a large army-surplus tent. The spaciousness inside the tent housed the men's sleeping quarters, the kitchen, and the workbench for repairing and fine-tuning the chain saws. A large wood stove made from a fifty-five gallon drum in the center of the plank platform on which the tent was mounted kept the place toasty warm on the late winter mountain cold nights.

The men worked in pairs, one man dropping and limbing the trees and other hauling them out with one of the large skidder machines. One of these machines, with its five-foot high tires and hydraulic winch, could drag out roughly fifteen hundred of pine logs in one hitch. With the girth of the trees they were cutting, each hitch contained only three trees. It wasn't hard to see why Scheutz and Pelletier had been sent this far from home. These trees averaged two and half feet in diameter at shoulder height with no limbs at all for the lower thirty feet. Scheutz's guess was that the area had been logged over about fifty years before, and then select cut allowing for maxim regrowth. The Canucks had two Timberjack skidders of their own, and The Brockton Mill's own John Deere skidder arrived later that morning on a tandem trailer driven by the mill's driver, Olavi. Throughout the next three weeks Olavi trucked out over two hundred and fifty thousand board feet of grade A spruce, white pine, and hemlock. Another two hundred thousand feet of lesser quality logs were hauled out by trucks from the Rolland Paper Company to be used for paper pulp.

Scheutz and Pelletier worked the upper ridge that first day, Scheutz felling the tall pines so they pointed downhill. Pelletier worked the skidder, winching in the trees in bunches of three and skidding them down the slope to add to the huge piles already on the landing. Scheutz worked in late-winter snow up to his knees, stamping it down at the base of each tree before making the first cut. The steepness of the approach to the ridge reminded him of an uncleared ski hill. By the end of the day, riding down on the skidder with the last hitch, his leg muscles burned with fatigue.

In early March, that first day in Quebec the sun had gone down already by five-thirty. The inside of the tent resembled a dimly-lit cave, with kerosene lamps hung from tent poles. Apparently, the generator the Canucks were supposed to tow up from Notre Dame des Bois was on the blink and would not arrive until the next day. The old cook, Rennie, made a wonderful stew on a wood-burning camp stove. In one corner of the tent were stacked several cases of Molson beer. A shower bag hung from one of the tent's ridge poles, but even with the heat from the central wood stove, it was still too cold to strip for a shower. Scheutz put a flannel shirt on over his long johns and shuffled around the plank floor in the felt linings of his boots, tuning up his two Husqvarna chainsaws for the next day.

At supper, he and Pelletier sat across from each other at one of the wooden picnic tables set up for eating. The Canucks, five in all, sat at the other table, carrying on in French, shouting over each other. Pelletier's attention leaned almost totally toward the other table. He even added his own interjections—so uncharacteristic for him—that made the Frenchmen laugh. Scheutz understood barely a word being said. Many of the men's sentences ended in "la" in the manner of Quebecois country folk, and the national epithet "E'Christ" seemed to punctuate every other comment. One phrase he did catch was "e totalement fuckee" the bilingual Canadianism meaning something was totally fucked up.

He asked Pelletier what they were talking about and received one of the man's Gallic shrugs for an answer. Pelletier had drifted away from him and attached himself to his countrymen. The scene reminded him of being in the mountains of Cuba years earlier. His only friend there, Enrique, had drifted away towards his countrymen in the same manner, leaving Scheutz virtually alone with the sensation he'd often had in his life of existing inside, or part of a group but completely separate from it.

He wondered again whatever happened to Enrique. People did that; they drifted away. Gerry had done that; drifted slowly at first and then faster until she was finally gone altogether, as if over a falls. Dan was gone, and Marty was now absent from home more, only a matter of months until he disappeared down the same river as his mother and brother. Marty seldom even ate the food left for him in the refrigerator. He'd grab a pizza after school or he'd eat at his girlfriend, Regina's house. These last few months, Scheutz spent his evenings alone. The only way he knew Marty was still around was the way he knew deer were present in the woods, he'd read the signs. Marty left signs, dirty towels and such, in the bathroom, or Scheutz might see his coat and boots in the mud room on the way out to work in the morning. He didn't miss Marty yet the way he missed Dan, but he could see it coming.

At least here in the logging tent, the unintelligible chatter of French provided a better companion than the god-awful emptiness of the television screen at home. He was a foreigner here but then, he didn't mind it as much as sitting alone in his own home. In a way it was nice that there was no electricity up here yet. Otherwise, they'd all be sitting here watching that television set over on top of the beer cases, the thing blaring out something even more inane than his own because it was inane in another language.

With supper over, he could barely keep his eyes open. The heat from the wood stove, a long hard day in the snow, and the lack of sleep the night before driving three hours to get up here, all conspired to shroud him in drowsiness. He opened his sleeping bag on one of the unoccupied cots and climbed in, removing only his boot liners. He'd brought a book to read, just as he read every night in bed before nodding off, but the light from the kerosene lamp was too dim to read by. He'd just nap for a little and then maybe get up and try socializing, having a beer with the Canucks. Other than the babble of voices at the picnic table, the world inside and outside the tent lay swathed in a blissful silence.

He awoke slowly to strange sounds. His face, turned toward the kerosene lights, felt burnt by heat from the wood stove. His sleep must have been deep because he found himself in total confusion as to where he was. In his half-awake state he opened his eyes in fear that he was caught in some weird tale he'd read once in a comic book as a child where a person awoke in hell without even knowing he had died. On the other side of the wood stove, shadows moved rhythmically back and forth in front of the lights and maniacal laughter accompanied sounds of a running chain saw engine. A high-pitched, alien music bounced on top of the engine sound. He cringed further into his sleeping bag and blinked his eyes to help orient himself.

In the middle of the plank floor, between the kitchen and sleeping areas a big Husqvarna chain saw with the chain and bar removed, ran, but roughly, out of sync, rumbling in sort of a five-eighths time. Seated on one of the picnic tables with his feet on the seat, Rennie's arms pumped in and out on what looked like a small concertina. The music created a manic background to the singing of one of the other loggers, a man who had been introduced earlier as Donat. The end of every line rhymed in a sing-songy shout. The other four men, including Pelletier, all danced back and forth with high-kicking steps in what looked like a polka. Once he got over his fright, Scheutz found himself entranced by the performance. In all the years he'd known Pelletier, he'd never seen him like this. The same as the other men dancing around him, he laughed out loud, occasionally letting out a French version of "Whoop," with his arms encircled in front of him and his feet stomping the planks in time with the out-of-sync chain saw engine.

Scheutz pushed the sleeping bag down off his shoulders. The scene before him may have looked like some version of hell, but it was just a bunch of guys enjoying themselves. He lay his head on his crooked arm and watched. Empty beer bottles crowded the picnic table that Rennie perched on with his concertina. A couple other loggers carried open bottles in their hands, and the singer snatched sips from his bottle between song verses.

Nanda would say this kind of dancing was religious. Everything was religious to Nanda. Sitting at a poker table was a communal ritual to the God of Chance. Churches held bingo nights for the same reason. Eating together, sleeping together, or walking alone on the tundra, all had religious undertones. All you had to do was pay attention to what you were doing. What was it she said? "Quakers, fakirs, shakers. Kosher bakers, Hadj makers, mescal takers, Lazarus wakers, and God's little acres. It's all the same thing, man. Just pay attention to what you're doing and you'll be in the state of grace." In Nanda's view, these guys dancing to the rhythm of the chain saw would be plugged into their collective unconscious, the Gothic—or Gaulic—tribesman in their cave at night, celebrating the day's release of the spirit of the trees.

Nanda really gets carried away sometimes, doesn't she?

Yeah. Well. My old buddy Pelletier is something, huh? Dancing like that. Who'dda thought it?

I'dda thought it. You must know, I'm sure, that the only reason he's such a stick when he's around you is because he's around you.

Because I don't dance?

Because you've grown a shell on you like a turtle. And you move about as gracefully as one.

Nanda wouldn't agree with you.

Nanda? What the hell does she know about it? She's never seen you move. When you guys do that tantric sex thing, neither one of you moves a muscle.

Nanda and I might look to you like we're not moving when we have sex, but there's a lot else going on.

Fine. So, let's get her in here to explain it to us.

You're the only voice allowed inside my head.

Chapter 5

Mountain Laurel

He turned off the hardtop onto a weed-choked dirt road barely visible from the highway. Twenty yards in, the land dropped steeply, the road, at times nothing more than a wide space between trees, descending for almost a half mile to a narrow stream. A low-lying mist obscured the stream itself and gave to the tall pines an illusion of growing out of some mythical dreamscape. He inched slowly through the shallow stream bed. Pelletier rolled down his window and hung his head out, peering through the mist, looking, as he did every morning, for the trout he had once seen hiding back under an outcrop of rock.

On the other side of the stream the road rose again until they ascended out of the fog onto a road became steeper and more rutted, washed away in places. Weed growth was not as clogged, and inside a patch of thick hemlock it was obvious the ground never saw the sun year-round. Climbing for about a hundred yards, they eventually crossed with the main logging road, also dirt but much less overgrown. Following this bigger road, they came to the "landing" at the base of a ridge known locally as "The Throne." Scheutz parked next to a newer pick-up truck belonging to Brockton's kid, Freddie.

Frank Upperman, another logger, stood behind his one-ton dump truck, parked on the other side of Freddie's. He held a Stihl chainsaw in one hand while adjusting the carburetor, using a tiny screwdriver. From the sound of it, he'd get it running smooth, and then as soon as he revved the motor it would fall off again. He threw the saw on the ground in frustration and then picked it up and tried adjusting it again. Upperman, lean and raw-boned, sported a chainsaw scar running the length of his left cheek. It gave his face a kind of Atilla-like appearance. He lived with his brother on their family farm over in Walpole, and sold firewood on the side. The childishly hand-painted letters on the door of his truck contained the letters 'F.U.', one on each side of a raised middle finger, and the word 'firewood'.

The landing, as it was called, a euphemism left over from the days when logs were transported as river raftings, consisted of roughly an acre of cleared ground near an old stone fence separating it from the logging road. Stone fences bordered both sides of the road, and ran up through the woods at right angles.

The landing itself was choked with piles of pine logs, each pile sixty feet long and over fifteen feet high, with hardly enough room to get a grapple truck in to take them out. The two crews—Scheutz and Pelletier in one, and Freddie and Upperman in the other—had been at this cutting site for the past month, getting timber down too fast for Olavi, to keep up with trucking it out. The work went fairly easy on this woodlot, with some pretty decent timber for this part of New Hampshire. The Throne was owned by the Brockton family and had been logged off by Freddie's grandfather back in the forties, just after the war. Unlike a lot of other tracts, it had been intelligently forested which was why their yield was so good now.

Pelletier pointed out to Scheutz deer tracks in the dust of the landing near a pile of hardwood logs waiting to be cut for firewood. The single set of tracks was big enough to have been made by a cow, but were obviously the marks of the wily old buck Pelletier had been stalking unsuccessfully for several years.

The sound of Freddie's skidder drifted down from the ridge. In the other direction, from the logging road came the distinct sound of Olavi's grapple truck laboring its way up from the highway. Upperman finally got his saw adjusted to his satisfaction, shut the engine off and threw it onto his shoulder like soldiering a rifle. He picked up his gallon jugs of gas and bar oil, waved at Scheutz and entered the trees on the uphill border of the landing. Pelletier went to crank up his John Deere skidder while Scheutz finished off his coffee and took his time opening the back of his truck bed cap and lowering the tailgate. With all that wood on the landing it made no sense for anybody busting their ass getting more out. He clamped the bar of his chainsaw into the vise mounted on the tailgate and, with a round file, touched up the edges on the teeth. The diesel on the John Deere chugged to life and a few minutes later, Pelletier, without so much as a nod to Scheutz, started his way up the hill at the far end of the landing, the choker chains hanging off the back clinking against each other and the ground stones.

Don't you usually ride up with him? What's wrong with him now?

Who knows. He's probably got his nose out of joint again about something. Maybe he's pissed about me teasing his dog again. You never know about that guy.

You shouldn't be teasing his dog in the first place.

Olavi's truck pulled into the landing and parked next to the largest pile of pine logs. He threw Scheutz his huge grin as he climbed down from the cab. That's what Pelletier's problem was again this morning, Scheutz realized. Pelletier and Olavi did not get along at all, going back to the time five years earlier with Olavi yelling at Pelletier in that Finnish accent something about Pelletier and Olavi's wife. Pelletier would never talk about it, but speculative gossip and jokes went around at the mill about how Olavi's youngest child was dark-complected like Pelletier, in a family of otherwise Scandinavian blondes.

Scheutz bent to sharpening his saw, hoping to deter Olavi from talking with him. Not that he was in hurry to get to work, but once Olavi started in on his reportage of daily gossip, it was hard to get away from him. It might have been different if Scheutz cared a jot about following the lives of all those connected with the mill, or if Olavi's thick Finnish accent left Scheutz understanding more than thirty percent of what the man was saying.

Olavi limped over to Scheutz's truck. He was a mountain of a man who had once been Brockton's most productive logger. He had had a reputation in that part of New Hampshire as "The Finn Machine," averaging twelve thousand board feet a day. A skidder accident that smashed his ankle left him with a pinned-together leg and an unshakable belief that God was punishing him for abandoning his parents' Apostolic Lutheran religion. This on top of his wife being deflowered—his definition of her already non-virgin seduction—in a wooded glade by Satan's representative here on earth, the 'French-ugly' Pelletier.

"Boy, is Freddie's mom mad at him," Olavi opened with.

"You know, Olavi, we can't pile any more logs on the landing until you get some of this timber out of here." The only way to deal with Olavi's incessant gossip was to ignore whatever he said and change the subject.

"I know, I know." Olavi flapped his hand. "I have to do what they tell me. But I finished hauling from that other site. All day today, I will haul from here. Okay? Does that make you happy now? But, Freddie. Ha. Ha..."

"We're starving at home, you know that? My little children have nothing to eat," Scheutz said. The way to Olavi's heart was through a child's stomach. Loggers were paid piecework, so much per thousand feet, but only after the timber arrived and was scaled at the mill. Olavi's major focus in life had always been the feeding of the children his Apostolic Lutheran wife pumped out year after year after year. Including the dark one.

"You bullshit me. You don't have kiddies to feed."

Scheutz smiled and waved his round file in Olavi's face. "How do you know? How do you know Dan doesn't have a dozen whelps scattered across the countryside?"

"That is no way to talk." Olavi waved a big finger as if parrying a thrust of Scheutz's file. "And your boy Dan should keep it in his pants. I tell my two girls, I better not catch them with Dan. I speak no disrespect for you and your son, but that boy has maybe lessons from that Frog." He tilted his chin in the direction of the noise of Pelletier's skidder.

"I thought your girls were too young."

Olavi shook his head. "No. My wife has her first when she is fifteen. And my daughter Karen is a freshman when your son Dan is a senior. She comes home with moons in her eyes over this tall, blond boy, and I tell her I knock his block off if he comes around my house."

"Yeah, well. These days he's plying his trade in a more fertile valley."

"Yes, but he leaves his friend Freddie Brockton behind to carry on in his name." Olavi's head wagged up and down and left and right as if it couldn't make up its mind between yes and no. "I am telling you, poor Mrs. Brockton, she is a saint to put up with that wild one."

"Freddie's okay." Scheutz finished his filing and released the saw from the vise. "And besides, he's engaged to that girl, Samantha."

Olavi shook his head. "One day he is and the next day he is not. Those kids do not know what they are doing. But, yes, I must say, Freddie is a good kid." Olavi's head went into its cross-wag again. "Some day he will be our boss. But he drinks too much."

"But he works hard."

"Yes, he works hard. Maybe some day he marries that girl, Samantha" Olavi said.

Scheutz shrugged. "Eh. Maybe. Be good for him, but not for her. The girl deserves better." He set his saw on the tailgate and went to the cab to retrieve his hard hat. "Hey, bring us back some coffee on one of your runs, will you?" Olavi waved an "okay" and walked back to his truck. Scheutz buckled on his tool pouch and gathered up his gas and bar oil containers. With his chain saw on his shoulder, he set off up the hill.

He skirted the skid trail, avoiding the deep ruts, for about a hundred yards and then veered off in a more direct but steeper route toward where he'd left off cutting the day before. The woods under the pines was thick with mountain laurel, sprayed at this time of year with beautiful white and violet tinted blooms against the dark green pods of laurel leaves. Added to the sound of the two skidders up on the ridge came the yipping of two, or maybe three dogs, moving between them. The tone of their bark sounded like they were running a deer. Maybe that was what Pelletier was in such a rush about. He'd heard the tone of the dogs—he could hear things normal people couldn't—and was afraid they were after his buck. Mountain laurel, even when it was not in bloom, was a beautiful sight when viewed from a distance. Up close, though, trying to get through it was like trying to slog through a giant spider web. He angled off to the right of the laurel.

Paying attention to nothing more than where he put his feet in the thick undergrowth, he could feel himself relax a little. The pathless woods. There was a line from a poem with that phrase. What was it? He couldn't place it. Some Romantic poet. Back in the days when he and Gerry used to read aloud to each other, she often requested some seventeenth or eighteenth century poet. He climbed steadily. It reminded him again of the canopy of tall trees in the mountains of Cuba. The rays of the sun did not penetrate there. The chain saw rested on his shoulder the same way the carbine had rested back then. In Cuba it seemed to never stop raining and the closeness of the heat was like a palpable force field. Here it was dry and, with the sun getting higher, just now beginning to warm up. He'd trade this for that any day, except that….except that, there he had at least felt alive. Here he felt like he'd been slogging up the same hill with the same saw, cutting the same tree for the last ten years.

It's your own fault, you know.

I did it for you and Dan. And then Marty.

Don't act the martyr. It doesn't suit you.

I didn't know what else to do.

He could see them again in Mexico, Gerry and little Dan, almost three and learning to talk, the two of them on the dock at Isla Mujeres, walking toward him, Gerry striding in that purposeful way she always put on, especially when she was afraid and unsure. And Dan, zigzagging, turning in circles, unable to take in all the new sights and sounds the world held out to him. The sight of the two of them like messengers from heaven sent to bring him home. He had climbed off the fishing boat with nothing more in the world than the clothes he stood in. He had left the weapons with the Mexican who owned the boat. He had even traded his heavy boots for food. Having escaped from the over-lush, green inferno that was Cuba, his two angels, Gerry and his son brought heaven with them. There was no other way he could describe it. And he didn't require much from heaven; heaven was merely to be in their presence. And then, as the years went by, first Gerry was gone. And then Dan. And, after today, Marty. And here he would be, left alone again in hell.

Where was he really? Forty years old. And he felt old. You're not supposed to feel old at forty. This kind of physical labor for eight to ten hours a day for ten years probably took it out of his body. There were not a lot of old loggers around. But even worse, chugging along with your spirit on half-light will use you up faster. He was a like a truck engine running with only a six volt spark. He was doing nothing more than coasting through limbo.

Wouldn't it be great to be like Dan. Twenty-two years old and just throwing himself into anything interesting that passed in front of him. Of course, his mother, the real Gerry, not the one in his head, seemed so conflicted about Dan and what he did with his life. She would say she wished he'd settle on something and somebody that he really liked. He was still her beautiful little boy, but he'd grown into such a…What was it she'd called him? A cocksmith. Adding one more chauvinist pig to the world. Nanda, on the other hand, had no ambivalence about Dan's perennial girlfriending. She let Scheutz know quite directly how much she disliked his son. Early on in their relationship, Scheutz had taken Dan and Marty with him to party at Nanda's house in Claremont. Dan immediately began hitting on some Dartmouth freshman girl who had only recently come out of the closet. The girl carried on as if Dan were some fiend with long fingernails trying to drag her into an alley. According to Dan, all he did was compliment her on her nice tits. Scheutz and Nanda had argued over the incident and did not speak to each other for a month after it.

But if Dan was still Gerry's sweet little boy, he meant even more to Scheutz. More than a child, he was, like his brother Marty, an eternal friend. Scheutz had learned how to be young through his sons. He had learned to wonder at the world while showing those wonders to his boys. He had learned some of the joy and exuberance of a carefree adolescence, those years he himself had spent in a juvenile detention home. Yes, Dan and Marty had gone through the same day-to-day little agonies that all teenagers must go through. But without the underlying curse of no one or nothing to bounce off of, they had won the struggle with a self-assurance that Scheutz had never attained. And Scheutz had tried his best to give his son, both his sons, something to bounce off of, and something to measure themselves by. What he remembered most, though, were not the struggles, there had been plenty of those, but those little moments, especially with Dan, when the two of them would just stop, look at each other and then burst into a laugh over something they both knew and agreed on but did not need words to define. Those moments were the punctuation of joy. And the absence in his life left a palpable ache.

Just as Marty's moments would be when he left. But Marty was different. His teenage struggle was quieter and more consistent than Dan's. Dan's was all peaks and valleys, and Marty's seemed more like a steady climb. It was as if he could see the end of it and so planned for it day after day. There had been no fits and starts like his brother's, no throwing himself into anything that came along without understanding exactly what he was getting into. Marty had one steady girlfriend, Regina, with her tight compact body and direct manner, in contrast to Dan's dreamy-eyed girlfriends that came and went with the phases of the moon. But both boys, each in a very different way, had inherited so much of their mother.

And, if Dan's relationship with Nanda was strained, Marty's was almost non-existent. He never said one way or the other whether he liked the woman or not, but he tried not to be around whenever she was present. When he was around, he spent much of his time with his eyes raised to the ceiling over something Nanda had just said.

Maybe she should to get used to it. Tha boy's been doing that to me since he was four years old.

Oh, there you are. I wondered where you got to.

And don't kid yourself; Marty does it to you too.

Yeah, well, that's not surprising, considering how he never agrees with anything I say.

Ahead of him lay another large pod of mountain laurel that he needed to skirt, causing him to strain with slower steps where the terrain was steeper. The flowers on the laurel brought back the day of Dan's graduation, four years ago, in the same season as now. From a table on a restaurant patio, he had sat daydreaming, looking off to a slope about a half mile away where a forest's edge sported a ring of mountain laurel in bloom. They'd all gone to lunch that day, to a natural foods restaurant in South Strafford, Vermont. Samantha, one of Dan's classmates, had told Gerry about the place. Gerry and Georgina, rode in the car driven by Samantha. Scheutz followed in the truck with Dan and Marty. Georgina's daughter, Sharna, had begged off going with them for, as far as Scheutz could tell, the same problem she always had with being around Dan. The warm, sunny day on the hillside, gave them just enough of a breeze to allow them to forget about the overlap of black-fly season with mosquito season.

He knew he'd have trouble with the A-frame constructed restaurant the moment he walked into the building and saw all the hanging plants. There seemed to be an inverse ratio between the number of hanging plants in a restaurant and how good the food tasted. Sure enough, the menu was strictly macrobiotic and contained nothing that appealed to Scheutz. The balding, full-bearded waiter, the waitperson, as Scheutz preferred to think of him, who introduced himself as Bruce, finally agreed to make him a grilled cheese sandwich. The others, including Marty who looked like he was having a hard time keeping a straight face, each entered into a too-long discussion with waitperson on the correct balance of yin and yang in the dishes offered. It was during these discussions that the laurel on the next hill reached out to grab Scheutz's attention. The blossoms stood out sharply against the deep green background of the forest and a foreground of eroded dirt and rocks where the hillside had been washed away. The harshness of the landscape only served to accentuate the powerful force of the transient delicacy of the flowers. He was being given a peep at raw beauty on a far hillside.

Scheutz sat silently, waiting for his sandwich, long after everyone else was served. His attention flipped from the laurel to the people at the table and back again. Gerry, still as thin as she was in high school, wore tight Levi's and a tank top the lilac color of the laurel blossoms. The long, brunette hair, obviously lightened in a New York salon, bronzed somewhat, hung straight down her back the way she had worn it since she was pregnant with Marty. She ate with exaggerated slowness, taking her time chewing, and talking with Dan between bites. She seemed jumpy, though, with all her slow chewing, nervous about something. He'd noticed it when she first arrived that morning in the car with Dan and Samantha who had picked her up from the train station in Bellows Falls. Excited to see her, Scheutz waited at the passenger door to greet her as she stepped out. Almost as tall as him, she stared straight into his eyes, giving him that look of conspiracy he had been so familiar with since high school, the look that said they could get away with anything if they did it together. He reached his arms to give her a hug and she started for him, but then, as if remembering some warning, she stopped and looked away, turning back into herself.

Georgina sat between her and Scheutz at the table on the patio. She wore a high-waisted, sleeveless print dress that exposed too much of her too-light skin. Samantha, in between Dan and Marty, wearing a tie-dyed t-shirt and jeans, did her best, as always, to imitate Gerry. Her hair was not quite straight enough to get the same effect as Gerry's, but it draped nicely in ash-blond waves onto her shoulders. Her eyes darted to Gerry's face and then away, watching the way she ate, tilted her head, held her fork. The same movements, so graceful on Gerry, gave Samantha a kind of clumsiness. Her emulation dated back to the summer she had visited Dan in New York during their short-lived fling at age thirteen. Since that time she'd also become a regular visitor to the house in Acworth, even when Dan was not there. Her younger brother, Joe, rode the school bus every day, and was in the same class as Marty. The two of them, Joe and Samantha, could often be found still hanging around at supper time when Scheutz came home from work.

The boys, Marty and Dan, along with Joe and Freddy Brockton might be out in the barn messing with some old car, or out riding their dirt bikes on the unused logging roads on weekends or after school, but even then Samantha often stayed in and kept Scheutz company. She would cook dinner, or help Scheutz prepare it. He found her a pleasant person to have around, except for those times when her Gerry poses, got on his nerves.

"So, are you riding back to New York with us?" Gerry was saying to Dan. Why did Scheutz get the feeling that she asked that question for his benefit?

"No. I've got some stuff I have to take care of. It'll be about a week," Dan said.

"You're going to New York?" Scheutz asked. "That's the first I've heard. When will you be back?"

"I don't know. I might stay down there."

"What do you mean, stay down there?"

"You know, like for good."

"What? No. You can't do that."

"Yes, he can," Gerry said, leaning in over her plate to point her face in Scheutz's direction. "In case you hadn't noticed, Clement, he's a grown up. He can do whatever he wants."

"Mom. Please." Dan put a hand on her arm. "I don't need an advocate here."

The table fell quiet. Scheutz listened for Gerry's voice in his head, but it was silent. She always chickened out at the wrong times. What should he do now? Of course Dan was right. Gerry was right. But... "What were you planning on doing, sneaking out without telling me? Leaving me a note saying, Hasta luego, it's been fun?"

"Oh, Clement, come on," Gerry said. Clement again. She put her fork down, looking around the table at all the faces, as if looking for support. No one gave her any.

Waitperson chose this as the moment to drop the plate with the grilled cheese sandwich onto the table in front of him. Scheutz wanted to slap his smug little, hipper-than-thou face. He pushed the plate toward the center of the table.

"You going to register for the draft up here or in New York?" Marty asked Dan. Your timing is great, as always, Scheutz thought. Leave it to Marty to make any tense situation a little worse. Where Dan made any effort he could to smooth over differences between his mother and father, Marty, never one to abide any unspoken argument in the air, and bred on Scheutz and Gerry's many disagreements, poked at them as he might a hornet's nest in the barn.

"What draft? There's no more draft," Gerry said. "Didn't you see that whole thing on television a couple of months ago with them evacuating Saigon? The war's over, thank God. Finally."

"There isn't a draft, but all the boys have to register when they reach eighteen," Georgina put in.

"You're not going to register," Gerry said. "Look what it did to your father."

"I enlisted," Scheutz said. "I wasn't drafted. And what do you mean, what it did to me?"

"Well...you know...you know how you are."

"No. How am I?"

"Dad. Calm down," Dan said in an even voice. "Mom. Shut up for a minute, will you."

"Don't tell me to shut up." Gerry said.

"Don't talk to your mother like that," Scheutz said.

Marty smirked, shifting his eyes back and forth, waiting for the next outburst. Georgina pushed her chair back as if she were ready to run. Samantha lowered her head with her hands in her lap in an attitude of waiting for it all to blow over, as she often did when Scheutz and Dan started to argue at home.

"Look," Dan said. "If you all just cool it for a moment, I'll tell you what I'm gonna do." He spread his hands. His used-car salesman routine. "I'm going to New York, but I'll come home on weekends. Okay? And..." His eyes moved back and forth between Gerry and Scheutz as if to say, 'have I got a deal for you'. "I will register up here, but if they think up another war, they'll never find me in New York."

Scheutz listened again for Gerry's voice to tell him what to do, and at the same time, watched the real Gerry's face across the table to see what she would do next. Neither of the Gerrys was giving him a clue. This was one of those times when he wasn't sure if he was crazy or not. Gerry unwound her long body slowly from the chair and walked from the patio to the lawn that sloped away on the hillside. Samantha looked up, at each person in turn, and then went to join her.

Georgina made to rise also, but stopped and placed her hand atop Scheutz's where it lay on the table. "Whew. Sitting between you two feels like being inside a magnetic force field. Even when you're not paying attention to each other, there's a lot of energy going back and forth betwee you two." Marty raised his eyes to the cloudless sky.

The three women sat on the grass facing away from the patio. Waitperson took their order and brought out three iced teas for the women, then two organic root beers for Dan and Marty, and a cappuccino for Scheutz. Scheutz asked waitperson if he was sure the coffee was properly balanced with yin and yang, The bearded one merely gave him a 'go fuck yourself' look and scurried off to his kitchen. Dan moved around to sit next to Scheutz, so the three faced the afternoon sun and the backs of the women on the lawn.

"So what do you plan on doing in New York?" he asked Dan. Ever since Dan's junior year at the district high school, the two of them had been having an on-going, but disjointed conversation on the subject of what Dan planned on doing after graduation. At one point, Dan had snapped back at him, "So what do you want me to do, have a career?" inflecting the word 'career' with the same disgust one might put on the word 'syphilis'.

Dan sipped his root beer and shook his head slowly.

"What does that mean?" Scheutz asked. "Nothing? You don't know? Or you don't want to have this conversation?"

"All three." He met Scheutz's eye. Scheutz said nothing. What a shitty day this was turning out to be. He let his eyes drift back to the mountain laurel. "Okay?" Dan asked. Scheutz nodded. "I'm sorry," Dan said. "I don't know what I'm going to do in New York. Mom says I should take a year off and think about what I want to do. You gotta stop hounding me about this, okay?"

Scheutz nodded again. He had to give Dan credit for one thing, the kid certainly could stand up for what he wanted, even if he didn't know what he wanted. "You are going to live at your mother's, right?" Gerry had moved two years before into a duplex in the top two floors of a renovated brownstone in the Park Slope section of Brooklyn. Her career as a graphic designer had finally taken off and she could afford to leave the apartment on 2nd Avenue and East 6th Street across from the old Fillmore East in Manhattan. Before she sent Dan and Marty back up to New Hampshire to live with him, it had made Scheutz almost sick to think of the two of them living in that neighborhood. Dan apparently loved the old apartment on the Lower East Side, but Marty's eight and nine-year-old mind could think up the grossest details to feed Scheutz's paranoia about it whenever he talked to Scheutz on the phone or came to visit in the summer.

"He's moving into the hippie pad," Marty put in.

"Stop, will you?" Dan told him. "Mom's home is not a hippie pad, okay?"

Scheutz turned to Marty. "I thought you told me the new apartment was very nice. All new furniture, and a marble fire place. Didn't some interior designer friend of hers do over the whole thing for her?"

"So, now it looks like a classy hippie pad." Marty said.

"Dad, don't listen to him. The new place is very comfortable. Park Slope is an excellent neighborhood. All kinds of middle class people. And professional people. Mom's a professional. She works her butt off for all those ad agencies."

"She's still a hippie. She listens to the Grateful Dead." Marty in full taunt mode.

"So do you. What does that prove?" Dan said.

Marty tilted his chin in the direction of where the women talked and laughed on the lawn. "Look at them. They all look like they stepped right out of the Mod Squad. It's still 1966 over there."

"How would you know?" Dan said. "You were only five years old in 1966."

"Hey, I was there. She may be a little shorter, but Mom hasn't changed a bit. Isn't that right, Daddy-O?"

Scheutz smiled. "No." he paused for effect. "She's as tall as she was then."

Dan and Marty gave each other that side-long look they shared whenever they thought Scheutz had missed the point. Then they all three laughed. Gerry turned back toward them, not hearing what was being said, but obviously enjoying their laughing together. She grinned and winked at him. He could feel his body react, like he'd just taken a whiff of some potent drug. He knew his face was flushed and he turned aside, toward Dan, to hide it. But then, seeing the look on Dan's face, it became obvious to him that Gerry had been looking past Scheutz, winking at Dan. Scheutz stood, turned his back to the table and walked inside to see what time it was getting to be. "We should be going," he called out to them.

Plodding up the slope of The Throne, well inside the woods now, with his head down, concentrating on the steepness beneath his feet, he didn't see the deer. He had shifted the weight of the chain saw on his shoulder as he veered off to the right of the laurel patch. The deer sprang from the laurel, hitting Scheutz head-on with his muscled chest. Scheutz, his mind elsewhere and the earmuffs down on his hard hat, hadn't heard the buck. It wasn't till he stopped somersaulting backwards that he realized what had just happened to him. The deer bounced off him at an angle, like a billiard ball, and sprinted off down the hill in another direction, disappearing into another laurel patch. From the glimpse Scheutz had of the deer, there had to be at least seventeen points on his rack. Must have been Pelletier's old buck. Now the dogs came, yelping down the hill, running low to the ground, and then circling the laurel on the other side.

Scheutz had come to rest with his shoulder against a tree, his legs splayed uphill. His shoulder hurt where it hit. His hard hat, saw, gas and oil jugs, and hand ax marked the trajectory of his fall. He sat up, rubbing his shoulder.

I hope the deer got away.

What about me?

You're all right. Don't be a baby.

Chapter 6

White Buffalo Woman

He dripped with sweat. Drops fell from his forehead and mixed with the gas he poured into the chain saw's fuel opening. With his hardhat off and the chain saw not running, mosquitoes buzzed in both ears. He removed the bandanna he wore under his hardhat and rung it out like a dish rag. His heavy felt gloves squished like they'd been dunked into a pail of water. The still, muggy air under the trees closed in on him more as the sun rose higher, more like the Cuban rain forest. The weather forecast on the radio in the truck that morning had said cloudy with possible thunder showers. He wouldn't mind a little rain today. The hard physical labor of dropping tree after tree gave him a loose, pleasurable sensation, but not the struggle against the heat.

You know, you might clean the house a little better.

Where the hell does that come from? You're becoming the master of the non-sequitur.

It follows. Tidying up the forest, tidying up the house.

That's a stretch.

But since we're on it....and since Dan and I are coming over this evening. You could get in some groceries fit for human consumption. God, I can't believe the way you and Marty eat.

We burn it off.

But it would help if you ate something healthy once in a while.

What, you don't think olive loaf is healthy?

You might not think that was anything to joke about if you read what they put in that stuff. On the other hand, maybe you would.

I know what's in it. It's got olive and it's got loaf. Besides, I put mustard on it. Don't tell me that's not healthy. Sometimes I put mustard and ketchup.

Gerry's voice had grown more insistent in the last few months. She popped up everywhere. Driving his pick-up truck, felling a tree, washing dishes, there she was. Under the guise of giving him advice, she carped, she cajoled, she cautioned—*Careful now!*—she warned of possible dangers, and she was driving him nuts. He had noticed his hands shaking ever so slightly on the steering wheel of his truck. In the woods with the chain saw running, he had taken to yelling at her, telling her to shut up, arguing with just about everything she said. The yelling kept his hands steadier on the saw.

He couldn't even pretend to enjoy himself in the woods today. The anxiety radiating out from the pit of his stomach caused his movements to become jerky and he had to stop often just to settle himself down. Of course, the moment he did stop, the world around him crept in. The sweat, the mud, the bugs. He preferred cutting in winter time. Between ten and twenty degrees above zero was optimum; the body wasn't expending so much energy keeping itself cool.

Early June saw the final days of black fly season, overlapping the first days of the mosquito onslaught. And, due to the upcoming social evening necessitated by Marty's graduation ceremonies, and Gerry's arrival that very afternoon in person, he could not allow himself his usual garlic routine. Pelletier had taught him an old Canuck trick, which worked for keeping insects away. At the beginning of black fly season and on through the summer, consuming loads of garlic in his food gave his sweat an odor that actually repelled biters. Pelletier's little joke was that the garlic worked well on repelling three things—bugs, vampires, and people. Gerry complained once that the Acworth house in summer smelled like a Paris subway station. Nanda, on the other hand, loved garlic and, all year round, gave off a faint aroma of it herself, mixed with patchouli and some other unidentifiable feminine scent, much like moss in a forest.

He replaced his bandanna, the wetness of it cool against his head, and then his hardhat, adjusting the ear protectors and the face screen. He touched up the edges of the chain saw blade with his round file. The saw started on two pulls of the cord and he moved on to the next tree. Even though he reminded himself to slow down, his efficiency in dropping a seventy-foot pine had become second nature to him.

Nanda was the only person who took him seriously when he had talked with her about Gerry's voice. He mentioned it to very few people, partially out of fear that they would think he was nuts but, more generally, because he felt it be a topic no one else was interested in. And, even if they were interested, it was none of their business. He had interrupted Gerry's voice in the truck one evening after work to tell Pelletier about it. Pelletier listened as he always did, staring through the windshield with his eyes half open.

Pelletier said, "That is not your wife's voice."

"Okay. Well, whose is it then?"

"It is the White Buffalo Woman."

"The what?"

"She is the mother of all mankind."

"What is that, some part the Micmac Indian lore?"

"No."

"Well, where'd you get it?"

"I saw this thing on television. A Paiute was telling how the ghosts of our ancestors lead us to the good hunting ground."

He should know better than to ask Pelletier anything. Pelletier had no opinion at all on most things, but the few he did have could always be traced right back to his television set.

Nanda's explanation was much more complicated. She decided that Gerry's voice was "the personification of the female side" of Scheutz's character, the one he allowed up from the oppressive abyss where he kept her, except for when he was either making love or was dealing with his children.

Scheutz could picture Marty raising his eyes to the ceiling on hearing that one. "But why Gerry?" he asked Nanda. "She doesn't even like me."

"Because she is a very powerful Bodhisattva for you."

"A bodey what?"

" Bo-dhi-satt-va." She turned her head, mouthing the syllables into his ear the way a language teacher might sound out a new vocabulary. They were lying side by side on their backs, in the soft wake of making love, the only time they ever talked anymore. "The Buddhists believe that there are people you meet now and then in your life that have the wisdom you need. They're called Bodhisattvas. Could be anybody. The trick is to leave yourself open to them. That's what you are for me."

"Whaaat? I'm not anybody's Bodhisattva." Even though he protested, that might just be the nicest thing anybody had ever said to him. "No shit, you really think so? And here I thought I was just a piece of ass."

She snorted. "You are anything but just a piece of ass."

"So what do these Bodhisattvas do when they're at home?"

"Same as anybody else. The Buddhists believe that these people are very close to nirvana, but they hang around to help out the rest of us."

"Then I know that's not me. Gerry maybe, but not me. I'm so far from nirvana I couldn't even find it on a map."

He made the scarf cut just above the root swell on the next tree and then moved around for the back cut. The land sloped at such a pitch right there that, on the back side, he was actually standing below the tree itself. He'd gotten well into the cut when the chain saw tilted at just enough of an angle to throw the chain off the bar and whip it around with such a force that it caught the front of his upper thigh. He swore at it as he pulled the bar out from the cut and threw the saw on the ground. Flipping up his face screen, he first made sure the tree was not cut so deeply as to be in danger of falling. Then he knelt on one knee and opened the new rip in his pants in order to see at the gash in his leg.

About an eighth of an inch wide bite, an inch-and-a-half long, not too deep into the muscle. It hadn't started oozing blood, and still seemed to be too traumatized to start hurting yet.

He swore at himself; he could have preventive on two counts. He could have, should have, worn his chaps as he usually did, except when the temperature grew too hot and they made his legs drip with extra sweat. And secondly, he should have stopped and tightened the tension on the chain before cutting into this tree. What was the matter with him today? This was a hell of a time to start self-destructing.

He shut off the chain saw motor and, using the tools from the pouch on his belt, replaced and tightened the chain. Before going back to work on the tree he inserted a wedge into the back cut and tapped it in place.

Whoa. Hey. Hey. Hey. Wait a minute. What about your leg?

What about my leg?

Clem, you have a gash in your leg.

Didn't you just tell me not to act like a big baby? I'll fix it at lunch time.

No, this is different. You should stop and fix it now. It'll be infected by lunch time. What's wrong with you today?

You know what's wrong with me today.

No excuse. No excuse. Sit your ass down and deal with that leg.

Yes, mother.

For chrissake, you sound like you're six years old. You act like it, too. Come on, get the pants off.

He unbuckled his utility belt, lowered his suspenders and pushed his pants down to below the gash in his right thigh. From the first aid kit on his utility belt, he opened a packet of antiseptic salve, applying it to the cut.

That needs a stitch.

I can't do that. That will hurt.

Aww. Pobrecito.

Why don't you go away and let me do this by myself.

Actually, it needs two stitches.

Gerry, goddammit, you're making me crazy. He realized he was shouting aloud into the empty woods. The burning water in his eyes was not sweat now, but tears. The cut on his leg began to burn. He was happy to feel it, at least it made sense. *Today's the day, Gerry,* he said aloud.

What day?

Graduation day.

I know. Marty's graduation day.

And mine.

What's that supposed to mean?

I'm graduating today. I've told myself for years that when Dan and Marty are grown, there are two things I will never have to do again. First, I will never have to go back to work in the woods. And second, I will never have to have anything to do with you. Ever again.

I know you've told yourself that. But it's bullshit. First, you don't know how to do anything else but work in the woods.

Oh, yeah? I know how to do a lot things. I can fix a truck. I can frame a house, do wiring, plumbing, roofing. Lots of things.

But not make a living at them unless there's a housing boom in this neck of the woods, which I doubt will happen in your lifetime. And, as to your second point, you wouldn't know how to take care of yourself without me. Look at your leg, for example.

Just shut up, okay? Do you really think I need somebody to tell me how to live my life?

Yes.

Name one thing you ever told me that helped me out.

What about cooking? You even had a hard time with Campbell's Chicken Noodle Soup until I came along.

Well, okay. Cooking. But...

And that's just for openers. You want the whole list.

Sometimes I hate you.

No, you don't.

You don't know.

Yes, I do. You love me. That's why you let me in. And I've always loved you, that's why I'm here. You're too much of a burden to actually live with, but I'm doing what I can.

Humph. Your idea of love is like the line from that stupid movie. Love is never having to admit you're wrong.

According to your friend Nanda, that's what Bodhisattvas are for. If you thought I was wrong, you wouldn't listen to me.

Yeah, well. You'd be a lot easier to listen to if you weren't so smug.

He extracted the needle and thread from its sealed packet and gritted his teeth against the pain of sewing two stitches across the gash in his leg, pulling the two sides together. He tied the ends off and applied more antiseptic salve and a gauze pad, held in place by tape wrapped around his leg. After pulling his pants back up and hooking his suspenders over his shoulders, he replaced the utility belt, flipped his face screen down and picked up his saw. Before resuming his cut, he stood for a moment, wishing it was lunch time. This had already been a hell of a morning.

Chapter 7

The Blue Ox

He hated to admit, even to himself, that Gerry's voice could, bring bring tears to his eyes. But he did feel a little more relaxed and freshened. His leg wound ached, but he was more attuned to what he was doing.

One afternoon when they were lying in bed, Nanda had brought up the subject of Gerry's voice in his head. She had read a book, she said, recently published by a professor at Princeton who proposed a theory that Greek warriors like Achilles in the Iliad, and people like Moses actually heard the voices of different gods in their heads. It made sense to her that they heard them just as Homer, or whoever, reported. "Those are the earliest records we have of a conscious awareness in a primitive mind," she told him. "And besides, there is some scientific evidence to show that it's neurologically possible."

"I'm not sure I want to hear all this."

"Yeah, you'll love it. Just shut up and listen." She bounced up onto her elbow, her breast resting on his arm. While she talked, she drew diagrams with her finger on his bare chest. "See, in the human brain, in the temporal lobe, there is an area called Wernicke's Area that controls speech. In both hemispheres the area governs understanding of speech but only one governs the individual's response. These primitive minds took in voices, probably auditory hallucinations, and sent them across the connecting bridge to the opposite hemisphere."

"Uh, yeah. Maybe you want to skip over the wiring diagram and get to the layman's translation. So what?"

"The Greeks were the first people we know of to reach any kind of self-awareness, which is what makes them so cool. All those yogis and buddhas and sufis, and Lao Tsu, those guys actually came after the Greeks. But the Greek mind was still very primitive. And the neural impulses through the amygdala came across as auditory sensations so that the people actually heard voices talking to them. You see it in the Bible, too. Like where Moses hears Yahweh's voice in a burning bush."

"And people still do that?"

"Well, yeah. Some people. Schizophrenics do it. At least the one's who aren't all doped up on some kind of phenothiazine. Some people on LSD hear voices. On peyote, things like that. Who else? People who have heavy-duty religious experiences do it. And people under stress, like combat."

"So you're saying I am nuts."

"No. No. No."

"You're saying I have a primitive mind?"

"Yes. That's what I love about you, sweetie."

That conversation had happened not too long before the night in the truck when he had told Gerry that he had been having a conversation in his head with her while she herself sat in the passenger seat. He was able to mention it to Gerry after all those years because Nanda had finally all but convinced him that he wasn't crazy for hearing her voice. In fact, he kind of liked the

Greek warrior image. If Achilles and Moses weren't crazy, then maybe he wasn't?

That was the last time he'd seen Gerry. Or Dan. Last Christmas when they both came up to visit Marty. Dan drove up with a friend of his, but Scheutz had picked Gerry up at the train station in Bellows Falls. He was so used to her voice in his head whenever he drove his truck, especially in the dark, that it took precedence over whoever might be riding with him. The more uptight he was, the more predominant the voice became. And Gerry's actual presence in the truck certainly made him uptight. He could feel the tension in the back of his neck and down the muscles alongside his spine. Nanda called these the 'Gerry muscles'. Whenever she massaged his back and shoulders, she could tell when he had recently talked to Gerry in person on the phone. Sometimes these muscles tensed up just thinking about her. All Nanda had to do was touch one of these muscles lightly with her fingers and it caused him to wince in pain. Nanda had told him that kind of tension came from his wanting to do something and simultaneously not wanting to do it. That would certainly describe anything having to do with Gerry, ever since she left him to move to New York.

"So, how've you been?" Gerry had pulled her head out of her sweater enough to ask in the truck that night.

"Huh? Oh. Okay, I guess. Life lumbers along."

"Is that a pun?"

"What do you mean? Oh, I get it. 'Lumbers along'. Ha ha."

"Wouldn't you like to know how I've been?"

"Well, yeah. You know, yes and no."

"All you have to do is ask. You could say something like, 'So, Gerry, how's it going?' or else, um, whatever you guys say. 'So, how they hanging?'"

How about va t'faire chier? That was something Pelletier taught him.

What does that mean?

I don't know. Pelletier says it a lot.

Careful now. Don't say it aloud.

You're such a smart-mouth.

There was a time you really enjoyed her...my, smart mouth.

I see where Marty gets it.

Maybe you could have the kind of conversation we used to have years ago. Remember when we talked over everything we did, or thought about?

Yes. I also remember you getting bored by it. Finishing my sentences, like you knew more about what I was saying than I did.

I usually did know more.

See, that's what I mean. And even if you did know more, it's just common decency to let a guy finish what he has to say.

Not if you've said the same thing over again for the tenth time.

Yeah? Well va t'faire chier to you, too. Nanda had told him once that in the Zoroastrian religion in ancient Persia, it was considered a major sin to be boring. They thought of it as a 'little death', and if a person was boring enough, they'd put them out of their misery by whacking their head off. He could understand the feeling of wanting to whack someone's head off because he was so boring. Television made him feel like that. But being told by your own wife, the most important person in the world to you, that you are boring is like being told you are some kind of pervert.

So, talk to her. I don't think you're boring.

To her I would be. What did she say when she moved to New York? She had to be closer to the 'heat source'. I'm sure I'm just Mr. Tepid up here, cutting trees and raising kids.

You've got a point. That doesn't mean you can't talk. What would she think, by the way, of you're having two conversations with her at once? One with her and one in your head with her. That's pretty interesting, wouldn't you say?

So he tried it. He told Gerry, sitting in truck, about the weird phenomenon of having a conversation with her in his head while the two of them sat side by side in the truck cab.

"Well, speak up, boy." Gerry said. "Don't be shy."

He clammed up at that. She was just sitting there waiting to whack his head off.

By the time they arrived at the house the sun had been gone for a good hour. Every window was lit, plus the floodlight between the house and the barn. Marty's Plymouth and Dan's partly-restored GTO sat in their usual spaces in front of the barn. Freddie Brockton's pick-up, which had been there earlier, was gone. Gerry, shivering in her city-stylish coat, ran straight from the truck to the door of the mud room leaving Scheutz to grab her overnight bag out the back of the truck. He hung his jacket on a peg in the mud room and carried Gerry's bag into the kitchen. Just inside the door, Gerry, still wearing her coat and gloves was being hugged by Marty.

Regina, a foot shorter than Marty, strode into the room from the front hall, lightly bouncing on the balls of her feet while she waited in line to hug Gerry. "Hi, Mrs. Scheutz. Oh, it's so nice to see you again."

"Please don't call me Mrs. Scheutz."

"Gerry, Berry, Foferry..." Marty intoned.

Regina slapped his arm. "Show a little respect for your mother."

Gerry laughed. "You should have heard him when he was little." She waddled in a circle like a toddler. "He'd go 'Momma Bomma Fofamma'."

Dan, who had driven up from New York three days before, took his time coming down the front stairs. "Hi, Mom. Good trip?"

"Not too bad. Where's Livia?"

"Upstairs. She's coming down."

Scheutz stood for a moment between Gerry's back and the kitchen door. When Dan led her over to the wood stove to warm up, Scheutz slid around the whole home-coming scene and carried Gerry's bag out to the hall and up the front stairs to the small room in the back where she usually slept when she visited. In the hallway he almost bumped into Livia, the astonishingly beautiful Puerto Rican woman who had accompanied Dan on his two-week vacation in the country the previous summer. Dan's latest short-lived love affair. Scheutz nodded and smiled at her. She lowered her head and smiled back, obviously still a little embarrassed about being thrust into this alien environment where she felt she didn't belong. Pushing his way through the guest room door, Scheutz felt a twinge of compassion for the woman. He'd seen so many in her situation since Dan reached puberty, lovely, intelligent women, with that special gleam in their eye for his son. A gleam that he knew, as Dan's attention drifted elsewhere, would fade to a longing, and then to a dull ache, and eventually to a cicatrix that would eventually be chalked up as one of life's little lessons. In the three days they had spent all together in the same house the previous summer, he had found her to be particularly wonderful. And vulnerable. She majored in history at Columbia University, and, on some weekends, sang with a salsa band in clubs around the city. He would have liked to be able to clue her in on how she could keep Dan, but he hadn't a clue himself.

He dropped Gerry's bag onto the bureau in the small room. Like the other two bedrooms on this end of the house, the room had no heating vent of its own, but relied on convection from the rooms below and one large vent in the second floor hallway. Earlier in the week, in anticipation of Dan's and Gerry's coming for the holidays, Scheutz and Marty had begun warming this end of the house, keeping a fire in the wood stove in the double parlor below. For that week, if Marty was out, Scheutz stoked the fire and sat in there, reading or sometimes just daydreaming, pretending, while telling himself he wasn't doing it, that Gerry was already there. He could not hear her voice in his head at those times, but could almost feel her presence curled into the chair on the other side of the stove the way she had done for so many years, here and in Santa Fe, reading intently, her fingers absent-mindedly fiddling with her hair.

The day before Dan's arrival with Livia, Scheutz had turned up the thermostat for the oil furnace and opened the second floor vent. Dan's old bedroom, with the queen-sized bed and a floor vent directly over the wood stove in the room below, became the toastiest room in the house. The little spare bedroom that Gerry used was certainly not as warm as the hallway but was a comfortable sleeping temperature. Scheutz stripped the single twin bed in the room and, with clean sheets from the free-standing linen closet in the bathroom, remade the bed. He stood a moment, looking out the window, thinking about Gerry's comment in the truck, calling him 'boy'. Livia's high-heeled boots clicked in the hall outside the doorway and then down the front stairs. Voices came up from the open door to the kitchen. The thought flitted through his mind that he wanted to leave. Just put his coat back on and walk out and get in his truck, and drive....Where?

Well, that's a pretty stupid idea. Was that Gerry's voice saying that? No, it was his own. Gerry's voice hadn't said boo since his exchange with the real Gerry in the truck. "It's Christmas, for chrissake," he said aloud to the empty room. "Stop feeling sorry for yourself and enjoy the kids." He said this to his reflection in the window, then waited for Gerry's voice to put its two-cents worth in. Nothing. Outside, the headlights of a car pulled in off the road and up the long dirt driveway to the house.

Scheutz left the room and descended the staircase. He entered the kitchen, surprised at seeing Samantha and her younger brother Joe come in the back door. Samantha ran toward Gerry, letting go a squeal before abruptly cutting it off and imitating Gerry's composure. As the two women hugged Scheutz sensed Gerry's impatience with the girl and her almost cloying imitation of her.

Joe stepped up and shook Gerry's hand as his sister backed away. "Hey, Marty's mom, how you doing? Merry Christmas. Good to see you."

"You guys aren't home on Christmas eve?" Gerry asked them.

"We told the 'rents we had a dinner party to go to," Samantha said. She had been at the house helping Scheutz cook dinner for most of the day while the rest of the young people were playing hockey with Freddie Brockton and a few others down on the frozen river. She had loaned her skates to Livia, who Dan had promised to teach enough to get her up and moving around on the ice. That afternoon, in the wood-stove-warm kitchen Samantha had greased the turkey pan, cut vegetables and made two pies, all in high spirits at the thought of her hero, Gerry, coming that evening. Scheutz himself had been excited, looking forward to Gerry's arrival. Music blasted from the stereo in the front parlor, and Samantha danced around the kitchen, even pulled him into dancing along to Santana's *Black Magic Woman.* The girl always made him so self-conscious doing things like that. The few times she had been able to catch him in a light enough mood to push him over the line into actually relaxing a little and enjoying himself, as on that particular Christmas eve, were like tiny bits of stolen pleasure that actually made him blush to remember them. By the time the sun dipped, around four o'clock, when the crowd stomped their snow-covered boots in the mud room behind the kitchen, the dinner was done.

Freddie, shorter and stockier than Dan, slammed his way out the kitchen door only a few minutes after they all came in from skating. He and Samantha had had a not very carefully modulated argument in the front parlor on the recently reopened side of the house. The two of them had been engaged to be married, and then not and then engaged again and, apparently, not again now. Samantha left in tears a few minutes later saying she and Joe had to go home, relatives were coming that evening. Now here she was back again.

"I thought you had company this evening," Scheutz said to her as she stepped back from hugging Gerry.

Samantha made a face. "It's only our aunt and uncle from Boston. All they ever do is sit around and talk about what kind of wax to put on their cross-country skis. I can't stand it."

"Well, Mom's finally here, let's eat," Marty broke in.

Scheutz had earlier spread a white cotton tablecloth over the long deal table in the middle of the kitchen. While Gerry was upstairs putting her coat and travel bag in her bedroom, the kids all helped prepare the table and bring out the food. Regina went around asking each person what they wanted to drink. Marty and Joe dragged in extra chairs. Dan brought more firewood up from the basement and fed the wood stove. Samantha set her pies, one apple and one blueberry, on the brick shelf that extended behind the wood stove, over the old, closed-off warming oven that was part of the chimney.

Scheutz pulled himself out of the scene and leaned back against the counter, his arms folded across his chest, just watching and listening to Livia oohing and aahing about how it all looked like some television Christmas special. Scheutz had to admit to himself that, yes, it was pretty special. He forgot for a moment about his nose being out of joint over Gerry calling him 'boy' in the truck. This was about as perfect as he imagined it could get. His sons, Gerry, himself, Samantha, his whole world really, all together. They were happy, they were healthy. And in the future, when the boys were gone, this is what he would be left with, a memory like this. This and others. Years ago he had tried explaining this feeling to Gerry, but he didn't have the words, so it came out like the worst sentimental cliché.

In the front parlor, Regina had found an oldies rock station out of Brattleboro that was now doing a truly dopey song called *Rocking around the Christmas Tree.* Gerry walked into the room from the front hall and clapped her hands in delight at the beauty of the table. Marty held a bottle of beer in the air and shouted, "I propose a toast. This Christmas Eve dinner is dedicated to the old folks. Parents. Long may they reign." Everyone except Scheutz and Gerry walked to the table and took up whatever sat in front of their plate to drink. They waved their bottles or glasses first in Gerry's direction and then in Scheutz's.

"Here, here."

"To the parental units."

"Viva las taitas."

Gerry waited graciously for the toast to be over, and then when everyone went back to putting the finishing touches on the table, she walked around to Scheutz and leaned next to him against the counter. She nudged his shoulder with her own and said low into his ear, "Nice kids, huh?"

He turned to her, drinking in the familiar aroma of her body, closer to him than it had been in so many years. And there was that conspiratorial smile of hers that said, that had always said, "I can't believe we're actually getting away with this." All he could manage in response was a nod of his head.

"You raise good sons, Big Daddy," she said.

He couldn't answer. His throat felt clogged on the surge of gratitude that she actually gave him credit for being something more than Paul Bunyan's blue-collar ox, which she'd called him once, years before. He nodded his head again slowly. In a gesture of what he meant to be friendship, since they were right there together, observing the kids, he put his arm across her shoulders and pulled her sideways into him. They stood like that for a few moments before the totally unexpected happened. They both began to breathe heavy, in unison. Scheutz had never experienced such an immediate sexual excitation. And he could feel that she felt it, too. Her chest heaved and he could see her eyelids flutter.

Without looking at him, she broke away and walked briskly to the other end of the table where she took a seat at its head. Or foot, depending on how you looked at it. Scheutz watched her face when she turned to sit, but she had regained her composure and did not meet his gaze. Of all the young people in the room, the only one who saw what had just happened was Samantha. Her eyes widened and she came toward him. Standing squarely in front of him to block everyone else's view, she took his hand and said, "We're ready to sit down." He let her lead him to the chair at the head, or foot, directly across from Gerry, and took the seat next to him.

While the noise of dishing out food and eating and talking and laughing went on around him, he ate slowly and tried to bring himself, the soul of himself, back into the room. The inane little question of which one of them sat at the head and which one at the foot of the table blotted out everything else. He finally forced himself to stop thinking about it. What the hell difference did it make? There had never been a head or foot, just like there had never been a head of the household. They were the same. He forced himself to think about what had just happened over next to the counter. It made no sense. It was such a small moment, why had he reacted to strongly? Why had it happened at all? How could that feeling be there between them so strong and immediate without them knowing it? Maybe Gerry did know it, and that was why she had to spend so much effort maintaining that cool citified demeanor she had always projected since she moved to New York. If that much feeling was under there, what else did it mean? What else did she feel for him that she hid so expertly?

He realized that Samantha had been at his elbow, talking to him. Something about the Christmas tree they were planning on decorating that evening after supper. He nodded to something she said without knowing what he was agreeing to. They were distracted by a burst of laughter from the other end of the table, and Gerry laughing aloud while exclaiming to Marty, "How can you say that?"

"I can say that because I know you. I've known you all my life, remember?" Marty said.

"The first two or three years you didn't know shit, buddy." Gerry poked her fork in his direction.

"Yeah, I did. I was watching you; you just didn't know it."

The silliness of the banter between Marty and Gerry had infected everyone else at the table, with Dan, Regina, and Joe adding commentary, Livia relaxing and laughing with the rest. Even Scheutz had to smile watching the other end of the table. It was like listening to a free-form jazz piece, nothing important being said, but each comment coming like a short riff from a different instrument.

And then it came to him that here he was again, the only one not part of it all, not playing with the group but outside it, just watching the show. A touch on the back of his hand made him turn to look at Samantha sitting to his left. She was also not playing with the group, but sat as if alone, eating slowly and smiling, being entertained by the rest the same as himself. And something about her made him very sad. He'd never given much thought to the girl, except to notice that she always seemed to be there, and that her presence was comforting in some small way. But now that he thought about it, it did seem very sad, her imitation of Gerry, her staying stuck in this small town, her apparently awful on-again-off-again engagement to Freddie Brockton.

Thinking about the girl made him a little less alone. And yes, she was a small comfort to him. And yes, there were those little bits of pure pleasure with her dancing in the house that embarrassed him. But he couldn't think about that now with Gerry here. Actually, he could not allow himself to think about it ever.

Chapter 8

The Man with the Hoe

What had set off the memory of last Christmas? Scheutz stood for a moment, looking down the slope. That was it, the slope. He'd been cutting from the bottom, creating an opening for the skidder to yard out the timber through the area already cut. Without the trees the opening would make a nice ski trail, all the way to the landing, probably all the way to the stream bed below the landing and the logging road if that were cleared.

He'd gotten sidetracked to Gerry again from the image the slope had opened up in his mind. It was actually the next day, Christmas Day. They were all in the pasture behind the house. Under a thick blanket of snow, the hay field dropped away at about a forty-five degree angle to a tree line below. The day was clear and cold, a little windy, the sun glinting off the snow field. Dan was off to the left trying to teach Livia, on Samantha's downhill skis, how to snowplow. He followed her on his own skis, Mr. True Balance, as always. Livia progressed down the slope ten yards at a time before she tangled the skis and fell, squealing, into the powder. Samantha skied alongside Gerry, who wore an old, puffy, down vest that had been left in the attic. Side by side, both on cross-country skis, they hot-dogged down the steepest part of the pasture, traversed the bottom and worked their way up the shallower incline on the other end, then completed the circle again.

Marty and Joe had gotten hold of two "snowboards" as they called them. The boards were some new kind of skiing idea and were made by some guy over in Vermont. Both the boys had become fairly adept at using them. Marty had an edge over Joe since he had spent a good deal of time on a skate board when he lived with his mother in New York. He traded off every other run with his girl friend, Regina, who also looked like she had the form down pat, leaning gracefully to the rear and then alternating to lean over the front edge of the board. The way Regina did it, it looked more like some fluidly exotic dance. All three of them were certainly more beautiful to watch on their boards than anyone he'd every seen on skis.

Marty and Regina began pestering Scheutz to try the board. After his third refusal he finally gave in. Marty showed him how to lean into first the front and then the back edge of the board. "This'll be easier for you than skiing, you don't have to worry about getting all tangled up in your skis. If you go out of control, just sit down." The second winter they spent up here in New England, when Marty was seven years old, Scheutz and Gerry had taken both boys out on cross-country skis, packing a lunch and spending hours on old logging roads in the woods. By the time Dan and Marty moved back to Acworth from New York, that gentle form of winter entertainment had lost all its appeal. From then on it was nothing but the glitzier world of metal-edged skis and black-diamond slopes. The recent development by the Burton fellow in Vermont and some guy named Sym in New York State of these new snowboards, had put Marty and his friends into a buzz of excitement.

Scheutz slid his boots into the footholds of the board but then, even though he tried propelling his body forward with a hula type movement of his hips and legs, could not move. Marty and Regina pushed him slowly to where the pasture slope dropped off and then let him go, whereupon he pitched face forward into the snow. Rolling over and sitting up, his first sensation was the sound of Marty's and Regina's shrieking laughs. Marty had fallen to his knees and Regina bent onto his shoulders, both convulsed in laughter. Joe stood aside, trying to be polite, biting his glove to keep from laughing aloud.

"Dad—(laugh, laugh)—Dad—(laugh, laugh). That was the funniest thing I've seen in—(laugh, laugh)..."

Scheutz wiped the snow from his face, flipped the board away from him and struggled to his feet. Gerry and Samantha had appeared behind Marty and Regina.

"What's going on? What's so funny?" Gerry asked.

Marty pointed at Scheutz but, before he could get a word out, broke into guffaws again. Scheutz walked up the few feet to the top, smacking the front of his coat to knock the snow off it. He had to admit, from their point of view, it must have looked pretty funny in a pratfall sort of way. But, instead of it being funny, he could feel the tightness of anger in his chest. Everything he did when Gerry was around made him feel like a dope and a doofus. She grinned inquisitively at him, infected by the kids' glee, but still not knowing what the joke was. Her red cheeks radiated the beauty of the bright winter day, a dark strand of hair sticking out from under her knit hat in contrast to the clear pink complexion of her face. Her glee felt to him as an accelerator to the blackness of his anger.

"Stupid fucking sport. What's the point? Skiing, snowboarding, what's the difference between this and riding in an elevator? You go up, you come down, you go up, you come down." He couldn't stop himself. Even as he was saying it, he knew how idiotic it sounded to the people on the hill in front of him. The whole world, everyone but him, found some kind of joy in moving their bodies. They danced, skied, raced, swam, skated, climbed mountains, jumped out of airplanes, and did handstands on parallel bars, and what did he do? He plodded day after day, through his life from one fucking tree to another to another.

As if to punctuate his own outburst, the entire group at the top of the pasture broke up laughing. Even Joe stopped biting his glove. Scheutz turned and stomped away, as much as one can stomp though drifted snow, toward the house.

He could not remember what happened after that on that day. He remembered walking by himself to the house, leaving them out there. It was a small, insignificant thing, them all laughing at him like that. But he'd almost lost it. The deep pool of anger that had built all these years had, for such a small thing, threatened to break its dam. He could never remember being so angry. It frightened him. He found himself listening for Gerry's voice to say something to calm him. But she was not there. Probably knew better than to show up at a time like this.

Here came snatches of memory: sitting rigidly in front of the wood stove while watching through the window as everyone else flung themselves about like disgustingly healthy snow bunnies. Then Samantha, in her polypropylene vest and cross-country ski shoes, bringing him a hot lunch of leftovers and acting just a little too chipper for the occasion. Then Gerry, bending her head and pushing out her lower lip to mock his pout. "Poor widdle Daddy," she said. Goddamn, they made him angry. All of them. Just because he acted like the family retard, didn't mean they had to treat him that way. He pushed the memory of Christmas from his mind and bent to the next tree to make the first cut just above the root swell.

You know, you shouldn't be so hard on yourself.

Easy for you to say.

It's all over and done with, it's past. Forget about it. It's almost like you drag all this stuff up again just to prove to yourself that you're not worthy of me.

I don't drag stuff up.

Then what's it all doing here again?

What are you doing here again?

I'm trying to help you out here. Stop acting like an idiot.

See? You do think I'm an idiot.

Oh, for chrissake. I do not think you're an idiot. Is that what you're fishing for? Okay, I will say it. You are not an idiot. Now you can stop acting like the man with the hoe.

What man with a hoe?

You don't remember the painting I showed you? The one by Millet? And the poem by whatsisname, Markham? Bowed by the weight of centuries he leans upon his hoe…ta-dah, ta-dah, ta-dah...and on his back the burden of the world. Who made him dead to rapture and despair…ta-dah, ta-dah…stolid and stunned, a brother to the ox?

Yes, I remember. That's how you always thought of me.

I never did. But I got really fed up with you thinking that's what I thought of you. And, anyhow, here it is a beautiful warm summer day in the woods, your favorite place. What the hell are you doing spending so much mind time thinking about a cold Christmas past?

Fair question. What was he doing remembering Christmas? Not that he had any control over what he remembered whenever the routine of working in the woods set his mind free to float. He took a shot at trying to bring up something he could dwell on that was positive, or at least interesting, and he came up with Christmas again. Years ago. Ten or eleven years. In New York City of all places. What was there in New York that could even remotely interest him? That was the Christmas Eve he'd ended up at a penthouse party in a building on 5th Avenue, down near Washington Square.

Gerry had, only a month before, moved the kids out of Acworth and into an apartment she'd taken in the East Village. She suggested he come down and spend Christmas Day with them. It was their first holiday without him, and Marty especially was having a hard time about the whole thing, coming out of the cocoon of his daily sulk only to zing his mother with his own brand of caustic comments. One of his favorites, apparently, involved the line of argument he'd used often on Scheutz, that she had no right to tell him to do anything, like clean up his and Dan's bedroom, because she didn't own the apartment, only rented it from that old Polish guy on the first floor. Dan, on the other hand, had nothing to say about any of it, which was even worse, according to Gerry. He was all of sudden, Mr. Cool, spending hours in the bathroom, combing his hair, and striking pre-macho poses in the mirror. Gerry said on the phone that maybe the kids would be comforted by him coming down to spend Christmas Day with them.

The problem was, no way Scheutz could even think of driving his old truck down to the city, especially on Christmas Day when no garage was open anywhere, just in the likelihood the Chevy decided to succumb to one of its many ailments en route. And the Amtrak schedule could not get him there early enough in the day. So, he decided to go down the night before. Unfortunately, she did not have a phone yet, so he could not call and tell her this. She had given him directions from Penn Station, a crosstown bus and then another down 2nd Avenue, but it was confusing and, since it was raining, he decided to take a taxi across town. The driver, a young man with shoulder length hair knew exactly where 2nd Avenue and 6th Street was. "Must be right across from the Fillmore East," he said, leaning his head toward the back of the cab. "Cool spot."

"From the what?"

"The Fillmore East, man. You heard of the Fillmore in California, right?" Scheutz shook head as the cabbie peered at him in the rearview mirror. "Well, it's only the absolute grooviest place on the planet to hear good, I'm saying the best, rock music in the world, man. Janis, Jimi, Jerry, Joanie, they all played there. And now, coming to you live, right here in our little burg, you can hear the same people at the Fillmore East. I'm telling you, man, the planet gets smaller...." He stopped his rapid monologue for a moment, his head cocked to one side. "Oh, it's my song." He began a rhythm with his right hand on the steering wheel. "Dadda da dah. Dan dan da dadda. Dadda da dah. Dan dan da dadda." He turned up the cab's radio, blasting the rock group Cream playing *In the Sunshine of Your Love.* The song struck Scheutz, in this cab on the rainy streets of this city, as some kind of cruel joke.

Gerry's apartment was on the fifth floor in the front. He could see the light on. After a somewhat frightening ride in the very rickety wrought iron cage of the building's elevator, he walked the dimly lit hallway to knock on apartment number 502.

On leaving the house in Acworth and driving to the Amtrak station in Bellows Falls, he could not shake the image of Orpheus descending into hell to bring back Eurydice to the land of the living. And then, as the train descended down through Massachusetts and Connecticut into the Bronx, and the evening sky darkened, the beautiful white snow turned to a cold gray rain. He was deposited into the underground, the graffiti-laden inferno of Penn Station. The crowds frightened him, all those people pushing, rushing to get out of the city to celebrate the pagan festival of lights with a breath of clean air. And then the taxi driver, delivering him across town, the streets in between the East Side and West Side flowing like the River Styx. The radio in the artificial pine scent smelly cab taunted him with a song of sunshine that probably never dared to show its face in this morbid land.

At his knock, Gerry's voice sang out from inside, "Come in. It's open. I'm almost ready."

Well, at least she sounded happy to see him. Inside, a short hallway ran beside a sparsely furnished kitchen and into a larger, completely empty room with a hardwood, parquet floor, raised molding on the walls, and two windows that looked out onto what had to have been East 6th Street.

Gerry tapped down the hallway from the other end of the apartment and stopped dead in her high heels, a smile dropping from her face as she saw him. "What are you doing here?"

"You told me to come in." He had never seen her in high heels. Nor with such a gauzy, flowing, knee-length evening dress, her beautiful dark hair, obviously teased on the top before it fell with an added fullness down her back. This was a new person, one he'd never seen dolled up like this. From the day she and Dan met him in Mexico there had been nothing but the paint-spattered jeans and sweatshirts he always loved her in.

"I thought you were someone else," she said. "Is he here?"

"Is who here?"

"Bentley. Are you in the kitchen, Bentley?" No answer. She turned to Scheutz. "We agreed you were to come tomorrow."

"I couldn't get a train early enough. So, I came down tonight. What's the big deal?"

She let out an exasperated snort. "The big deal is, I'm going out tonight."

"Okay. I thought we could all spend a nice evening together. But, if you have to go, I'll stay here with the kids. Why don't you have any furniture in here?"

"I don't want you to stay here, Clement. As you can see there is no furniture, nothing to sleep on. Now, just go and come back in the morning. But not too early."

"Where the hell am I supposed go? Where does somebody go in this city? I don't know anybody. I thought for sure you'd put me up for one night."

"I told you, I can't."

"I'd put you up if you came to see the kids at my house."

"This is different."

"Can I at least see them before I go."

"Marty's asleep. Dan's watching TV with the baby sitter. And I have to go out." Someone knocked on the apartment door. "Oh, shit. Can't you just wait till tomorrow?" She lifted her voice toward the door. "Hang on, I'll be right out." Scheutz walked toward the inner hall leading to the front of the apartment. "Dammit, boy, I said no."

"Don't call me boy."

She glared at him. "Get out of here. Now."

"I'm going to say hi to Dan." With heels on, her eyes were at his level. They held each other's gaze for a long moment. Her lips quivered. He imagined them forming the word 'boy' directly behind them. What was the big deal? She could give him a blanket on the floor or something for the night. "Dan would be upset if he knew I was here and didn't say hi." He pulled himself away from her eyes and walked into the front room. The room was obviously Gerry's bedroom. Her clothes were piled against the wall and spilled out of the room's only closet. The only furnishings were a double mattress on the floor and a small black and white television set, also on the floor. Dan sprawled on the bed next to a cherubic young woman, only a few years older than him, who was tall for his twelve years. They both looked up at Scheutz when he entered.

"Hey Big Daddy, what's happening?"

"Came to say hi. What's on?" He went to sit down on the mattress next to Dan.

Gerry called from down the hall. "Clement. Goddammit, no. Out. Come on, this is not fair."

Dan looked up at him, giving him that look he and Dan and Marty shared whenever they knew they were doing something Gerry would not approve of. He stood and took hold of Scheutz's arm, nodding his head toward the front of the apartment. "Come on, Dad. It's bad enough. Don't make it worse, okay?" They moved into the hall a few steps before Dan stopped and motioned for him to bend down so he could whisper to him. "I hate to tell you this, but Mom's got a date."

"Looks that way." A date? Gerry had a date? He stood stock still in the little hallway with his hand on Dan's shoulder. He had to think about this. Is that what people did here in hell, they went on dates? The idea of Gerry going on a date didn't fit anywhere. Dan took his hand and looked up at him, waiting for some response. His son needed him to give him some reassurance about this. How awful it must be for him that his mother was going out on a date with someone besides his father.

Dan motioned for him to bend down again so he could whisper to him. "And another thing, Dad." Scheutz leaned in to hear better what the boy was saying. "See that baby sitter?" Scheutz frowned, glancing into the front room where the young girl watched the television with intensity. "She's a stone hippie, man. Not only that, but she's a 'stoned' hippie. Mom's leaving us alone for a few hours; you know what that means?" He bugged out his eyes and waved his hands at the sides of Scheutz's face. "Free-love, Daddy-O."

"What? What do you mean, free love?"

"I mean....if Mom isn't here, and Marty's sleeping, I'm going to have some fun tonight. So, you can't screw it up for me by hanging around. Know what I mean?"

"You're only twelve, for chrissake. What kind of a Sodom and Gomorrah is this? My family lives in the middle of Sintown, USA. There's no furniture in the apartment. An irresponsible hippie is supposedly babysitting, while one of her charges, this little boy is trying to get in her pants. GERRY."

She appeared at the end of the hall. "Hush, Clement. You're going to wake Marty." She turned to a man standing behind her. "I'm sorry to put you through this, Ben. He showed up here about two minutes before you arrived."

Scheutz clamped his teeth together to make himself calm down. "Dan, take a piece of fatherly advice," he whispered, not moving his teeth or his lips. "Let that girl alone. Go to bed." Then in a low voice, letting up on his tooth-clamp. "I'll see you in the morning. It'll be Christmas. We'll have fun. Okay?" He gave Dan a hug, and tried propelling him toward the closed door that was probably their bedroom.

Dan let himself be pushed to the door but not through it. "Okay, I'll take your 'fatherly' advice and go to bed on one condition—that you do like Mom asks you and come back tomorrow. Deal?"

Scheutz looked at Gerry, standing at the end of the hall, and then at Dan in the doorway to the bedroom. Beyond him, inside the room, Marty lay curled under a quilt. Scheutz didn't believe for a minute that Dan would not be back in front of the television with his 'sitter' the moment the apartment door closed. He smiled at Dan. "Well, why don't I just keep her company for a while?"

Dan's eyes shifted first toward his mother at one end of the hall and then toward the sound of the television at the other, as he gave his head an emphatic shake. In a voice too low for his mother to hear, he said, "You just want her for yourself, don't you?"

Scheutz felt a spasm of laughter escape from his throat. He hugged Dan to him. Damn, he loved this kid. The idea of having sex with a stoned teeny-bopper in front of a television set struck him as truly unappetizing. But the idea of competing with his twelve-year-old son for the attentions of said teeny-bopper was hilarious. "I give up," he said into the hair on the top of Dan's head. "I'll see you in the morning. Just don't catch the clap."

"Clap? What's that?" Dan squinted in question as he prodded Scheutz through the bedroom doorway.

Back in the empty living room, Gerry introduced him to Ben. Bentley. That was his name. Scheutz had met him before, in Hanover, at a Dartmouth College film festival. He could never remember the guy's name, even though Gerry talked about him from time to time as being a newly acquired friend. He was kind of a pasty looking dude, as if he spent all his waking hours inside the same dark movie theater where Scheutz met him. Another name popped into Scheutz's mind when they were introduced that crowded out his real name.

"Listen, why don't you go to the party with us?" the guy was saying. What was the name that Scheutz had tagged him with that night in Hanover? "I'll know lots of people there, and just maybe I can find someone who could let you have a couch for the night."

"That's all right. I don't really like parties. Don't worry I'll find someplace to go."

"I doubt it," Gerry said. "Now you've got me worried about you. You don't know anyone here in the city and you're liable to end up in some homeless shelter covered with bedbugs."

That patronizing—or was it matronizing?—tone of hers could be so annoying. "Why don't I just stay here until you get back. And then…."

"No."

"Oh, why not?" Bentley asked.

Gerry raised a palm toward Bentley. "Stay out of this. I said no. It'll be much worse finding a place a two o'clock in the morning than it will be now. Besides, I don't want to come to home and find my children are on a train back to New Hampshire."

"You think I'd do that?" The thought had crossed Scheutz's mind.

"Look." She turned to Scheutz. "I want you to go to the party with us. I do not want you to stay here when I am not here. If Ben can't find somebody to put you up, I will. I promise. I don't want you out wandering the streets till all hours. You're a country boy."

"I grew up in a city, remember?"

"But it was a lot friendlier than this one."

Through the drizzling rain outside the taxi window, Scheutz kept track of the street names so he could find his way back. 2nd Avenue to 5th Avenue and then two blocks down to the arch at Washington Square Park. Only six blocks away, but the penthouse of the building on the corner of 5th Avenue was as sharply defined a contrast to the apartment on 2nd Avenue as the light and shadow of some old Fritz Lang movie.

Chapter 9

Orpheus Descending

The penthouse apartment glowed just like an over-lit movie set with a long backdrop of windows looking out over the park and Greenwich Village beyond. At least that's what Gerry told him he was seeing from where he'd retreated very soon after entering the apartment door. He'd moved to the window immediately, sidling along the wall at the edge of the chattering crowd that threatened to swallow him. She left him there and pushed her way into the mass of people as he watched her, taller than most of the revelers, worm her way toward Bentley in the middle of a group of other expensively-dressed party people.

Bored finally of peering through the blurred, water-spotted glass, he realized he was hungry. He had not eaten since that morning. He made his way down the length of the window to a food and drink table that ran perpendicular to it. There he placed himself between an enormous silver champagne bubbler and a tureen of what looked to be scallops and shrimps in a cream sauce. The party, in a maelstrom about him, left him in a cocoon with his own little picnic. The room gyrated with moving bodies to the sound of Gracie Slick screaming *Don't you want somebody to love? Don't you need somebody to love?* On the other side of the champagne bubbler a short-haired blonde beauty in a skimpy black sheath ranted into the ear of a middle-aged man in a tweed jacket about the Republican conspiracy that had recently elected Richard Nixon and assassinated both Martin Luther King and Robert Kennedy. The stoop-shouldered pedant listened and nodded like one of those little dolls people put on their dashboard with its head on a spring. The minute she drew a breath, he launched into her with his own conspiracy theory about the relationship last spring between the Prague massacre in Czechoslovakia and the Tet offensive in Viet Nam.

Scheutz filled his fluted champagne glass again with his left hand and speared another scallop from the tureen with his right. No matter how you looked at it, 1968 was a bad year. He had his own conspiracy theory. The Bentley boy Gerry was now dancing with over in the corner was behind her moving herself and the kids to the city. He had gotten her the job as a paste-up artist for Milton Glaser at his Pushpin Studio. He had found her the apartment on the fourth floor of the building on 2nd Avenue and East 6th Street. He was responsible even for Scheutz being at this party tonight. What the hell was his name? Bentley. Bentley what? 'Buttwad', that was the name Scheutz had made up for him upon meeting him in Hanover the first time. Bentley Buttwad was some relation to old C.S. Mott who owned the controlling stock shares in General Motors, and who left the whole Buttwad family well provided for. Of course, Bentley wouldn't be caught dead driving a General Motors car. Couldn't you guess it? He drove a Bentley. Kind of a buttwad beige color. Bentley could be seen flapping his pony tail in rock and roll rapture. Scheutz speared another scallop pretending it was a Bentley eyeball.

"Hi, how are you doing?" The voice came from a very pretty face with brown eyes, and framed by long, straight black hair. The woman smiled up at him from the height of his shoulder, as she extended her hand. "My name's Renee."

"I'm Clement," he said and realized, squinting down at her, that he was a little light-headed from the champagne. He put the scallop spear in his mouth and shook her hand. "This your party?"

"Yep. And I'm glad you could come." She wore a white angora sweater with two holiday pins, a tiny menorah and a miniature holly wreath, over the left breast like combat ribbons in the campaign against the solstice gloom.

"I'm here with my wife," he said.

"Oh? Who is she?"

"That's her over there. See the tall one with the dark hair dancing with the pony tail guy?"

"With Bentley? You're kidding. I thought she was his date."

Scheutz speared another Bentley eyeball from the tureen. Besides being a little drunk, he must have had a touch of flu. His head hurt behind his eyes and his body felt all achy in the joints.

"You know you shouldn't put that pick back in there after it was in your mouth. You're putting your germs back in the Newburg."

"You want one?"

She tilted her head to the side and smiled up at him. "Sure. Why not? Make it a shrimp."

With a new plastic pick he speared a shrimp and placed it between her perfect white teeth. "That's some very delicious food," he said.

"I know." She talked around her mouthful of shrimp. "I'll give you the name of my caterer, if you want." She flapped her hand. "He's wonderful. He's such a funny guy, too. You'd love him. He's like really, really conservative." Right hand flap. "But he's also really, really swishy." Left hand flap. She paused, gave him a quizzical look. "So...what do you do?" She put a hand on his arm. "No, let me guess. You're an actor."

He took another sip of champagne and shook his head.

"You can't deny it. You look so familiar. Don't tell me, let me guess. I've seen you in something. No, no, don't tell me." She waved her finger like a scolding school teacher. "Aren't you in that new Stanley Kubrick movie, *2001*?"

"No. Really. I'm just visiting in the city."

"I could have guessed that. You work in California. That's why you have that healthy complexion."

"I live in New Hampshire. And I'm not an actor."

"Oh, I love New Hampshire. *Ski trails down a mountainside. Moonlight in*...no, that's Vermont isn't it?" She giggled. "What do I know? I'm a little...you know." She waved her hand in circles. "They've got some great ganja in the bedroom. So, come on, you want to dance?"

"Not really. I don't dance."

"Come on. Put your glass down. Here, let me have it."

"No. Really. I don't want to dance." He lifted his glass out of her reach.

"Listen, I'm the hostess, and I say you have to dance." She tried to push him away from the table without any success. "Jesus, what're you made of, brick? You're built like a brick shithouse." Another fit of giggles. "You some kind of a fitness nut?"

"No. I work as a logger."

With her hand still on his waist, she stopped pushing and looked off toward the corner of the ceiling. "A logger? What do you do, write in a log book or something?"

"No, I cut down trees."

"You mean you're a lumberjack? No shit? I never met a lumberjack. You don't look like a lumberjack. Aren't you supposed to have one of those checkered shirts or something? Hey, I know a lumberjack joke. You gotta hear this, it's really funny. Um, let me think. What is it? Oh, yeah. What did the lumberjack's wife say when he...something...I forget. Anyhow, what did she say?"

He shook his head. And smiled in spite of himself. This woman was getting to him. She was so cute.

"She said, 'Don't let your lumber jack off.' Hah. Isn't that funny? You get it?" She laughed aloud, then giggled again. And he laughed, at her, not at the joke, which he'd heard twenty years ago. "Listen," she said. "I have to go in the bedroom for a minute. I'll be right back. Don't you move. What am I saying, you probably can't move. Okay?" She patted his chest, then squeezed his arm muscle before moving off.

He felt his heart flutter in his chest. And he had an erection. He held his glass under the stream of the champagne bubbler again, drank, and looked in the direction of the bedroom, already wanting her to come back. He looked over at Gerry and the Buttwad dancing slowly in the corner. The Beatles sang, *Hey, Jude, don't make it bad. Take a sad song and make it better. The minute you let her into your heart, then you can start to…*The tingling started in his hands. His chest muscles tightened and his breath came short. The noise of the party faded around him and all he could see was the Buttwad in the corner, his head draped onto Gerry's shoulder. He could feel his fingers masticating the man's bones like soft spines of canned sardines, his insides oozing out between Scheutz's fingers like lily-livered oatmeal.

He blinked. He couldn't do this. He had to get away from here, get away from that gorgeous but dangerous siren whose party it was, and who infused into him enough spirit to bring him back to life. This antidote to his being a zombie flicked open the cellar door to his rage. He could feel it welling up in his throat. And the Buttwad was not even fair game. If the man had any kind of personal force, or even if he was as physically large as Scheutz, it might have been okay. Forget about the fairness in squishing a scallop, he wanted to do it. He imagined Gerry's shock in seeing him come to life after all these years, but he could also see beyond it to the horror she would feel.

Renee, the siren, entered the periphery of his vision, moving toward him through the crowd. Squishing the Buttwad would certainly spoil the party, and he couldn't do that. He also could not let himself get turned on to the siren the way he could see was happening. This was what treason must have felt like. Like some kind of violation of his longing to have Gerry back.

He could not hide from the siren in her own house. He also had to get away from the sight of Gerry in the arms of the Buttwad. He set down his champagne glass and moved away from the table, working his way through the crowd till he reached the corridor leading to the front door of the apartment. In the foyer, in the middle of a pile on a chaise lounge, he found his sheepskin coat. He fled through the front door and donned the coat while waiting for the elevator.

Outside, the rain had lessened to a light drizzle. He stood on the corner next to the building, wrapping the sheepskin tighter around him. Now what? Going back to the apartment on 2nd Avenue was out. He could not take the chance that Gerry would bring the Buttwad back there after the party. He could see himself grinding the creep into the bare parquet floor with his children watching and his wife screaming at him to stop.

His head hurt, his joints ached. He couldn't tell whether the flush he felt was from the champagne, or the rage, or if he had a fever. He had no idea what time it was. Probably not long before midnight. The large cathedral across the street and up a block piped Christmas music out into the street. *O come all ye faithful, joyful and triumphant...* Well, that left him out. On three counts. He wasn't one of their faithful, he wasn't joyful and he certainly wasn't triumphant. Not yet, anyway. He could not remember the ending of the Orpheus and Eurydice story. Had Orpheus been successful in spiriting Eurydice and her children back to Acworth. Gerry must have seen already how difficult it could be, living in this city and trying to raise two kids on not much money.

Of course, he had not counted on the Buttwad still being in the picture. His money and influence could throw a considerable redoubt around Gerry's defenses. But he'd work on it tomorrow. He had no idea what plan of assault to make, but whatever he did he had to bury the rage again. He'd play it by ear, tomorrow. Offer her the same thing he had always shown her, friendship, stability, love for the children, love for her, certainly. What else? He couldn't give her the one thing she really wanted right now, the stimulation, the chance to find wherein her 'sparkle' lay, as she had said. But is that worth putting yourself in a place like this? Is it worth putting your children in a place like this?

Well, he couldn't stand there all night. Maybe he should just go back to the apartment on 2nd Avenue. It was not that far a walk from where he stood. Even if she didn't bring the Buttwad home, nobody would be awake, and the teeny-bopper would probably not even remember having seen him earlier, so she wouldn't let him in. Even if she did, he'd have to sleep on the floor in his wet coat. Then when Gerry finally got home, she'd certainly pitch a bitch at him. Maybe he should go back up to the party.

No. He'd rather die here on the street. The party probably wouldn't break up till three o'clock in the morning, anyhow, by which time he'd be dead from the flu he surely had. He turned in the opposite direction from that of Gerry's apartment and walked into Washington Square Park. Here and there people moved along the streets and on the walkways inside the park. He came out of the park into a series of blocks that no longer had streets and avenues with numbers for names, MacDougal, Bleecker, Cornelia. Finally, not even knowing what street he was on, there glowed a long, vertical neon red sign that read "Greenwich Hotel."

Inside, a man with a Spanish accent behind a heavily barred window, gave him a room key in exchange for $11.36. Scheutz lost track of how many flights of stairs he climbed, four, maybe five. There was no elevator that he could see. On the right floor, he followed a labyrinth of plywood paneled walls until he found, first a public toilet with a filthy piss-trough, and then a wooden door with the same number as the one on his key. There was no window in the room and the only light came in through a wire mesh about a foot wide that ran between the top of the plywood wall and the ceiling.

My God, what a shit hole. But he was beyond caring. He had to lie down. Without disturbing the one blanket on the bed, or unbuttoning his coat, he lay on his back with the knuckles of each hand resting against opposite walls. The joints of his body ached.

His head throbbed with stuffed sinuses. His mind swirled with images of the day, that apartment with no furniture, Gerry dancing with the Buttwad, the hostess in the white sweater, Dan whispering to him about the stoned baby-sitter, the taxi driver. That song on the radio while splashing through the rainy streets on New York. There were probably a lot worse places to be in this world, but right now he couldn't think of any.

This was all his own fault. If he hadn't been such a....what the hell was it he'd done anyhow, to put his children and Gerry in such a place? She had said that he died on her and that she was dying in that house in Acworth. She could not stand the thought of another winter there, where it got dark by four thirty in the afternoon and the cold numbed her brain. She had been happy in Santa Fe, and in Mexico. Even Cincinnati was better than New Hampshire, she had ranted at him. But he didn't get it till it was too late. He considered winter to be the best time of year, working in the woods, cozy inside their old farmhouse. Acworth was just this side of heaven. But you have to die to go to heaven, she said.

You have to die to go to hell, too. And that's just what he felt he was doing, here in this shit-hole. And it served him right. Because all he could think of, even now, was how beautiful the snow had looked when he had left home that morning.

Chapter 10

Christmas in the City

He woke with a mouth that tasted like he'd been sucking the ashes out of his wood stove, and a bladder inflated to the size of a blimp. When he finally figured out where he was, he realized that all the little noises he had heard earlier, beyond the wall of his own private dungeon, had ceased. Staring up at the paint-blistered ceiling, he wondered if maybe he might be dead. The room was certainly small enough to resemble a coffin—his knuckles still rested against each wall. But the dim glow of the hall light still shone through the wire mesh at the top of his wall. That was a hopeful sign. The thought of stumbling down the hall to that horrible pissoir he'd seen the night before, and then back to his little cubicle made him almost wish he was dead. That, along with the image of Gerry dancing in the arms of the Buttwad.

He sat up, expecting every ache to return, but was surprised to find that he felt much better than he had when he had locked the door to his room the night before. His headache was gone, but he did feel a little lightheaded. The rest was overshadowed by his burning mouth and overblown bladder. He stood and unlocked the door. Outside in the hall, nothing had changed except for a barred but dirty window at the far end, which now showed a square of daylight.

Out on the street, the sun was too bright. The air had turned colder, as if the city could have had a white Christmas if only the clouds had hung around. By the time he reached St. Mark's Place the full realization came to him. He knew he would not be successful in convincing Gerry to leave the city. Why ruin the holiday? He would enjoy the kids. Act happy to open the presents they got for him. Accept their hugs. At least Marty's hug, since Dan had considered himself too old for that even before he left for New York. Smile as they opened the presents he had sent down the week before.

Dan answered his knock at the door of apartment 502. He wore pajama bottoms and a t-shirt. With the door to the outer hall still standing open, Dan did something he had not done in over a year. He put his arms around Scheutz. "You came back," he said into Scheutz's chest.

"Why wouldn't I?"

"I don't know....I was just worried that you wouldn't."

Scheutz pulled the boy into his chest with one arm. "Is everybody up?"

"No. Mom's still sleeping. Marty and I are watching TV in our room. Come on." He led Scheutz past the kitchen and empty living room to their bedroom. The door to the front room, Gerry's room, was closed. The apartment, as Scheutz had noticed the night before, was warm, almost too warm.

"Is the Buttwad here?" Scheutz whispered.

"The what?" Dan stopped just inside the bedroom door.

"You know, the boyfriend. Whatsisname, Bentley."

Dan let out a hoot. "Did you hear what he called Bentley?" he said to Marty who sat sideways on his bed with his back against the wall, watching the little black and white television that sat propped on the foot of the other bed, Dan's bed. He was also in pajamas.

"Dad!" Marty jumped up onto the bed and leapt at Scheutz, throwing his arms around his neck. Scheutz squeezed Marty's young body to him. Marty said, "Mom said Santa Claus might not make it, but you were coming instead."

"So, is that good or bad?" Scheutz teased him.

Marty squeezed his neck harder in reply. "Are you going to take us home?"

That stopped him. He could feel tears come to his eyes. What should he do? He could take them. Right now, before Gerry woke up. They could be on the train to New Hampshire and home for supper. His mind raced with the scenario. Gerry would wake and find her children gone. She'd be frantic. She'd find the fastest way to get to Acworth. And then what? The tug-of-war would start. He could not let that happen. He certainly could not keep them from their mother. He couldn't make them have to choose.

"Is the truck here?" Marty asked.

"No. I took the train."

"Well, let's go. I'll get Mom up and you guys start packing."

"Mom's not going back to Acworth, you dope," Dan said.

"But I hate it here," Marty said.

Dan and Marty would certainly not ever leave their mother. For themselves and for her; they wouldn't do that to her. What should he do? If there were someone he could ask about this....Gerry was the only one who came to mind. He had always turned to her, whenever he'd had a problem like this he couldn't work out. But, obviously, he couldn't ask her about this one. He stood there, frozen, holding Marty, the sound of some zany reindeer cartoon coming from the television.

"Let's talk about this, okay," he said softly to Marty. He leaned over and set the boy down onto his bed. Marty nodded without saying anything. The two twin beds were the only furniture in the room. There was no closet; the boys' clothes were piled in the corners of the too-small room. Scheutz sat sideways on the bed next to Marty. Dan sat on the other side of him, his shoulder and hip touching Scheutz's. All three stared at the idiotic antics of two reindeer—Dancer and Prancer—on the television. Scheutz was too stunned and too jammed up to know where to even start. The stark reality of this room reminded him of the room he'd just spent the night in at the Greenwich Hotel. This was where his children now lived. True, it was more space than Dan had in the little one-room house where the three of them had lived in Taxco before Marty was born. But that was different; they were all there together. They had all three slept together in a pile on the mattress making the place the coziest nest Scheutz had ever known. As Gerry become larger in her pregnancy with Marty, the mattress grew smaller and they had to sleep even closer together, protecting her from the cold mountain night air. But this…

When the cartoon was over, Dan said, "I'm going to get a glass of milk. You want some, Marty?"

"I want some cereal."

Dan squeezed by them. He returned, saying, "The milk smells bad. That refrigerator doesn't get very cold."

"I'm hungry," Marty said.

"And there's only a little bit of cereal."

"I hate this place."

The next cartoon started, this one about a bunch of mice scurrying around a pile of Christmas presents under the tree before the family woke up. They watched the mice, dumbly, nobody speaking for a long time.

He had to stop this. Stop this obsession with the hell he was wallowing in. If he was going to figure out how to deal with the situation, he needed to be a little more objective, at least to think a little clearer. It might be a few hours until Gerry got up. She was probably out late partying with the Buttwad, and she never was an early riser even in her most domestic mode. Meanwhile, he could be spending time being with the kids. But he couldn't just be with them as long as he was indulging himself with his Orpheus fantasy. "You guys mind if we turn the television off for a while?"

"There's nothing else to do here," Marty said.

"We could talk."

"Talk is cheap. I want action."

"We can't do anything about anything until your mother gets out of bed."

"We already talked with her about it," Dan said. He reached across the beds and turned off the television.

"And?"

"She says we have to stay here." Marty said.

"This place really does kind of suck, Dad," Dan said. "I mean, I thought it was going to be this great adventure. At least Mom said it was. But it's not."

"It's not as bad as that tiny place we had in Mexico."

"I'm talking about outside. Yeah, there's a few cool people out there, but there's a lot crazies running around this neighborhood. You can't go out at night, and there's nothing to do inside except sit around listening to Mom and her friends talk about art and stuff like that. Like anybody cares."

"When do we open our Christmas presents?" Marty asked.

"We have to wait till Mom wakes up, don't we?" Dan said.

"Do we?" Marty turned to Scheutz.

"Well, yes, if we're all going to spend Christmas together, we should wait till your mother is with us."

"Maybe it's not even Christmas," Marty said. "It doesn't seem like Christmas."

"The guy on the television said it was," Dan said.

It certainly didn't seem like any Christmas Scheutz had ever seen. The three of them sat side by side on Marty's bed, leaning with their backs against the wall, staring at the blank television screen. A movement high up on the opposite wall caught his attention. A cockroach wandered in a slow arc toward the ceiling.

"Why don't you guys get dressed? Let's get out of here."

"Where we going? What about Mom?"

"I don't know. Let her sleep for now. We'll be back. We'll go get some breakfast or something. We can't just sit here. Is there a place around here where you can buy a Christmas tree?"

"Yeah." Dan stood up and moved toward his corner, his pile of clothes. "Over in the next block. On 1st Avenue."

"Good. Let's go. Come on Marty. Up, up, up."

They creaked down in the elevator, and out onto the empty streets. Across the street a large coffee shop with the name Ratner's showed some activity inside but the front door was still locked. Marty held Scheutz's hand as they walked the long block of East 6th Street. Dan talked about some of the people they'd met so far in the city. Scheutz noticed he carefully avoided mentioning the stoned hippie baby-sitter from the night before. What would have been a very inexperienced frontal assault was probably repulsed by her, or else he would have dropped some hint by now of what happened. Good.

The store on 1st Avenue that sold Christmas trees was closed. As were all the other stores on the street. A few scraggly little trees stood outside on the sidewalk, leaning against the building. Marty picked out the best one. The least objectionable one. He and Dan carried the tree while Scheutz tagged behind pondering the inverse ratio of trees to people between New York and New Hampshire. Back on 2nd Avenue, he could see that the little corner store with the name Gem Spa was open a block up on the corner of St. Mark's Place.

They stood the tree against the building while all three squeezed into the little store past early customers, men looking for newspapers, cigarettes, magazines, candy. Scheutz bought a bag of individually wrapped hard candy in different colors. He offered the chubby man behind the counter five dollars for the strand of colored Christmas lights strung around the inside of the door. "Teke it. Teke it." The counter man said waving his hand. "It has to come down today anyway. It's for the kiddies, right? Teke it." Scheutz paid him the five dollars plus money for the candy, plus Marty had found a comic book he wanted.

Dan helped him pull out the staples that held the strand of lights to the door frame. They rolled it up and put it in the bag with the candy and the comic book. Scheutz carried the bag and the boys carried the tree back to the apartment house, crammed the tree, which was a little taller than Scheutz but not nearly as bulky, into the rickety elevator. Trapped in a corner by the branches, Marty giggled because the pine needles tickled him.

There was no tree stand so Scheutz stood the tree on the floor in the corner of the empty living room. With twine that Dan found in the kitchen, he tied it to a curtain rod hook on the window frame on one side and to a small nail on the top of the door frame leading to the kitchen on the other. Marty and Dan strung the lights. The cellophane on the hard candy was twisted on both ends and, by rewrapping them, it was possible to make a little hook of the wrapper to hang it on a branch. The branches on the tree were so skimpy that the candy and the lights were enough. Dan found an oven mitt in a kitchen drawer on which he drew an angel face. Scheutz placed the mitt onto the spindly stem at the top of the tree. Dan plugged the lights in and they all three stood back against the opposite wall and viewed their creation.

"Der Scheutzbaum," Scheutz said

"I like it," Dan said.

"Let's show Mom," Marty said.

"Maybe we better let her sleep some more." Scheutz laid his hand on the top of Marty's head. "Where are all the presents, do you know?"

"I know," Dan said. "They're in the closet in Mom's room."

"All right, let's do this. Very quietly so you don't wake her, bring all the presents out here and put them under the tree. Then, since there is nowhere to sit in this apartment, and no food either, we will go across the street and get some breakfast. And if your mother is still not up when we get back, we'll wake her. Okay?"

Dan and Marty slunk silently back and forth across the front room bringing already wrapped presents of various sizes from the closet to the where Scheutz stood at the open door, careful not to disturb the rumpled lump of Gerry's unmoving form at the far side of her bed. All he could see of her was a mass of dark hair spilling out from a disorganized pile of sheets and blankets. As the pile of presents grew in his arms, he could only stand mesmerized by the form in the bed. There was nothing else, nothing else he could think of that he wanted more in his life than to wake up every morning in the nestled warmth of her sleeping body. The constriction in his chest he'd felt since getting off the train in Penn Station the day before now turned into an ache. Yes, he would move to this hellacious place if it meant he could wake up every morning next to Gerry.

Dan closed the door softly and they all three carried the presents down the short hallway to the living room to pile them under the tree. The tree and the presents made, a corny but lovely tableau. Marty ushered them out the door to go get breakfast.

The waitress in Ratners', a middle-aged woman with a face resembling a tired old hound dog, and with what sounded like a Yiddish accent, flashed them a smile that he would never have thought possible coming from such a mug. "And what are you gonta heve, sweetie?" she asked Marty. What Marty was going to have seemed to Scheutz like more food than could possibly be crammed into an eight-year-old. And Dan also dug into his pancakes and sausages like he hadn't eaten in a while. Scheutz watched them silently as he sipped his coffee and ate his eggs.

The initial hunger slaked, they fell into the easy pattern of conversation that characterized breakfast at home on the weekends when Scheutz wasn't off in the woods at the crack of dawn. Marty missed his friend, Joe, he said. But not as much as he missed their home in Acworth, and his and Dan's big bedroom with all his stuff in it.

Dan sipped on a cup of coffee. This was something new. Scheutz had never seen him drink coffee before. Another new thing. Right in line with Dan's interest in hitting on the baby sitter the night before. He didn't look like he was enjoying the coffee, more like he was posing with it, trying it out, doing what the big guys did. Puberty rearing its ugly head. It was not Dan, but only Marty who was pushing to go back home to Acworth. Even though Dan told him he hated all it down here, he was loving this New York adventure. He had been talking for a few months before they left about moving out of the bedroom he shared with Marty, about wanting to make himself a room in the attic, leaving all the little-kid things behind. Being plopped suddenly in the middle of

New York City's Lower East Side, a heat source, as Gerry called it, of free love and flower power, must seem like a teenager's wet dream come true.

Scheutz looked over at the waitress who had just straightened from placing something on the next table. She caught his eye and gave him another one of her beaming smiles, as if she was congratulating him on his insight about Dan. And suddenly he felt very tired. Whatever counter forces he faced in his struggle to rescue Gerry and the kids from the depths of hell had just doubled. More than doubled. He had lost an ally in Dan who had gone over to the other side. Gerry and Dan were doing the same thing, moving from the known, the safe, the comfortable, into the Land of Nod. In Dan's case it was nothing less than a force of nature, not a whole lot different from what Scheutz himself had done at age thirteen, running away from home with his little brother Willi, the two of them hitch-hiking to Florida.

How can you tug against something like that? He watched Dan, watched the way he ate, the way he took a bite of sausage and then a bite of the toast he'd folded in half just the way Gerry did. And then watched the way he looked around the room to see if anyone was watching him as he sipped the coffee. Their eyes met and Dan smiled, the smile self-consciously adolescent, but carrying a glimmer of recognition of the whole new relationship he and Scheutz were about to enter into. How could Scheutz not let him have this? Yes, it was awful their being dragged off to live in the hell-hole of New York City, but taking Dan back at this point would be like dragging him back into his childhood. He had to ask himself again why he was doing this. Was the heroic Orpheus really saving Eurydice from hell or was he merely trying to fill the void in his own life that she had created by her descent. Hell, after all, is in the eye of the beholder. Maybe it was his own hell he was trying to save her from.

The kids having finished off an astonishing amount of food, Scheutz asked the waitress for coffee and two knishes to go, to feed Gerry when she woke up. They hustled across the sunlit street whose traffic was starting to pick up. Inside the apartment, it was clear from the quiet that Gerry was still not out of bed. Marty declared he could not stand it any longer, and took himself into his mother's bedroom to wake her up.

She came down the hall with her poofed hair from the night before matted flat on the left side of her head, wearing the ratty old green chenille bathrobe she'd had since Santa Fe. She rubbed her eyes with her fingertips as she walked into the room. On seeing the tree and the presents, her eyes filled with tears. Scheutz laid his hand high on her back just below the nape of her neck, and she turned into him. She nodded just slightly, that old smile playing on her lips, and moved toward him. She lifted her face and he made to kiss her lips but she shifted so that his lips landed on her cheek. Then she moved her face back and planted a quick peck on his lips. Her sleepy, half-opened eyes reminded him of mornings waking next to her. She looked down at Marty standing beside her and then looked back up at Scheutz. It flitted like a wisp but he saw it in her eyes, the thing that they shared with no one else, the knowing that any happiness they were able to garner from the world, was theirs only because they conspired together to winkle it out of its hiding place. And then the moment was gone and she turned away to put her face in her hands.

"Are you all right, Mom?" Marty said.

"Yes, I'm okay, honey." She bent and hugged Marty.

"What's wrong?" Dan wanted to know.

"Nothing's wrong. It's just…." She straightened, still holding Marty to her side. She shook her head and looked at the tree, her eyes swelling to tears again. "That is the absolute worst….And the most beautiful Christmas tree I've ever seen."

Dan let out a laugh and Gerry reached for him to give him a kiss. Then she turned to Scheutz again and leaned in to kiss him, on the cheek this time. He reached his hand to her shoulder to put his arms around her but she backed away. Her hair, Scheutz noticed when he had hugged her did not smell like her. It smelled of hair spray. Ugh. She had once made a joke about the similarity between hair spray and insect repellent, and now here she was wearing it. A Scheutz repellent. In the look-at-me-but-don't-touch-me nether world of the big city.

Marty hugged her around her waist. "Can we open our presents now? Please. "

Dan brought out from the kitchen for his mother the only chair in the apartment. While the kids opened their presents, she sat on the chair and ate her knish and drank her coffee. Scheutz sat on the floor, leaning against the opposite wall, sipping the take-out coffee he'd bought for himself along with Gerry's. And it was suddenly like every Christmas they'd ever had together. The place didn't matter. The Christmas in Mexico with Gerry's father before Marty was born, the three years in Santa Fe, the one Christmas in Cincinnati, and then the three winters in Acworth. In all these they seemed to carry nothing from one to the other except themselves. This moment, right here in this living room, was all that existed in the world. Everything else was just details.

And the day went on like that. Gerry took pictures with the new camera Scheutz had gotten for her, a single lens reflex Pentax he had paid half price for by sending away to the Asahi company in Japan a month earlier. Dan wore his new fringed leather jacket all day long. He and Marty, almost immediately after the presents were all opened, began putting together one of the plastic car models Marty had received. Tolstoy's remark about all happy families being alike could also be extended to those moments when even unhappy families take a break from their sturm und drang. After sitting a while with Dan and Marty and the plastic chassis of the '55 Chevy, Scheutz drifted into Gerry's room where he found her hanging out the opened front window, taking pictures of the street below. She glanced back at him as he entered the room, and grinned. "This internal light meter is fantastic," she said. He sat on the edge of her bed and just watched her. She turned from the window, pointing the camera at him, and adjusting the focus and the f-stop. "This'll be a nice shot of you with the light from the window on your face."

"You like that camera?"

"Oh, yes. What a wonderful present. Thank you. I already know where I can get a good deal on some lenses for this kind of camera. A ninety millimeter, and a wide-angle."

"You have money to spend on lenses?"

"Well, I will have."

"Seems like there's a lot of other things that need to be bought before you go spending money on camera equipment."

She brought the camera down from her face and raised the index finger of her left hand. "Clem, please....don't start."

"Don't start what? I'm just...."

"I just knew you were going to do this."

"Do what?"

"Look. We're having a nice day here with the kids. I don't want to get into this kind of shit with you now."

"But...."

"But nothing. We no longer live together. You have no say in what I do with my money."

"When it involves the kids, I most certainly do."

"The kids are fine, they're...."

"The kids are not fine. The first thing Marty said to me this morning was how much he hates this place."

"Oh, Christ. Can't we just have a pleasant Christmas morning without hauling out all this?"

"There is no furniture in this apartment. How the hell can anybody have kids living in an apartment with no furniture?"

"Furniture is coming. As soon as the holidays are over. Until then, we are camping out. What is so wrong with that?"

"Why couldn't you just leave the kids at home till after the holidays?"

"This is their home now. Get used to it, Clem."

"Okay, so why couldn't you leave them with me until after the holidays?"

"I had to get them settled. I'm starting that job the day after New Years. They are already registered in school and will start the day after New Years. This is the best thing. Believe me."

"They have schools in this place?"

"Stop, will you. There is, in fact, a very good public school, P.S. 41, in the Village. And it's one helluva lot better than that goddamned grade school in Acworth."

"In the Village?"

"Greenwich Village."

"This morning when we went to get that Christmas tree, we passed a school right down the street."

"I've checked them all out. This one isn't very good. Technically, we are not in the district for P.S. 41, but I gave them Bentley's address not far from the school, and it's really not that many blocks to walk over there in the morning. In the afternoon, they can go to his house and Bentley's cook will babysit for them until I get off work."

"Well, why don't we ask the kids where they'd rather live?"

"We've been through this." Gerry's voice took on a sing-songy tone. "You do not ask an eight year old child to make decisions like that."

"Don't make fun of me."

"And, believe me, you would not want to hear Dan's answer to a question like that. He's having the time of his life down here."

He turned away from her to look out the window at the theater marquee across the street. What the hell did he think was going to happen here? When had he ever in their entire relationship won an argument with this woman? What she said made sense. She had obviously thought out this whole move into the city. She had it covered. And what was he doing? Wandering around in some vague fantasy about Orpheus and Eurydice. It was he that needed rescuing, not her and the kids.

"Clem, cut it out, will you? You sit there with that look on your face, pulling your Eeyore act on me again. I'm not going for it. So, just quit. I feel like I've been dragging you around behind me for ten years, like some Sisyphian stone. I can't do it anymore. I won't do it anymore."

"Really? You dragged me around? That must been such a burden. Almost as heavy as all those delusions I've been laboring under. Like the one about how we loved each other and built everything together, and…."

"Don't do this to me, Clem. Please? Yes, we built everything together." She turned toward the window. He waited till she composed herself and turned back. "And now we have to do this together."

"This?"

"This separation. You've got to help me make this work. We'll die without it."

"That's the silliest goddamned thing I've ever heard."

She lifted the Pentax to her face like it was a shield. Or a weapon.

Chapter 11

Noise in the Attic

Pelletier waved the thermos at him from the seat of the skidder. Picnic time. Coffee break in the woods always felt like a picnic, whatever weather that particular day brought. Even in the coldest days of winter, Scheutz's body generated so much heat, it took lounging for a full coffee break to cool down to the shiver point. The thermos-full of coffee was courtesy of Olavi who had stopped at Georgina's on the run back up to The Throne at mid-morning. Some days it happened, some days it didn't. After three days of no coffee break, the surprise heightened the pleasure of it. Today, there were donuts, two apiece, in the bag with the styrofoam cups and little individual creamers.

Scheutz propped his saw against the butt log of the last tree he'd felled. Like his gloves and the front of his clothes, the body of the saw was black with the pine sap so abundant at this time of year. The stumps and the ends of the logs were sticky with the stuff, almost like blood oozing from a severed foot. The sap, running clear from the timber, turned black as creosote where it clung to non-tree surfaces. He lifted his face screen and removed his hardhat, then the bandanna he wore under it. Pelletier had also brought him a two-liter plastic soda bottle filled with fresh water that he used to first soak the bandanna and then his head. He tied the bandanna, as wet from water as it had been with his sweat, back onto his head. The black flies and mosquitoes drove him to replace his hardhat and pull down the face screen. The little bastards were vicious this time of year.

Pelletier hopped up to sit on the log, then set the cups out to pour coffee into. He left his hardhat on, but didn't need to worry about the bugs so much because his sweat reeked of garlic. Scheutz chose a donut, broke it and dunked one half into the coffee. The morning's work so far had tired him just enough to take the edge off his anxiety. He could relax a little and enjoy his break. The weather wasn't bad, hot but not too hot. The work was going okay, each tree giving a sense of something having been done smoothly and well. It was days like this that made him think he ought to just keep working in the woods. Even cutting his leg this morning wasn't that bad. He could barely feel it now.

With no work to occupy his mind while he sipped his coffee, he let it drift away, watching the sap ooze from the butt end of a log facing him. The rings were narrower toward the outside; growth had slowed in the past few years. Forests like these became like root-bound plants if they were not thinned. But it was the rings themselves that fascinated him now, the different shades of light and dark wood. People's lives were like that; certain days, like this one for him, showed up how time had passed and how cycles came full circle. Probably why the ring was such a sacred symbol to the old Germans and the Norsemen who lived in the forests before the Christians got to them. Wodin created the first human out of an ash tree and an alder tree? Probably why it felt so satisfying being in the forest.

The middle of a forest was such a pleasant place to be. It must feel the same for a fisherman out on the Grand Banks, or a farmer operating a combine out in the middle of a vast sea of wheat. On the one hand, you are dwarfed by it and on the other you become immense by being part of it. It was like being both small and large at the same time, and the idea of that gave him a little thrill.

You sure get thrilled over the weirdest things.

I do? I hadn't noticed.

You do. And this is one that gets to you a lot, in case you hadn't noticed.

What, big and little together?

Not just that. Anything that involves two opposites. You're not just a blue ox, you're a blue oxymoron.

Very funny.

He sipped his coffee and peered at the spot between the trees that held Pelletier's gaze. Nothing moved there that he could see. Pelletier could see things no one else could. A picnic in the woods with Pelletier ranked right up there with the top ten little things Scheutz looked forward to in a day. Companionship without the blather. As opposed to Gerry's voice where he got the blather without the companionship.

I could take offense at that.

Does that mean you'll go away?

The only reason I'm here is because you want me here.

Really? I thought you were here because you loved me.

I do love you, Clem. You're my reason for being.

Did he like having Pelletier around because the man did not intrude on Gerry's voice? Or did Gerry's voice merely seep in to fill the vacuum left by being alone or, being with Pelletier, which often amounted to the same thing. Or did it matter?

With their coffee break over, he helped Pelletier set the choker chains on the three nearest logs, and when the skidder had winched them in and begun its way down the slope, Scheutz went back to his chain saw.

I need to talk to you about Samantha.

What brings her up?

Well, she's like Pelletier.

Huh? Boy, that's a stretch. How is Samantha like Pelletier?

Haven't you noticed that when she's around, you treat her just like you treat Pelletier? She can sit in your parlor, or your kitchen for hours with neither of you talking, each one of you in your own little world.

What's wrong with that?

What's wrong with that? You're like two ruminant deer standing in the same field.

What's wrong with that? We don't have a lot to talk about. She's only a twenty-two year-old girl.

Woman.

Woman. She's only a twenty-two-year-old woman. And I don't imagine she's got any more on her mind than Pelletier does.

And you don't see the difference. Come on, Clem. Think about it. Pelletier is a woodsman. This is his chosen life. He lives more by instinct than thought. And he's happy here. Samantha is depressed. She has her whole life ahead of her and she spends her time hanging out in the house of a forty-year-old man with whom she has nothing in common. Don't you think there is something wrong with that?

Well, now that you mention it. But it's not my problem. I've got two kids of my own to worry about.

And you haven't learned anything raising those two kids?

Listen, my house is a comfortable place for her to be away from her family, which I guess is kind of awful.

You're not helping her.

I'm not hurting her.

If you're not part of the solution, you're part of the problem.

Oh Jesus. Now I've got Mrs. Huey Newton in my brain. What is all this anyhow? The girl...

The woman.

The woman. I can't stop thinking of her as a girl, any more than I can stop thinking of Dan and Marty as boys. They're kids, okay? They'll always be kids. What I was saying was...the girl is not your child, so what do you care? You don't even like her.

What I'm saying is...the woman is in your house. She's in your life. And for that reason alone you have some obligation to care. How can you see someone almost every day who is in pain and not want to do something to help her?

It's easy. I do it every day. Look at Uppermann. I see that asshole almost every day, and almost every day he has to tell us how awful it is that his wife threw him out of the house. He's hurting for sure, otherwise he wouldn't go on about it. But do I give a shit? No.

That's different. Uppermann is beyond help. Besides, you're right; he is an asshole. But, think about Samantha a minute. What is she really doing in this small town at her age?

She's engaged to Freddie Brockton.

No, she's not. Don't you think there's a reason why she's always breaking up with him?

Yeah. Because he's on his way to being the kind of asshole Uppermann is. The state government should make them register, you know, like sex-offenders. They have to sign up at town hall and have it put on their driver's license, First Class Asshole.

I just wish Samantha could have hung on to Dan. They would make such a wonderful couple.

Samantha and Dan. They were a couple once, weren't they? When they were too young to be. Scheutz tried to remember why he had gone up into the attic the day he'd found Dan and Samantha up there. The first time he'd ever really noticed Samantha, apart from being just another member of a group of kids that came to house to hang out with Dan.

It was in the fall. The weather had turned cold—they'd had a few good frosts at night already—and the attic was warm with the heat from the wood stove in the kitchen drifting up through the house below. It got a little too stuffy up there in the summer, being right under the roof with the sun on it all day, but in the fall, winter and spring, the attic was the coziest place in the house. Dan would have been fourteen then. And it was definitely before Dan moved out of the big bedroom over the kitchen he had shared with Marty, turning the attic into a teen heaven, complete with ping pong table, beat up sofas and a stereo blasting out Neil Young or Jerry Garcia.

It was the small noises he'd heard that brought him up there that day. Taking a shower in the second floor bathroom after work, he'd heard a soft rhythmic thumping above and, thinking maybe some kind of varmint had gotten in up there, after toweling off and dressing, he went up to check. There, on a bare mattress in the middle of the attic were Dan, naked as the times his diaper had been changed, and this girl, all gawky elbows and knees, reminding Scheutz of Gerry in high school, equally naked, both of them fucking away like rabid rabbits. What he'd heard from below was apparently her heel hitting the wooden floor next to the mattress. Scheutz was shocked. That's the only way he could put it. He'd never considered himself much of a prude, but he could see how someone might become one.

Once it registered what he was seeing, he immediately turned and retraced his steps down to the second floor hallway and closed the attic door. He wasn't sure whether the coupling couple had heard him or not. They didn't show any signs of it, by breaking rhythm or anything. Even though only his head had risen above the attic floor level—giving him a very weird perspective on the proceedings—Dan, at least, must have heard him, the attic stairs creaked so loud.

Scheutz stood in the back hallway next to the attic door, listening for the soft thump, but not wanting to hear it. What should he do? Should he go stomping up there and tell them to stop it this minute? He could picture himself standing there red-faced like an irate father, upholding the Christian morals that supposedly held society together. He could also picture the two teenagers totally ignoring him as teenagers do, especially Dan.

Or should he just not say anything about it. He never was very big on Christian morals, and it would be hypocritical of him to use that as a justification just in case what he felt might be nothing more than jealousy on is own part that his child was enjoying himself so much while he, Scheutz, hadn't gotten laid in over two years. Since Gerry left. But no, that wasn't all of it. Aside from his own problem, he actually did have a problem with those kids carrying on like that. She could get pregnant. Or even more probable, she could get terribly hurt by all this. From what he knew of Dan's attitude toward just about everything in general, this was nothing more than fun and games to him, nothing serious intended. But was it to her? What if it wasn't just fun and games, what happens then? Or was that any of Scheutz's business? He didn't even know the girl.

He walked down the hall to the boys' bedroom and knocked.

"Yeah?" Marty's voice in don't-bother-me mode. When Scheutz stuck his head in, Marty looked up from the plastic model he was building. "What?"

"Why is the window open?"

"It's too hot in here."

"Then why don't you leave the door to the hall open?"

Marty shrugged. "Is that what you came to ask?"

"No. I was just wondering if you knew where Dan was?"

Marty delicately touched a bead of glue on a tail pipe section and put it in its place on the undercarriage of what looked like one of those sixties muscle cars. Without looking up, he said, "No, I don't know where Dan is."

"Is there some girl visiting him?"

Marty let out a half grunt, half sigh. "There's always some girl visiting him."

"You know who it is?"

"Why?"

"Why? I'd just like to know, that's why. Is there some big secret going on here?"

"No."

"That's not a very convincing 'no'."

Marty put the tube of model glue down. "The girl of the day is Samantha, okay? You know Samantha? She lives on the road going down the hill. On the other side. Her parents have the cross-country ski lodge."

"Oh. Those folks. What does she look like?"

"I don't know. She looks like a girl. She's tall and she's real skinny. Giggles all the time." He waved a tiny muffler in the air. "

Scheutz stepped back into the hall. He had meant to tell Marty about the scene in the attic, but…Was he really meaning to talk to a ten-year-old kid about the problem of what to do about his fourteen-year-old brother screwing another fourteen-year-old in the attic? That was all wrong. Even though Marty surely knew a lot more about what went on with Dan than Scheutz did. Even if Marty was old enough to talk to about something like that, his two sons stuck together like thieves in the Casbah. It reminded him of himself and his little brother when they were kids, but now he was being….what was the word?….marginalized on the outside of the same kind of cabal.

"Hey, Dad."

Scheutz stopped and turned. "Yeah. What?"

"Close the door, will you?"

Downstairs in the kitchen, he dropped into his chair and propped his feet on the little pile of firewood next to the chimney. Supper was just going to have to wait. The quiet in the house seemed to gain in intensity. Outside, the early-growing dusk of the fall evening held the world in stillness. No music played upstairs, which was odd in itself. Rock and roll always seemed to come from somewhere in the house whenever the kids were home. Marty's model-making in the room above was, as usual, a quiet activity. What would Dan and the bony girl be doing by now? Lying side by side and talking quietly like people did after making love, if what they were doing could be called that. Or maybe she was crying, having just been ravaged. He heard in his head the noise of that soft thumping of the bony girl's heel while she had bounced under Dan.

What had Marty said her name was? Samantha. He tried, but could not differentiate her face from those of the other kids who came to the house. He knew her parents, and didn't particularly like them. The father, whose name he couldn't recall, told Scheutz once at a New Year's Eve party that the family had moved here from New Jersey in the late sixties. He had a smarmy feel to him that Scheutz didn't trust, and he told much more about himself and his family than Scheutz wanted hear. Both he and his wife were the beneficiaries of trust funds. They felt an obligation to use their money for good causes, he said, seasoning the pronouncement with a dash of parochial smugness. They had bought nearly a thousand acres of second-growth forest in Acworth for the purpose of opening a cross-country ski lodge. Not because they needed to earn a living, he said, but because they both enjoyed the sport, and because they felt this was an excellent way of utilizing the land while preserving its ecology.

And what would these trust-funders do if their fourteen-year-old daughter came home in hysterics because she had just lost her virginity to the budding Priapus up the road. With all their money, and their proclivity toward fighting for equal rights for Blacks, Indians, and certainly women, Scheutz could see them waging a major offensive against Dan for statutory rape. Was that possible if both kids were the same age? And if not statutory rape, then all it took was the bony girl's accusation of regular old rape if her heart was broken by Dan's bip-bam-thank-you-ma'am approach to undying love.

Scheutz needed to talk to someone about this. The problem with the trust-funders was bad enough, but there was something else that bothered him even more about the scene in the attic, something that lurked just beyond the wall of his consciousness that felt life-threatening. But he couldn't put his finger on what it was. Again, if he could sit down and talk with someone about this, it would come out. He tried to think of who he could talk to.

Georgina? No, she wouldn't do. She was somewhat of a friend, yes, but....she had a reluctance, it seemed, to talk about things like this. Georgina was voluble on certain subjects, like being a single parent, or the practical day-to-day needs of running a restaurant. She could and would talk at length about the struggles of womankind in patriarchal societies.

What about talking to Pelletier? Forget it. To him it would be no more than two foxes fucking in a field. What's the big deal? And not his girl friend, either, who'd probably think the whole thing was very funny. Gerry had once described the girlfriend, Nicole, as a 'trailer-park skank' who adhered to the philosophy that human relations never rose above 'cocks and cunts'. "If she had a brain any larger than a lima bean," Gerry had said. "She'd make the perfect Freudian analyst."

He ran through every one else he knew. Old man Brockton had kids, even had a son the same age as Dan. He could tell Scheutz about how to deal with a potential court case from the trust-funders, but not anything else. Olavi? Nice guy, but no. He'd see this as some major catastrophe, and then spread it around as a juicy gossip story throughout the lower half of the state. Who else was there? Mrs. Alcott at the store? Nice old lady, but no. And there, too, was the gossip factor. One of Dan's teachers at school? Scheutz didn't personally know any of them. The preacher at the Congregational church? No, it had nothing to do with religion.

Whatever did he do before when he needed someone to talk to? He'd never needed anybody; he always had Gerry. Maybe if he talked to her about this. He dialed her number on the phone that hung on the wall next to the sink. She'd be home from work now, probably having supper. But he got nothing more than her answering machine. He left a message for her to call him, that it was important he talk to her this evening.

Rather than go back and stew in his chair, he started dinner. He set a pot of water on to boil and took the remains of last night's chicken carcass out of the fridge, dropping it whole into the water. He pulled out potatoes, carrots, onions, and green beans, washing them and setting them out of the cutting board. Cooking for him had become as ritualized as cutting trees. Chunking up carrots and potatoes even had a model-sized feel similar to bucking up an oak log for firewood. Like cutting wood, cooking wasn't something he enjoyed, it was something he needed to do. And it showed; the kids both said his meals all had pretty much the same exciting flavor as sawdust. That was all right, they ate it. Most of the time. Except for when they could get their hands on a pizza.

What was it that bothered him so much about that scene in the attic? It really wasn't so much the problem with the girl's parents raising hell about it. Yes, that was a problem he'd have to find a way to deal with. But there was something else about seeing his son actually fucking a girl that bothered him worse, something he couldn't put his finger on. It had something to do with Gerry. Where the hell was she? Why wasn't she home eating supper where she should be? So she could take his phone call and talk with him about this.

The pile of vegetables in the middle of the cutting board gave him such a pang of emptiness, the like of which he hadn't felt in as long as he could remember. It was like the day just after high school, when she had left her mother's house to go off to college and he'd tried to write her a letter so she'd get it when she arrived at school. But he couldn't do it. Whatever he thought of to say in the letter was so anemic it mocked him. Just as her not being home for supper just now mocked him.

He was blowing this whole thing with Dan and the bony girl out of proportion. He should just pass it off like Gerry had taught him to do with so many things the kids did. Don't make a big deal out of it, she might say. It's just life. Would she really say that? It felt like so much more than just life.

Dammit, he had to stop this obsessing. Just go ahead and fix supper and take it as it comes. That's what she would say. He could almost hear her saying it. Let it go, Clem, she'd say, treat it like a dance partner. If you just move with it, stay in step with it, feel the rhythm of it, you'll work it out.

"Oh, hi, Mr. Scheutz." The bony girl walked into the kitchen with Dan right behind her.

"Daddy-O. What's up for supper?"

"Cooking supper, huh?" the girl asked.

Scheutz turned away from the cutting board to stare her. She beamed. A scrawny bean pole topped by carefully combed straight dishwater blonde hair and a radiant grin. Was this the same pile of knees and elbows he'd just seen thrashing about on a bare mattress? He remembered her now, could picture her on a bicycle with her base ball hat on backwards, not yet pushed over the line into womanhood.

"Looks like you got a chicken soup going, huh? Here, let me

help you." She took the cutting board off the counter and carried it to the table and then began transporting vegetables to the board. Scheutz turned to Dan, raising his eyebrows. Dan gave him one of those New York gestures with his hands, and a facial expression that said, "Hey, why not?" Samantha sat down at the cutting board with the rectangular Chinese cutting knife and expertly began pulling first carrots and then potatoes from the pile and bucking them into soup-sized chunks. Scheutz and Dan stood on either side of the table watching her as if mesmerized by such expertise in an otherwise seemingly clumsy person.

Dan's affect appeared not his usual self since entering the kitchen with the girl, a little distant, almost stunned. "Sit down, Dan," he said. "let's have a talk."

" 'Bout what?" His demeanor changed to alert but casual.

"About the attic. Sit down."

"What about the attic?"

"Sit." Scheutz pulled out a chair and sat at an angle to Samantha, then waited for Dan to sit across from him. The ensuing silence made Scheutz think of the old expression he'd heard his aunt use once to describe a pregnant pause—'an angel passed between them'. Interrupted only by the sound of Samantha chopping carrots into fancy angled bits.

"You guys were just up there, right?"

"Up where?" Dan said.

"The attic. What else are we talking about?"

"The attic? When were we in the attic?" He turned to Samantha. "Were you in the attic?"

She looked up at Dan, widened her eyes, and shook her head. Then turned toward Scheutz, compressed her lips and shook her head at him, before going back to her cutting.

"You weren't in the attic just now?"

Unified head shakes all around.

"Then where were you just now?"

"We were in the bedroom helping Marty build his car model."

"Come on, Dan, don't give me that shit. I was just in Marty's room and you two were not there."

Dan and Samantha exchanged a fleeting look. Samantha held the cutting knife with the tip resting on the board. "Oh, I know," she said to Dan. "That must have been while we were downstairs in the parlor looking for that record album."

Dan pointed his finger at her. "Yep, that must be what happened."

Now what? What the hell should he do now? The muscles in Scheutz's back and shoulders tightened as the anger rose up inside him. He clasped his hands together to keep them from banging on the surface of the table. Dan's eyes met his with a look of studied innocence that defied any attempt at branding him a liar. He knew that Scheutz knew he was lying—what was the term, bald-faced, boldfaced?—and another dark angel passed between them to the tune of the girl's snicks on the cutting board. Furious and confused, Scheutz groped for the image of Gerry's face, her voice, to tell him how to handle this. His son, who he loved more than life, sat serenely opposing him, pushing him out to his arm's length, turning him into an adversary. Even in the face of his controlled anger he had to admire the kid's nerve, the sheer ballsiness of that façade of innocence. The girl, at least, had some human chink in her armor as her eyes filled with tears. Or was that merely from the onion she was dicing?

Scheutz placed his hands, callused but shaky, on the edge of the table and pushed himself backwards, the chair scraping against the wide-planked floor. He had to give in, let the kid stare him down. There was no winning this. At the stove, he lifted the lid on the boiling pot with the chicken carcass. Behind him, Dan whispered something to the girl, who emitted a snuffly giggle. How many years had it been since he consciously wanted to smack someone? Both of them.

Take the chicken bones out of the water, Gerry's voice said

He dropped the lid back, covering the pot. Then turned toward the outside door, expecting to see her there. When she wasn't, he looked around the room. No Gerry. But he'd heard the voice, the same as if she was standing next to him. "Did you say something?" He directed his question to Dan and Samantha, with their heads together at the table.

"No." Dan looked up. "We're just talking about school."

"Did you say something about the chicken, um, Samantha?"

She turned her head halfway around at him. "No. I'm doing the vegetables."

What the hell was going on? He heard the goddamned voice. And there was no question it was Gerry's voice. He knew it like he knew his own. It still retained the same Cincinnati flatness of tone that his own voice had never lost. And it wasn't something he imaged she would say, he actually heard the goddamned voice. As inane and stupid as it felt doing it, he lifted the lid off the boiling pot to see if the voice came from there. Nothing. Just the bubbling water and the bones now floating on the surface. Perhaps he should take the bones out.

With a serving fork he transferred the carcass to a large bowl and then fished out the loose bones with a tea strainer. His anger at the kids had been dissipated by his newfound fear that he might be going nuts, hearing voices. Maybe he even hallucinated the scene in the attic, and he was unjustly accusing a couple of innocent kids. Was it possible that his own loneliness was driving him insane? Was it possible to miss someone that much? Was it himself and Gerry he'd seen in the attic, as they were in high school on the floor in the spare room of her mother's house?

It's all right, Clem. Relax, it's okay.

There it was again, the voice. Jesus, he really was going insane. He stood, petrified, holding the strainer and staring into the boiling water. My poor children, living in a house with a raving maniac. No wonder Gerry took them away when she did. She probably saw him going crazy and feared for their safety as well as her own. What should he do now?

Put the vegetables in the pot. Gerry's voice sounded like some cop's voice on a police show saying, 'Put the gun down'.

Okay. He needed to carry on, act as if life was still somewhat normal. He turned to the table. "Um, Samantha?"

"Yes?"

"Can I put the vegetables in now?"

"Well, you can put the carrots and potatoes in, but I'd wait before putting in the onion and green beans. They don't take as long to cook as the others." She and Dan scooped up the carrot and potato chunks in their cupped hands and carried them to the stove. Scheutz stood aside and let them insert the vegetables into the water without splashing. "What kind of spices do you usually put in your soup?" she asked.

"Spices?"

"Yeah, you know? Bay leaf, a little garlic. What?"

"I don't know. I never put spices in soup."

Dan widened his eyes in a Barney Fife imitation. "Well, there's your problem, right there."

Samantha returned to the table and continued cutting the onions and green beans. Scheutz waved Dan away from the stove, and then began picking the meat off the chicken carcass to toss back into the burgeoning soup once the carrots and potatoes were soft. He was too upset to stand face to face with his son right then. But he couldn't tell whether he was still angry at him for lying so easily, or if he was ashamed for possibly accusing the boy—and the girl—of something that he had manufactured wholly from out of his own sick mind. He'd seen a bumper sticker once in Hanover that said, "Warning! I brake for hallucinations."

Let it go, Clem, Gerry's voice said. *Do the soup. Whether you actually saw them in the attic or not, you should let it be.*

But....

It came to him then what really upset him about seeing Dan and the girl in the attic like that. His son was moving away from him. The fantasy that he had created about his two sons returning from New York to live with him, filling the void left when they and Gerry moved away, that fantasy was to be short-lived. This was Dan's first step toward complete independence. At least the first step that Scheutz let himself be fully cognizant of. And this first step had smashed the little fantasy like a sledge hammer, not giving him time even to get used to Dan's maturity over a long term of adolescence. Of course there was no one to blame for it, it was just life. Like Gerry's leaving. He couldn't blame her for that; she was dying here with him, her life spirit was dying here in this little country town. But it left him like that Salvador Dali painting of the form with a large, odd shaped, see-through hole in the middle of it.

The torso of the chicken burned his fingers when he picked it up, but instead of dropping it, he crushed it, strangling it with both hands.

Quiet, Let it be.

Jesus, I miss you. So much.

Let that be, too.

Chapter 12

It'll Get Better, Won't It?

On the landing, Olavi's grapple truck stood off to the side, already loaded. Freddie Brockton was just pushing up the last of his log hitch onto the pile, while Uppermann stood at the tail gate of his truck, still fiddling with the carburetor adjustment on his chain saw. Pelletier waited for Freddie to clear out of the way and then pulled up next to the log pile. Scheutz had ridden down from the ridge for lunch break, and now helped Pelletier cut the their latest logs into eight, ten, twelve, or sixteen foot lengths.

By the time he retrieved his lunch from the dashboard of his truck, and a cold ginger ale from the cooler in the cab of Olavi's truck, Freddie Brockton and Olavi were already perched on a long butt log about half-way up the pile. Olavi talked with a mouthful of food, gesturing and describing with his hands while Freddie, his mouth also filled with food, seemed to be having a hard time keeping himself from laughing. Scheutz opened his own sandwich bag in which the cheese slices in each of his olive loaf sandwiches had melted with the sun shining on them all morning through the windshield. The cheese had run all inside the lunch bag, coating the large handful of Doritos he'd thrown in before closing it.

Pelletier parked the skidder, grabbed his own lunch from the cab of Scheutz's truck, and then a Coke from the cooler in Olavi's truck. Uppermann continued to fiddle with his chain saw over on the tailgate of his truck, visibly more agitated with each attempt to set its idle correctly. Scheutz watched him, waiting for the explosion, picking Doritos out of the melted cheese. Uppermann had a short frustration fuse, and it was only a matter of time till he would let go.

It seemed to be all around him, people just waiting to explode. Olavi had stopped his monologue in mid-sentence to stare at Pelletier while the Canuck climbed the log pile. Pelletier avoided his gaze with a studied concentration. He sat himself next to Scheutz on the side away from Olavi. The day was going to come, and it was not that far off, when Pelletier would stop avoiding Olavi's hostile stare and the two would have it out.

But the explosion came from Freddie, of all people. Olavi had finally given up staring at Pelletier and returned to his latest tale of woe. Freddie, the only one listening to him, apparently could not hold it in any longer, and let out a laugh that sprayed the bottom of the log pile with tiny bits of half-chewed sandwich. Freddie laughed in that way he had that made his life seem like just another episode of Romper Room. Freddie's glee level rose to where he was pounding his thigh with the hand that held his sandwich, and his caulk boots performed a staccato tapping on the log below. "You gotta hear this," he hooted at Scheutz and Pelletier, rapping Scheutz on the leg with his same sandwich hand. "Tell 'em." He hit Olavi's shoulder with his other hand. "Go on tell 'em."

"Well, I start over." Olavi lowered his Coke and paused, looking toward his feet, sighing with what they recognized, and often imitated, as the standard preamble to the latest chapter in the unrelenting saga of Why Does Our All-Powerful and All-Knowing Lutheran God Visit Upon Us So Many Trials? He looked up at Scheutz and then at Freddie. "It is not funny."

"The pig house burned down." Freddie hooted.

Scheutz looked away before Olavi caught his eye. Freddie, who had been attempting to take another bite of sandwich, began to convulse. Pelletier, with a mouth full, grinned. He always grinned whenever he heard of the next bad thing to befall his nemesis. Scheutz did not want to laugh, but couldn't help the little chortle that escaped.

You know, it isn't really very funny. That man and his wife raise blue-ribbon pigs. The loss of a pig sty could be....

Yeah, yeah, yeah.

No, don't brush it off like that. You guys act like a bunch of pimply-faced sixth graders. You think this is all very funny, but that kind of a loss could be critical to someone like Olavi and his wife. Those prizes obviously mean a lot to them, and the pigs could even be a source of revenue, and probably food.

Yeah, yeah. But every day it's something else. What's the latest? Their truck died and they had to buy a new one, but they just missed out on the dealer discount so they don't have money for more insurance than the basic liability just to get registered.

They probably don't have the pig sty insured either.

"...so, my wife, she runs out to save the pig. The hose does not reach, so I fill buckets and run them to the pig house but it is no good. I yell for the kids to help, but she yells the kids are off to school already. She runs around with carrying this pig which is as big as she is with nowhere to put it. It will run off if you put it down. All the other pigs run off. They are squealing in all directions, running down the hill into the woods. I yell to her, 'go get a leash for the pig'. She puts the pig into the cab of the new pick-up truck and closes the door. Better it is the new truck. The door on the old truck would not close tight."

Olavi's voice had fallen into his Scandinavian singsongy monotone, as he wagged his head like an old bear with the telling. Freddie's laughter took off again, which Olavi seemed to have no trouble ignoring once he got into the cadence of the story. Even Pelletier was laughing now. Scheutz held himself in check. Gerry was right. That poor couple was about the two hardest luck people he'd ever met. He ought to get up and carry his lunch over to eat in the cab of his truck so as not hear this and insult Olavi by laughing along with the others. But he stayed.

"...so the pig jumps around inside the truck. I am afraid it will shit in there on my new upholstery. So I let the fire go and run to get the pig out of the truck. When it sees me coming it jumps with its front paws up and down, you know, like a person in a panic, and then accidentally pushes down the lock button on the door. So, I run around quick quick to the driver's side to open that door but the pig runs over to me at the window and before I can open the door, it pushes down that button, too. By this time my wife runs out of the house with the dog leash but it is too late. 'Get the keys', she says. But the keys are in the ignition of the truck. 'Why did you not get another set of keys?', she says. 'I did', I says. 'I put them in the glove compartment so I will not lose them'.

"Haaa." Scheutz felt it all let go, as if all the tension in his body had been pulled back in the pad of a slingshot. Whatever control he'd kept on himself blew all at once. His mouthful of sandwich did an encore of Freddie's, all over the log. *You pig.* He wiped his face on the sleeve of his t-shirt and snorted out a piece of olive that had gone up the back of his nose. Freddie had given up trying to eat and Pelletier was struggling. Across the landing Uppermann raised his chain saw above his head and heaved it at a small outcrop of rock.

"...so my wife is so mad she is whipping the truck hood with the leash. She yells at the pig to calm down and just sit down till we can get it out. I am speechless. I try to think, what do we do now? I think, what would Clement Scheutz do? The fire from the pig house is so hot I can feel it on my backside. The fences are burning. The trough is burning. I am thinking, I hope the heat does not break the windows on my new truck. But then I think, I will anyhow have to break the side window to get the pig out. So I go to the tool shed to bring back a hammer to break the window.

My wife is now next to the truck window and is talking soothing things to calm the pig down. But the pig is still jumping around. When the pig sees the hammer, he goes, how do you say, berserk. He's a very smart pig, you know, and he is afraid the hammer maybe means he is going to get beaned. So he jumps around even more, like a big pink crazy balloon, against the windows, against the dashboard and the steering wheel and then the back of the seat again. And then the worst happens...."

Freddie hung onto Scheutz's shoulder. Scheutz could only listen and laugh, Gerry's voice nowhere to be heard.

"...so the pig hits the floor shift with his paws. The truck shifts into neutral and begins to roll down the hill. My wife screams and jumps out of the way, but I hang on to the door handle to try to stop it. It does not stop. It rolls past the burning pig fence and then dips down and picks up speed. I fall off and hurt my back, which I do not notice till later because I am watching my new truck rush and bounce down the hill toward the woods. The pig is in the back window wishing he was still safe in his mudhole with his loving owners caring for him. The truck comes to rest against the front of the big white oak at the edge of the woods. It comes to rest so hard that the door pops open and the pig is so scared it runs off into the woods. My wife runs off down the hill to go after the pig. I go to look at the truck which has the whole front end smashed, the radiator, the windshield, the hood, the quarter panels, tie rods, maybe even the four wheel drive axle, I do not know yet.

The talk of Olavi's smashed pick-up truck had a sobering effect, at least on Freddie, who'd done in more than one truck on a Saturday night. Pelletier muttered something in French to himself between the last dregs of laughter bubbling out of him. Scheutz made himself stop laughing and was glad to do so. Eventually, all four fell silent, Olavi staring off into space, and the other three casually watching Uppermann hacking away at his chain saw with a double-bladed ax. This day was getting weirder as it went along.

You should be ashamed of yourself.

I know I should. You're absolutely right. The poor guy.

His poor wife.

The poor pig. Scheutz started laughing again. The laughter rolled out on a life force of its own. He could see Olavi's wife, with her enormous bosom and round red face running in circles with the overflowing pig in her arms. And then, of course, Freddie and Pelletier got going again. Olavi shook his head slowly. "Pffaah. You guys. You don't know nothing."

Uppermann left off destroying his saw and turned toward them. Probably thinking they were laughing at him, he took a theatrical bow and then struck an awkward muscle-builder pose. He lifted the chain saw and, with it in one hand and the ax in the other, walked toward the wood pile, stopping just below where they sat like an audience in an amphitheater. He had chopped the saw to pieces, bar, chain, engine, carburetor, handles, muffler twisted and wrecked, all somehow still clinging together like a piece of modern sculpture. Uppermann held the saw aloft with one hand like some alien species of forest creature, oil and gas dripping from it like its life's blood. With the other hand he raised his ax, letting out his version of a victory roar, looking and sounding like some small-brained Homo sapiens.

What an idiot. Scheutz and the men beside him fell silent. There was nothing funny about this performance. Purposefully destroying a perfectly good Stihl chainsaw—okay, maybe needing the carburetor rebuilt—was a stupid waste. Any one of the men on the log pile would gladly have bought the saw from him and had it fixed.

He's anathema to you.

He's a what?

Anathema. He's your opposite. You know, I always told you that you obsess but you don't compulse. Uppermann is too compulsive but he doesn't obsess about anything.

Hngh. Nothing stays in his brain long enough. So, what's better, obsessing or compulsing?

Well, you notice he's always bemoaning the fact that his wife threw him out of the house, but in the next breath he'll tell those stories he's so proud of. Like the time he chased her cat around the house for not using the litter box and finally ended up cornering it under the dining room table and shooting it with that pistol he always carries. What does he expect?

Yeah, well in case you hadn't noticed, Gerry dear, I don't have a wife either. And I'm not compulsive like that.

I know, and that's too bad. Whatever spontaneity you had just oozed out. You died on me, Clem.

Still here aren't I?

Yeah? And would you call this living?

It has its moments. I don't need to be in the city like you to feel like I'm alive.

I'll give you that. I'll bet you rack up at least a good fifteen minutes a day feeling alive out here.

He finished the last of his second sandwich, and washed the Doritos down with the ginger ale. He capped the bottle and leaned it back against the log, then leaned back himself, turning his face up to the sun. Fifteen minutes a day, huh? It might be nice if Gerry would shut up right about now. He wanted to think about Gerry herself. Something about Olavi's story bothered him. Yeah, the pig story was sad, and yeah the two of them seemed clumsy, but they did it together. And yeah, maybe Olavi's wife had a little fling with Pelletier, she and Olavi were still working together. That's what bothered him; why couldn't he and Gerry have continued to do that? He could feel her voice squeaking to get a word in edgewise, but he shut it out. It surprised him that he could do that. He'd just shut it down, refuse to hear it.

But…

Hush.

He closed his eyes and felt some of the tension leave his body. This was nice. The woods around the landing was quiet in the noonday sun. Next to him Freddie and Olavi engaged in conversation about replacing front end parts on a truck. Across the landing, Uppermann made small clanking sounds at the back of his truck, probably preparing another chain saw for the slaughter. Scheutz tried relaxing further the way Nanda had taught him, to envision himself on a beach someplace in the sun. No, that wouldn't work. That particular image never did much for him; he could always feel the sand in his underwear, and too often the image reminded him of that awful time in Cuba with his brother, Willi, the two of them trying to escape the fidelistas closing in on them. Instead, he tried to envision himself in the woods, on a hillside under the tall white pine or spruce.

What came was not the voice, but a memory of Gerry, her hair tied back off her face, hovering above him as he reclined back in his easy chair at home. "Clem? Clem, wake up." The bright light of his reading lamp had been turned on and the television set buzzed its snowy screen in the corner. "Come on. Get upstairs to bed." She nudged him gently.

He smiled up at her. She was home. He reached up to touch her but she brushed his hand aside.

"What are you doing sitting here? Why didn't you go to bed?"

"I was waiting up for you."

"You shouldn't have. Are the kids in bed?"

He nodded. He had let them stay up until eleven to finish watching some movie on the television. Not that he had any control over the situation. Ever since he'd started working in the woods six months before, he usually fell asleep by seven o'clock in the evening. If Gerry wasn't home, which happened more and more often, the kids just let him sleep in his favorite chair in the living room, and went to bed whenever they pleased. This evening, though, he had awoken when the eleven o'clock news came on, and he packed them off to their room. Dan gave him guff about how there was no school the next day and it was important for them to keep up with late-breaking news events in the world. Scheutz could almost hear Marty's voice behind that argument. That was normally not Dan's way. Marty would argue about anything, but not Dan. Dan did not give a justification for anything he did, he merely continued on with what he was told to stop doing. Infinitely more frustrating for Scheutz.

Seven years old and bigger than all the other kids in his first grade class, Marty had no inhibitions about telling anyone else, including his parents and older brother, what they ought to be doing. But his over-developed sense of justice did not extend to altering his own behavior at anyone else's request. There were times, in the face of such an often illogical stance, that Scheutz did not bother to repeat himself, but just picked the kid up and carried him to his room or to the dinner table.

Marty had repeated the argument about how they needed to keep up with the latest breaking news developments. He and his brother needed to be taking on some of the more adult concerns of the changing world they were growing into. At least that was what Scheutz, in his not-quite-awake state understood him to say. That had been Marty's rap, or variations on it, since before kindergarten. Even Dan had once used the same argument when he wanted to drive Scheutz's truck around the meadow behind the house. Where do those kids get that stuff? was the last thing Scheutz remembered thinking until Gerry shook him awake.

"So how was the exhibit?" he asked her.

"It was good. We went out afterwards. A bunch of us."

"Oh? Where to, a bar?"

"Yeah. That real nice place in Brattleboro near the river."

"Brattleboro? I thought the show was in Keene."

"No, no. It's that gallery in Brattleboro. I told you that."

"No. You told me it was Keene."

"Whatever. Come on, let's go up. I'm pooped." She clicked off the television and went around turning off lights. He pulled himself up out of the chair, and as he did so, the book he'd been reading before he fell asleep slipped off his lap onto the floor. Gerry picked up the book and laid it on the arm of the chair. "Marty says you always snore louder when you fall asleep reading a book than you do when you fall asleep watching television,"

"I wouldn't know." He picked up the book and followed her into the kitchen where she turned out that light.

She walked ahead of him up the back stairs. "He says you ought to read in a different room. He can hardly hear the television with your snoring. He's got a point, you know"

"No, he doesn't. It's much nicer to spend time in the evening together, in the same room. Even if everybody is doing something different."

She stopped in the hallway, turning to him in front of the door to their bedroom. "Clem, since you have been working as a logger, you don't spend time with anybody in the evening. You come home dead tired, shower, eat, go to your chair and book and you're out cold by seven o'clock. I'm sure that for the kids, sitting in a room with you in the evening is not a whole lot different than having a big dog snuffling in his sleep on the hearth."

"Is that how you feel about it, too?"

"You want to know the truth?"

"No."

Gerry turned on the light. Their room was only half the size of the house's master bedroom over the kitchen that Dan and Marty slept in. But, the kids needed the room size to store all their toys, games, models and kidhood paraphernalia, which they were not allowed to leave lying around the rest of the house. Scheutz and Gerry's bed and night stand were an antique set that they'd found in a junk store in Troy, New Hampshire for ten dollars. Under a coat of age-darkened shellac, Gerry had uncovered sumptuous hand-painted flowers on the head and foot boards of the bed and the front of the drawers in the night stand.

Once in bed, Gerry turned on her side, her back to him. He lay awake, staring into the dark of the ceiling, the left side of his bare body touching the back of Gerry's. He knew she wasn't criticizing him about him not being with them in the evening, but her remark tugged at him. What did she want? That was all he could do right now. Logging was the only kind of work he could find in this corner of the world. Or was that quite true? Is certainly was the least objectionable kind of work to be found here. But, boy, did the logging wear him out. Things would get better, once his body became attuned to it. It was decent money and he actually kind of liked it, being in the woods all day by himself. What was the line from that Byron poem she liked so much? *There is a pleasure in the pathless woods. There is a rapture on the lonely shore.*

Once he got in the kind of physical shape the job required, he wouldn't be so tired and he'd have his life back. And Gerry and the kids would have him back.

"Would you rather I had gone to that gallery opening with you tonight?" he asked the back of her head.

"No, that's all right, Clem. Don't worry about it. I know how hard you work."

"Maybe the next one, okay? It's just that....well....Georgina's work...you know, I didn't think I could take another exhibit of art photographs of rain falling on ferns against a mossy tree trunk."

Gerry rolled over onto her back, her voice sleepy but still clear. "You would have liked this show. It's a whole new direction for Georgina. The photos were all about people. Very clear, very direct. People standing posed, looking into the camera, or just caught in the middle of working. I was very impressed. The whole show wasn't consistently good, but she's got hold of something."

"What kind of people?"

"Oh, local people. New Hampshire, Vermont people. Doing things like cleaning tables in the lounge at a ski resort, or stacking boards in a lumber yard."

"You mean, like Diane Arbus kind of shots?"

"No. These people are more normal than that; they're not odd...you know...They're like the kind of people you see around here every day. They're just people that live in the country in New Hampshire and Vermont. But yeah, in a way, they are a little like Arbus's people in that they have that same...how do you say it?...that same kind of, this is who I am and this is all I'll ever be."

"My kind of people."

"Oh, stop." Her voice took on an edge.. "This new job you have is taking over your whole personality?"

"That's not so. But this is just who I am. And those people you're describing in the photos are just like me."

"No, not like you. They're not people who go around hiding behind some bogus image as a working-class hero."

"Is that what you think I do?"

"I think you're a lot more intelligent than you like people to believe."

"And what if I wasn't? What if I was really just a Joe Sixpack, going around trying to keep up with all you arty people?"

"Arty people?" She rolled back again to her side, facing away from him. "That's a stretch. I wouldn't exactly consider myself one of the 'arty people'." She let out a long sigh. "Have you noticed that, since we moved up here to New Hampshire, I have not finished one painting?"

"No, I hadn't noticed."

"Think about it; when the last time you sat in a room with me and read aloud while I worked?"

He thought about it. "Now that you mention it…I guess it was way back before we left Cincinnati. Wow. That's a long time. But, we've been so…."

"Busy. I know. The house, the kids, money. Your stupid job in the woods. I feel like I'm turning into some kind of Calvinist pioneer housewife." She turned back toward him. "I can't take it, Clem. We have to change this life we have. The only time I feel alive any more is when I'm not here. Like tonight. I can't tell you what that was like, talking with them about art, about what?; just anything, just…you know, politics, people, the way people think, why they do what they do." She propped herself up her elbow. "Say something."

"What?"

"What? You're asking me what to say?" Her head shook slowly in the dim shadow of the room. She stayed silent for a long time and then rolled over away from him again.

"What?"

"Nothing. I don't know. I don't even want to think about it. I'm too tired." Soon her breathing grew deeper into sleep.

Scheutz lay alone in the darkness, their two bodies touching. It seemed lately he needed to touch her physically to feel that she was still there. It was difficult knowing what was bothering her. She wanted something from him that he couldn't give her right now. But it would get better. He knew that. It was just that right now was a rough time.

But it was more than that. It seemed as if some space had opened between them and it frightened him. What had changed? It wasn't that long ago, only within the last year, that he always felt her there. If he was with the kids or if he went to fix something, or change something about the house, he had the sensation of seeing that thing, or thinking of that thing as though both he and she saw it together. But lately…just a few days ago, he stood outside looking at the old wooden gutters on the eaves and wondered what she would think about his pulling them off and replacing them. That was new for him, wondering what she thought. Since they began restoring this old house two years before, even before that, in Ohio and in New Mexico, he always felt they shared a kind of folie a deux. Both of them knowing what the other wanted, or knowing what the other wanted to do.

It felt like they were no longer in the same boat. Maybe in the same fleet, heading in the same direction, dealing with the same weather, but not in the same boat. When he had asked her again about the gutters, she responded in a way that made him think she was not at all concerned about them. "Whatever you think is best, Clem." That wasn't like her. And because she didn't seem to care, he wondered if he should care. Maybe the gutters were not important. But they were rotted, and leaking in several spots. And the rot would spread, especially where the wood of the gutters touched the wood of the eave. The damp wood would attract carpenter ants and….

He had to stop thinking about this. If he continued to lie there, letting his mind go, he'd have half the damned house falling down and the other half filled with bats and squirrels. And really the only reason he was obsessing about the house right now was to keep himself from thinking about how Gerry was drifting away from him. He rolled toward her and snaked his arm around her till his fist nestled between her breasts. She did not respond. Her breath had evened out in sleep.

Chapter 13

The Rapture

He awoke that next morning with the windows gray from the coming dawn. Gerry had not moved. She never did. She always slept on the edge of the bed with her back to him, not moving her position all night, her hair all but covering her face. He awoke on his side, turned away from her. The realm of silence reigned, unbroken by Gerry's sleeping breath or a settling squeak from the house. No birds. No animals. No cars out on the road. This was his time of beauty. This kind of early-morning stillness he came to appreciate only after he began working in the woods. There were days in the winter when it got light later, before the engines of the skidders and chain saws were started up, when the men's voices fell silent, overwhelmed, by the immensity of the quiet in the woods around them. Scheutz stood in awe of it, but it frightened the other men—except for Pelletier—to the point where they seemed to be driven to crank their engines, revving them to dispel the silent fingers that reached for them in the half-light.

Even though it was Saturday and he did not have to go to work, he dressed and then walked outside. He lifted the two chain saws from the bed of his truck and carried them inside the barn to set them on the workbench. Later that day, he would break them down, clean them both of the oil and sawdust and pine sap, change the spark plugs, clean the air filters, and put a new chain on one of them.

The thought of not going to work for a couple of days, to spend time with the Gerry and the kids, rested on him like the light from the growing dawn. And maybe they could get those old wooden gutters off this weekend. But it would be hours before anyone besides him would be awake. He stood outside the barn door for awhile and watched the ridge of trees to the east, almost sure he could see it get lighter as he stood there. It was just a fantasy, but watching the eastern sky at dawn always made him feel the earth turning beneath him. When the top edge of the sun was about to touch the top of the trees he left off and got in his truck to go for coffee and the newspaper.

In Georgina's, the same people were there that sat in attendance every morning, the farmers, the nurse, the used car salesman on his way into Keene. Since it was not a school day, Georgina's daughter, Sharna helped out. Her long cook's apron, tied high on her chest, reached to just above her shoe tops. Scheutz watched her moving between the tables, carrying plates of eggs and sausage to the three old farmers in the corner table. She carried herself and the plates with an unusual grace for a ten-year-old. He'd never be able to get his own kids up this early in the morning, let alone get any work out of them.

"Hi," she said as she passed Scheutz's table heading toward the kitchen, giving him a little wave with her empty tray. He smiled back to her. Before the kitchen door swung closed, he heard, "Mom, Mr. Scheutz is here." He sipped his coffee and scanned the front page of *The Boston Globe.*

As he finished poring over the front page article about the Tet offensive in Viet Nam, Georgina herself set his omelet plate in front of him. She then went to the sideboard to refill his coffee cup and get a cup for herself. He continued with his newspaper while he ate. She sat across from him and read the *Keene Sentinel.* "You ride down with Gerry last night to your show in Brattleboro?" he asked her.

He expected her usual, "Ayuh." But she lifted her coffee cup before she answered. After a sip she merely nodded her head a few times without saying anything and suddenly developed a keen interest in some article in her newspaper. Scheutz waited for her attention to come back to him, but it did not come. He went back to his paper, but not before noticing that she was blushing all up her neck and the side of her face. Scheutz smiled to himself. Something must have gone on in Brattleboro for her to blush like that. Gerry had said that they went to a bar after the gallery opening. Georgina had been divorced since Sharna was just a baby and, as far as Scheutz knew, the few guys she'd gone out with since that time never lasted for more than one date. But it was none of his business. Besides, she'd tell him about it sooner or later. Just a matter of time till the blush wore off.

And that could be as early as tomorrow. On Sundays when they met for coffee and the New York Times crossword puzzle, she often prattled on about everything that had happened to her during the week. Even very intimate things, as if the Sunday puzzle were some kind of religious service that evoked confession and the purging of the soul. The purging was always one-sided since he felt no compunction to do the same. Talking to Georgina about himself had the feeling of dumping his soul into a meat grinder. Probably the reason she felt so at ease in telling him about these things was that she sensed his distance from them, the way a priest is so distant from his confessees. Listening to her was a little like reading the Metro section of the Boston Globe, interesting but with no affect on his own life. He went back to his omelet and newspaper.

Gerry was up when he returned to the house, at the stove in her bathrobe, cooking french toast for the kids. Dan sprawled on one elbow in his spot at one end of the long deal table, reading a comic book and forking a piece of eggy-bread, as the kids called it, into his mouth. Yelps and bams of Saturday morning television cartoons forced their way in from the front parlor where Marty indulged in his own weekly religious observance. A brilliant morning sun poured in through the row of windows he and Gerry had installed over the counter, exactly what they had envisioned two years earlier in the midst of the debris of the gutted room. He stood directly behind her and buried his face in the uncombed mass of hair, kissing the back of her head and savoring the unbathed smell of her.

"Hi, hon," she said. "Want a piece of eggy bread?"

"Sure."

"Marty, get in here." She yelled as she scooped two pieces of bread from the skillet onto a plate. The sound reverbrated through the back of her skull into his nose and lips.

"I want to eat in here." Marty yelled back.

She moved away from him, laterally along the counter. Without turning her head, she yelled again. "No. Turn it off. You can go back after breakfast."

Scheutz plucked a coffee mug from the cupboard and poured half a cup from the pot on the stove. "You want some more?"

"Yeah. Here." She handed her empty cup to him behind her back, still without turning around. "I just can't seem to get awake this morning."

He put the folded newspaper at Gerry's place on the table opposite from Dan, and then sat in his own chair on the end. "Yoohoo, Dan my son, good morning there."

"Daddy-O," Dan mumbled without skipping a beat on the comic panels.

Gerry set Marty's plate on the table directly across from Dan and next to her own. "Marty. I'm not telling you one more time. Now get in here." She put a plate in front of Scheutz and then brought her own plate of toast and her coffee cup to the table.

Scheutz got up and went into the parlor to click the television off. Before he could lift Marty up by his armpits, the kid stood and did his gorilla stomp into the kitchen. At the table, Marty picked up the maple syrup cruet just as Dan, without looking, reached for it. Feeling it move away from his hand, Dan looked up, grabbed the cruet from Marty's hand.

"Hey," Marty said to Dan.

"Hey, yourself," Dan said to Marty.

"Put the book away," Gerry said to Dan.

"Give me your glass," Scheutz said to Marty, and poured him some milk.

Dan put the comic down and poured syrup on his french toast, then pushed the cruet across the table to Marty. Scheutz put cream in his coffee. Gerry flipped over the Boston Globe to read the front headline.

Marty sipped his milk. "Put the paper away," he said to his mother.

"Oh. Sorry," she said, giving Marty a yes-master smile, and taking a sip of her coffee. They ate quietly, chewing and sipping almost in unison.

"Beautiful spring day," Scheutz said finally. "Supposed to be nice tomorrow, too." Gerry nodded with her mouth full. Dan raised his eyebrows in agreement. Marty continued to eat. Scheutz paused for sip of coffee. "If we get right on it, we can get those wooden gutters off today and get the other ones up. I checked at the hardware store in Keene. They have everything we need."

"Can't," Gerry said. "I've got to work."

"What do you mean you have to work?"

"I've got to spend the day in Lebanon, at that little ad agency. They've got a big job due at the printer first thing Monday morning." Gerry hired herself out to design studios, ad agencies, and local printers, as a freelance paste-up artist. She had worked at the place in Lebanon before. With not that many ad agencies or design studios in the area, there was not a lot of that kind of work. But when she did work, the pay was decent.

"When did this come about?" Scheutz asked. "We talked about these gutters a couple of days ago."

"I just heard about it last night…at that gallery opening." She paused, studying the look on Scheutz's face. "What? Come on, Clem, I can get two whole days work at that place."

"You're working tomorrow, too?"

"Yes. Those folks are en charrette. I'm sure I can get twenty hours in this weekend."

"I just wish you would've told me."

"When? Last night when you were half awake? Beside, what's the big rush. If we don't do the gutters this weekend, we'll do it later. We've got all summer."

"No, you're right. It's just that…well, it's going to be so nice. Too bad you have to be chained to a drawing table all weekend."

Gerry laughed. "I'll be fine. You guys do something fun all weekend."

"We'll do the gutters. Okay, guys?"

"Not me," Dan said. "You remember I told I was going to Freddie Brockton's house today. A whole bunch of us are getting together."

"To do what?"

"Stuff."

"So, it's me and you, Marty." Scheutz drained his coffee cup.

Marty nodded. "I'll help you. Can I be the one on top of the ladder?"

"We'll see how it works out."

"No," Gerry said. "You will not be up on the ladder." She tilted her head at Scheutz. "He's not to be up on the ladder, okay?"

Scheutz smiled at her. "Not to worry, dearheart." To Marty, he said, "I'll tell you what. You help me this morning—I'll go up the ladder and you hold it. Then this afternoon we'll do whatever you want to do. Okay?"

"The green slime."

"Say what?"

"That's what's at the Saturday matinee in Keene," Dan said. "He wants to see the movie called *The Green Slime.*"

"It's really cool." Marty spread his fingers, talking around a mouthful of french toast. "It's about this spaceship that comes back from another planet, only it accidentally picked up this slime on one of its tail fins and the slime starts eating people on earth and you can't kill it and the more it eats the bigger it gets and then it breaks off into little slimes."

"Sounds like the Revenge of *Soylent Green*," Gerry said.

Dan laughed. "Good one, Mom."

Marty asked, "What's Soylent Green?"

"It's a sci-fi movie with that guy, Moses, in it," Dan said. "See, they put people in a vat and make this green glop out of them but nobody knows the glop is human flesh, so they all eat it 'cause there's a food shortage, and they like the taste of it."

"What does that have to do with *The Green Slime*?"

"You don't see it? Instead of the green glop eating the people, the people eat the green glop."

"It's not glop, it's slime."

Dan dropped his fork onto his empty plate. "What the hell's the difference?"

Marty separated two pieces of french toast on his plate, then pointed at each one in turn. "Slime oozes. Glop goes plop."

"I'm sorry I brought it up," Gerry mumbled. "Dan, if you're dressed by the time I am, I'll drop you off at Freddie's on my way out of town."

After breakfast, Marty followed Scheutz into the barn as Gerry's rusted old Pontiac descended the driveway toward the road. Scheutz stopped for a moment at the barn door and watched the car, feeling an unusual sense of loss. What the hell was wrong with him? It was a beautiful spring day that he could spend with Marty, and then Dan later on. He had a whole weekend ahead of getting something done he'd been thinking about all winter. Gerry had found two days work at a better hourly rate than he could ever make. He'd see her tonight. What was wrong? For chrissake, he spent all week alone in the woods, what was the big deal about not having her here to work with him for the next two days?

Well, for one thing, he was not in the woods. He was at home. He had been alone in the woods all week and would be alone in the woods all next week, and in between, it would be nice not to be alone for two days. But, what the hell, he had Marty, a whole trip unto himself.

Marty put his foot on the bottom rung of the extension to secure it while Scheutz hand-walked the ladder down from where it leaned up into the hayloft. They carried it, one on each end, with Scheutz more toward the middle leaving less weight for Marty to handle, out to the front of the house. They spent the morning removing the gutters and square wooden downspouts from each corner of the house. Scheutz, on the ladder, detached the downspouts from the forged spikes driven into the clapboards while Marty steadied them below. By the time they got to the gutters themselves Marty's attention drifted and he developed a need to know how high on the barn roof he could bounce a stone.

The front gutter came off in pieces, breaking at points of the worst rot. Scheutz called down to Marty to drag the smaller pieces away from the house and pile them with the downspouts. Marty had taken off his gloves so he could throw stones and, grabbing a rotted gutter, got himself a splinter from the first piece of wood he picked up. He let out a yelp of pain that brought Scheutz down from the ladder. Scheutz brought him into the kitchen to remove the splinter, which was a good half inch long and in fairly deep. As he got tweezers and a needle and antiseptic salve from the drawer, Marty limped around the room holding is palm out as if begging for alms.

"This will hurt," Scheutz told him. "But it will hurt a lot less if you don't move your hand while I'm getting it out. Okay?"

"Aaagh."

"You can yell all you want. But don't move that hand. Got it?"

Marty nodded his head, dancing in place like he had to go to the bathroom. But his hand stayed solid and unmoved in Scheutz's hand. He screamed as Scheutz touched the splinter with the tweezers. "Aaagh. It's killing me."

"That's okay. Go ahead and scream. Just don't move the hand." The splinter finally came out with trickle of blood behind it. Scheutz went to put a band-aid on the palm but Marty, sobbing the while, insisted on something larger, something more in line with the suffering he had just undergone. Scheutz wrapped it in a gauze bandage but drew the line on the arm sling. Once the hand was wrapped, Scheutz pulled him onto his lap and held him close against his chest. Eventually, he stopped snuffling into Scheutz's shirt and wanted to know what was for lunch.

By the time they'd eaten, Marty had given up his wounded lion cub act and was back to his demanding little self. Now it was time for The Green Slime. Scheutz phoned the Brockton house to see if maybe Dan and Freddie might want to go down to Keene with them. "Dad," Dan said when he got him to the phone. "Can I stay overnight? A couple other kids are staying over."

"Well, yeah, I guess. If it's all right with Freddie's parents."

"Yeah, it is. I'll see you tomorrow. Mr. Brockton said he'd bring me home."

The Saturday matinee and *The Green Slime* were about what Scheutz expected. Marty met some other first-grader from Acworth who Scheutz didn't know. The boy, almost as big as Marty with thick bangs that hung into his eyes, seemed to have a problem controlling his giggle fits. The two boys fell immediately into their own little two-person cabal, leaving the adults behind. The boy's mother, a wispy blonde woman wearing a calf-length denim skirt and a peasant blouse, asked if her son, Joe, could sit with them in the movie while she went shopping at the local health food store. Ten minutes into the movie, Scheutz wished he had beat Joe's mother to the punch by asking her to watch the two kids. The movie was awful. But then, Marty and his friend were like a show unto themselves, like bear cubs, wrestling in their seats, jumping up to hang their heads over the balcony rail in front of them, squealing, laughing, hiding on the floor at the scary parts of the movie. Scheutz slouched in his seat with his feet up on the balcony rail. Instead of the movie, he watched his son. There, in that squirming ball of ceaseless energy, was his rapture.

On the way home, he stopped at Keene's only Chinese restaurant and got a take-out dinner for Marty, Gerry and himself. Gerry would be too tired to cook when she got home.

By seven o'clock she still wasn't home, and hadn't called, so he and Marty ate the Pupu Platter Marty had insisted on, complete with lighting the little sterno cup that came with it. At seven-thirty, Gerry called to say they were still working away. The company had brought in Chinese food for everyone.

"And what did you order?" Scheutz asked her.

"Moo Goo Gai Pan."

"I'm jealous. We're having Chinese kid food."

"Clem, listen," Gerry said. "We're going to be working until really late. And then we get going very early tomorrow again. So, I'm thinking I'll just crash here for the night. I'll be really too tired to drive home at midnight. And I'll just have to get up at six and drive back. Do you mind?"

"Well, yeah, I'll miss you. But you have to do what you have to do. You're getting a lot of hours in, huh?"

"Yep. And there's more coming up later in the month. These are good people to work for. We'll be walking in tall cotton, honey bunch. How're the kids?" They talked for a few minutes longer before she had to get back to work. He wanted to hold her there on the phone for as long as he could. After he hung up, he tried to remember the last time they had not spent the night together. It was the night Marty was born.

At bedtime, he brought Marty into his and Gerry's bed where Marty snuggled in against him while Scheutz read to him from the *Prydain Chronicles*, the adventures of Taran, the lowly Assistant Pig Keeper on a great lord's estate. Taran wanted to be a hero and left the estate to travel with his favorite pig, to confront the forces of evil in the world. Somewhere in the middle of the night Scheutz woke to find the book still open on his chest and the light still on. Marty slept soundly on Gerry's side of the bed, the covers half off. He tucked the around him and turned out the light.

On Sunday morning, Scheutz was up early as usual. Careful not to wake Marty, he was dressed and downstairs in the kitchen before he realized that he could not just take off and go down to Georgina's for his usual coffee and crossword puzzle. Marty was too young to be left in the house by himself. He'd wait until Marty woke so they could both go down together. But he should call Georgina and tell her so she wouldn't wait for him before having a go at the puzzle herself.

"That's okay, I'll wait," she said when he called. "I'm not too wide awake, anyhow. I got in late from that party last night."

"Oh, what party?" She must be working herself up to telling him about what had gotten her blushing the morning before.

"At that professor's house in Hanover. You know, whatsis-name? That guy, that friend of Gerry's, the one that teaches art. I'm surprised I didn't see you there."

"Well, you know, Gerry had to work. It wouldn't be fair.

"Oh, yeah. Right."

He piddled around in the barn for awhile with the new gutters he'd planned to put up that day. When he came back inside, the television blasted away in the parlor, with Marty still in his pajamas. "Hey, I'm hungry," Marty yelled at him.

"Don't 'Hey-I'm-hungry' me. Get off your butt. Turn that thing off; we're going out."

"No."

Scheutz turned off the television. "Go upstairs and get dressed."

"Why?"

Here we go. You start the day off arguing with this kid and by noontime you want to kill yourself. "We have an appointment."

"What appointment?"

"We have to meet someone. I'll tell you about it on the way. You want breakfast, then get dressed."

On the way down the hill in the truck, he explained to Marty that the important appointment was with a band of gypsies who were traveling through looking for kids.

"No. Tell me for real."

Scheutz laughed. "For real, we have to get breakfast."

Marty leaned his elbow out the window of the truck cab. "You made me turn the cartoons off for that?" He shook his head. "I can find my own gypsies, you know."

Inside the diner, Scheutz poured himself a cup of coffee at the sideboard and carried the New York Times to the table. Sharna brought Marty a glass of milk. He wanted pancakes, and when Georgina brought out his plate and Scheutz's eggs, she and Sharna sat with them. Georgina opened the Sunday magazine section to the crossword puzzles and placed it on the table between them.

"Why didn't you go to the party last night?" Sharna asked Marty.

"There wasn't any party," he answered.

"Yes there was. We went." Sharna lifted her head to display her most imitation of the sophisticated adult woman.

"Sharna, honey," Georgina said. "Can you go in the kitchen and make sure I turned the stove off."

Sharna stood up. "There were lots of kids there. We had a'wonderful' time. Your mother was there."

"Sharna. Go. Please." Georgina watched her daughter walk toward the kitchen before turning her face back to Scheutz. The blush of yesterday was back. And suddenly Scheutz understood—she was not blushing for herself, but for what Scheutz was not supposed to know about Gerry.

Chapter 14

In the Wind off the River

There may have been a pleasure in the pathless woods, but there was also a sameness to it. Every tree, every hour, every day differed from the one before only if you looked close at the small details of what you were doing. Not being able to see the forest for the trees was not always such a bad thing. But then, missing the small details of a tree could hurt. A difference in the angle of lean could make a big difference in the way it fell. As could the direction of the wind against the bush at the top. If a tree twisted the wrong way, it could bind the saw blade between the trunk and stump, with no hope of moving it until the skidder arrived to push it over. And if it twisted too far or split up the middle as it fell, the cutter could be in danger.

But cutting trees all day was like a musical counterpoint. The details of felling each tree were like treble semitones, and the number of trees on a hillside like a bass rhythm. There was a pleasure in the sameness of the work. On the hillside, in the early afternoon, inside the cocoon of the chain saw noise, Scheutz could actually feel his anxiety leave him. The buzzing cloud of foreboding that had overtaken him during lunch dissipated into wispy horsetails as he focused on the cut and fall of each tree. But, as anyone who works out-of-doors knows, horsetail clouds always foretold a coming storm. For now, at least, the pathless woods soothed him, as it always had done. The fear of the powerful, violent chain saw in his hands, and the tons of timber rising above his head helped to stave off that greater, unnamed fear of what could not be seen. The saw and the timber could at least gain his respect, but he couldn't respect what he couldn't see.

The free-floating anxiety that had been his companion since he awoke that morning had moved its camp deeper into the forest before lunch. But then, sitting on the log pile listening to Olavi's story about the pig house fire, his belly had turned queasy again. Maybe it was just the olive loaf, maybe he should find something healthier to eat for lunch. Nanda never ceased criticizing the stuff he ate, declaring most of it to be, like the olive loaf, unfit for human consumption. "Soul food," she called it. "Since it has no nutritional value for your body, your only reason for eating it must be that it soothes your soul in some perverse way."

Come on, Clem, you know better than that. It's not the olive loaf. It's the pig.

The pig?

Yes, the pig. The story of the pig reminded you of the story you read to Marty that night.

Scheutz had to stop in the middle of the tree he was limbing. He set the running chain saw on the trunk and leaned his knees against the bark of the horizontal tree. Yes, that was it. That night signaled the beginning of the end. That was the night Gerry went to the party in Hanover after telling him she would be working until the small hours.

You're wrong, Clem, that was not the beginning of the end. That was only when you first noticed it.

That was only the first time you'd caught yourself in a lie.

No, I never lied before that night.

Then what do you mean?

That the beginning of the end came years before, and that night only marked the end of when I couldn't stand it any more.

Stand what?

You dying on me.

What? What kind of bullshit is that?

You died on me, Clem. Every time I turned around. One minute you were there with me and the next time I looked you were gone. I don't know where you went all the time, but I couldn't reach you.

I never left you. I still haven't left you.

Yes, you did. I never noticed it really until we moved from Santa Fe to Cincinnati. It got a lot worse when we moved to New Hampshire. And when you started working in the woods, I knew.

Knew what?

I knew you were off on your own, and that you'd visit once in a while. That you'd be there with me and then I'd be alone for days, weeks at a time. You became a shell, walking through the house, a golem that ate, and farted, and snored.

Yes, he did that sometimes, what Gerry had said, the going off on his own. But he didn't think anyone else noticed. He would be gone for such a short time…actually, he didn't know how long his mind would just take off and leave the room. All he knew was that he'd be with someone, or even alone, like here in the woods, and then realize he had tuned out, his mind gone somewhere else. He'd stay focused on a task with one part of his mind while the rest of him went off. He'd been doing that for so long, had first noticed it years ago. In Cincinnati, when they'd gone back there after Gerry's mother died.

Not long after they arrived. That day by the river he had not heard her calling him, did not know she was there until he felt the touch of her fingertips on his back. "What are doing down here so long?" she said. He wasn't aware he'd been there a long time, standing in the waist-high grass, about where the old black man's cabin had been, staring at the current of the river.

He turned to her, turned his back on the river, and embraced her. The day was cold but sunny. She was so warm against him. He had gotten chilled, and her warmth made him realize how cold he'd been. She stretched her arms around him and beat a rhythm on his back. "My God," she said. "You're like an ice sculpture. What have you been doing out here?"

"Just daydreaming," he said. "How did you know I was here?"

"I guessed. You come down here a lot."

"Where are the kids?"

"Dan's in school. Marty's up at the house by himself. We don't want to leave him alone, so come on. Let's get something done today." She held out her hand for him to take. "I have everything you wanted from the hardware store."

He held her hand and they walked away from the river. He stopped her at the spot where the old man's cabin had been. It was hard to tell exactly, the remains of the old tar paper shack had been removed so completely. He could remember, though, almost the exact angle of the view to the river, and in the other direction, exactly were it was in relation to the railroad switching station. Now there was nothing, only the same tall, winter-brown river grass that covered the entire bank.

She stopped with him and stood silently beside him, waiting, replacing, as she had been doing for years, all those memories that pestered him. With her he had no past. So, why was he here? What was he doing standing by the river, in the same place he'd stood years ago with the old black man, finding a solace in the stories of the old man's life, unable to take his view away from slow-moving current of the Little Miami River.

He and Gerry had never talked much about this place where they had both grown up, not until the night they crossed the Ohio River on the suspension bridge into downtown Cincinnati. They rolled in like an Okie family in the Chevy pickup with the kids asleep in pull-down bunks inside the truck's camper bed, crammed with all their belongings. That night they began to reminisce about their old high school in Mariemont. Since then this area itched like some open sore on the earth's skin he couldn't stop picking at.

In the two months they'd been here he noticed the scab picking didn't affect Gerry as intensely as it did him. She talked about her past life here the way she might talk about running into an old acquaintance in the hardware store. For Scheutz, though, especially in places like here at the site of Renfro's old cabin, or the neighborhood where Scheutz and his brother had shared an attic room, the cankerous sores in these places snaked out fibrous tentacles that tugged at him. He'd find himself coming back to Gerry's mother's house—now hers—at supper time, not sure where he'd been for four hours. Except that he had found himself sitting behind the wheel of the Chevy, parked in some neighborhood or in some city park that stabbed him with familiarity. He'd stir as if from a deep sleep, not knowing for a few moments where he was. But then slowly he'd come to the awareness that the street outside the truck cab windows had altered slightly in the last ten or twelve years since he was there last, changing behind him and encapsulating, as if in amber, the overlaid scenes of his childhood. To be more accurate, scenes of his and his brother Willi's childhood, because he could not remember ever being without him. These images stifled him, the tentacles enshrouding him like roots holding him in river-bottom silt.

But even worse were the times he'd found himself sitting in the truck at the curb across and down the street from his older brother Hank's house. The other memories of Willi or Renfro merely held him in place because he could not go back there, but Hank was alive in the present. He knew Hank's address from the two letters that had found him in New Mexico and which he never answered. Sitting in his truck, he had seen Hank's wife Evelyn come and go from the house with three small children. He'd even seen Hank himself once and put his hand on the truck's door handle, but froze there before he could open it. Why couldn't he bring himself to just get out of the truck and greet his brother?

He stared at the grassy patch of empty ground where Renfro's cabin had been until Gerry squeezed his hand in hers and nodded her head in the direction of the house. She knew. It was uncanny the way she knew. She knew what was wrong with him. Did she also know that she alone was the antidote? That she replaced everyone, Willi, Renfro, Hank, even herself at age seventeen? Was that too much of a burden for her to bear? She stood shivering in the wind off the river.

She let go his hand and, wrapping one arm around his shoulders, pulled him in the direction away from the river. He went willingly, lifting up the bottom of her heavy sweater and pushing his bare hand into the back pocket of her Levi's. They walked that way through the grass, across the railroad yard tracks, past the switching house and up the railroad's steep, winding driveway to the house on Miami Bluff Road.

Gerry had backed the Chevy into the driveway so that the truck bed with the copper tubing and the other plumbing supplies sat next to the side door of the house. They had removed the camper cap from the bed when they arrived two months before and it now sat on wooden sawhorses in front of the little one-car garage at the end of the driveway. Mr. Bright from next door had complained that the camper and the scabrous Chevy truck with its washed-out paint finish and New Mexico license plates gave the property the look of hillbillies moving into the neighborhood. It apparently cut against the grain of the community's aspirations toward middle-class affluence. Indeed, since Scheutz and Gerry arrived, the square, little brick house had taken on the aura of an Appalachian construction site with piles of lumber and old appliances and other junk sitting out in the yard. Gerry assured the man that all would be well. That they were, in fact, renovating and restoring the house, built in the early 1920s, but let go by Gerry's mother for so many years.

Inside, the house was warm. Too warm for Scheutz's taste. The kids sat in t-shirts, squabbling in the living room over something or other. Wait a minute. Why wasn't Dan in school? It was the middle of the morning on a school day; why was he home?

"They sent me home," he said. He flicked a long, blonde strand of hair from his face and looked up from where he sat on the living room carpet with his back against the sofa. He and Marty had a Monopoly board and its accoutrements spread out between them on the floor. Both boys were dressed alike with white t-shirts and worn jeans, except that Marty was barefoot and Dan wore his beloved cracked and scuffed cowboy boots that had to be too tight for him by now.

"Would you like to expand on that a little?" Scheutz asked.

"Come on, Clem, help me unload the truck." Gerry came up behind him in the doorway. Then she saw Dan. "What are you doing here?"

"They gave me the day off."

"They did not," Marty said. "They kicked him out. And we all have to go up and talk to the principal to get him back in."

"They don't want you there," Dan said to Marty.

"Well, I'm going. I'll tell them all about you. You're a big bully and you cheat at Monopoly."

"Hold on," Scheutz said. "Why do we have to go up and talk to the principal?"

"He got kicked out 'cause he was fighting." Marty said in full taunt mode. "He beat up some kid in front of the school."

"I did not beat up some kid in front of the school. It was in back of the school."

"What?" Gerry's voice slid up into the treble range. "Fighting? You were fighting?"

Marty raised up on his knees. "Yeah, and the kid was bigger than him, he was in the fourth grade, and…"

"Marty, hush," Gerry said. "Dan?"

"What?"

"Don't 'what' me. You were fighting? I can't believe this. You were sent home from school for fighting in the school yard? My God, I can't believe this. Clement?"

"What?"

"What do you mean, 'what?'? Say something. Our son is going to end up a mercenary soldier just like his father, and all you can say is 'what?'? Say something to him."

"Did you win?"

"Sure he won," Marty said. "He's the toughest kid in the school."

"Aaagh." Gerry stomped across the room and lifted Dan up off the floor by his left arm, sitting him on the sofa. "You will not do this, Daniel. I will not allow you to act like some tough punk."

"Gerry. Honey. Calm down. Please." Scheutz touched her back and she turned to him.

"Clem, you promised me."

"I know. And it's okay. Don't be so upset. We haven't even heard Dan's story yet."

"I'll tell you the story," Marty offered.

"Marty. Shut. Up." Scheutz put his arm around Gerry and pulled her to him. "Come on, hon, this is not a major catastrophe, okay? Dan's only nine. He got in a school yard fight. It happens to the best of us. That doesn't mean he's signed up for the Wehrmacht."

"God, I hate coming back to this place," Gerry said, moving away from Scheutz. "I can't wait till we get out of here. They must use animosity for fertilizer in this town. If we were still in Santa Fe, you wouldn't fighting in school."

"I wouldn't be too sure about that," Marty said.

"Shut up, Marty." Dan swiped the back of Marty's head with his open hand.

"Now you're hitting your brother? Clement."

"Dan, don't hit your brother."

"Is that all you're going to say to him? Do something."

"What do you want me to do, spank him for hitting his brother?"

Her shoulders sagged. "What I really want is to get us out of this town."

"Well, let's get the work done. Sooner the house is finished, the sooner we can leave."

An hour later, sitting in the principal's office, they learned that Dan was not the only boy suspended for the day. Mr. Kaiser, the heavily jowled principal leaned forward over his desk telling the story of the fight. More of a melee of third and fourth graders swarming around the back stoop of the school building, pushing and shoving. Dan and the other boy were the only ones actually fighting. The story did not differ appreciably from the one Dan told earlier at home. "You must know that no one wanted to single out Dan in this fracas, but we had no choice." He peered at Gerry with his hands folded in a Buddhist-like manner, pausing for what appeared to be dramatic effect. "We all still miss your mother, Geraldine. And, of course, when Dan came to us, we all welcomed him with open arms. But…and you will have to admit this…the boy is a handful."

"I'm sorry, but I don't admit any such thing," Gerry said.

Scheutz could feel Marty, sitting on his lap in front of the desk, fidgeting his way up to some pronouncement on Dan's being a handful. He quietly clamped a hand on Marty's arm and whispered in the boy's ear, "Whatever it is, Marty, don't say it. Just keep a lid on it till we're out of here."

"Geraldine." Mr. Kaiser leaned back in his chair, laying his hands flat on the desk. "I always remember you as one of the most well-behaved students I have ever had in my school. And, of course your mother, God rest her soul, could have won awards as the best school librarian in the state. So we all here expect any child of yours, any grandchild of Cynthia Rieker, to be a model of obedience. Perhaps our expectations are too high."

"Well, Mr. Kaiser." Gerry switched into what seemed to Scheutz to be a perfect imitation of her mother. "We shall all make the greatest effort to live up to those expectations. I can assure you that Daniel will henceforth bring to your school—our school—the same joy we all feel at home with him there."

Dan slouched in his chair as he had done throughout the entire meeting. His eyes moved from his mother's to Mr. Kaiser's and then to Scheutz's. He held Marty in a long look and then made the circuit again around the room. It was hard to know what he was thinking, but Scheutz had no doubt that Dan grasped what was going on in that office. This was a game they all needed to play. Mr. Kaiser was, in his own way, inviting them to belong to the community. But they didn't belong, and they wouldn't. The familiar twinge of foreignness visited Scheutz again, sitting there with Marty on his lap. He'd always felt most foreign in Cincinnati, the one place that should have felt most like home. Being in Mexico did not feel as foreign, nor did living in Santa Fe. That sense of differentness and isolation, woven in and out of the riveting memories he had been having since coming back to Cincinnati, was what made those memories so acute. Back then, sitting in that shack by the river with that old black man, who was himself some kind of weird alien form, he had felt more at home than he had ever felt at home or in school.

Mr. Kaiser was smiling and saying to Scheutz. "And Clement. Of course I remember you on our football team. And I shall always remember the pleasure of knowing your aunt. A wonderful woman. A great supporter of football."

Scheutz nodded and smiled. Marty turned to Scheutz with a wide-eyed, look as if some great secret had been revealed to him.

With the front door of the school building closed behind them, on the way down the front steps, Gerry growled through her teeth. "That patronizing son of a bitch. God, I can't wait till we're out of here."

Marty flung himself from the bottom two steps, cackling with delight. "Your aunt was a football player, Dad?"

"No, she was a rooter."

"Hah. Aunt Roto-Rooter."

Scheutz took Gerry's hand as they walked through the square and the four blocks back to Miami Bluff Road. Dan had gone back to his classroom after they all endured a long lecture by Mr. Kaiser. Marty ran on ahead of them and then stopped on each street corner to wait for them before crossing. The midday sun warmed the January air and the wind of the morning had dropped. With Gerry he felt no foreignness, no matter where they were. The four of them belonged to each other, they were their own community.

Chapter 15

RENASCENCE

After lunch, he and Gerry got to work. Marty amused himself with his toys in the kids' bedroom. Scheutz and Gerry's first job for the day was to isolate the pipes going to the small bathroom in the basement. That was the one they would use while they removed all the old iron pipe and replumbed the rest of the house. By the time Dan got home from school, they had installed copper tubing in the second floor bathroom, Gerry measuring and cutting the pipe and Scheutz sweating the joints.

In the two months they had been in the little house, they had completely rewired it with new Romex cable. The furnace in the basement had also needed replacing. The original coal furnace, installed when the house was built, had been later converted to gas. The new one Scheutz and Gerry put in was a quarter of the size and left so much room in the basement they decided, when-everything else was finished, they would build a recreation room down there. The restoration was being done with an eye toward getting as much money as they could for the place. At least that was what Gerry said, but Scheutz knew she actually enjoyed building this nest with him as much as she had enjoyed renovating their old adobe house in Agua Fria, the little town on the edge of Santa Fe.

Dan slammed his way in the side door, dropped a reader and a three-ring binder on the kitchen table and said he was going over to his friend Tommie's house till supper.

"Why don't you take your brother along?" Gerry said.

"No." He slammed his way out again.

"I wish he'd stop that," Scheutz said He lay under the kitchen sink. "Makes me sorry I ever taught him how to open a door."

Gerry lightly kicked the bottom of his shoe. "You should talk. I think he inherited that slamming business from you."

"Didn't we decide to replace this whole sink? This is a mess under here. And the floor's all rotted."

"Is it? Well, maybe we should. The one thing Gaither stressed of the things people go for is a nice shiny kitchen." Tom Gaither had been in Gerry's class in high school and, instead of going off to college on a football scholarship, he had become a local real estate whiz. "I know where we can get a good deal on a sink and a dish washer," Gerry said. "That place over on Duck Creek Road where I found the stove. So, yeah, why don't we just the rip the whole thing out and do the floor the same time we do the pipes."

"Hah. Didn't Mr. Bright next door say we had everything in the yard but the kitchen sink?"

By supper time the area under the kitchen window where the sink had been resembled a gap left by an extracted tooth. Gerry cooked while Dan, back from his friend's house, helped Scheutz load the sink as well as the old stove into the back of the Chevy so he could transport them to the dump the next day. Marty was given the task of carrying a clean milk bottle down to the bathroom in the basement and filling it with water to use for cooking.

After the meal, Marty helped carry dishes and pots downstairs where Scheutz washed them.

"I've got to work tonight, Clem," Gerry said as he hauled the wire tray of clean dishes and pots up from below. "I really have to finish that piece and get it sent off."

"Want me to read to you?"

She titled her head and smiled. "That would be nice."

With Dan and Marty in front of the television in the living room, Scheutz and Gerry moved themselves upstairs to her studio. Of the three bedrooms on the second floor, the kids got the largest, which had been Gerry's room as a child. Scheutz and Gerry slept in the smallest room, which had been her mother's sewing room, and they had cleared out her mother's bedroom for a studio for Gerry. The antique pencil-post bedstead, the one the old woman had died in, was stored with much of the other furniture from the house, out in the little one-car garage. They covered the hardwood floor with a doubled layer of painter's drop cloth to protect it and moved in the worn overstuffed chair from the living room. Gerry's easel, with its four by six foot canvas, held court over the room.

The only thing left from her mother's time were the bookshelves and the hundreds of books that lined every wall. The woman, a librarian to the core, had sorted and marked each shelf according to category, and alphabetized according to author's last name. There were novels, and books of poetry, volumes on history, art, philosophy, and one very tiny section of books, the only trace of Gerry's father in the house, on civil engineering, drainage systems, surveying, and geological exploration.

Her mother's books had dominated Gerry's childhood. As far back as she could remember, she had said, back to the time when she first learned to distinguish a book as an object different from all the other things that made up her environment, her mother had read to her from her books. Her earliest memories involved being curled up next to her mother, straining to understand what her mother was reading. There was no *Uncle Wiggly* or *The Little Train that Could* or Beatrix Potter; it was Byron and Keats and

Shelley that first penetrated the miasma of her budding awareness of the world.

Gerry adjusted the light from the lamps she had set shining on the painting. During the day the room got some southern light, but not much at this time of year. The painting she needed to finish was a horizontal view of their old house in Agua Fria. She had been accepted for a group show in Taos, the theme of the show being "Southwest Exposures." In the painting the house and surrounding courtyard wall are rendered in the sandstone color of the actual house, blending with the neutral colors of the surrounding countryside. The prominent figure against this background is the old man they had bought the house from. The man is seated, and wearing a shirt of bright Mexican design. Near and above him, much like the floating characters in many of Chagall's paintings, there is the spirit of the man's dead wife who he had told them haunted the house, prompting him to sell it. If her spirit was there, Gerry had said after they lived there for several months, it was certainly a benign one. In the painting, the yet unfinished spirit embodies both the neutral-colored background and the brightness of the man's clothing.

"So, what do you want to hear?" Scheutz scanned the shelves, only a few books even remotely familiar to him. From the beginning, he had left it to her to choose reading matter, since the extent of his literary exposure before meeting Gerry had been limited to the *Marvel* comic books or *Tales from the Crypt* comic books he shared with his younger brother. Occasionally, he had come across a *Classic Comics* rendition of a story such as *The Prisoner of Zenda* or *Huckleberry Finn.* While they lived in Santa Fe, at Gerry's urging, he had audited two evening adult education classes, one in English Literature, and one in American Literature. Since he had never finished high school, he could not officially sign up for the classes, but showed up every night and read everything on every list they handed out.

"I need something...I don't know." Gerry paused, looking up from the canvas. "...something feminine and spectral."

"Feminine and spectral?"

"Yeah." She moved one the lamps again and stood with her legs spread and her arms akimbo, staring at the painting. "What do I see?" Her tone was musing. "All I can see from where I stand is…That's it. Edna St. Vincent Millay. See it? Right there in the poetry section."

He settled himself in the overstuffed chair and thumbed the pages. He knew which one she meant. He had heard it before.

"All I could see from where I stood
Was three long mountains and a wood."

She mixed paint with a palette knife and then began to apply it. "I think I'll call the painting *Renascence,*" she said.

"I think you should call it The Spirit of Cold Water."

"La Espirita de la Agua Fria. Yeah, that's nice."

The reading ritual had started not long after Marty was born. At first, it was her reading to him. She read excerpts from *Justine*, the first book of *The Alexandria Quartet.* The cadence of Durrell's writing, she said, begged to be read aloud. He took over reading to her when she tired and, by the time they finished *Balthazar*, he was reading to her while she painted. Once he started the adult education classes, he realized there existed so many beautiful things he could never read them all to her before they died. She had even done a painting of him in the manner of Mary Cassatt, with his leg hooked over the arm of a chair, reading to a small girl with long dark hair.

"The sky, I thought, is not so grand;
I 'most could touch it with my hand!
And reaching up my hand to try,
I screamed to feel it touch the sky."

"Have you been giving much thought to where we want to go when we leave here, Daddy-O?" she asked him, looking up from her painting.

"Not really. I just assumed you'd want to go back out west."

"You do agree that we can't stay here, don't you?"

"Absolutely. I feel buried in this place. Like I can't move and I can't breathe. Did you see that sign painted on the tower of the Baldwin Piano factory over on Gilbert Avenue?"

"No. Whatsit say?"

"It says, 'Impeach Earl Warren. Join the John Birch Society.' With a huge American flag waving."

She looked up from the canvas. "About says it all, doesn't it?"

"I saw and heard and knew at last

The How and Why of all things, past,"

"And present, and forevermore," Gerry added.

He had picked Gerry up at the airport in Albuquerque when she flew back to New Mexico after attending her mother's funeral in Cincinnati. Riding in the Chevy north to Agua Fria she told him that the house in Mariemont was theirs, with no liens or mortgages. They could sell the house in Agua Fria and use the money to fix up the Mariemont house. It made good financial sense. It was a nice neighborhood with a good school. In the city there was a good art museum, a few galleries, and lots of jazz clubs.

"I don't know," he said. "I didn't lose anything in Cincinnati I need to go find. I guess I have more reason to stay away from there than I do to go there."

"It doesn't matter, Clem. We can live anywhere, you know?"

"Well, if had my druthers, I'druther think about that place in New Hampshire your friend Georgina told us about. We could sell both houses and have enough to get a great place up there."

"So, what's so great about New Hampshire?"

"Trees. They got trees up the gazoo there. I feel like I haven't seen a tree since we left Mexico five years ago."

"Hell a of a reason to move someplace."

"Better reason than moving to a coffin in a midwestern suburb." He gestured toward the surrounding neighborhood.

So, they compromised. They would try living in Mariemont and see how it went. They got a decent price for the adobe house in Agua Fria, packed the kids up in the Chevy and drove east. But by the time Christmas was over, Gerry was as ready as Scheutz to move on. The town hadn't changed since they both went to high school there. Maybe that was the problem, because Gerry had changed. And it wasn't that the town wasn't nice, or the people weren't friendly, or the school wasn't good. Scheutz had left the place years before with a pocket-full of bad memories that did not really start rearing their ugly heads till he hit town again. For Gerry, it took a month and a little more for the politically conservative aura that sat like the unmoving smog in the basin of the city and emanated out to the suburb to serrate the edges of her soul. She groaned aloud the third time someone said to her, "You know, Cincinnati's a real sports town."

"And so beneath the weight lay I
And suffered death, but could not die."

He read and she painted. From downstairs the sounds of Batman and F Troop drifted up along with the kid sounds of laughter and occasional banging around during commercials. Winter night wrapped them as if in a cocoon. If they were entombed in this neighborhood, at least they stayed happy inside their tomb. This was okay; he could live with this for now, even with the memories that crept up to haunt him. He and Gerry did this for each other. She replaced whatever scraps of love he had before, which were gone forever. And he tried to replace her mother's reading that both soothed and invigorated her as a child. In this way they could go on forever.

He thought of Dan that morning, sitting in the school principal's office, watching his mother and Scheutz, and coming to an understanding of the game they played for his sake. It seemed to be all right with Dan that they were alien to this place. Scheutz remembered old Renfro once saying, "Chilluns ride on yo' back. Where you go, they go. If you happy, they happy. They be like puppies, they don't care where they live. They only care that they be with you."

It was early March before the house was ready to be sold. Tom Gaither came and made several suggestions about little final touches that would catch the eye of a potential buyer, like paint on the outside of the window trim. At least in the front of the house. On one of the first warmish weekend days, Gerry and Dan painted the trim on all the windows. Scheutz pruned the overgrown shrubs around the front and back porches, and repaired the garage doors before Gerry painted them. In the middle of March it rained for a solid week and when the rain stopped, they all, even Marty, painted the outside of the garage. Mr. Bright from next door beamed and waved at them from his yard where he was getting an early start on his lawn care.

The house was lovely. Tom Gaither said so. "Just lovely," Marty said in imitation of him that night at supper. Gerry smiled and nodded, spooning green beans onto her plate. "Not very interesting, but lovely," she said. The old wallpaper had been removed in the living room and the upstairs bedrooms, the plaster repaired and painted neutral colors. Most of the bookshelves had been taken out of Gerry's mother's old room and Gerry's studio was dismantled. It became just another not very interesting, but lovely, room.

It was as if their suburban tomb had been thrown open to public scrutiny. Anything not essential for daily life was toted out to the garage. Their lives became constricted by the self-conscious awareness that their home had to be open for inspection to potential buyers at any time. So saith the Gaither. A "For Sale" sign went up on the front lawn. People stopped in cars and looked at the house and then drove on. Some stopped and asked if they could look around. Tom Gaither made appointments to bring young couples in to walk through the house, pointing them first to the "lovely" kitchen with its new sink and appliances and linoleum flooring. He called Gerry with offers that people had made and advised her that she should take a few thousand less than what she wanted just to get the house sold. She would not come down, so she and Scheutz and the kids remained on public view until the middle of April when a young couple from Binghamton, New York met the offer. He had taken a new junior executive position with the Cincinnati Milling Machine Company and they needed something fast because she was seven months pregnant with their first child.

Scheutz and Gerry had a week to move out of the house. They secured the camper back onto the bed of the Chevy and repacked it with the tools, clothes, art supplies and toys they had brought six months before from New Mexico. They rented a U-Haul trailer and packed it with the furniture they wanted from the house, the old pencil-post bedstead without the mattress, the kitchen table with the legs removed, and other odds and ends, kitchen-ware, chairs, lamps. They packed in roughly a third of the books Gerry's mother had amassed and various pieces of art she had collected over her lifetime. The Salvation Army came and picked up the rest.

It was all finished ahead of schedule. Time to leave. They hung around, puttered, in a house that was no longer theirs. Tom Gaither had attended the closing, the money was deposited in the same account they had opened when they came to town, the account into which Scheutz transferred the money from the sale of the Agua Fria house. So why didn't they leave?

"What are we waiting for?" Gerry asked him. "Just because we don't have to be out until day after tomorrow, that doesn't mean we have to stay until then. Let's get on with it." Georgina wasn't expecting them in New Hampshire for another week, but that didn't mean they couldn't head out that way. Maybe they could take the kids to see Niagara Falls, or visit New York City for a few days. Gerry had always wanted to go there—The Museum of Modern Art, the Metropolitan, the Guggenheim, the Whitney.

"You want to drive that truck and trailer into New York City?"

"Don't be silly. We could leave the trailer and the camper at Georgina's and then just drive the truck in. Don't you want to get out of here?"

"I do, but..."

"What? But what?"

Exactly. But what? He wasn't ready to leave this box. Not just yet. Something held him, and wasn't letting him see what it was. They walked down to the river on a beautiful, sunny spring day. They showed Dan and Marty the place on the shore where Scheutz had first kissed Gerry.

"That's where I came from, right?" Dan said.

"Well, not exactly," Gerry said. "That happened a few months later on the roof of a moving boxcar."

Marty thought that was very funny. "Like Doctor Strangelove riding the bomb."

"That wasn't Doctor Strangelove, you doofus," Dan said. "That was the bomber pilot."

Standing on the spot of Renfro's old cabin, Scheutz watched Gerry and the kids chasing each other along the riverbank. This was all gone. Everything was gone. He really didn't need to hang on to any of it any longer. He had so much now, what need did he have for these crumbs? That did not mean he wouldn't keep them as part of himself, Renfro, his little brother Willi, even his old aunt Adelaide, the football rooter, but he really didn't need them.

Chapter 16

RENASCENCE II

The only thing that kept him from leaving now that the house was sold was seeing his brother Hank. When he'd first come to town he tried to make himself go over there, or call him, but always found something else that needed to be done instead.

For six years, since Willi died, he had been fighting the need to visit his older brother. It took a few months afterward to even bring himself to write the letter to Hank telling him about it. That letter had been short, informing him of their brother's death without going into any detail about it, without telling how Willi had been shot in their attempt to escape from the Cuban army. Scheutz blamed himself for bringing Willi to Cuba in the first place. And he knew Hank would blame him. For six years he had run the conversation with Hank through his head, always coming to the same end, Hank's angry accusation of Scheutz's irresponsibility, that putting himself in harm's way was his own business but he had no right to drag his brother along.

Gerry again insisted they leave. Nothing held them in this place where even the new spring flower buds in Mr. Bright's yard took on funereal overtones. She didn't have whatever her mother had in her, she said, to continue even another minute in this suburban confinement. They camped out in the living room on what was sure to be their last night in this neighborhood, the kids in their sleeping bags, and Scheutz and Gerry snuggled close under the last of the unpacked blankets.

The phone had been shut off so he used a pay phone in the drug store on the square. "Oh my God," Hank's wife Evelyn said when he told her who he was. "Where are you?" No, Hank was not home but she would try to get hold of him at work. He would be so thrilled; he'd been so worried about Scheutz all these years. Yes, they should come over that evening. She was dying to meet Scheutz's wife and children. They have three children of their own now. It's been, what?, six years since they saw him. 1959, wasn't it?; before she and Hank were married. Did he know where they lived now in Golf Manor. Scheutz repeated the address without telling her he'd already been past the house a few times. She gave him directions and said she expected them for supper. "Come early and stay late," she intoned, sounding like a professional hostess.

"I know you have to see your brother, Clem, but can we leave then?" Gerry said. She sat pinched against the truck cab door with an arm around Marty next to her. Scheutz had stopped for a light on Red Bank Road, only ten minutes from Hank's house. Dan sat between Marty and Scheutz, his legs hiked over to the right to avoid the floor shift lever. "What if, after dinner with your brother, we just went back to the house, hooked up the U-Haul, and left town. We could drive all night and it probably would put us at Niagara Falls sometime tomorrow afternoon. And then the next morning we could be in New Hampshire."

"So, when do we sleep?"

"I feel like I've been asleep for six months," she said. "I want us to get on with our lives."

"So, these kids are our cousins?" Dan asked. "That's weird."

"What's so weird?" Scheutz asked.

"I don't know." He shrugged. "Like they're not part of our family, but they are."

"Yeah, I guess you're right. That is weird. What do you think about it Marty? You're awful quiet for a change."

"I'm not quiet. I have nothing to say." He snuggled his head into his mother's shoulder. "I don't want to meet any cousins. What do we need cousins for? I want to go see Niagara Falls."

This visit was going to be rough. Scheutz tried to remember if they had, as a family, ever gone to visit anyone. Before Marty was born, Scheutz and Gerry and Dan had visited and then stayed for a year with Gerry's father in Mexico, but that was different. Scheutz had met Hank's wife only once, when they announced their engagement, before he and his brother Willi left town six years earlier. Hank had answered his letter from Mexico when Scheutz wrote to tell him Willi was dead, and had written back an angry, sad letter, telling him that their father had also died, a fact that Scheutz already knew. The tone of the letter stopped short of being accusatory, but Scheutz read it that way. He couldn't even bring himself to answer Hank's next letter which followed them to New Mexico a year later, telling him that their old Aunt Adelaide had died suddenly of stroke, and that Hank's and Evelyn's first child was born.

Hank's house resembled Gerry's mother's house, the same size and shape but with vinyl siding instead of brick. The lawn in front was smaller. There was no car in the driveway and no signs of movement in the house itself. Scheutz parked the Chevy at the curb. He sat there, they all sat there, looking at the house. "I really don't want to do this," Scheutz said.

"Good. Let's go," Marty said. "Niagara Falls." He punched his fist forward.

"Marty, calm down," Gerry said. She reached a hand across the back of the seat and touched Scheutz's shoulder. "Clem.

Honey." He turned to her. "I know it's hard but you have to do it. This has been eating at you for such a long time."

"It has? How can you tell?"

"How could I tell? How could I not tell? I've been inside your head for years, you know?"

He nodded, then looked away from her toward the front of the truck. Dan, next to him, put his hand on Scheutz's arm. Scheutz looked down into Dan's face and Dan gave a slight tilt of the chin toward the house.

"Let's get this show on the road," Marty said.

Scheutz pushed open the truck door and walked alone to the front of the house. Evelyn opened the front door and smiled as she opened the storm door. She hadn't changed much since he'd seen her the evening six years earlier, the night they had toasted her and Hank's engagement. She was maybe a few pounds heavier but still slim, shorter without her high heels, with maybe a little tiredness around her eyes. She wore a dress with a simple pink and light green pattern and over it an apron hemmed with ruff, looking like a 1950s magazine add pitching a kitchen appliance.

She shook his hand and then leaned forward to peer at Gerry and the kids in the truck cab, waving them in. She held the storm door open while a small boy joined her in the doorway. Gerry and the kids disengaged themselves from the truck and she herded them up the front walk. Scheutz stood aside as Gerry and Evelyn shook hands and introduced themselves.

"And this is Martin," Evelyn said with her hand touching the back of the little boy's head. He was the same height as Marty who stared at him as if encountering a new species of spider he hadn't seen before.

"That can't be your name," Marty said. "That's my name. Nobody has that name but me."

Evelyn laughed. "Why don't we come inside. Hank isn't home from work yet. He should be here any minute. Come, come."

It was obvious that the floor plan of the house was the same as the one they had been working on and living in for six months. The only difference seemed to be that the front door and the stairway to the second floor were on the right side of living room here, but on the left in the house in Mariemont. Two pink alabaster flamingoes hung in relief on the wall. Another wall was taken up with family photos, Hank and Evelyn's wedding, recent pictures of the three children, Evelyn's mother who Scheutz had met once, her brother Joey, a photo of Scheutz's father wearing a vest and a fedora and smoking a cigar. There were even school pictures of Scheutz and Willi in about the sixth or seventh grade.

Evelyn introduced a little girl of about three years old named Rosalie. She picked up another little girl who was barely walking, wearing a pretty dress the same color as the flamingoes, saying her name was Connie. Dan went in turn to Rosalie and then Connie, gently shaking each one's hand and smiling into their faces.

"You want to see my room?" Rosalie asked him, holding onto his hand.

"Sure, why not?" The ever-charming Mister Dan.

Marty and Martin still had not been able to let go of the similarity in their names and they seemed to be stalking each other in the middle of the living room like two wary gunfighters feeling each other out. If Scheutz remembered correctly the last letter he had received from Hank put his son's birth within a month or two of Marty's.

"But my name in Martin Scheutz," Martin said.

"Da-ad," Marty pleaded. "He says his name is the same as mine. That's not true, is it?"

"Must be," Scheutz said.

"What a strange coincidence," Gerry said. "We both named our little boys Martin."

"It's not really so strange," Evelyn said. She nodded toward Scheutz. "Their mother's name was Martina."

"I didn't know that," Gerry said, turning toward Scheutz. "I guess you never told me your mother's name. I never knew where you came up with the name Martin."

"It's not fair. He stole my name," Marty said. "See. I told you we didn't need cousins."

"Marty, stop that," Gerry said. "Be nice."

"I've got G.I. Joe," Martin said.

"All right." Marty looked up at Gerry, silently asking for permission. She was so against all these action-figure dolls that seem to promote nothing but violence. But she nodded, and the two boys ran off.

The front door of the house opened behind Scheutz and there was Hank. No different than Scheutz last saw him with his tailored suit, starched shirt and bright tie. Hank looked at the end of a work day as fresh as if he had just walked out of the house on is way to work in the morning. Scheutz was struck once again by the incredible resemblance between Hank and their father, even to the way he wore his hair combed straight back from his forehead and the way he moved his hands.

"That your rig out there at the curb?" Hank said, in the chiding tone all three brothers had always used with each other. "Looks like the gypsy's landed."

"Nice to see you, too," Schetuz said. He motioned toward the suit. "You have a new job as a store mannequin?"

"How are you, Clem? God, it's good to see you." He came close and put his arms around Scheutz. Scheutz stiffened; it was such an odd thing for Hank to do. Hank was easily four inches shorter than Scheutz but as heavy in through his torso. Holding Scheutz's arms he stood back, looked up at him and smiled.

Scheutz eyed him warily, expecting at any moment to be hit, which he had no precedent for since Hank never hit him, even when they were kids. If nothing else, he expected Hank to at least stop smiling and begin cursing him, which would be worse than hitting him. In spite of himself, he couldn't help smiling at Hank. It was wonderful to see his brother again. He wanted to hug him but he couldn't. The fear froze him in place.

Hank turned toward Gerry and extended his hand to her. "Welcome. Any wife of my brother is a friend of mine." Gerry laughed and took his hand. "You're from New Mexico, are you?" Hank said to her.

"No I'm from here. we knew each other in high school."

"Oh, out there in, um…what was that town you lived with Aunt Adelaide?"

"Mariemont," Scheutz said.

"Mariemont. Nice little town. I just went through there a couple months ago. Going out Wooster Pike, right?"

"Well, dinner's all ready," Evelyn said. "Hank, why don't you change clothes and we'll round up the kids and get the table set. Come one, Gerry."

With the smaller children distributed around Evelyn and Gerry, the corner of the table Scheutz, Dan and Hank occupied felt almost secluded. Hank's idea of changing clothes had meant nothing more than taking off his suit coat and tie and putting on a gray crew-neck sweater. The two women talked about the only thing they had in common--children. They fed the little girls and laughed among themselves. Evelyn had thrown out a few quips early on about what it was like being married to a Scheutz, but Gerry didn't pick up on them. The quips seemed more like part of a repertoire that went back and forth between her and Hank, the same kind of thing Hank, Scheutz and Willi had always done amongst themselves. But this sort of joking always made Gerry nervous and so she and Scheutz never indulged in it. Besides, there had existed, ever since Scheutz and Gerry had first met, a reluctance on both their parts to talk about each other to other people, even to Dan and Marty.

Hank laughed when he found out that both families had a son named Martin Scheutz. "I'd like to calculate the odds on that one," he said. Marty had overcome whatever problems he had with the liberal use of his name and the two boys had difficulty focusing on anything that went on outside their new-found friendship. Hank then turned his attention to Dan, asking him how old he was. He looked from Dan to Scheutz, not asking the obvious question, probably for Dan's sake. The boy had been two-and-a-half years old when Scheutz left Cincinnati six years earlier. Hank asked, "Had you been married with a child the last time I saw you? I don't recall you saying anything about it."

Scheutz said, "It's a long story." Dan had already heard all about it. "Dan was born while I was in the army. I didn't really know about it until I came back. And then after Willi and I..." He couldn't go on.

Hank moved the conversation to Mexico and New Mexico. Scheutz told him about their travels, Gerry and Dan meeting him in Mexico and their search for her father, the year in Taxco, then their house in Agua Fria. Dan added color, telling anecdotes, funny stories about mistakes made due to the family's difficulty with Spanish, which Dan seemed to have mastered better than both his parents. Hank hung on every word, and let Dan do as much talking as he wanted. Dan obviously reveled in the attention. And Scheutz had a hard time talking at all, over and above one or two word responses to Hank's questions. This whole conversation felt like audience chit-chat while waiting for the public execution to begin.

They got onto the subject of Hank's present occupation. Yes, he was still partners with Evelyn's brother, Joey Palmieri. They were transportation brokers, booking cargo loads on trucks moving in and out of the greater Cincinnati area. They supervised a varying number of individuals who did nothing more than man telephones in a large office down in the Over-the-Rhine district. But, strangest of all, their third partner was their old nemesis, Dmitri Saranas. Six years earlier, Willi, who worked for Hank and Joey, severely beat Saranas's son, Nicky, in the middle of a turf war for control of gambling interests in the city.

"So what's this trucking business a cover for?" Scheutz asked.

"What's that mean?" Dan asked, looking up from his plate.

"What are you referring to?" Hank asked.

"Well," Scheutz said. "Any enterprise involving you, Palmieri and Saranas has three to one odds against being even marginally legal. What are you guys really doing?"

Hank took a sudden interest in his mashed potatoes. The other end of the table had become suddenly quiet as Scheutz realized that Evelyn was staring at him in silence. Dan looked back and forth between Scheutz and Hank, knowing that something had just happened, but not knowing what. Only the two Martins kept up their chatter. A squeal from little Connie in her high chair as she threw a piece of bread crust at her sister broke the long pause. Hank forked potatoes into is mouth, shrugged and shook his head. The little joke Scheutz made, referring to what he knew of Hank's past endeavors, was apparently not a little joke. The conversation on both Hank's end and on Evelyn's end of the table picked up after the pause, but changed from lively chit chat to constrained politeness.

Hank announced to everyone before they all got up from the dinner table that he had to go out again for the evening, some very pressing business that he could not leave to anyone else. But, he said to Scheutz, he did very much want to talk to him alone before he left. Dan followed them down the stairs to a small basement den room that smelled faintly of old cigar smoke. The room contained not much more that an octagonal poker table with a green felt cover.

"Can I come in, too?" Dan said behind them, standing in the doorway.

Scheutz looked to Hank, who shrugged. "No, I don't think so, Dan," Scheutz said. "You go back upstairs with the other kids."

Dan made a face. "There's nothing to do."

"That's all right. I'll only be a short time."

Dan looked back and forth between his father and his uncle. "What is it, some big secret you guys have going on?"

"No, it's not a secret, exactly. It's just something Hank and I have to discuss that I'd prefer, and I know your mother would prefer, you not to sit in on."

"I thought we didn't have secrets in our family."

"Well, we don't. But this has to do with our brother Willi, and it doesn't really have anything to do with our family. Okay?"

Dan looked quickly at Hank and then back. He put his hand in Scheutz's. "You gonna be okay?"

Scheutz had to laugh. God, he loved this kid. He squeezed his hand and motioned for him to go back upstairs. "Why shouldn't I be okay? This is my brother I'm talking to."

"Yeah, yeah. I know what talking to a brother is like. Talking to Marty sometimes is really cool, and then sometimes it's a real pain in the butt."

Hank laughed. "This will not be a pain in the butt, I can assure you."

"Well, take it easy on him, okay?" Dan turned at the door. "He's not too good at talking to people."

With the door closed behind them, Scheutz and Hank sat facing each other across the poker table. Hank folded his hands in an attitude of prayer, touching his hands to his forehead and staring at the green felt of the table top. Scheutz waited, tense, ready to counteract anything his brother had to say. "When Evelyn and I were married," Hank began slowly. "No one from my family was there. No one was left. I wanted to invite Aunt Adelaide, but I she was already in the hospital. Within a matter of a few months, my family was gone. First Dad died, then I get the letter from you that Willi had died, and then letters to you began coming back as undeliverable. You just disappeared. Getting married to Evie was the happiest day of my life. But it had a hole in it." He stopped, put his hands down and stared across the table at Scheutz. "I don't talk about these things to people. Not even to Evie. But I've wanted to tell someone for a long time."

He talked and Scheutz listened. Hank told him about his life, about his children. He talked about his work, about Evelyn's brother, Joey, about Saranas. "Whatever passed between us and Saranas is just that—past. No matter how the cards fell in a previous game, this is new. A new game, new odds." Hank passed his fingers over the green felt in front of him. He slowly handed Scheutz short pieces of information, as if he was dealing cards across the table. Nicky Saranas was a paraplegic. This came as a result of Willi's beating. It broke Dmitri Saranas's heart. When the word came that Willi had died, Hank and Saranas, who had met for "business" reasons, each began to talk about their loss, and ended finding a bond between them. Hank convinced Joey Palmieri that merging the two organizations would give them a chance to be major contenders in the underground, mobile card and dice trade in the Ohio River Valley. The transportation business came a few years later, when they needed a place to invest their profits.

Hank talked about his home, about what it meant to him, about his children, Martin and the two little girls. This was also a new game. Whatever life Hank, Scheutz and Willi had had with their father was old, dead and gone, not to be dwelt on. Another round of poker. If you watch what you're doing, watch the way the cards fall, you can play the odds and come out ahead. But they're still just that, odds. Chance is the only God.

This was how Hank survived here. He had adopted the religion of their father. Just like a late-night poker session in a smoke-filled room, he paid homage to only what was being played out in front of him. Whether he won or lost in the past or would win or lose in the future had no bearing on how the present game was going.

But his religion was not Evelyn's religion. She had never approved, from the beginning of her brother's or her husband's involvement in the gambling business. To her it was dangerous, it was illegal, and it was heresy. But, like her mother before her, she had an excellent filter. As long as she didn't choose to look at it, the gambling was not there. Hank and Joey ran a legitimate trucking business. Evelyn looked no further than that. Which was why Scheutz's little joke at the dinner table had upset her.

"Well, I'm on Evelyn's side," Scheutz said. "Gambling is a bad business. That's why I could never work for you years ago, the way Willi could."

"That's your prerogative. I personally think that gambling is less insidious than selling your services as a soldier."

"I don't do that any more. I quit when Willi died. Actually, I quit before Willi died. And I agree with you, that's also a nasty business. I guess you want to know how Willi died."

Tears came to Hank's eyes. He looked down and shook his head, saying nothing.

Scheutz stared at him across the table. This was it, this question coming from Hank, asking him to account for Willi's death, the thought of Hank putting this question to him had scared him for years. And here it was. And he could not bring himself to speak. Being buried here in this basement room with his brother, in this city that throbbed with the past and laid in wait for its errant sons to come near enough to smother them again in its smog-filled air, there was no release, no survival. Immobilized on his side of the green-felt poker table, he strained to be let go. Lines from the Edna St. Vincent Millay poem he'd read to Gerry came to him.

Sleeping your myriad magics through,
Close-sepulchred away from you!
O God, I cried, give me new birth,
And put me back upon the earth!

What held him, for God's sake? This hand he'd been dealt for six months here in this tomb of a city. He was sick with it. "Willi…" he said.

Yes, that would be God's hole card. "Yes, I'll tell you about Willi," Scheutz said.

"No, stop," Hank said. "I don't need to know about Willi. I cried when you wrote me Willi had died. I don't need to know how he died. Just that he died."

"But I need to tell you."

"Why? To relieve your guilt? It's okay. You're absolved. For your penance, say three *Pater Nosters.* Now, go in peace."

"But…"

"I don't want to hear it, Clem. If you tell me about it, I will see him dying, and I don't want to see him dying." Hank leaned in toward the center of the table, looking into Scheutz's eyes. "I know you, Clem. I helped Dad raise you and Willi after our mother died. I know you feel guilty, or at least responsible for Willi's death. But, forget it. Forget about it. Forget about all of it, it doesn't matter any more."

"You don't want to know how he died?"

"No. I knew Willi as well as I know you. I know how he was. I know about him and Dad, what happened between them. I know that Willi beat him up behind that pool hall, and that that eventually caused his death. And I think I know why he beat him. I know you helped Willi get out of town. Whatever happened, I know you tried to help him in any way you could. You two were like twins, you could not not help him."

"I had the feeling you blamed me."

"I did. I blamed everybody. Dad. Joey. Aunt Adelaide. Saranas. Even Evelyn. Mostly myself."

"And so what did you do? You just got over it?"

"No, I didn't just get over it. I forgot about it, but I didn't get over it. You don't get over your life."

It was late by the time they left. And it was raining. Marty nodded off in Gerry's lap in the cab of the truck. Dan leaned against her with her left arm around him. Back in Mariemont, at the house that was no longer theirs, Scheutz backed the truck into the drive and Dan helped him hitch the U-Haul trailer to the ball on the back bumper. A light came on in Mr. Bright's house next door. "It's after midnight, you know." Mrs. Bright's voice came from an upstairs window.

"We're just leaving," Gerry said up in response. "Two minutes and we'll be out your of hair for good."

She put the house keys in an envelope, which she deposited in the mailbox on the front porch. "You guys hop in the back and go to sleep," she told Dan and Marty.

"I want you to come, too," Marty said, pulling her hand.

"I've got to keep your father awake."

"I'm scared," Marty said.

"I'll sit up front with Dad," Dan said. "I'll tell him a story."

Scheutz laughed. Dan's long, involved, overly detailed stories could put him to sleep faster than a thump on the skull with a sock full of sand. Gerry kissed him, and then Dan, before climbing into the back of the camper with Marty. The rain poured harder as Scheutz turned onto Wooster Pike. Traffic was light but slow moving because of the rain. He kept to the slow lane once he'd picked up Route 22 heading north out of the city. The truck did okay pulling the U-Haul, but the 350 engine was such a gas hog; he could almost see the fuel level gauge drop as he drove.

Dan's head drooped before he could even start a story. By the time they reached the Warren County line, he was curled up in the passenger seat with a light blanket over him, sound asleep.

Scheutz drove through the night. The windshield wipers barely kept up with the rain. The right headlight only worked on high beam, so that when he dimmed them for oncoming cars, he had to slow even further to make out the road ahead on only the left beam. But the traffic thinned even more as the night went on, and the road past Columbus became straighter and less hilly, stretching across rolling farmland. The trailer created an extra strain on the Chevy's engine on the uphill and extra push from behind going down. He was not in a hurry, and the further he got from Cincinnati, the more he relaxed into the drive. Peace settled into the truck cab. He smiled at the latest hand he'd been dealt. It was okay to smile, no one was watching. He was alone where he liked to be, and yet with all those he loved there with him. Well, except Hank, but Hank was a different deck of cards altogether.

Upset each cloud's gigantic gourd
And let the heavy rain, down-poured
In one big torrent, set me free,
Washing my grave away from me!

A passing truck splashed the windshield, obscuring vision for a moment. At this time of night most of the vehicles on the road were semis. He kept to the right on the four-lane highway, took his time and let the big rigs pass. Even with the strain, the Chevy's engine hummed. When the windows began to fog he turned the heater on low and the truck warmed like an incubator. Dan slept with the top of his head against Scheutz's leg.

At least Scheutz thought he was asleep until his voice punctured the silence in the truck cab. "Hey, Big Daddy?"

"Yeah?"

"Can I ask you about what you and Uncle Hank talked about? I asked Mom but she got really upset about it, like it was a big deal or something."

"Well, it's not really a big deal. I can see how it would be to her, but it's not worth talking about. It's all over and gone."

"So why can't you tell me?"

Scheutz stared ahead at the wet road. Why not tell him? If he didn't, Dan would make it bigger than it was. "You have to never tell your mother I told you about this, okay?"

Dan jumped into an upright sitting position next to him, pulling the blanket around his shoulders.

"Hank and I were talking mostly about our brother, Willi. You know, the one who died?"

"And it was your fault?"

"How'd you know that?"

"I know how you are."

"We were soldiers, fighting in Cuba. That's where Willi died. And it was my fault. I shouldn't have dragged him into it in the first place."

"You were Cuban soldiers?"

"No. We were mercenary soldiers." He stopped, not sure if he should go on. He had never told anyone this story, not even Gerry. She hadn't wanted to hear the gory details, she said. All she really wanted from him was his promise that all that was finished for him. And it was. All except Willi's death, which ate at him still. "You remember being in Mexico?" he asked Dan.

"No, not really. I remember going to Santa Fe, to our new house, but I don't remember where we lived before that."

"Well, this all happened just before I met your mother and you in Mexico. I had just come from Cuba on a boat. Willi died a couple of days before that. We were trying to escape the Cuban army and he was shot. Once I got to Mexico, I was like in a state of shock. It took me about a week to do anything more than lay around and eat soup."

Dan patted Scheutz's shoulder. "Pobrecito Papa." And they both laughed.

"Yeah. Pobrecito mio. Your mother finally helped me out it, got me back among the living. She's a hot shit, your mother."

"Yeah, yeah. But I still want to hear the story of what happened in Cuba."

So Scheutz told him the story, how, after Castro's take-over, the group had been hired by a big sugar company to destroy some newly patented refining equipment in a recently nationalized plant in Mercedita. They had accomplished one phase of their mission before being chased by the Cuban army into the cordillera. Scheutz, the only one to survive, escaped on a fishing boat after Willi died.

Dan had been quiet throughout the story, and when Scheutz took his eyes off the road for a second to look at him, realized the boy was sound asleep. He had not noticed how, miles before, his son's body had slumped against his own.

Somewhere in northwestern Pennsylvania the light had changed enough for Scheutz to notice the faint outlines of fences along side of the highway and the houses in the near distance. The rain had stopped somewhere back near the Ohio border. The grit of tiredness watered his eyes but otherwise he felt relaxed and full of energy, as if he could drive on into infinity.

I know not how such things can be!—
I breathed my soul back into me.

In New York state the highway ran along Lake Erie to his left, the dark gray waves all but absorbing the first rays of the sun rising beyond the flat land to his right. What a lovely day for a tourist visit to the falls, the same kind of day they had had when they stopped to visit the Grand Canyon on their way east from New Mexico. The kids will love it, and he and Gerry could pretend they were on a belated honeymoon.

The world stands out on either side
No wider than the heart is wide;

Dan sat up, his hair sticking out from the side of his head which swiveled from left to right. His mouth hung open and his eyes opened to only half-light. "Wow. Where are we?"

"Far away."

Chapter 17

Happiness Ain't All it's Cracked Up to Be

"I see you tonight, eh?" Olavi said. With a lopsided limp he descended the ladder on the side of the truck from the control handles used to operate the grapple. "I see you at Georgina's, eh?" he said to Scheutz.

"Why at Georgina's?" Scheutz asked.

"You know. At the party for the kids after graduation."

"Oh, really? Why didn't she say anything to me about it?"

"She has it every year. Everybody knows that."

"At least anybody who goes out of their house at night." Freddie, standing next to the truck, jerked his thumb in Scheutz's direction. He and Olavi laughed. They stood in the shade of the truck which, piled high with logs, rose like the twenty-foot high wall of a building. Olavi busied himself with a chain tightener, putting tension on a thick chain that ran up over the top of the logs. He was obviously in a hurry to get out of there. His daughter was also graduating in Marty's class that evening. Freddie opened the passenger-side door of the grapple truck to get at the cooler on the seat. He handed Scheutz a cold can of Budweiser. "Hey, Frank, want a beer?" He shouted to Uppermann.

"Ayuh." Uppermann left his truck to cross the open landing and accepted a can of beer from Freddie. Dust from the landing stuck to the sweat of his face and his shirt. Scheutz knew that he himself looked as dirty as Uppermann. But he also knew he didn't smell as bad as Uppermann who could go day after day working in the woods without ever taking a shower in between. Freddie, on the other hand, would often, like today, still smell of laundry detergent after a day of work.

They stood in a small group near the open door of the grapple truck, Scheutz and Olavi both sipping, and the other two sucking on their cans. This had become a ritual over the years, one beer at the end of the day. For Uppermann it was the opening glug that would have him drunk within an hour after leaving the landing. Freddie, in the last few years, seemed to be heading in the same direction, though for him the drunken state would come later in the evening at some bar. Olavi opened his can of beer each day and took two sips just to be sociable. Even then, he beat himself up with guilt because of the beer's violation of his Apostolic Lutheran upbringing. Pelletier deigned each day to lower himself to drinking the one Budweiser whose homogenized flavor could never match that of his beloved Canadian brands.

Scheutz's limit for the day was one for the after-work ritual, and then maybe one more beer with supper. "I cannot abide a drunk," he'd told Uppermann once when the man asked him point blank why he didn't like him.

He finished off the can of beer and tossed it into the pile of cans on the floor of the truck cab. He was tired and sweaty. They had knocked off early, which they often did on Friday. It was only about three o'clock, just past the warmest time of day. If Pelletier would quit dicking around with the engine of that skidder, they could get home. Gerry was coming up from New York for the graduation today. And Dan.

"Dan's coming up for the graduation, right?" Freddie said.

"Yeah, he said he was."

"Good. We're all going out and party after."

"You mean at Georgina's?"

"No. After that. Remember that great party we had after Dan and Samantha and I graduated? Up in your barn. People still talk about that party. Man." He shook his head. "I was so drunk that night. Whoo. I was even dancing; can you picture that? That fucking Samantha, though. I'll tell you, that girl can get so stubborn sometimes. She got on such a crying jag. Couldn't shut her up, you know? All I wanted to do was get laid, but nooo. Wouldn't even tell me what she was crying about. Just sat there in that horse stall and bawled and bawled. Damn."

A simple little thing like a high school graduation was a major event in Acworth. At Dan's graduation four years ago, he had recognized several people who had no kids and no connection to the school at all. They clapped and cheered when the kids got their diplomas, and chimed in heartily as the band raggedly played the school song. It was the same thing in the fall with Homecoming Day when the soccer team almost always lost to the team from Sunapee. Even though Scheutz had not paid much attention to it, Georgina had started giving parties the year Dan and her daughter Sharna graduated and kept up the tradition year after year. The party was probably still the same, a pot-luck supper with parents supplying more food than anyone could ever consume in a lifetime. And the kids always ate quickly and ducked out to someone's barn party where they could spend the night drinking beer and playing bootleg Grateful Dead cassettes.

Pelletier finally shut his machine off and joined them, accepting his can of Bud from Freddie without a word. Close to the longest day of the year, it wouldn't get dark until after nine. The weather for the graduation was almost perfect. "You ready to go?" Scheutz asked him. He was anxious to get out of there, get home. Gerry might even be there already.

"A couple of minutes." Pelletier spat out the first mouthful of Budweiser, then held up the can and shook his head

Olavi reached in front of Scheutz and grabbed the can from Pelletier's hand. "You don't like our beer, why don't you go back where you come from."

"Whoa. Come on, Olavi," Scheutz said, extending his arm in front of Pelletier's, who had taken a step toward the man. "This is social hour. You don't want to ruin it."

"I don't feel social with a damned Canuck."

"You gonna take that shit offa him?" Uppermann said to Pelletier.

"Shut up, Frank," Scheutz told him. "Or else you'll have the whole bunch of us rolling around in the dirt, here."

"Whoo, I'd like to see that," Freddie laughed and clapped.

Pelletier had dropped his hands to his side. His face had fallen into a quiet repose, even more than his usual stillness, only his eyes moving in heightened alert. Scheutz had seen him that way before, a large predatory cat ready to pounce. Scheutz moved in front of him, put his palm flat on Pelletier's chest, and held him with his eyes. "Stop it."

Pelletier slowly came to life again. Without looking at Olavi, he tilted his head toward the skidder. "I still have to check the hydraulic fluid."

Scheutz said to Olavi. "Maybe you should settle this thing with him when the rest of us are not around."

Olavi poured the contents the can he'd taken away from Pelletier into the dirt. Uppermann reached into the truck cab to extract another can of Budweiser, popped the top and stood smirking at Scheutz. Just one wrong word right now, a look, anything, could turn this little after-work social ritual into a brawl. It never ceased to amaze Scheutz, the impetus to fight that lurked just under the surface of men like this. Himself included. For the second time that day, Scheutz could feel his right hand tingle. Uppermann was big enough, with a raw toughness that made him a good match. The smell of bile tugged at Scheutz. One small word from Uppermann could tip him over right now, could release the spring that had stayed coiled for years inside him.

What was it, twenty years since he could remember smacking someone just for the hell of it. Not that he hadn't wanted to in all that time. But he had promised. He had promised Gerry right at the beginning that he would never again give in. As time went on it had become easier and easier to swallow the urge. The wisdom of it made sense. What was the point? Even now, smacking Uppermann, or anyone else would be nothing more than a childish indulgence. A lot like splashing around in a rain puddle. So, what had started out as something he gave up for Gerry—and the kids—became something he adopted for his own reasons. The more he thought about it, the more he realized that what had gotten Willi killed was nothing more than a childish indulgence in what was nothing more than random violence, an act of revenge on the part of the company that had hired him and his brother. But on this day, the day when his last child was officially grown and his connection with the boys' mother was officially ended, the need to hold himself back felt as if were losing its grip.

But the moment passed. Uppermann carried his can of beer across the landing to his truck. Olavi slammed the door of the grapple truck and walked around to the driver's side. Scheutz relaxed his muscles and walked to his own pick-up truck. His chainsaw and other gear had been stowed in the back. He sat with the door open, changing his spiked boots for his regular work boots. Then he backed the truck out and up the grade of the landing to stop in front of Pelletier's skidder, and sat idling, watching the men each going their own way. In the dirt near his truck, wherever it had not been disturbed by the tracks of the skidders, he could make out the huge hoof prints of the old buck that had run him down that morning.

The anxiety of the morning had eased with his physical tiredness. He couldn't wait to see Gerry again. And he wanted to get away from the wood cutting scene and the men he worked with week after week. His normal Friday let-down seeped in, when he allowed himself to look at what lurked in the recess of his mind day in and day out. This job, ten years old now, bored the living shit out of him.

So. Why. Don't. You. Get. Off. Your. Ass. And. Do. Some. Thing. About. It.

He tried to relax himself the way Nanda had taught him to do, make his mind go blank, focus on his muscles starting with his toes and working upward. Yes, it was boring, but...the other side argued. This wasn't so bad. There were worse ways to make a living. Especially on a day like today.

If only he could untie this knot, this life he'd been seduced by and bored by for so many years now. His brain had gone dead on this job years ago. But it refused to just lie down in peace. It haunted him. His own brain haunted him. Not to mention Gerry haunting him. Another knot. He wanted her there and he didn't want her there. And then the Nanda knot. Doing their yogic sex thing, was great, but whenever he and she were not in their alpha mode, her personality, not to mention that whole Goncharov circus, grated on him.

And today's graduation presented its own knot. He looked forward to not having to be a responsible parent any longer, to have conversations with Marty as an equal the way he and Dan now talked with each other, but those long lonely nights in front of the television...

Pelletier climbed into the passenger side door. " Let's go."

Scheutz gave Olavi a wave as they left the landing. A hundred yards along, he turned off the main logging road, downhill onto the overgrown shortcut. Just before the stream bed, Pelletier told him to stop.

"I really need to get home," Scheutz said.

"Just a few minutes." Pelletier got out and walked around front, up stream a little from the truck. He signaled for Scheutz to cut the engine. From his pants pocket he took a plastic baggie, and from that a roll of fishing line with what looked like a fly on the end. He put his finger in front of his lips, telling Scheutz not to make any noise and then slunk upstream a little farther. According to Pelletier, not only could trout hear you talking, they understood everything you said. He dropped the fly onto the top of the water and let it float down to a point in front of the truck, then, with a flick of the line, popped the fly upstream and let it float down again.

Scheutz sat quietly in the truck cab. Yes, he was anxious to get home, but there was something so idyllic about just sitting there watching Pelletier. The fly came down and went back up again, each time passing by a small flat rock that cropped out over the clear running water. Without realizing at first what he was seeing, he became aware of the shadow of a large fish just sitting under the rock. The fly floated past but the shadow did not move except for a gentle wave of its tail fin. Like the buck up on The Throne, the trout seemed a little too large for its environment. Probably been around for a long time, too, just like the buck. Scheutz found himself rooting for the trout, urging him silently not to fall for Pelletier's phony fly.

In a wave the whole damned thing got to him, the lovely day, this beautiful stream with its crafty trout, that buck up on the ridge maintaining his realm. He couldn't remember where he'd read the phrase "edenic splendor" but this was certainly what those early Bible writers must have had in mind. This was so….

Goodness. Aren't we happy all of a sudden?

What do you mean, happy?

Oh, I forgot. You don't do happy. Coulda fooled me, though. But then maybe it's you who is the one that's fooled. You wouldn't know happiness if you fell into a vat full of it.

You're the one who quoted me that stuff from Goethe. How did that go? "Don't think that your time is special.. Throughout all the ages and in all countries, people have been miserable, always in fear and in trouble, bringing each other pain and torture. Life is thus."

Life is also this. Give yourself a break, Clem.

"No fish?" he asked when his partner finally gave up returned to the truck.

"He must be out to lunch."

"Good for him."

At Pelletier's trailer, Nicole, his overweight girlfriend with no upper teeth, sat outside on a car seat petting that awful dog of theirs. Scheutz waited until Pelletier was half way across the yard and then opened his door, causing the dog to leap towards the truck, snarling, his lips pulled back from his teeth. The dog almost pulled the girlfriend off the seat and all but knocked Pelletier down tearing past him. Scheutz laughed and slammed his door. The dog reached the end of his tether causing one of those all but strangling flips that landed him on his back. Pelletier shouted "E'christ" at him and then a string of rapid French as Scheutz drove out of the yard, laughing.

You do this when you're happy? You pick at some poor dog?

Happy's got nothing to do with it. I pick at that fucking thing when I'm unhappy, too. You ever notice that people always pick at whatever they're frightened of.

Chapter 18

Divided by the Light

An unfamiliar car, a red late model Saab, sat next to the barn where Marty usually parked. Scheutz parked in his own spot and sat for a moment looking at the Saab. It must be Gerry's new car. She always liked Saabs. Either that, or she rode up with a friend. The warm, tingly excitement he had been holding at bay for the better part of the afternoon spread itself throughout his chest and down into his lower belly. He climbed out of the truck.

Wait, hold on. Don't get yourself too excited, Buster. That may not be her, or rather my, car.

Yeah, yeah, yeah.

Well, don't make an ass out of yourself, just because you're glad to see her.

She was always accusing him of being such a dull ox. Wouldn't Gerry, the real Gerry, like it better if he was an ass for a change.

He wiped the sweat off his face with the short sleeve of his t-shirt, left his caulk boots in the truck and strode, keeping himself from running, through the mud room door. And there she was, inside the kitchen, standing, as he remembered her, with her back to him at the kitchen sink, washing vegetables. She was here. Something tugged at him, trying to keep him from, as Gerry said, making an ass of himself by rushing to hug her, but he pushed it aside. With one more step into that kitchen he could turn the last ten years back as if they had not existed. She was here. Without a word, he crossed the room till he stood directly behind her and put his arms around her long, thin waist, diving his face into the dark hair until his nose, mouth and chin pressed against the back of her skull.

Her body went slack in his arms as she leaned back against him, the mass of hair engulfing his face. He melted into her as the old feeling of excitement, comfort, familiarity, the confirmation of who he was and who he belonged to, filled him. Her smell was different—could a person change that living in New York for ten years?—but the softness of her buttocks against his rising erection and the animal ripple of her back muscles against his chest increased the pull of his arms. Was he trying to pull her inside of himself or pull himself inside of her?

Her body sagged and she seemed to lose the strength of her legs. A momentary flash of fear that he had hurt her somehow. It was the same as the first time he'd kissed her in the little clearing by the river when they were in high school. Back then it was a real scare because he had never seen her or anyone else do that before. Since then he came to know that the meltdown was often her way of letting herself go completely.

That's bullshit. I never in my life melted like that.

Oh yeah? You don't know because you were like shutting your brain down when you did it.

"What are you doing?" she said. Her voice came low and husky, the way he remembered it from when they were young. She stood tall again, turned toward him, pushing against his arms.

But it wasn't Gerry. He stepped back in shock. It was Samantha. He stood in front of her, trying to put together what had just happened, realizing that his mouth was still hanging open. He tried to control his panting breath, and hung his thumb over his belt buckle with his fingers extending downward in an attempt to hide his erection.

Samantha's eyes darted around the room. She took a deep breath and put both hands to her flushed cheeks. One hand held a carrot and the other a vegetable scraper. "What are you doing?" she repeated.

"I'm sorry. I'm sorry. I thought you were Gerry."

"You thought I was Gerry?" she gave a small, embarrassed, tinkle laugh.

"I…uh…you dyed your hair."

"You like it?" She touched the top with the back of the carrot hand.

"It looks just like Gerry's."

"There's worse things to look like."

He backed away from her. "Is that your car out there?"

"My dad's new car."

He could see now, through the window, that the Saab had a New Hampshire license plate, not New York. What an idiot he was. He wanted so badly for it to be Gerry's car he had not even noticed the plate. He kept his face turned toward the window so she could not see his embarrassment. The tingly excitement drained out of him and left him with nothing but the gritty tiredness beneath it. He needed to take his nap. He went to sit next to the now cold wood stove where he always took off his boots. He could not look at the girl next to the sink. God, what a stupid thing to do. If she said anything he could be charged with molesting a child. "Where is everybody?" he said to the boots he was removing.

"Marty was here a little while ago, but he went over to his girlfriend's house."

"Dan call?"

"Yeah, he did. He should be here in time for the graduation. He's got a girl with him. I don't think it's the same one he had here at Christmas."

If Dan was bringing another girl up from New York, what the hell was Samantha doing hanging around here? Why was she always hanging around, anyhow? It was very clear Dan had no intention of taking up with her again. Besides, wasn't she supposed to be Freddie's girlfriend? And was the engagement on or off right now? He could never keep track. On or off, either way it never seemed to affect the amount of time she spent in Scheutz's house. Not that it wasn't nice having her here, but having a beautiful girl hanging around in the house of a lonely old man was like leaving a can of open sardines on the floor and expecting the cat not to indulge himself. What was it Gerry called it—tropism? Moth to the flame.

The girl did liven the place up a lot, especially when Marty wasn't home. She had a nice laugh and was always dancing around the kitchen. But, for Christ's sake, she was only…what?…how old was she anyhow? She'd be the same age as Dan. What was that—twenty-two? What the hell was a twenty-two year old girl doing hanging around in a tiny town like this at all. Why wasn't she out somewhere going to college or jet-setting to Europe or something?

We already talked about this, Clem.

Yeah, yeah, I know. She needs a father because that super-liberal dickhead she's got at home can't stop whining like a baby himself. I'm sorry, Gerry, I don't want to be anybody's father.

You could help her a lot.

I did the father thing. I don't want to do it any more.

He threw his boots to the side of the chair and looked up at where Samantha still leaned with her back to the sink, watching him. In all the years she'd been hanging around his house, he'd never really looked at her. She was just this kid, mixed in with all the other kids. She didn't look at all like Gerry from the front. Gerry's face was square and Samantha's was long, but with a nose that looked like it had been fixed, it snubbed slightly. Her mouth was smaller and her eyes set closer together, almost as if Gerry's face had been put in a clamp and squeezed together at the sides. The face was just as pretty, but more delicate than Gerry's. Maybe it was the age difference. "I'm really sorry," he said again. "Don't think I was trying to get fresh or anything, okay?"

"Don't worry about it." She started to say something else then stopped and just stood there with the carrot and scraper in her hands looking at him. He looked away, wanting to find something to say, but came up nothing. She must be in a state of shock or something. He certainly was. A kid like that, coming over to his house to find an atmosphere she could feel relaxed in and now it was ruined because she has this horny old goat to contend with.

Clem, give it a break will you? You're blowing this a little out of proportion.

No, I'm not. Aren't you the one says I should be trying to help her? Does this look like help?

It was a mistake. She knows that. Come on. And stop with the old-goat-attacks-little-innocent-child routine. First of all, you're not an old goat, you're only forty.

I feel like an old goat.

And she's not a little pre-schooler. Look at her. She's a twenty-two year old woman. I had two kids by age twenty-two. Besides, isn't she the one you found screwing Dan in the attic years ago?

Dan was screwing her.

Same difference. This is not Saint Theresa, the Little Flower cleaning vegetables at your sink.

Still....

Samantha turned back to the sink without saying another word. Little pieces of wood chips stuck to the back of her t-shirt and one in her hair. They must have come from his shirt and beard. He could feel the warmth of her back seeping into his chest again and stood to leave the room. At the doorway to the front hall he stopped, his hand gripping the jamb.

"Gerry was talking to me about you, today," he said.

"Oh, is Gerry here already?"

"Um, no, that's not what I meant. I mean...I was thinking about what she might say about you."

Shut up, idiot. You want her to think you're nuts?"

He stepped through the doorway.

"She talks to you, doesn't she?" Samantha said. "When she's not around."

"Why do you say that?" He turned to look at Samantha's back.

"I've seen you talking to her. In your chair in the parlor, in your truck. You do it all the time. Your lips move." She turned around to face him again. No carrot or scraper this time. "It took me a long time to figure it out. Who you talk to, I mean. I finally figured it must be her. You even move your hands sometimes, and you get this look on your face like you're trying to convince somebody of something."

"You make me sound like I'm crazy, or something."

"No, I'm not. Mr. Scheutz, believe me, I don't think you're crazy at all. Mrs. Scheutz talks to me, too."

Scheutz took a step backward, further into the hallway, not taking his eyes off the girl next to the sink in the room he'd just left. She took a step toward him, away from the sink, body straining toward him, her face expectant. What did she want from him? He looked away, scanning the front hallway to the left and right, and then found himself eyeing the painted-over indentations on the door frame where the hinges had been removed. Where was that door? He and Gerry had removed it years ago so that the warmth from the kitchen stove could move into the unheated hallway and up the main staircase. The door itself must be in the basement with a lot of other building materials. Why hadn't they left it where it was and then just open it during the winter months?

What was this girl doing to him? She was invading, that's what she was doing. Who the hell was she anyway? She'd wormed her way into his home years ago--using Dan to gain access—to the point where he could no longer imagine this house without her in it. She modeled herself after Gerry and now she was pushing her way into his psyche.

Isn't that what Gerry had done, pushed her way into his psyche so that he couldn't imagine what it would be like without her there? That was different, though, wasn't it? He loved Gerry, she was his wife. Well, not any more, but she had been. They had been like the same person, so it made sense that she still lived inside him. But she couldn't live inside this girl also, could she? What the hell was going on here? Was Gerry some kind of witch? No, she couldn't be, she didn't believe in witchcraft. What was this girl saying? How many other people did Gerry go around talking to in their heads?

Samantha walked toward him, moving around the table in the center of the kitchen. He could feel the fear rising and knotting in his chest. Not only was she not put off by his mistake in hugging her from behind, but in saying what she did about Gerry's voice and now walking toward him with that expectant look on her face, she seemed to be pushing open a door that he certainly had no intention of even looking into.

"You're wrong," he said.

"About what?"

"About my talking to Gerry. I don't know what you think you've been seeing me do, but it's not that."

"Then what is it?"

"It's got nothing to do with you. Sometimes I just…nothing. It's none of your business."

She stopped next to the table, looking like he'd just slapped her. "Oh," she said.

"I'm sorry," he said. Was he going to spend the rest of his life apologizing to this girl? "Forgive me, I'm kind of upset about today, what with Dan and Gerry coming, and Marty's graduation, and…what are you doing, making a salad?"

"Yeah. A big one. Georgina asked me to bring it tonight for the party. She just has too much to do."

"Well, I've got to take a shower and lie down for a little nap. I'm really bushed. What time is the graduation?"

"I think it starts around seven."

He nodded. "Look, why don't we just pretend the last fifteen minutes or so didn't happen, okay?"

She stood there next to the table, just watching him, not saying anything, her face showing nothing of what he was sure must be running amok inside her head.

"Okay?"

She nodded.

Upstairs, he stripped and stepped into the hot shower, listening, as had become his habit, for noises above him in the attic. Then, wrapped in a towel, he carried his work clothes into the bedroom. He pulled the blind and climbed between the sheets that still smelled of Nanda from the night before.

Getting a little paranoid, aren't we?

What do you mean?

All that shit about Samantha worming her way into your psyche. Next thing you'll be convinced the CIA is implanting a bug in your brain.

No, actually, I'm getting electronic wave signals from the planet Venus. They're telling me to go forth and…

She's pretty smart, isn't she, to have figured that out?

Figured what out?

That you've been talking to me.

So, have you been talking to her?

It's all in her mind.

As opposed to what? Isn't that what we do?

You know what I mean. She just thinks I talk to her. It's a euphemism for daydreaming.

And what are we doing?

This is different. I'm a part of you. Always will be. And I'll let you in on a little secret. In real life, in New York, I hear your voice in my head. You'll always be part of me, too.

A knife-thin ray of sunlight found its way between the edge of the blind and window jamb and drew a line across the floor next to the bed. He watched it through half-opened eyes, curled on his side with his face at the edge of the mattress. It was as if the line of light separated his bed with him on it from everything else. Nothing could touch him. What a nice thought. Or was it?

He came up out of a dream of Samantha kissing him. But it was not Samantha. It was Nanda. He knew before he opened his eyes. The smell of her, so familiar to him. She lay next to him, her nipples touching his bare chest, her long-fingered hand caressing his cock. He opened his eyes and saw hers only inches away. "I'm so glad it's you," he said. She smiled and kissed him lightly on the lips. She had done this many times before, on her way home at the end of the day, walking into the house, saying hello to whoever happened to be in the kitchen, bee-lining it to his bedroom for what she called her most relaxing Tantric meditation.

She moved, slowly, deliberately, hands not touching him, positioning him onto his back with her body. He knew what came next; it was always the same. Watching her through half-lidded eyes was like watching a Japanese Noh drama. It was always the same, every time, and the deep pleasure was in the sameness. The satisfaction of the flesh comes only with ritual. Like the pleasure of the pathless woods. No surprise. No frenetic movement. No bays, beaches, and rock-bound coast. Only the rapture of the unbroken lonely shore. Her leg extended across his body to kneel above him. He watched the triangle of hair between her legs as her pelvis made its searching movement and then finally found his cock, lowering itself onto him.

She rested there, her back straight, her hands on her thighs, her head tilted. She would stay like that, unmoving till the orgasm came, if it came. The means did not necessarily justify an end. He felt the length of his back against the mattress. The sensation of his cock inside ruled over all else. He could feel himself drifting down, giving in. The rabbit gives in to the fox in that last sublime moment before its death. He searched for Gerry's voice but it was not there. He had gone beyond that. He wafted down, lolling on the edge of that lonely shore.

He could will himself into an orgasm but chose not to. Let it continue. It was lovely here with the Sybil on him. There we no knots here, only the calm of the Garden before the snake. The line of light from the sun had moved all the way across the room, no longer cutting him and the bed apart from everything else. Noises came from downstairs—Marty's voice. Samantha's. A door closed. A car started in the driveway. Nanda's weight shifted ever so slightly. She moved her pelvis, once, twice, and then stopped.

But this was not what he wanted. He wanted someone to hold him. To put her arms around him and press the warmth of her chest against his own. To be with him. Not to fuck him. Not to masturbate herself on him. He listened for Gerry's voice again, tried to see her as she had been ten years ago, but all he could see was Samantha.

Chapter 19

ZARATHUSTRA

He came awake slowly. What a day. This would make the third time he'd woken up today. If he did nothing else on his son's graduation day, at least he could say, against superior odds, he had awakened. Not that being awake was necessarily a good thing. Consciousness was highly over-rated. Perpetrated and promulgated by people who are awake. They want everyone to share the misery. Sort of like Christian missionaries who go around the world trying to drag everyone else down to their level. Share the misery, share the guilt. You were born in original sin. Who made that shit up? He drifted slowly downward again toward sleep.

"Clem."

He opened his eyes. A pair of feet lay on the pillow next to him. He was being addressed by a pair of feet. The air coming in the screened window had cooled a little, nudging the curtain and blowing gently across his sweaty back.

"Clem, wake up."

The voice came from the other end. Without moving his head, he looked down the length of the legs, past the pubic hair, the flat plain of the belly, the small breast nipples framing Nanda's face, propped against a pillow at the footboard of the bed. He'd never seen her from this angle. Kind of pretty. Longer than her normal height.

"Clem, are you awake?"

"Yeah."

"You don't look awake. C'mon, open your eyes. I have to talk to you about something."

Marty's GTX rumbled outside. It sounded like it was coming from inside the barn. How did that thing get up the driveway without waking him? Voices outside. A woman's laugh. Was Gerry here? Maybe he should get up. He opened his eyes. Nanda sat in the middle of the bed, hunched over, looking at him, her small breasts now hanging like sow dugs. The shaft of sunlight in the room had moved all the way over so that only the window frame glowed. What did she say? She had to talk to him about something. Not, Clem, we have to talk to each other, but she had to talk to him. That's Nanda all over, isn't it?

"Look at me, Clem. I have something important to say."

"Fire away." He folded his left arm under the side of his head.

She sat with her back straight, legs folded in a half-lotus. "Goncharov has gotten really out of control. She's back, you know. Banging on my front door, my back door, my windows. She's following me around. She shows up in my classroom. She knows where all my friends live. I'm sure she's been by here looking for my car. I actually hid it in the barn this time."

Marty's engine revved, fell off, and revved again. Sounded like he was adjusting something on it. And, from the echo, it was definitely in the runway of the barn. And given the almost complete lack of communication between Marty and Nanda, it would be just like Marty to push Nanda's car out of the barn before he put his own in. Which meant her car was probably sitting in plain view. Which meant that any minute he could expect the mad Russian screaming on his lawn again. He closed his eyes. For this, she woke him up?

"Clem. Listen to me. Are you listening? This involves you. I can't get rid of her. I can't convince her that I do not love her any more. I even told her I stopped being gay. I told her you and I were getting married."

Gerry? Hey, where are you?

Right here. I'm listening.

"And…?"

"And she doesn't believe me. She says there's no way I could take up with an *aslayo*p like you."

"Aslayop? What's that mean?"

"It's Russian. It means 'donkey-fucker'. Somebody that doesn't know what he's doing."

Goncharov was as big as Uppermann. And she made her living as a mud-wrestler. Scheutz might really enjoy punching her out. He rolled over onto his back.

Nanda laid a hand on his chest. "So, I need your help. I need to get her off my back for good."

"You want me to beat her up?"

She let out a hoot of laughter. "Does this all stoke some kind macho bad-ass image you have of yourself? Come on, Clem. What I'm saying we should do is get married. That's the only way she'll leave me alone."

Feel free to jump in any time, Gerry. I could use your Ann Landers thing right about now.

I'm stumped.

Never thought I'd see the day.

The woman's asking you to marry her.

Yeah, I got that.

And do you get that the Goncharov fiasco is just a flimsy excuse?

You mean she really wants to marry me?

God knows why.

"Um. I'm sorry Nanda. I don't think I can get married. I never got a divorce from my wife."

"You told me you and she never officially got married."

"Uh, well....um. Yeah, technically that's true. But..."

"But....?"

"But....I didn't think you went in for that sort of thing."

"I don't. But this is an emergency."

He shook his head, trying to think of something to tell her. "You know, mixed marriages don't ever really work."

"Mixed marriages?"

"Yeah. You know, like mixed company, men and women."

"Are you turning me down? I'm asking you to marry me and you're blowing me off. I don't believe this."

"Well, it's all so sudden. Let me think about it."

"Think about it? Knowing you, Clem, that could take fifteen years. Come on. It has to be pretty quick. Goncharov is on the prowl. I'll give you till tomorrow morning."

"This is sort of like a shotgun wedding, huh?"

"It's not funny." She turned away from him, got off the bed, and began putting on her clothes. He watched her move around the room in a kind of reverse strip-tease. First the panties, then a chambray work shirt, no bra—she never wore a bra—then cut-off jeans, and finally her sandals. The more clothes she put on, the sexier she looked. She stood in front of the dresser mirror for a few moments to readjust her single plait of hair before tossing it back over her shoulder. She looked at him in the mirror without turning. "Maybe I'll see you tonight. Depending." She was not looking at him but at his crotch.

"Depending?"

"On whether the mad Russian shows up. So, think about what I said, okay?"

"Your proposal?"

"Yes. My proposal. I'm proposing to you."

When the door closed behind her, he rolled onto his stomach, pulled the sheet over his body and listened to the voices coming up through the screened open window from the driveway in front of the house. From the angle of the sun, it must have been after five o'clock. Be nice to go back to sleep for another hour. Gerry's voice—the real Gerry—was not among those downstairs. That didn't necessarily mean she hadn't arrived.

Boy, for someone who doesn't have any women in his life, you sure have a lot of women problems.

No shit, huh?

Gerry, Samantha, Nanda. Anybody else?

Yeah. You.

I am Gerry, remember?

No you're not.

Now, don't start pouting again. God, I hate it when you sulk.

I'm not sulking. I'd just like to have another hour of sleep.

No such luck, Buster. Your ever-loving wife—me in the flesh, who as you've been reminded, is not actually your wife—will show up here at any time. And you better wash Nanda off your dick before she does show up. You smell like a whorehouse.

What would it mean if he married Nanda? Or, to be more exact, if Nanda married him? He'd just be doing her a favor is all. Nothing else would change. It didn't really mean anything. Any more than not being officially married to Gerry meant anything. And, once Goncharov was gone, if he didn't like it, they could file for a divorce. There wouldn't be any property or kids involved. And what the hell, it might help spur him on to changing his life. He'd be a faculty spouse at Dartmouth, maybe get better health insurance coverage and invites to hoity-toity cocktail parties. "Hi, nice to meet you. And what do you teach? Oh, really, how interesting. No, I don't teach, myself. Supportive spouse and all that. Actually, most of my time is tied up in meditation. Personal friend of the Buddha."

What would his kids think of such a thing? They'd hate it. The opportunity for them to interact would be minimal. But, it would be the idea of the thing, that their father was married to a) someone not their mother and b) someone they truly disliked. Well, what the hell, they were both grown-ups now—Marty, officially as of today—and they could just suck it up as "that's the way life goes." Of course, he'd talk to them about it, but he already knew what they would say, both of them. "Yeah, sure, whatever."

Hey, whoa. What does this train of thought mean? Are you actually thinking seriously of marrying that woman?

No, I was just musing.

I'm not hearing any musing in the opposite direction.

Well....yeah, maybe I am thinking positive about it. I mean, I don't want to end up a lonely old man who has to bring that mangy barn cat into the house just for companionship.

Will. You. Stop. It. Please. For Chrissake. That wacko lesbian you're musing about will suck out whatever life is left in you, and you'll still end up with the barn cat. What's that word her friend called you, aslayop? Sheesh.

I take it you don't approve.

Approve? Listen, numbnuts, I so don't approve I think you'd be better off married to Goncharov.

Come on, I'm trying to have a serious discussion here.

That would be funny, though, wouldn't it? You and the Russian together, the two of you going around trying to out-macho each other.

You're not helping much. The only reason I let you in here is so you can help me figure these things out.

The reason you let me in here is because you can't keep me out.

And you're just here to make fun of me.

No, I'm here because I love you.

Nanda's voice came up from the driveway, yelling something at someone, he couldn't make out what or to who. Probably at Marty for pushing her car out of the barn. Then Freddie Brockton's voice yelled back. What the hell was he doing here? Probably waiting for Dan to show up. And to see Samantha. Scheutz could feel his face blush hot against the sheet with the thought again about his little encounter with Samantha. Hope she doesn't go telling anyone about that. A car door slammed and Nanda's Volvo started up, then moved away down the driveway. Good. Glad she was gone.

Wait a minute. You're thinking of marrying her and yet you're glad she's gone. What's up with that?

The duality of nature. Action-reaction; plus and minus, the forces of good and evil.

Which one's which?

Depends on your point of view.

Stop with the bullshit and get back to your feelings about Nanda.

There was something so pushy about her. She always seemed to know exactly what she wanted and, at least when it came to what she wanted from him, seemed so predatory in her single-mindedness. Here he was wandering around like some dumb Bambi in hunting season. Which was fine when it came to that version of tantric sex she visited upon him without his having to take her on dates, buy dinner and flowers, or whatever it was that guys usually do to open the petals of the flower. Because the sex was delicious. But this marriage proposal was something else again.

Now we're getting somewhere. Here come the arguments from the other side of the aisle. And what else?

What else what?

What else is bothering you about the predator?

That's about it. I'm not sure I can handle being her cabana boy.

That's not what else is bothering you about Nanda.

You sound like you're jealous. Are you jealous because Nanda and I have better sex than you and I did when we were together?

No, you schnook, I'm not jealous. Our sex life was just fine. In fact, towards the end, that was the only way I got your attention.

Okay, so what else are you saying is bothering me about Nanda?

Come on, it's right there. No? Let me give you a hint. Samantha.

That was it. That was the other reason he was glad to see Nanda go. He did not want her around Samantha, who was either downstairs in the kitchen or outside in the barn with the rest of the kids. Nanda had quizzed him a couple of times in the past month or so about Samantha and, now that he thought about it, there did seem to be that little predatory gleam in her eye. With Goncharov out of the picture, Nanda was surely casting about for someone else on whom to practice her kundalini yoga, or 'cunnilingus' yoga, as she called it. And there was poor Samantha, in an even deeper fog than Scheutz himself, still emulating Gerry, her high school hero, and probably just waiting for someone to come along and fashion a new identity for her.

He had better stop all this and get his ass up and out of bed. His train of thought was getting kinkier by the minute. He rolled off the bed, wrapped himself in a towel and headed across the hall for another shower. Then he dressed in a pair of shorts, white painter pants with the legs cut off, and a bright red t-shirt.

The kitchen was empty, a large clear-plastic bag of mixed salad sitting on the table. It looked like enough greens to feed a battalion of rabbits for a month. The driveway in front of the barn looked like it had always looked when Dan was in high school here, filled with cars and trucks. Freddie's new diesel pick-up truck sat behind Samatha's Saab. Joe, Samantha's brother and Marty's friend, had parked his Barracuda behind Scheutz's truck. The car, gleaming bright yellow in the late afternoon sun, was another relic of the sixties that Marty and Joe and a few other friends had restored to a better-than-new condition. It had spent its requisite six months inside the barn while a gang of teenagers tinkered like an army of North Pole elves, replacing parts, welding, sanding, sipping cans of beer, and blasting their eardrums with speakers spewing Eric Clapton, Neil Young, or Jerry Garcia.

Behind Joe's car was parked a green and white Volkswagen minibus with New York plates that Scheutz had never seen before. So Gerry must be here. He retrieved a pair of flip-flops from his shoe pile beside the wood stove and headed for the barn.

Marty's GTX sat in the runway of the barn with its hood up and Marty's and Joe's heads under it. Wooden-slated animal stalls still lined both sides of the concrete-floor runway even though no animals had occupied them since well before Scheutz and Gerry had bought the farm twelve years earlier. Above the stalls, what had once been a hay loft, had been converted to storage area and a large party room replete with couches, ping pong table, and television, all dating back to Dan's sophomore year in high school. At around the same time the party room was being furnished, the far end of the lower level had been converted into a mechanic shop with tool benches, floor jacks, jack stands, an engine hoist, acetylene torches, MIG welder, and air compressor. The kids had mounted speakers in every corner of the barn so that the decibels emanating from either the radio or tape player could drown a crowd of teenagers in sound. Now, at a reasonable level, it aired a female vocalist, whose voice Scheutz didn't recognize. The woman actually sang, as opposed to the shouting that usually came from those speakers.

Marty had turned six the year they moved into the farm and Dan was ten. Gerry had the wonderful idea, which proved to be overly romantic, that growing children would just love having their own horses to ride across the hayfields and through the woods on old logging roads. Great idea for girls maybe, but both Dan and Marty had no affinity whatsoever for anything that was not powered by an internal combustion engine. What started as go-carts powered by old lawn mower engines, grew to minibikes and then dirt bikes and street bikes—Ossa for Dan and Kowasaki for Marty—and right on up to Dan's first automobile, an early Beetle at age fourteen, that saw a lot of service in the hay fields and on logging roads.

Scheutz had tried to allay Gerry's fears of all this smoke-belching speed by reminding her of a statistic he read somewhere that teenagers who wipe themselves out on the nation's highways were, almost to a man, not the kids who worked on their own cars. Over the years, this statistic had held true in their own section of New Hampshire. All the high school and college frat boys from Dartmouth who were killed on the roads wouldn't know intake from exhaust. Kids who built their cars had an appreciation for what they could and would do with that car. But Gerry never stopped fighting against the shop in the barn, tsking it, all but sneering at it, switching to a new topic every time the subject of engines came up amongst them.

It was not till after the kids came back from New York to live with him in Acworth that the shop and the teen party room in the hay loft took shape. But the seeds had already been planted before then.

Samantha and Regina, in a tie-dyed t-shirt, leaned against the side of one of the scarred and cribbed wooden stalls, each holding a bottle of beer and involved in an animated conversation. Freddie sat on a wooden crate next to Samantha, but talking across the runway to Dan standing on the other side with the Puerto Rican girl, Livia, who'd been here with him last Christmas.

"Dan, hi. When did you get in? Hi, Livia."

Livia grinned and flapped her fingers at him. Dan met him half way in the middle of the runway and returned his hug, squeezing his back like a wrestling hold. "Hey, Big Daddy. How you doon, man?"

"Pretty good. How are you? How's life in the city? Where's your mother? She came up with you, didn't she?"

"No. I haven't seen her in a couple of months. I've been staying over at Livia's." He touched the girl's arm and she gave him and then Scheutz another toothy grin.

"You moved out of the apartment in Park Slope?"

"No. My stuff is all still there. Livia's apartment is really small. And I have so much shit. Mom's cool about it."

"She is coming up, though, right?"

Dan spread his palms. "Are you kidding? Miss her baby boy's high school graduation?"

Marty's voice came from under the hood of the car. "Baby boy. Up yours."

"What did she tell you, Dad?" Dan asked. "Didn't she tell you when she'd be here."

"Well, we don't normally talk about stuff like that."

Samantha and Regina moved from the stall to stand with them in the center of the runway. "I can't wait to see her," Samantha said. "Be nice to talk to her in person, right, Mr. Scheutz....Clem."

His head snapped around to look at her. She gave him what he could describe as a conspiratorial smile, an off-center imitation of the same kind of smile Gerry often gave him. What was with the "Clem?" This girl, this woman, had never called him anything but Mr. Scheutz as long as he'd known her. Did that little mistaken interlude in the kitchen this afternoon all of sudden put them on a different footing? That thought was almost as unsettling as her saying to him that Gerry spoke to her in her head the same as she did with him.

Regina tilted her head to see around Samantha. "Hi, Mr. Scheutz. You want a beer?"

"Uh, no. Thanks. Not on an empty stomach." He turned to Dan. "That your van out there?"

"It's Livia's. Like it? She got it real cheap and I helped some guy in Brooklyn fix it up for her. You should've seen it, man, it was a mess."

"Looks good now," Scheutz said, turning to Livia. "You going to keep it in the city?"

"No." She shook her head and grinned at him. "We have big plans."

"Do you have any idea what these things go for in Puerto Rico?" Dan said.

"But you're not in Puerto Rico," Freddie said, joining them. "And I'm sure you're not going to drive it there."

"No, but listen to this. Livia's off school for the summer, so we're driving down to Florida. We have to pick up a friend of hers in Philadelphia and then we're all going to Key West."

"In the summer?" Scheutz asked. "You're supposed to go north in the summer and south in the winter."

"No, wait. Listen. We're only staying in Key West a few weeks and then we're going back up to Jacksonville. It's all worked out already. We can ship this van to P.R. for six hundred dollars, and pay a few hundred dollars for import tax. Then we sell it in San Juan for a thousand dollars profit." One of Dan's little schemes in New York was selling cars in Queens. He worked for a guy with a used car lot, but they parked cars on the street within a twenty block radius with "For Sale" signs on them. Dan would act like he was the owner and it was a private sale, leading people to believe they got a better deal than buying off a lot.

"So, you're going to Puerto Rico?" Scheutz asked Dan.

"Yeah, for a little while. Stay with Livia's folks in Mayaguez."

"It's so beautiful there," Livia said, hugging herself to Dan's upper arm. "And we have to talk to my parents about....you know....the big news."

"What big news?"

She looked up at Dan. "You didn't tell him?"

"Wellll....I was going to, but...."

"You bum," she said.

Marty laughed. He and Joe were now leaning against the front fenders of the GTX. "Go on, Bro, tell him."

"Tell me what?"

"Welll....we might have a baby coming."

"No might about it, pendejo." Livia squeezed his arm with both hands as if she was choking him. "And....?"

"And....we might get married."

"Might?" Livia turned to Samantha and Regina, "Aren't these guys awful."

"That's so neat," Regina said. "We're going to be sisters."

"Uhhh... wait a minute," Marty said.

Samantha grabbed Scheutz's arm in the same way Livia held onto Dan's. "Isn't that wonderful, Clem. I think it's so romantic."

Nothing to say, Gerry? Silence. Oh, shit. It was all too much. He was going to be a grandfather? He felt old, but not that old. Dan, who had never stayed with one girl any longer than a week in his entire life, was....

Dan was getting married. He was too young to get married. He was only twenty-two. He was going to get married and have a baby and live in New York City. Impossible scenario. "Well, I guess you'll all have to move up here," he said. "This is a great place to raise a kid. And that house is so big, you can...."

Dan and Livia, and Marty over next to the car, all burst out laughing.

"What the hell is so funny?" Scheutz wanted know.

Dan stopped himself in mid-laugh. "That's exactly what we all said you would come up with once you heard we were getting married."

"Why is that funny? I think it's the perfect solution."

"It's funny because you're so predictable. Besides, we don't need a solution."

"Well, you can't raise a child in New York. Unless you're really rich, and you're not."

"Dad, don't take offense, but…."

"But, what? Every time someone says, 'Don't take offense, but….' they're about to say something offensive."

"Come on, don't get all mad, now. But, we couldn't live in this town. What the hell would we do here?"

"You could come work for the mill," Freddie said.

Dan looked at Freddie, and shook his head slowly. "And do what? Handle boards as they come off the saw? Ooh, wow." He raised his eyebrows and spread his hands in wonder. "Maybe. Just maybe, if one of the old sawyers dies in twenty years, I could even progress all the way up to running one of those big band saws. What a future ahead of me!"

"Hey, man, don't make fun. It's a good life."

"For you, yeah. You're going to own the mill someday."

"I'll make you my manager."

"Great. And what do we do in the meantime, get drunk together every night?"

Freddie gave him a look like Dan had just slapped him. Dan was right, of course. How stupid of Scheutz to even suggest they live up here. It would tear his heart out to see his son go the way Freddie was headed. He should be happy hearing that Dan was getting married, but he wasn't. What it would mean to him, to Scheutz, was that his son, his buddy for all these years, was one step further away from him, with his own family.

And, what the hell was Samantha doing hanging onto his arm, and calling him Clem, and saying it was so wonderful that Dan was getting married? That blew apart Scheutz's analysis of why the girl had been hanging around their house all these years—hoping it would somehow get Dan back again. Then why was she there? It was too much to think about.

He turned to look at Marty, laughing with his head back, the car's hood yawning behind him. And then everything shifted.

Samantha still hung onto his arm, but it was not Samantha any longer, it was Gerry there. Dan and Marty had not moved at all but they were tiny children, with a group of other small children. And they were all no longer in the barn in New Hampshire but in the living room of the adobe house in Agua Fria.

Everyone was laughing. Dan, Gerry and himself, even the other little kids and a few other parents at the birthday party were all laughing at Marty, laughing because the way Marty laughed was so funny. It was his first birthday and he didn't even know how to talk yet, but already he had everybody going. Gerry squeezed Scheutz's arm and roared, bouncing her forehead against his shoulder. Dan doubled over and fell onto the floor, beating his feet against the carpet. Scheutz's eyes filled with tears and he began to cough, but he could not stop laughing. Then came a lull as the laughter tapered off, accompanied a lot 'ahems' and 'whoos'. Marty, sitting in the middle of his presents with cake all over his face, silently watched the crowd, obviously knowing he was causing everyone's reaction. With the same sly look as Gerry's conspiratorial grin, he tried it again—Ho. Ho. Ho. And it set everyone off again.

Until Marty got old enough to walk and talk back and generally do things on his own, he might as well have been Dan's baby. Dan would never do the diaper thing, but he'd rock him to sleep at night and give him his bottle, although with an occasional suck on it himself. He played with him and never tired of showing him things, things that moved on their own, or fell down after being piled high, things made noise, or that bounced or popped up. Dan had helped Scheutz wrap Marty's birthday presents, most of them ending up looking like wads of paper with Scotch tape holding them. You'd have thought it was his party the way he got so excited.

And then the time shifted again and they were back in the barn. Marty was still laughing. And Scheutz could picture Dan with his own son, or daughter, being with him or her the same as he had cared for Marty. His family was not going away, he realized, it was merely expanding. Before the day Marty was born, he remembered now having that same fear, that the tight little nexus created between Gerry, Dan and himself would be blown apart with a new element. But it did not blow apart, it merely expanded to include Marty.

And it was Dan who had opened that expansion up to him on that day, eighteen years ago. They were cast onto the side a dusty road in New Mexico, with his old pick-up truck broken down half way between Madrid and Santa Fe. Gerry about to give birth any minute, groaned inside the cab, and four-year-old Dan stomped about, making little dust geysers in the middle of the deserted roadway.

"I can't find what's wrong with this thing, honey," he said to Gerry through the open window of the truck cab. "Maybe if we let the engine cool down, it might start again."

"Ugghh. I don't have time to let the engine cool down."

Dust rose on the road behind them before the noise of an engine reached his ears. From around a small hillock came a truck, an even older, rattier one than Scheutz's Chevy. Five men stood up in the stake bed on the back of the truck. Scheutz grabbed Dan from the middle of the road pushed him inside the Chevy's cab next to Gerry, telling him to stay put. "Take care of your mother. Hold her hand." And then he placed himself in the middle of the road to wave down the on-coming truck.

"Habla usted ingles," he asked the driver when the truck stopped before him.

The man with a large mustache and straw cowboy hat shook his head. "Que pasa?"

"Por favor. Mi esposa esta embarazado. Dara a luz a muy presto. Por favor, nos triagas a la hospital en Santa Fe."

The stocky middle-aged woman in the cab of the truck opened the passenger door, got out and hustled herself around the back to Scheutz's truck. She motioned for Dan to get out and then helped Gerry onto the road and then into the front of the chicano's truck.

"Subasen detras." The driver motioned for Scheutz and Dan to climb onto the bed in back. All the way into Santa Fe, he could hear Gerry alternate between grunting and screaming in the front seat. Dan made a game of running back and forth across the bed of the truck from one man to another on each side. He and the men in the truck bed all seemed to find this very funny. Exhaust smoke mixed with road dust billowed up from the tailgate, making it hard to breathe. Scheutz was convinced the truck owner had removed any semblance of springs or shock absorbers, and the driver seemed to know every rut and pothole for the entire ten mile stretch into Santa Fe. He tried concentrating his mind on sending Gerry a mental message to keep her knees closed.

Her water broke in the wheel chair heading into the emergency entrance of the hospital. The woman from the front seat applauded while the men in the truck bed behind hooted and cheered. Gerry acknowledged them like a queen with a smile and a small wave. Dan jumped up and down with his fists in the air, returning the cheers. Scheutz gave the driver a twenty dollar bill. "Para la gasolina."

Inside the air-conditioned foyer, he dragged Dan into the bathroom near the registration desk, washed his face and hands, and tried brushing some of the dust from his hair with a paper towel. Before giving the receptionist the information she needed, he bought Dan a cold soda pop from the Coke machine in the waiting room.

"It's cold in here," Dan said.

"Yeah, it's air-conditioned."

"What's that mean?"

"Let's start with your wife's name," the receptionist said.

When they finished, he asked if he and Dan could go up see Gerry. The receptionist looked them both up and down and shook her head. "I don't think so."

"No fair," Dan piped up. "Mom said I could watch."

The receptionist laughed. "Well, your mom's going to be real busy for awhile, muchacho. So, why don't you guys go have a seat."

Before Scheutz had a chance to drag Dan away from the swinging doors that led into the emergency ward, the nurse came to tell him he had a new son--ten pounds, eight ounces. They could come see Gerry and the baby in the morning, but they'd better clean themselves up first.

At the Salvation Army store in the center of the city, he bought Dan a new t-shirt and shorts, and a cotton shirt and jeans for himself. They had tacos and enchiladas in a nearby restaurant and checked into a motel with television in the rooms. By the time he'd finished washing out their underwear and rinsing off their huarachas in the shower, Dan was sound asleep. Scheutz snuggled in bed next to him and watched a really dumb movie until it settled him down enough to fall asleep himself. Since Gerry and Dan had come to Isla Mujeres to meet him a year and a half earlier, he had never slept without her next to him. Most often, Dan slept with them, sometimes in the middle, other times on his side or on her side, the three switching around like a shell game.

In the morning, both the underwear and huarachas were still damp, and Dan couldn't wait to get outside to warm up. By the time they reached the hospital, the huarachas were dry, and Scheutz could not tell whether the dampness of his underwear was from the washing or from his sweat. In the ward with four other women, they found Gerry nursing the baby when they entered. "Hi, sweetie," she said to Dan when Scheutz lifted him up to kiss his mother. Then Scheutz bent over and she caught his neck in a headlock, her face pressed against his, and her tears wetting his cheek. If Dan had not insisted they stop it, her wrestling hold on him felt like it was there for eternity.

"How was it?" he asked her.

"Imagine trying to shit a watermelon. That's a big kid."

Dan thought that was funny. "He doesn't look like a melon."

"Remember our deal," Scheutz reminded her. "You got to name the first kid. Now it's my turn."

"Have you thought about it?"

He had. A lot. He nodded. "Martin," he said.

"Martin? Where does that come from?"

He looked away to where Dan was now checking out the other new mothers in the room, walking from bed to bed to stand on tiptoes and peer at each baby. Scheutz shrugged. "I always liked the name. Hey, I didn't ask you where the name Dan came from."

Dan came back and stood on the opposite side of the bed, looking at his brother. Gerry leaned a little toward him to give him a better view, and Dan looked up into her face. He gave her a little punch in the arm and whispered, "We got the best one."

So, okay, Scheutz thought. He had always thought of Dan as the best one, but, looking down at the pinch-eyed little creature working away at Gerry's breast, maybe he'd just have to expand his idea of what 'the best one' meant.

"I don't know what this is going to cost us, Clem," she said, turning her face back to him. "But boy am I glad we're here. Imagine doing this in that shit-hole in Taxco." Gerry had waddled out of the clinic in Taxco de Alarcon, in the hills south of Mexico City, and announced to him that she needed to be taken back to the states as soon as they could get there.

Her father had died a few months before and there really was no other reason for them to stay in Mexico. Yes, they did have a few friends there, but....And they owned her father's house in Taxco de Viejo, which they sold within the next two weeks. It took them three days to Juarez in that old Chevy truck, but Gerry began to breathe easier once they crossed into El Paso. The truck was laboring by that time and it took another day to the ghost town in New Mexico called Madrid, to the home of a beatnik couple they'd met the year before in Taxco.

"Is Martin okay? You like the name?" he asked her. She nodded and squeezed his hand. "I mean, I thought you might want to name him after your father because he just died and all."

Gerry looked down at her new baby and then stared off toward the door of the ward. She shook her head slowly. "Nah." He mouth twisted. "He doesn't really mean anything. I never met him till I was twenty-one, and then...." She shook her head again. "And then he's nothing but an old drunk who needed a wet-nurse. No, Martin's just fine."

Dan stood up on his tip toes again. "He sure eats a lot, huh?"

Chapter 20

A Bird in the Hand

Marty, Regina, and Joe were due at the high school to don their caps and gowns and get ready for the graduation ceremony. And still Gerry had not showed up. Dan said he was hungry and they all trooped back inside the house. Samantha asked Freddie to help her take out some of the salad from the big bag, but he was on his way back out to his truck to retrieve a six-pack. Dan tried calling his mother's apartment in New York for the second time and left another message on her answer machine. Where the hell was Gerry? This was not like her.

Relax. I'm a very busy woman. I'll be there. Just not when you think I should be there.

How do I know you're not broken down on the road or something? Or even gotten mugged on your way out of the city. New York's terrible for that kind of thing, you know.

Will you stop? If I was broken down on the road, don't you think I'd call?

What do you mean 'if'? You don't know, do you? If you were really Gerry, you'd know. Who the hell have I been listening to all these years?

Clem, calm down. You're getting yourself in a state over nothing.

This is not nothing.

What was it that Russian woman called you? Aslayop? Stop acting like a donkey-fucker.

That's it. I'm not talking to you any more. Just shut up. Get out of my head. And when Gerry does bother to show up, that's it for her too. As soon as she gets here, I'm not going to have anything to do with her any more.

"Mr. Scheutz? Clem? Are you okay?" Samantha leaned into the counter next to him to place her face between his and the window.

He realized he had fixated his gaze on the end of the driveway, willing that vehicle, whatever she would be driving or riding in, to pull off the road. "It's over, isn't it?" he said to the girl beside him.

"What's over?"

He shook his head slowly. He couldn't look at her, and turned his head away to hide the tears that filled in his eyes. "It's all gone."

"What's all gone?"

He shrugged. "I don't know. My life."

Behind them, an eruption of laughter came from the table where Dan and Livia ate salad. After today, these kids would be all gone. Dan and Marty, his life for twenty years, all of his life really because nothing existed before them, before Gerry. They would all be gone.

Pick it up, Clem. Put a stitch in the gash and move on. It'll heal.

I thought I wasn't talking to you anymore.

You think I'm on a toggle switch you can turn off and on?

This is it for the rest of my life? Sitting in an empty parlor next to a wood stove, petting a mangy barn cat, listening to some disembodied ball-buster for all eternity?

Give me a break. I think I just might give up on you after all. You really are a donkey-fucker, you know that? You've got your life in front of you and you can't see it.

"Hey, Samantha, what happened to Freddie?" Dan asked. "I thought he was just going outside to get something?"

"I don't know." She turned to look out the window. "I don't see him out there." She shook head, and said quietly to Scheutz, "It's not even seven o'clock and I think he's drunk already. Every night it's the same thing. You think I should just give up on him?"

Scheutz looked at her. "I don't know about that."

"I would if you told me to," she said, leveling her gaze at him in the way she had seen Gerry do on more than one occasion.

"Don't lay that on me." Watching her the last few years, he didn't need Gerry to tell him how unhappy the girl was with that guy. But giving up on him?

Tell her what you think, Clem. I wouldn't be fair to her to let your feelings about being given up on get in the way.

"It's hard living with a drunk," he said softly.

"Tell me about it. He's just like my father."

"Really? I can't imagine your father being a drunk."

"No, my dad's a pothead. He doesn't get all slobbery and falling down like Freddie, but every night it's like hanging with Puff, the Magic Dragon." She ran a fingernail across his knuckle where his hand rested on the counter. "That's what I like about you. You're just who you are. All the time."

He put his hands in the pockets of his shorts and turned away from the counter. What the hell was wrong with this girl?

Maybe nothing is wrong with her. You might consider that.

Then it's me. I think about you and I get her.

"I guess we all better go," he said to Dan. "Or we'll be late for the graduation ceremony."

"What about Mom?"

"We'll leave her a note. She knows where the high school is. It's just that I was hoping she and I could go over there together." He glanced back at Samantha and then walked to the doorway into the hall. "I'll go and get dressed. I just hope she's all right."

He dressed in a pair of chinos and the old sky-blue guayabera he had not worn since Dan's graduation four years earlier. The shirt reminded him again of Mexico. He even remembered where he bought it. Actually it was Gerry who had bought it in a street stall in that town in the Yucatan. The shirt was in good shape and still fit him after twenty years. Of course, this was only about the fourth or fifth time he'd worn it.

The kids were already outside waiting for him. He grabbed his sunglasses off the chimney shelf and put them on before stepping out the door.

"Hey, Daddy-O. Nice shirt."

"Ay, que lindo," Livia said.

Samantha waggled her hips. "Hubba hubba." She still wore her shorts and sandals but had changed the t-shirt to a lavender raw-silk blouse. The darkly-dyed hair was piled on top of her head with tendrils falling on each side of her face, giving her long neck a Modigliani look. Like Gerry, she wore no make-up or jewelry.

Scheutz could feel his face flush from the unusual and, he felt, unwarranted attention paid to his change of clothes.

"You want to all ride in the van?" Dan asked.

"I'm taking my car," Samantha said. "Where the hell is Freddie?" She and Dan began shouting Freddie's name, but there was no answer. "Well, the hell with him," she said. "He's probably passed out in the barn someplace. Why don't you ride with me, Mr. Sch....Clem?"

Dan said he was going to find Freddie and walked into the barn. Livia went to sit in the van. Scheutz stood at the edge of driveway looking down toward where it met the road. Come on, Gerry. He'd better not wait any longer; he'd miss Marty's graduation. He turned back to Samantha. "Okay, I'll ride with you, but I might need to leave early."

She grinned at him.

The inside of the Saab smelled like it was still new. With the engine on, the radio blasted some unknown to Scheutz, rock band. "Do you want me to turn this down?" Samantha asked. He nodded. Even music he liked, he couldn't take loud like that. Out on the road, he looked intently into every car that passed to see if maybe Gerry would make a last minute appearance. The entire way to the regional high school in Alstead, Samantha kept up a running monologue about nothing and just about everything; about Freddie, Gerry, her brother Joe, Marty and Regina, Dan and Livia's engagement. He couldn't remember when he'd ever heard her talk so much. Maybe she always had and he just hadn't listened. But if this was what she usually talked about, maybe it was just as well he hadn't listened all these years. Now she brought his attention to what she was saying by tapping her fingernails on his knee. The second time she did it he moved his knee away so that she tapped in mid air.

Route 123A wound along the river, still up and babbling from the spring runoff. By August it would be nothing but small pools and a trickle between the boulders. On the right side of the road the heavily forested hill rose steeply in places with an occasional house built with its back into the slope and its front yard nothing but a graveled parking area. This was not a town where people got all fussy about mowing lawns.

The high school building of dark brick, built in the 1920s, dominated the center of Alstead. That is, if you could call it a center. But still it was more than Acworth had with its two stores, a combination gas station and mechanics garage, and an actual post office, unlike the small postal window inside the convenience store in South Acworth. According to Dan and Marty, the high school kids congregated in the coffee shop attached to the general store. In the evenings the place was kept clear by the town constable, a chubby little man named Ezekiel, who wore a huge pistol on his belt that he only ever took out of its holster to clean once a month.

Samantha drove slowly through the center looking for a parking place while Scheutz scanned each car and pick-up truck in the clotted crossroads for a New York license plate. By the time they found a spot at the end of a line of cars parked off the side of the road they were a good quarter of mile outside the center. Walking back toward the high school Samantha chattered on, pointing at different cars and trucks belonging to people she knew. There was her father's car, her mother's actually, since she herself had her father's car that evening. There was Mr. Bockton's pick-up truck, a man she liked and admired, unlike his son Freddie who was probably turning out to be drunk because his father gave him everything and spoiled him, di dah, di dah, di dah, on and on. Scheutz pointed with his chin toward a woman sitting in a truck cab almost hidden behind the general store.

"What?" she said, leaning forward to see better. "Who's that?"

"That's Olavi's wife. I wonder what she's doing just sitting there in the parked truck." The pickup truck was an old rusted-out heap Olavi had driven before he bought the new one. Scheutz related to Samantha the story of the burning pig sty that Olavi had told them at lunch. But instead of laughing as he thought she would, Samantha's reaction was pretty much like Gerry's voice had been—those poor people and their prize pig.

Ten yards past the store Scheutz could see the ratty old Buick belonging to Pelletier's girlfriend, Nicole, pullout from in front of the liquor store. Pelletier was driving, very slowly between the two lines of parked cars along either side of the roadway. With both hands on the steering wheel, and bent forward to look up and over it, he looked like a teenager with his first learner's permit. Scheutz waved at him but with the Canuck's attention riveted to the road, he didn't see him. Scheutz nudged Samantha again.

"What? Who's that?"

"Pelletier. You know, the guy that works with me?"

"I think I met him once. That guy with the French accent that lives up in the woods?"

"Uh huh. You know where he's headed?"

"No."

They stopped and watched the Buick make a left turn into the dirt driveway that went behind the General Store. "Assignation."

"No shit? Is that who he's going to see?" She stopped and walked back a few paces to get a better look. "Mr. Scheutz, I'm shocked. You're an old gossip just like my mother."

"Come on, we'll be late."

Chapter 21

Commencement and Decline

Tingly rays of anxiety emanated out from his stomach as they approached the high school building and walked around to the side. He stopped for a moment to take a deep breath. Samantha stopped a few steps ahead and turned to wait for him. The crowd of people thickened on the side of the building and then more so in the back as the playground gave way to the soccer field. Sharna walked toward them, nodded at Scheutz and then gave Samantha a little hug. The two women dropped immediately into a conversation about Sharna's boyfriend, Hubert. The young student from Keene State College seemed to be lost in the enormous crowd that came to the see the graduation. "He's so shy," Sharna was saying. "He went off to find the bathroom and he's probably afraid to ask anyone where it is."

"Come with me," Scheutz suggested. "I'm going to walk around and look for Marty's mother."

"I'm coming with you," Samantha said. "Where's your mom?" she asked Sharna.

Sharna shrugged. "God knows. She said she was going to finish up some stuff for the party later and then might come over, but..." She spread her palms and shook her head.

A small speaker's platform with a podium had been erected in front of the bleachers, which now held the entire graduating class of sixty-three students. Nothing had started yet. Everyone seemed to be waiting for something. The students in their caps and gowns talked and laughed among themselves or waved to the people sitting in folding chairs in the middle of the field facing them.

Scheutz walked between the two women, his head swiveling from one side to the other. Crowds of people made him nervous and, adding that to his anticipation of seeing Gerry again, he had to stop himself from bouncing on his toes. A shrill siren sounded from the loudspeaker at the edge of the field causing him to jump and spin almost in mid-air. A woman, on the podium fiddled with the microphone, sending out another long, high whistle.

"Excuse me, excuse me," she said too loudly into the mike. "Can I have your attention. We are sorry for the delay. The opening comments are to be made by Mrs. Drysdale, the superintendent of schools and she has not come yet. Does anyone....quiet please....does anyone know where Mrs. Drysdale is?" She waited, scanning the crowd, which had returned to its previous decibel level of chit chat. "Please," the woman said, sending reverberations of feedback through the mike. "Does anyone know where the superintendent has gone? We have tried her home phone but were told she'd left to come here. Anyone?....anyone?...."

Old man Brockton stepped away from a group of men he'd been talking to, and approached Scheutz. "Clement, hi there." He extended his hand for Scheutz to shake. "I don't get to see enough of you at the mill; you're always out in the woods by the time I get to work." Schetuz shook the man's hand. He liked Brockton. The man had a good solid feel about him. He was built like an older version of his son; the same big chest and shoulders but a little shorter than Freddie. Brockton turned to Samantha. "I thought Freddie was coming over here with you. Didn't he go to Clement's house to pick you up? Where is he?"

Samantha looked at Scheutz and then back to Brockton. "He's where everybody else is." She paused, looking dramatically from Scheutz's face to Sharna's, and back to Brockton. Brockton tilted his head forward and widened his eyes in question. Samantha paused a moment longer and said, "They've all been taken away. All our loved ones. Every year at this time. Haven't you noticed? They all get taken to that other planet...."

Brockton laughed and shook his head. "I love this girl," he said to Scheutz. He laughed again. "She's going to make a great daughter. If she can ever put up with my son. Huh, kiddo?" He gave her arm a little squeeze and turned to go. "Oh, speaking of that," he said to Scheutz. "I've got something I've got to talk to you about. But not here. You going over to Georgina's after the ceremony?" Scheutz nodded. "I'll talk to you there. Bye, girls. Sharna, nice to see you again."

"You too, Mr. Brockton."

She's here, Clem.

Where?

I don't know, but I know she's here.

"Where's Gerry?" he asked Samantha, and then wondered why he was asking her such a question. How would she know?

"Didn't you just hear what I told Mr. Brockton?"

Olavi limped out of the crowd behind her. "Hey, Clement," he waved and grinned. "Hey, have you seen my wife?"

Scheutz paused to think what he should say and then shook his head.

"That's where they all are," Samantha leaned close to whisper in Scheutz's ear. "Not on another planet. They're all behind the General Store, necking. Mrs. Drysdale probably has Freddie back there, and Gerry has Hubert. She likes the shy ones."

"Bye," Sharna said. "I'm going to look for Hubert."

"I never knew you were such a silly person," Scheutz said to Samantha after Sharna walked away. He began to scan the crowd again. She's here. She must be here.

"May I have your attention, please?....attention, please....hold it down. Ahem....As you all know, I am Jason Prysock, the principal of the Regional High School. These opening remarks were meant to be given by Mrs. Drysdale, the superintendent, as they are every year, but...." He held his hands out to the side of podium, palms up, much like Jesus suffering the little children to come unto him. "We'd best get on with it before it gets dark on us...." He then launched into the usual stuff about how endings are also beginnings and when one door closes, another opens. And then went on to tell everyone present what a wonderful school they had. Thankfully, he didn't have as much to say as Mrs. Drysdale would have.

The next speaker was the head of the school committee who, in almost the same words as when Dan graduated four years earlier, thanked all the members of the school committee and all those who voted for them. He then went on to congratulate each and every school committee member and said what a great job they were all doing here in this wonderful school they had.

Scheutz tuned out after the first school committee member's name and amused himself by finding first Marty and then each of his friends in the line-up on the bleachers. With that accomplished, he went back to searching the crowd for a hint of his ex-wife. That was strange; he'd never before that moment thought of her as his ex-wife. He listened for her voice in his head, but she wasn't there either. Instead came the sensation he'd had just earlier in the kitchen, a wave of longing and the emptiness of his life being over. But here he was, where he had always been, standing just outside the fringe of the crowd, his place of comfort, not totally in and not totally out. The only person here with him was Samantha, who, he realized now, also found this fringe a comfort zone. Off to the west the sun had lowered itself close enough to the horizon to turn red and had just begun pinking.

The crowd shifted and mumbled in its restlessness as the next speaker took the stand. This was a tall, skinny kid from the bleachers, his mortarboard hat sitting at a precarious angle on the side of his head. The valedictorian. He led off by thanking the principal, the superintendent, the school committee, his parents, and the town of Alstead, omitting reference to the town of Acworth altogether. He thanked President Jimmy Carter for showing everyone how an engineer could also be good leader. He then talked about what a wonderful school they had. It didn't sound like he meant it, though. His reasons for saying so seemed a little specious.

And then the kid got to the meat of what he wanted to say. It was a dangerous world we lived in, a tough place for graduating seniors like himself to venture forth into. He listed the recent evidence of this world: giant oil spills that were ruining the oceans, Three Mile Island which had begun spewing nuclear death throughout Pennsylvania, the overthrow of the Shah in Iran, the Jonestown death trip in Guyana, Nixon visiting China, and movies like *Apocalypse Now*. But, he said, there is an answer. He had found the solution to protecting ourselves. The computer. If we all had computers we could control all this. And he then launched into a detailed, technical description of his new Acorn 6520 Microcomputer Kit. This computer, for his own personal use, as well as the generations of individual computers to come after it would be the salvation of the world. This was the future. If he could, he said, his voice rising like an evangelist, he would give every graduating senior, a computer kit of their own.

"That kid sounds like my father after a few tokes," Samantha said. "If everybody had a computer, all our problems would be solved. The world would become a utopia. That makes no sense. What the hell are they teaching these kids today?"

The skinny young man retired to faint applause. Next up came the newly-found Superintendent of Schools, Mrs. Drysdale. She apologized for being so late, but said she had been unavoidably detained. "Smooching behind the general store," Samantha said from the corner of her mouth. The superintendent pulled out a prepared speech, putting forth pretty much the same thing that the high school principal and the head of the school committee had covered on the subject of what a wonderful school they had.

By this time, they were an hour and fifteen minutes into program and no one had as yet made even a glancing reference to the students who were graduating. Scheutz's feet began to hurt from standing in one place. Next up on the agenda was the school band. Seven seniors rose up from the bleachers and climbed to take their previous places with the rest of the band, after which they struck up the school fight song. All the seniors stood and sang along with many parents and members of the audience, who had themselves graduated from the same school. Scheutz never quite understood the importance of school fight songs, even in the high school he and Gerry had attended in Ohio. This particular song being sung here this evening seemed to defy all logic, though. It was all about football, a sport the school had given up many years before in favor of soccer because the equipment was a lot less expensive and playing-field injuries were held to a minimum.

Samantha nudged him and pointed to the edge of the crowd to the right. Dan, Livia and Freddie stood talking to Mr. Brockton, who was pointing in Scheutz's direction. Freddie nodded his head to something his father said, but made no move in Samantha's and Scheutz's direction. He was attempting to light a cigarette and even at that distance exhibited the disjointed feel of someone not too steady on his pins. Livia waved at them and Samantha waved back.

The sun was low in the sky as the school powers finally got around to acknowledging the graduating seniors. Awards were announced with the band giving drum rolls in appropriate and semi-appropriate places. Marty received an award for the most creatively artistic, with Mrs. Drysdale saying that Marty was going to make them all proud by heading off to New York City in the fall to attend the School of Visual Arts. The band broke out into a truly bizarre version of the Grateful Dead song, "What a Long Strange Trip it's Been" with all the horns swinging into a cacophonous noise that might have been a rendition of one of Jerry

Garcia's guitar riffs. You could pick out the various Deadheads in the crowd by their explosion of applause mixed with hysterical laughter. Marty grinned from the platform with his honors certificate in his hands, and then performed a few strokes of air guitar. Off to the right Dan and Livia hooted, while Freddie blinked to the left and right, unsure what all the noise was about.

In spite of himself, Scheutz broke into a grin. All the anxiety he had been feeling, all the emotional knots, the unsureness, the tiredness, left him. The sight of his beautiful son, up there on that platform, happy, accomplished, a little silly, zapped him in that moment with a dense microcosm of all the joy he had experienced over eighteen years of watching him grow. The rest of it did not matter. It didn't matter that Marty was going off, as Dan had done, and Gerry had done before him, and that he, Scheutz, would be left alone. That the last remnant of their little foursome that for so many years had sustained him was today being scattered to the winds. Marty, in that moment, was just who he was, nothing more. Harpo Marx with an air guitar, his cap and gown too small for him, as if he'd grown two feet in the last week since the caps and gowns were ordered.

He looked over toward Dan, to share the moment with him, but Dan was in the middle of laughing over some private joke between he and Livia. Before turning back to the platform, Samantha caught his eye. She grinned and said, "He's the best, isn't he?" He looked into her pale blue eyes. "Yes," he said. He could not share the moment with Gerry, but, for now, sharing it with Samantha was just as good.

And then an applause and a woman's shout off to the left revealed, finally, the presence of Gerry. There she was. And everything else faded from view. She glowed in the reddish hue of the descending sun. Without a word to Samantha, he turned and marched in the direction of this vision, not one hundred percent sure that what he was seeing was not some phantasm. Skirting the edge of the crowd, he became aware of Samantha behind him when she announced, "Oh, look. There she is."

He approached from behind. Gerry stood flanked by Sharna on one side and Georgina on the other, the three of them in an animated conversation that involved a lot of laughing. Gerry wore a dress he'd never seen her in. Her dark hair had been piled on top of her head, much like Samantha's but without the tendrils. The low back of the summer dress and the updone hair revealed the nape of her neck, not quite as long as Samantha's, but definitely the part of Gerry's body, like a painting of some 17th century geisha, that he found the most sensuous. She turned when Samantha blurted, "Hi, you guys. Hi, Mrs. Scheutz."

"Clem," Gerry said. "I've been looking for you. Where've you been? Hi Samantha."

"Where have I been? Where have you been?"

She laid a hand on his arm. "Looking for you." She searched his eyes with her own. The beige dress with spaghetti straps and large print flowers set off the city-dweller pallor of her skin. Her fingernails, while not painted, were precisely manicured and polished. What did he expect? All those years of high-end design and client presentations had all but obliterated the loose-jointed earth mother in paint-spattered jeans and sweatshirt. And the heels on her sandals raised her eye-level to his. "That shirt on you makes you look muy guapo," she said. "Is that the one I bought for you in Mexico?"

"You bought that for him in Mexico?" Samantha asked. "That is so cool. He's so handsome in it."

"And how are you, Samantha? I still haven't received a wedding invitation. I hope you and Freddie haven't already gone ahead with it and then forgot to invite me."

"No, I could never forget to invite you." She placed both hands on Gerry's upper arms and leaned in to kiss her cheek. "We have been looking for you like everywhere. He didn't want to leave the house because you hadn't shown up yet."

Gerry turned her gaze back to him. He waited. Then realized his breathing had stopped. Just give me the signal and I'll breath again. She gave him a small, sad smile. She knew. It was her, after all, who'd been talking to him all these years.

"Really, you should see him," Samantha chattered on. "Every time you come up in conversation, he gets like some little puppy."

Gerry turned to look at Samantha. A triangulated angel passed between the three of them. The graduation ceremony, the crowd on the soccer field, the evening sky around them shifted, leaving Gerry, Samantha and himself in what felt like a time-space warp. What could have been a moment, or a much longer time, he saw the three of them as three separate lines of music, like a Bach fugue, or else three strings, each on a different frequency, gyroing into harmony around each other.

"Don't say puppy. I don't need another puppy," Gerry said, breaking the pause. "I've got enough of them in my life." The look she threw to Scheutz, showed him how nervous she was. Her eyes softened for just a moment, before she caught herself. She put her hand on Samantha's arm. "I hope you've been taking care of him when he gets like that." Her conspiratorial smile, directed at Samantha, broke through her nervousness. Samantha looked at Scheutz and then smiled at Gerry. Gerry turned away from them, shot a glance at Georgina, and then looked back to the platform where the Superintendent had started handing out diplomas.

Scheutz was left staring at the back of her head and the nape of her neck. What had just happened? He looked at Samantha but she also was looking toward the platform where the capped and gowned students walked in single file to shake hands with Mrs. Drysale. He felt that sensation again which he recognized, that everyone else knew what was going on and he didn't. What was he missing? Not with the graduation, but with the two women and himself, just now. Something had passed between them which he did not understand.

He could feel himself becoming angry, but he did not know at what. At Gerry, certainly. Not at Samantha. Her part in this felt benign. But Gerry's remark about the puppy had the same tone as whenever she had referred to him as 'boy'. It was dismissive and demeaning. She was trying to tell him something without actually telling something. He wanted to touch that sensuous spot at the nape of her neck. To grab it and shake her loose from that imperious castle keep she'd locked herself into for the last ten years.

Gerry, Georgina, Sharna and Samantha where all clapping. He looked up to see the reason, and realized that Marty, in line up on the platform, had just received his diploma and was waving it as he walked back to his spot on the bleachers. Scheutz just stood and watched. He could not clap. This was it. This was the end. It was official now, he had no more children, he was responsible to and for no one.

Samantha took his hand and squeeze it. She leaned her shoulder into his and then away again, like a tap from a bumper car. Her touch irritated him. This was the third time since his faux pas a few hours ago that she had touched him in more than a friendly way. She seemed to be suggesting, or assuming, an intimacy he did not want from her.

Chapter 22

Evening by the Woodside

"Boy, everybody's here," Samantha said. She appeared at his side as he took a small bite of a taco, trying to keep its contents from spilling out the other side.

"Everybody? What do you mean, everybody?" He held the taco over a paper plate and looked around at the people gathered outside Georgina's diner. It was a large crowd for the small town of Acworth, certainly bigger than the annual Town Meeting. Cars lined the highway and were parked two deep on the grass at the side of the house. A long buffet table had been set up before the entrance to the diner, the table crowded with an array of cooked dishes and salads and desserts brought by the families in attendance. At an angle to that table, another held bottles of wine and soft drinks. Two galvanized wash tubs filled with ice and bottles of beer sat on the ground between the tables.

"I mean everybody in our community." She turned away to talk to Mrs. Alcott from the grocery store and Post Office window. With a mouthful of taco, Scheutz nodded hello to Sally Ann, the same as he did every morning in Georgina's when he got his coffee. He looked around for Gerry and saw her on the other side of the crowd talking with Dan and Livia, and a scruffy-looking young man with long hair he'd never seen before. The entire scene existed in an orange glow, given off by the paper lanterns Georgina and Sharna had strung in a criss-cross pattern over the parking area and the lawn at the side of the house. Beyond the lanterns, beyond the rows of cars parked along the highway, twilight had descended, shading the details of the trees and the hayfield up behind the house. Music from a Moody Blues album—something for the "older" folks--floated above the murmur of the crowd and seemed to add to the softness of the time of day.

Just about everyone he knew was right here at Georgina's. There were Olivi's wife and his daughter. And over there was Pelletier's girlfriend, Nicole. Pelletier was not in view but he was sure to be lurking somewhere near. Nicole stood talking to the old guy whose name Scheutz could never remember, who had been re-elected to every term of selectman since before Schetuz and Gerry moved to town. The man wore a tie with every outfit, no matter what time of year. Whether he had on his Sunday church clothes or bib overalls, in the heat of summer or in an ice storm, he sported any one of three different patterned ties, knotted right up against his Adam's apple. And over at the periphery, Uppermann had just walked in from the road between two parked cars, the orange light softening the contours even on his slack-jawed face. Just behind him and to his left stumbled his brother who was not quite as big but just as stupid. They both appeared to be already more than a little drunk.

Scheutz chewed slowly, pondering what Samantha had just said about this being a community. He supposed it was, but it did not feel like his community. Then again, he couldn't actually say what a community felt like. He had never aligned himself with one, never felt part of what could be called a community. All these people here were nice, they were harmless, and at times very helpful, but he was not part of anything in the town or the district other than having his name listed among the registered voters. And even voting he seldom bothered with. He could leave this place tomorrow and it would not bother him. He'd miss the house, and the isolated beauty of the countryside. Or he might miss that sense that one gets in rural New England that people are going to leave you pretty much alone if that's your preference.

"Clem." Old man Brockton's bass boomed behind him. "Need to talk to you."He emerged at Scheutz's elbow. "Mind if I steal your escort for a few minutes," he said to Samantha who, still in conversation with Mrs. Alcott, gave a little nod and a wave. Brockton put the slightest pressure on Scheutz's elbow and nodded toward the line of parked cars.

Schetuz carried his all-but-finished taco and his bottle of beer to the maroon pick-up truck with the words Brockton Lumber and a logo painted on the door. He set the bottle on the side of the truck bed and finished the taco waiting for Brockton to begin what he had to say.

"I'm making some changes at the mill." Brockton, as usual, got right to the point. Scheutz waited, finished chewing and took a swallow of beer. "I've given this some thought, and I think you're being wasted working out there in the woods. I'm going to make you my new forester."

Scheutz waited for more. His gaze drifted again to Gerry who, because of her height, was easy find in the crowd. The young, scruffy-looking guy talking to Dan and Livia seemed to have his hand casually resting on Gerry's hip. He wasn't sure what he was seeing until she, just as casually, reached her hand up to touch the dark curls of hair at the nape of his neck. He experienced a stab of pain in his stomach. The young guy turned back to say something that promoted laughs from Dan and Livia.

"I guess you need time to think it over, huh?" Brockton said.

"Oh, I'm sorry. I'm a little distracted today. What did you say about the forester?"

"I said that young forester I hired out of UNH just got himself fired. That's what I said."

Scheutz pulled his gaze away from Gerry. "Why is that?"

"Because he doesn't know shit about marking trees and estimating yield. I don't know what they teach these kids these days, but they don't spend much time in the woods."

"What does that have to do with me?"

"You been working in the woods for ten years. Maybe before that for all I know. And you're certainly the smartest chopper I ever met." He tilted his head back to observe Scheutz's face, like a doctor analyzing a new disease he'd never seen before.

Gerry moved away from Dan and Livia and the scruffy-looking guy. Maybe what he'd seen was a trick of his imagination, a stab of jealousy. He listened for Gerry's voice to tell him what was going on, but again she was silent. Now he really did not know what was going on. He watched Gerry make her way through the crowd toward Marty and a knot of recent grads. Samantha had left off talking with Mrs. Alcott and also moved in Marty's direction.

"So, what do you say, Clem?"

"About what?"

"About what we're talking about."

"I'm sorry. Can you run it by me again? I'm a little out of it here."

"I need a forester. You're it. Money's the same, but the hours are shorter and the work isn't as hard."

"I'm working piece-work now. Get paid by the thousand feet of timber."

"I know what you made last year, and it's less than the year before. And, you know, that little trend is going to keep up because you're getting past the age when guys are most efficient in the woods. What are you now, forty, forty-one? So, how about this? I'll pay you what you made two years ago. That's a raise. Next year it'll be a bigger raise with the same salary because I expect your piece rate would go down again."

"I'll have to think about it. What about Freddie?"

"Freddie's coming out, too. I'm putting him in the office. I'm cutting down to one crew. Pelletier and Uppermann. Frankly, it's less expensive nowadays for me buy timber from some of these little independent outfits. There's a man down in New Boston got one of those feller-bunchers the big paper mills been using in Maine. A man with a chain saw in the woods is fast going the way the sheep herder, for Christ's sake."

"I think I've seen one of those machines. Is that what they're called? Grabs the tree and saws it off the stump in one all in one operation?"

"Ayuh. What the guy in New Boston does is take the butt log off and then shove the rest of the tree into the biggest damned chipper you've ever seen, and then sells it all for pulp. A couple of men with those machines can select-cut a forest in a tenth of the time it takes a chain saw and a skidder." He shook his head in philosophical contemplation. "That's the way the world goes."

Scheutz took another swallow of beer. "I'll have to think about it. I thank you for the offer."

"It's not an offer. It's an order. I'm moving that guy's feller-buncher onto the next lot we're doing. You've got about a week's more chopping up where you are and then you're going to summer school classes over in Durham."

Near the buffet table, Gerry stood sideways to Scheutz with her arm around Marty's neck. Samantha looked in Scheutz's direction, and gave him a small wave. He nodded to her and then turned back to Brockton. "I have to go to school?"

"Ayuh. I'm sure you know most of it already, but I want to make sure you ain't missed nothing."

"I don't have any say about this?"

"You can have all the say you want."

"But...."

"That's right. 'But...' But, we're still going to do it this way no matter what any of you have to say. Freddie doesn't like it any better than you do, but that's the way it is. I need you to do this for me, Clem."

"It's your mill." It didn't seem right, somehow. But he couldn't fault Brockton. The man was actually trying to look out for him in the middle of all this change. "When I was in the army," he said. "The first sergeant had a little sign on his desk that said, 'The first sergeant isn't always right, but he's always the first sergeant.'"

Brockton bowed his head in reverence. "You see my point. Fact is, I need you in this job, Clem. You been the most reliable worker I've had for the last ten years. Certainly, more than my own son. And I need to sharpen this whole timber yield operation. Or close it down and buy all my timber from Canada. So, either way, you're out of the woods."

So there it was. This day just wasn't going to stop. He listened again for Gerry's voice, watching her--Gerry, the person—talking now to Georgina. Silence. What the hell could she tell him, any way? What could he tell himself? This was just the way it was. But it was beginning to feel like it was too much, too many changes all at once. All in one day. Marty graduating, Nanda proposing, Brockton promoting. Those were all supposed to be good things; he was supposed to be happy. He wasn't. Raising those two kids for the last twenty years had given a shape, a focus, a consistency to his life. Now who was he? Plus, being conjoined at the heart—or at the genitals--in holy wedlock with an overpowering tantric lesbian could only be like signing a contract to spend the rest of his life in oblivion. And if he turned her down. Then he would be running the risk of cutting off one of the very few people he considered his friend. And finally, here was Brockton taking away what had been for ten years, not just a job, but the only place in the world where he felt completely at home in his own skin.

"Wouldn't it make more sense to send Freddie to forestry classes?" Scheutz picked at the label on the beer bottle with his thumb. "I mean…I may not be around much longer. When Marty goes off to school in New York, that'll mean the whole family is down there." He looked up and at the party crowd, from Dan to Marty to Gerry. "Maybe I'll go there too."

"Is that what you been planning?"

"No. It just this minute occurred to me."

"What would you do there?"

"God knows."

"Well, you'd better let me know pretty soon what you want to do. The classes start right after July 4th. I got to send either you or Freddie. And I know Freddie is not going to do the job right. Not the way he's going."

If he did this, if he went to forestry classes, he'd be obligated. He'd be at that mill for the rest of his life, having breakfast every morning at Georgina's like those three old farmers. And if he didn't go to those classes, he'd be out of a job. In this neck of the woods, that was not a good thing to be. Around here you either had your own money or you worked at whatever your parents did before you. Even going off to someplace like New York held little prospect for employment. Who was going to hire a forty-year-old man with wood-cutting skills?

At the edge of the crowd, Samantha and Freddie came together for what looked, at a distance, to be a disagreement. She walked away leaving him staring sullenly after her. Brockton had been watching them also. He stepped to Scheutz's side and leaned his back against the bed of the pick-up truck. As Samantha joined another small knot of young people, Brockton folded his arms and dropped his gaze toward his shoes, sighing like a man with a lot on his mind.

"They have any plans for a wedding date yet?" Scheutz asked.

"Nobody's said anything to me about it. I sure hope they go through with it. If that girl can't straighten him out, nobody can."

"And I'm sure the mill business could always use a little financial help coming from her side of the family."

Brockton tilted his head and looked up sideways at Scheutz. "What do you mean by that?"

"Well, her old man's got all that trust fund money he's always donating to good causes. I'm sure he could donate a little to insure his daughter's and possible grandchildren's financial stability."

"Her old man's a goddamned communist, is what he is. I've tried a couple of times to get him to invest in the mill. He'd rather I shut down and go to growing pot plants like Pelletier does."

"Pelletier does that?"

"His girl friend does. Up there in the woods behind their trailer. Don't tell me you didn't know that."

"No, I didn't know that. But it doesn't surprise me."

"Tempting idea. You can get a hellova lot more per pound for dope than you can for spruce or pine. And I could get those goddamned environmentalists off my back."

Scheutz laughed. "You wouldn't be the first one. I read where a lot of those old cotton farmers down in the Mississippi Delta have been increasing profits for years that way."

"You know I'm just joking, right?"

"Yeah, I know you're just joking."

"You're going to help out on this forestry thing now aren't you? Say you'll do it, Clem. I need your help, and I don't want to lose a good man."

Where the hell was Gerry's voice when he needed her? "I've got to think about it. I don't do anything without talking it over with a certain party."

"You've got to let me know next week."

The people at the party moved in slow, kaleidoscope-like patterns, forming small groups and then dissolving and reforming again with others. The crowd comprised only those from Acworth; apparently, the other graduates, the ones from Alstead had their own graduation party in their own town. Here couples came together and then moved apart, husbands, wives, boyfriends, girl friends, talking, laughing, sometimes dancing with others. There were exceptions, like Dan and Livia, who stuck close to him because she felt awkward in this crowd, and Uppermann and his brother who were both awkward around anyone.

Darkness had asserted its dominion outside the circle of light cast by the paper lanterns. The music had changed to something younger and more strident. The noise of the crowd had sneaked up a couple of decibels as people relaxed into the mood. Even Georgina's breakfast regulars, Johnstone, not in his state trooper uniform, and the three farmers, peppering the crowd, all seemed to lose some of the New England sternness in their faces.

Freddie broke away from the crowd to sway his way toward his father and Scheutz where they continued to lounge against the side of the pick-up truck. He stood before them and fished a cigarette out of a pack in his shirt pocket, then held the cigarette in his hand, staring at it without lighting it. "Your girl's gonna be the death of me, Clem."

"What do you mean, my girl?"

"Oh, that's right. She's not your girl. I keep forgetting that. Well, she spends more time at your house than she does at her own." He spoke in the halted, broken manner he always slipped into whenever he had too much to drink.

"You don't treat her right, Fred," Brockton said.

"Oh, really, Dad?"

"Really." The muscles in Brockton's jaw twitched, his mouth pressed into a hard line.

"You ever notice how people tend to treat other people the way they get treated themselves?" Freddie stared hard at his father.

"Um..." Scheutz paused. "I need to have a talk with my kids' mother before she goes. I'll see you guys later."

"Wait a minute. Hold on." Freddie held his hand up in front of Scheutz's chest without actually touching him. "I need to...have a talk with you before you go."

"About what?"

Freddie looked at his father. "Did you tell...him?"

Brockton nodded. He stood away from the pickup bed, eyeing his son, his teeth clenched.

"And what...did he say?"

"I'm standing right here, Freddie," Scheutz said.

"So, what...did you say?"

"That I'd have to talk it over with someone and let him know."

"Who do you have...to talk it over with?...Samantha?" He giggled.

"No. But why is that funny?"

Freddie shrugged and looked from Scheutz to his father and then back, the look on his face Scheutz could only describe as supercilious. Or super-silly. "Why is it funny? She told me about the three-way conversations you two have with your ex-wife when she's not there. Doesn't that sound funny, Dad?"

"What?" Brockton said. "What the hell you talking about?"

"I'm talking about... how nutty your new forester-to-be is."

There it was again, that twitch in Scheutz's shoulder, the tingle in his right hand. He transferred the beer bottle from his right to his left hand. If he did let go and smack Freddie, at least he wouldn't have the beer bottle in his hand when he did it. He looked into old man Brockton's eyes, and could see that Freddie's father knew exactly what Scheutz was thinking. But maybe did not know how close he was to laying into his son. If he smacked Freddie, he might have both him and his father to contend with. Freddie may be drunk but he had a hockey player's instinct for fighting back. And Scheutz had witnessed on two occasions over the last few years, the meanness in him coming out in a fight. And he was younger and very strong. There was obviously not a whole lot of love lost between the father and son, but what father could stand by and see his own son get his ass whipped?

He moved away from the truck and stood sideways to it, facing the two Brocktons, keeping them both in full sight. Behind the old man a car's headlights slowed on the highway. As it entered the sphere of light shed by the paper lanterns, he could see the fake wood-paneled station wagon belonging to Goncharov, Nanda's ex-lover. Time seemed to slow down as he saw the Russian's bulldog face leaning over to scan the crowd, the car inching along. He entertained a momentary fantasy that she might be looking for Uppermann. The two did not even know each other, but what a pair they would make.

Brockton stepped between Freddie and Scheutz and put his arm around his son's shoulder. "I think, Freddie my boy, maybe you need to stop drinking so much."

"So…" Freddie said. "Dad? Who would you rather have for a forester, a nut or a drunk?"

Brockton turned Freddie so that his own body completely shielded him from Scheutz. "I think you better shut the hell up, boy, before I turn you over my knee." He turned to Scheutz. "Let me know by Monday, or at least Tuesday about the forestry classes." Leading the stumbling Freddie by the grip on his shoulders, he directed him away toward the crowd. As they walked away, Freddie turned his head and said, "We'll talk later, Clem."

Scheutz tossed his empty beer bottle into the bed of Brockton's truck, and leaned his fore-arms on the side of the bed, facing the roadway, awaiting the overdue lecture from Gerry's voice about his inappropriate caveman reactions to the world around him. Goncharov's station wagon disappeared around a bend in the road. The light from the paper lanterns stopped at the line of vehicles along the highway and, with no traffic on the road, the darkness beyond Brockton's truck appeared like some black war memorial with no names inscribed on it yet. Gerry's voice hid out there somewhere in that blackness, waiting. For what? Or maybe she had deserted him finally, completely.

Or maybe she was there and he just couldn't hear her; wasn't letting himself hear what she had to say. Ever since Samantha said what she had about Gerry's voice in the kitchen earlier, something had changed. The voice wasn't just his any more. He had not believed Samantha about the voice—in fact, Gerry had told him that it was only a euphemism for a thought process the girl used and not an actual voice she heard. But it must have more weight than a mere thought process if it was heavy enough for her to tell her boy friend about it. And now he had that twit, Freddie, going around saying he was a nut. Well, maybe he was.

Chapter 23

Let Me Take You Away

"What are you doing over here all by yourself?" A soft hand touched his shoulder. He turned to see Gerry standing behind him. "I brought you a beer." She handed him one of the two bottles in her hand.

"Thanks." Their eyes met, hers lingering on his with more feeling than he had seen from her in more years than he could count. "You look very nice tonight," he said to her. He lifted the bottle. "Here's to ya."

"Here's to us."

"What's that mean?"

"A toast to us." She touched his bottle with her own and then drank. "We did it. I should say, 'you did it.' Raised two healthy, happy boys. And gave them what they need to carry on."

She turned and leaned against the truck bed as Brockton had done, facing the party crowd. They both, simultaneously, as if on some hidden cue, raised their beer bottles in the direction of Marty who at that moment seemed engaged in an enthusiastic argument with another boy in his graduating class. Scheutz and Gerry looked at each other and laughed. Years ago they had often caught themselves doing or saying exactly the same thing at exactly the same time.

He sipped from his bottle. "We did it, didn't we?"

"I don't know about 'we.' I wasn't around for so much of it."

"Believe me, you were. A lot more than you know."

"That's sweet of you to say so. But…." She turned away toward the crowd again. He waited as she withdrew into herself. After a long pause, she took a deep breath and then turned to him. "It was really hard for me. I never wanted to send them back to Acworth. But I knew I had to. It was only a matter of time till Dan joined some street gang in New York. And the city would have eaten Marty alive. But, I've never really thanked you."

"Why should you thank me. They're my kids."

"I was so thankful that they had a place to go. That they had some one else who loved them as much as I did." She took a swig from her bottle. "I'm going to start blubbering here in a minute. Why don't you come and join the party? Your girl friend can't stop talking about you."

"My girl friend?"

"I'm joking. What has gotten into Samantha? 'Well, Clement says this and Clement says that.' You haven't started balling that girl, have you?"

"What?"

"I'm joking. I'm joking. But, look at her." As if on cue, Samantha turned away from the scruffy guy who had been talking with Dan and Livia earlier. She now stood very still, looking across the heads of the crowd at Scheutz and Gerry. "You are her new hero."

Scheutz shook his head. "That girl needs to get away from here. Brockton can't wait to get her married to his son. He thinks she's the one to save Freddie's life. It would just ruin her own."

"Poor kid."

"Why don't you take her to New York with you? You need an intern or an apprentice, or something like that, don't you?"

Gerry shook her head. "Just because I feel sorry for her, doesn't mean I like having her around. She drives me nuts. She dresses like me, she tries to talk like me. I've caught her trying to copy how I walk. She's even dyed her hair to look like mine. I look at her and I can see every flaw I've ever had. No, thanks."

The object of their discussion seemed to be at that moment engaged into what looked like a full-blown argument with her betrothed. She bent slightly at the waist, her face only a few inches from Freddie's snarl. He flung his hands about as he talked while her fists clenched in what looked like impotent fury, her voice rising in a simultaneous counterpoint to whatever Freddie ranted on about. Their two voices climbed above the murmur of the crowd, but still not to the level where Scheutz could make out what they were saying. People around them backed away silently, the way couples on a dance floor will form a circle to watch one couple that has transcended the mundane.

Gerry fell silent and they watched what they could see of the young couple's argument through the crowd of onlookers. On the other side of the crowd, on the lawn just off the gravel parking lot, people had started dancing to the rock music on the turntable. Mostly young people, moving like puppets on musical strings, but here and there the dance area was peppered with older folks, like Samantha's parents, dreamily out of sync, over-aged hippies still "feelin' groovy" and "blowin' in the wind." On their own side of the crowd, Freddie's and Samantha's pas de deux kept the frenetic rhythm of the background music.

"Did we ever look like that?" Gerry asked him.

"Which one?" He pointed with two index fingers, left at Samantha and right at her father.

Gerry looked back and forth. "Oh, God. I hope neither one."

"We had our own dance. Still do."

"We do, don't we? I mean…I should say, we did, didn't we?"

"We still do."

She tipped the beer bottle and sipped. They watched the argument progress. Freddie attempted to turn away and Samantha grabbed the sleeve of his t-shirt. He turned back to her, brushing off her hand, shouting. Samantha came back at him, impossible to make out because she was crying now, in his face with her tears, her fists still clenched, one raised as if to strike him.

"Don't do it, girl," Scheutz said quietly.

"Why not?" Gerry said. "He deserves a good smack."

"Whoa, listen to you. Miss anti-violence no matter-what."

"There are times...."

"A just war?"

"Oh, shut up."

"She'll win as long as she doesn't drag it onto a physical level. All she has to do is hit him once and it's a whole new choreography."

"And what if he hits her first?"

"Same thing. But a different dance. In that one she gets to keep the high ground."

"When did you get to be such a cynic?"

Dan moved away from the circle of spectators, approaching Freddie and stepping between him and Samantha. From the other side of the circle Joe stepped out to put his hand on his sister's raised arm. On the other side of the crowd, the dancers milled like unfed cattle when the music stopped. Samantha's parents gazed contentedly at those around them, her father in an Errol Flynn type pirate shirt and her mother, beaded like a gypsy, in a peasant blouse and ankle-length skirt.

"If those kids fight like this before they're married, think what they could do after," Scheutz said.

Gerry raised her eyebrows. "So then, what's the point?"

"You mean what's my point? Or what's the point of ever getting married?"

"I mean what's the point of ever getting married?"

"Why not? Men and women never see eye-to-eye no matter what they do."

"Jesus, Clem, you gotta come down out of the woods. What've you been doing up there all these years, thinking deep skeptical thoughts?"

"Well, you have to admit…have you ever known two people, I mean a man and a woman, who came at the world from the same direction?"

"Mmm. No, I guess I can't say I have. No, wait, what about Samantha's parents? They seem to always be on the same track."

They had known Samantha's parents for twelve years, ever since they moved to Acworth. But Gerry and he still thought of them as "Samantha's parents." Everyone they knew referred to them as such. Even their kids said, "my parents" never "my Dad" or "my Mom" or "Mom and Dad." As if they were not separate people, or even people at all, merely some kind of modular parental unit. Scheutz could not even remember their names. "Are you kidding me?" he said to Gerry. "That's not connubial bliss. That's cannabial bliss."

"Cannabial bliss?"

"As in cannabis. Or cannabliss."

"Oh. Hah. Or, how about 'Can of Bliss'."

He laughed. "What a great idea. We could figure out a way to can the stuff. That's what they did with Coke. We could make a mint." They both laughed now, and it felt to him as if the last twelve years away from her had never happened.

"But we're getting away from the main event." Gerry pointed her beer bottle in the direction of the Freddie and Samantha show where Dan and Joe were now having to physically restrain the two combatants. Samantha shouted over her brother's shoulder with her index finger pointed skyward, making points like a sermonizing preacher. Freddie meanwhile yelled back from around Dan's restraining arm, pumping his index finger downward, hammering away at his counterpoints.

"You have any idea what they're arguing over?" Gerry asked.

He shrugged. "Same dumb stuff they've been going on about for three years now. When she's at my house, she even tries giving summaries or wrap-ups on the latest chapter in the series. All I have to hear is word 'Freddie', or else 'Mr. Asshole', and I tune out. It makes no difference what they argue about—work, home, sex....."

"Yeah, I know," she said. "His parents, her parents, the kids...."

"What kids?"

"The ones I hope they never have."

"That's probably why they're not married yet. Not being knocked up is always a great deterrent to wedding chimes. Anyhow, it's all the same. They argue about the time of day. They even argue about how much they argue."

"I can't really tell, but it seems like it's getting worse, isn't it?"

"Yeah it is. This is the first time I've seen either one of them raise a hand to the other."

"Isn't there anything you can do, Clem?"

"Like what? I told you earlier, she's not my kid. What the hell can I do?"

"What do you mean you told me earlier? When did we have a conversation about Samantha?"

"Just today. This morning. You were saying...."

"I was still in New York this morning. What are you talking about?"

"Hmmm. I must be wrong." Of course he was wrong. But the voice was so real. Over the years, since he'd first heard her voice, it had become, and Gerry had remained, so much a part of his life. A person he hung out with day after day. "I'm talking about the conversation you and I had this morning when I was working up in the woods, up on The Throne."

Gerry lowered her beer bottle, stood away from the truck side and stepped backwards away from him. She stared at him, narrowing her eyes. "What....? What the hell's wrong with you?"

The little person who ran around inside his gut causing him all the acid reflux and stabs of anxiety was pushing his call button, demanding attention. He should have stopped himself, should not have run off the mouth about their conversation. He'd come to think of their conversations as some kind of telepathetic communication. He'd told himself that, of course, she knew about them. But the little man inside was telling him to shut up. Of course, she did not know about the conversations. Because they were not real, telepathy or not, they were not real. And the little man down inside knew it, had always known it. Yeah, maybe what Scheutz had been doing was a little crazy, but that little man saved him from being truly nutso. "You remember me telling you that I had conversations with you in my head? Don't you remember that?"

"Yeah. Last Christmas, wasn't it? Riding back from the train station? I thought it was kind of cute. You know, a way of thinking about me. I was flattered."

"You didn't sound flattered."

"Well, I was. I just didn't want to let you know it."

"Why not?"

She looked away and then back to him. "Clem." She looked down. "This is hard to say." Now she looked straight at him. "...the only way I can hold myself away from you... is to hold myself away from you. If I ever soften up toward you it'll make my life miserable."

"That doesn't make any sense."

"From over here it does. But that's beside the point. When you told me you had conversations with me in your head, you didn't tell me. I don't. You do know, don't you, that whatever goes on there has nothing to do with me."

"Yeah, I know. I know you don't send me these telepathic messages, talk to me while I'm working. But...."

She set her beer bottle on the side of the truck. "But, maybe you should come down out of the woods. Have you told anyone else about this?"

"Samantha. She says you talk to her, too."

"Oh, my God. And you and Samantha alone in that house together. All these years I should have been worrying about my children being in there. You didn't tell them about this, did you?"

"No. And I don't believe what Samantha says about it. I think she means it in a figurative way."

"But yours is literal? Yours is real?"

"I'd like to think so."

"You're getting weird on me, Clem. This is so fucked up. I don't know whether to be frightened or angry. You could just make up any old goddamned thing and tell yourself I said it. You could go around shooting John Lennon or people like that and tell the police I told you to do it."

"Better you than Jesus."

"What?"

"I'm joking, I'm joking. Come on, you know I wouldn't do that. The only things you tell me are good things, like, you know...like how to figure out some problem with the kids, or how to act with other people. The same sort of things you told me when we were together."

"But still...I mean.... You have to admit....Find somebody else to help you with that shit. What about your girl friend, what's her name?, Nanda?"

"Are you kidding? She's nuttier than I am."

Gerry shook her head. "I knew there was a good reason I got out of that house. Drive anybody nuts. Those long winter nights when it gets dark at four-thirty and the wind comes up over the hayfield and whistles like the ghost of that old woman we thought we saw on the second floor landing the first year we lived there. Remember her?"

"No."

"You ought to get out of here, Clem. Now that the kids'll both be gone. You could sell this place, give me my half, and buy a nice place where it's warm and sunny all year."

"You mean like retire to Florida. I'm only forty."

"I know how old you are. You've still got half your life to live. You want to sit up here and make yourself actually crazy?"

"See? If I had you around all the time giving me advice, I wouldn't need to have you in my head."

"I think we should join the party." She walked away from him.

The abruptness of her walking away was like a microcosm of what she had done years ago, moving to New York, leaving him with the same hole in the air next to him. You'd think that after all this time, that hole would have closed up. But it was just as strong as it always was. The only difference was that now it irritated him. No, not irritated, it pissed him off. *Where does she get the right to do that?* He listened for her voice to give him an answer.

Silence. Just as he had suspected. Gerry's voice didn't answer him when he was angry. Just as Gerry herself would never respond to him whenever he showed the least bit angry at something she did. And, even now, he wished he could say he didn't care, but he did care. And it did not look like that was about to change. For the voice maybe, but not for her.

The group of young people still formed a circle around the Samantha and Freddie show. The music had started up again. This one, at least, he recognized. Neil Young and something about rust. Freddie and Samantha had been separated, like boxers, each in a neutral corner, surrounded by their handlers. When she saw Scheutz reach the edge of the crowd, Samantha broke through the throng of people and ran to him, putting her face in her hands and her hands against his chest. Her thin body shook with spasms of sobs and she leaned against him. He froze, looking around at all the faces of the crowd watching them. Awkwardly, he raised his hands and placed them on her shoulders, not sure whether to push her away or comfort her.

Freddie broke away from where Dan and a few others had gathered around him. With a swiftness that belied his drunken state, he stopped behind Samantha, reaching out to grab her hair and pulling her head back away from Scheutz's chest. Scheutz reached around, grabbing Freddie's throat with one hand, squeezing his windpipe. Freddie let go of Samantha's hair and swung drunkenly at Scheutz who blocked his fist with ease. Freddie began swinging wildly with both hands, the blows falling harmlessly on Scheutz's shoulders and head, until he finally stopped, his body sagging from lack of air, his eyes rolling back in his head. Scheutz had to tell himself to let go of the throat, and still he did not, until Dan stepped up to grab hold of his arm.

"Dad," Dan said, looking into his eyes. Scheutz let go his grip. Dan, holding on to his friend, Freddie, to keep him from falling, never taking his eyes away from Scheutz's, tilted his head slightly to the side and gave him a look that said, "I understand how it is, but you can't do this." He led Freddie away, back to their group that now moved toward Freddie's car parked out on the highway.

A hoarse drunken laugh rose from Uppermann who had a ringside seat at the front of the opening in the crowd around the little scene. Scheutz found it somewhat disgusting that he had given himself up to something that Uppermann found to be so amusing. He looked around trying to find Freddie's father, hoping that the old man had not seen what just took place. He saw him walking toward his truck. There was no telling if Brockton had seen it or not.

Scheutz turned to look at Samantha who seemed frozen in place, her eyes wide with amazement. She watched Freddie being led away and then turned back to Scheutz, a look of both relief and fear on her face. "Thank you," she said, not sounding a bit like Gerry. She bent her head, and when she raised it, her eyes glistened with tears. She glowered out from under her eyebrows, looking first at him, then over at Freddie's car, and then to the lawn where her parents stood talking with a group of people. Coming back to Scheutz, she said in a barely audible voice, "God, I wish you'd take me away from this place."

"Why? Aren't you going to the party at your house?"

"That's not what I mean." She reached behind her head and rubbed her scalp with both hands, grimacing. Tears came to her eyes as she looked up at him. "That's not what I mean at all."

Over near the buffet table, Gerry gazed at the two of them standing there together. She caught his eye, shook her head and gave a snorting little laugh. He raised his eyebrows at her and shrugged. What choice did he have but to comfort this confused child who had climbed into his world without him wanting her there. Watching them, Gerry's eyes narrowed and, if he didn't know better, he'd think she was jealous. She pointed her two index fingers at him and Samantha and then, raising both fingers to point to her temples, she made the twirling motion that meant they were both nuts.

Chapter 24

After Forty Summers

"What are you doing making faces at me?"

"I wasn't making faces at you," Gerry said. She took a bite of cherry tart, holding it delicately to keep it from crumbling in her hand. The tarts were meant to be eaten with a fork, sitting at a table. Gerry held the napkin with the tart close to her mouth and picked at the pieces with her fingers.

"Well, what do you call that little gesture with your fingers, implying that Samantha and I are both crazy?"

"That's not making faces. That's giving you fingers."

"You know what I mean."

"I do." She sucked up the last of the tart. "And I apologize." She grinned at him as she wiped her mouth with the napkin. "Goodness, what would people think? An estranged couple not being polite to each other."

"I think you're jealous."

She spread her hands. "Of…?"

"Of Samantha."

"Spppt." The laugh exploded from her mouth sending tart crumbs onto his shirt. "Ooops." She swiped a crumb off the front of his shirt, leaving a tiny red cherry stain. "Don't do that to me, Clem. I'm supposed to be maintaining some dignity here as a visiting mom from the big city."

"Well, think about it. I mean, here she is, young, pretty, obviously enamored of such a cool guy as myself…."

"You're so cute when you're being an idiot."

"I'm not being an idiot. You forget, I know you better than anybody else in the world does."

"Uh. Huh. But what you don't know is the extent to which you're capable of kidding yourself in the service of your own ego."

"Mom?" Marty appeared at Scheutz's elbow, with Regina next to him.

"Yes, my son."

"You're staying overnight, right?"

Gerry nodded.

"So, we'll see you tomorrow. We're heading out to the party."

"I thought this was the party."

Marty shook his head. "This is the old people party. The real party's at Joe's house."

"Oh? As in Samantha and Joe's house?"

"Yeah. You remember when Dan graduated, we had the party in our barn?"

"Well, don't I get to go?" Gerry said.

"Mom. Did you go to the party when Dan graduated?"

"No, it was all kids."

"Well? Duh? Same thing here."

"That time I sat up half the night talking with your father." Gerry flicked a thumb in Scheutz's direction and made a face.

"What's so bad about sitting up talking to me?" Scheutz asked.

"I don't want to do that again. Besides, I've brought a date with me."

"You have a date with you?" Scheutz looked around.

"Mom, look. This party is still all kids. You wouldn't like it."

Gerry crossed her arms and studied Marty's face. "Are Dan and Samantha and all those people going to the 'kid's' party?'"

"Yeah?"

"There not kids."

"Well, they're not old…." The look on Gerry's face stopped him. "I mean…you know…they're not our parents."

Gerry turned to look at Scheutz. Scheutz smiled at her. "I'm sorry you had to learn the truth in this way. But, what Marty says is true. You are considered a parent. And as a parent, you must bear the same burden of discrimination that your own parents had to deal with."

"That's not funny," Gerry said and turned to Marty. "So, you're saying I'm not wanted. What goes on at those parties? You kids all have sex, drugs and rock and roll orgies in the barn?"

Regina laughed. Marty put his hands on his mother's forearms. "No. Mom. Please. Stop acting like a mom. The party is no different than this one. Well, maybe a little different. But, it's just a bunch of kids hanging out. You know? With other kids."

Gerry shrugged. "Okay. I just can't believe Jerome and I have to spend a Friday night out here in the boondocks listening to the crickets just because you and your friends don't like to have a parent around."

"Jerome?" Scheutz asked. "Who's Jerome?"

Marty pointed. "See the guy standing over there talking to Dan and Livia?"

"That's your date?" Scheutz looked at Gerry. "You do mean that kid with the orange tank-top and the big hair?" he said to Marty. Marty nodded. Scheutz grunted "I assumed he was a friend of Dan's from New York."

"He is. Sort of." Gerry said.

"You're old enough to be his mother. Well, at least you don't give me much to be jealous of." Scheutz grinned at her.

She gave him one of wihering looks.

"Uh, listen, guys," Marty said. "We gotta go. So, we'll see you tomorrow, Mom. 'Night, Daddy-O. Don't wait up for me again."

"Congratulations, Marty." Scheutz put his arms around his tall son. "Don't worry. As of tonight, I'm officially retired as your keeper. Just be careful in that damned car of yours, though."

Marty put his arm around Scheutz's neck and squeezed, turning Scheutz away from the others. In a low voice, he said, "Don't be so tough on Mom, all right? She's having a hard time with all this."

"How can you tell?"

"Trust me."

"Bye, Mrs. Scheutz," Regina said. She pinched Scheutz's elbow. "See you."

"Goodnight, Regina. Congratulations to you, too. You were the prettiest one up on that stage."

Scheutz watched them thread their way through the crowd back to where Dan and the others stood. And then he could not take his eyes off the kid, Jerome. He couldn't be any older than Dan. He had various colors of paint spatters on his jeans and he wore rubber flip-flops on his feet.

He could feel himself getting angry. At who? The smile on Gerry's face changed to one of mild alarm as she looked at him. The anger must have registered on his own face. He turned away from her, back toward the group that included their sons, and then away from them, dropping his head to stare at the ground.

"So everyone's going off to the party." The beatnik-looking kid, Jerome, stood in front of him, talking to Gerry.

"I'm not allowed to go, apparently," Gerry said, tilting her head and raising her eyebrows. "I've been informed that I am a restricting influence on my children's last fling at adolescence."

"Oh. Well, that sucks." He looked around as if searching the crowd for an answer to his new dilemma. "We come all the way up here so you can visit with your family and they tell you that they don't want you around?"

"It's not that. I know how they feel. It's okay."

"No, it's not okay. What the hell are we supposed to do for a whole night out here in the great north woods?"

"When this party breaks up, you could come home to my house," Scheutz said. "We could have a really groovy time sipping hot chocolate and listening to some golden oldie albums."

Jerome looked at him and then turned to Gerry. "This is the father?"

"Oh, yes," Gerry said. "I should have introduced you. This is Clem, my ex…husband, or Dan and Marty's father. Clem, this is Jerome, my…my…." She rotated her hands in front of her. "What would you say our relationship was?"

"I'm your…um. I can't think of a word for it," Jerome said.

"How about…twit? Does that word hold any meaning for you?" Scheutz asked.

"Hah." Gerry let out a barking laugh, and then, immediately laid a hand on Jerome's arm. "I'm sorry, I didn't mean to laugh, Jerome." And stifled another exhalation.

Jerome's glare met Scheutz's eyes. Without losing the glare, his eyes then slide sideways to Gerry's.

"Well, you have to admit," Gerry said. "You were being just a little childish there."

Jerome looked away and then back. "You know…I think I will go to the party. I'm obviously in the wrong generation here. You're staying here at your friend Georgina's house?"

Gerry nodded. "I said I'm sorry, Jerome. Stay here with me. Come on, don't' be like that."

"No, you stay here and have a 'groovy' time with your ex-whatever the word for him is." He turned away and walked back to where Dan and Marty and their friends were moving toward the cars parked along the roadway.

"It was nice meeting you," Scheutz called after him.

"Oh, God, what have I done?" Gerry covered her face in her hands. "Clem, you can be so crude sometimes."

"I'm crude? 'Is this the father?' Fuck him."

"I know. You're right. He is a twit sometimes. But he can be awful sweet at other times. He's nervous at being around you."

"Where'd you find him? He looks like some kind of bum."

"A very rich bum. At least his family is rich."

"As rich as your friend Buttwad? Whatever happened to him?"

She gave a little wave of her hand. "I haven't seen him in years. I have no idea what kind of money Jerome's family has. I know they pay for a very nice loft in Soho for him."

"He's an artist type?"

"One of the hottest up and coming painters in the New York art scene."

"Whoopie."

"Don't be a twit."

They smiled at each other. "So, is this serious, between you and him? I mean, he's so young."

"I don't know. I love his art. I love his creative mind. I've bought a couple of his pieces. He says I inspire him. You know, all that trite old crap about being a muse, or whatever."

They both watched the various cars belonging to the young people pulling away from the edge of the road. Freddie's truck had already left and Samantha climbed into the van with Dan and Livia. More than half of the cars and pick up trucks moved away from the party, their tail lights blinking as they formed a convoy. "But he is a kid. And a spoiled one at that. He can be a real pain in the ass. But I love his art."

She threw her hand out, palm up. "I thought he would change his mind and come back, but there goes his car." She walked to the galvanized tub, bent and plucked out a can of beer, then came back to where Scheutz stood. He handed her a napkin that she wrapped around the wet can. Then she pulled the tab and drank. "So I guess I'm stuck here at this wonderful party."

"You want to dance?"

"With you? Are you kidding? You're the worst dancer I've ever met, and I'm sure you haven't improved with age. No, I just want to get out of here."

"Want to go to my house?"

"What, and listen to you talk to the voice—my voice—in your head?"

He stopped himself from replying. What could he say? He could feel the anger rising again. Was it her he was angry at? Or was it the voice in his head? He waited for the voice to tell him. It didn't. He had forgotten that the voice didn't come when he was angry. Gerry sipped her beer, waiting for him to say something.

"You're a little scary, you know that?" she said. "Hearing voices the way you do."

"It's your voice, how could it be scary? Believe me, it is completely benign. It's only there to help."

"That doesn't make it any less scary. It feels icky, like some kind of invasion. Like you're stealing something from me."

"I'll stop. I mean I'll make it stop."

She took another drink of beer. "Just like that?"

He nodded. "I did something like that in Mexico, didn't I? Remember how frightened you were when we met on Isla Mujeres? So, I made myself change."

"That's right, I forgot about that. It took you a few days, but you did it, didn't you? I still remember feeling so…what?…so frightened, anxious, just being around you. For days. But then later, after we found my father, you totally changed. And it was okay. I was so impressed. You did that for me."

"And Dan."

"And Dan.

Chapter 25

Hope and Fear

He could see the Mexican's face with his huge teeth, explaining that the current in the Yucatan Channel was so strong he had to keep pointing the bow south in order to make land at Isla Mujeres. The small fishing boat churned all day and then still as the sun dropped over their starboard bow. The only light was the glow from the compass. During daylight, there was nothing to see but the expanse of water, so Scheutz wasn't missing much by not being able to see at night. And he was thankful to finally be out of the torturous hot sun.

He stretched out full length on the deck hoping to sleep. But it would not come. The boat pitched and rolled and an occasional wave hit them on the port side, big enough to send spray over the little open cabin. He was bone tired, but every time he started to drop off to sleep he saw his brother's face, screaming as the bullets from the guns of the Cuban soldiers ripped into him. Each time he awoke he looked at the position of the stars to see if an appreciable amount of time had gone by. But the stars never seemed to move. Once again he experienced the sense of being cut off from everything in the world, floating in a black hole somewhere. Just him and his brother, Willi. With Willi screaming.

The Mexican piloting the boat was no help. He had put out a plate of food, frijoles, rice, and bits of tasteless fried fish. The two of them occupied the same cabin but they might as well have been in different boats on different seas. Scheutz tried again to remember the guy's name. Angel; that was it. What a joke. This was no angel. Lerma was his last name. He had slapped the plate on the floor next to where Scheutz lay as if he were feeding his dog. But, as hungry as Scheutz was, he could not eat. Maybe the fish did have a flavor, but he could not taste it. The thought of eating turned his stomach. Maybe he was just seasick, but every time he went for a bite, his brother's face stopped him just as it did his sleeping.

At some point, though, he must have slept because when he startled awake, it was daylight and the boat had stopped its heavy pitch and roll. Lerma slouched on his seat at the helm, his mouth, normally resembling a large-toothed grin, now sagged with weariness. When he saw Scheutz sit up, he pointed to the land off the port bow and said, "Isla Mujeres." They must have been heading due west because the sun seemed to be rising off the stern. The boat passed through a narrow strait with a small island to starboard and a sandy beach to port. Out of the main current, the water still pushed them along. A long coast line beyond the strait must have been main land of Mexico.

He pulled himself up off the deck and almost fell from dizziness. His head ached. His whole body ached. His eye sockets ached. The pain in his head ran down the nape of his neck to the middle of his spine. His mouth burned from thirst and he had to piss. Whatever sleep he had gotten had not helped. God, he was glad that night was over. At least Willi's screaming had stopped. He drank from Lerma's water flask and then pissed off the stern.

Once out of the strait, the boat veered to port and ran along the beach, then turned to port again, heading south in the calm waters of bay. They were close enough to make out sandy beaches, vegetation and a few houses. The northwestern side of the island looked to have a small town. Thank God. All Scheutz could think of was getting off that boat.

As they pulled into the wooden dock that extended out into the water, a sudden panic gripped him. This place looked just like Cuba—same kind of fishing boats, same kind of palm trees and bohios, and small tiendas facing the water. "Eso no es Cuba, verdad?" he shouted at Lerma.

"No, no, senor. Esta es Mejico. Yucatan"

Scheutz scanned the shoreline for any sign of a uniform. Unless they were all hiding, the place looked peaceful enough. What few people were about seemed to be involved in nothing more than getting fishing boats into the water. Despite the island's name there were no women to be seen. On being told back in Cuba that they were going to the "Island of the Women" Scheutz had pictured something entirely different than what he now saw. Women meant peace, safety. Finally, he saw a woman, carrying a large bag and leaving one of the tiendas, a small store at the left of the village.

Lerma motioned for him to hop onto the dock with a line and tie the boat off to one of the wooden posts that rose above the dock itself. The movement hurt his body and reminded him again of how weary he was. Now the Mexican waved him off, shooing him away from the boat. He obviously wanted as few people as possible to associate him with the bearded Yanqui that had suddenly appeared in the town. There was nothing on the boat that Scheutz wanted. The only things he and Willi and Pilar had carried into the town of La Bajada back in Cuba were the guns, and those he had swapped with the Mexican for the trip across the channel. He gave the Mexican a tired wave and walked away down the dock.

So, here he was, in the middle of nowhere, on an island containing nothing more than what looked like a fishing village.

From the looks of two of the boats tied to the end of the dock, as well as Lerma's boat, there had to be occasional gringos coming here for deep sea fishing excursions. And Lerma had told him that there was a daily ferry back and forth from Puerto Juarez on the mainland. He walked to the end of the dock and then across a few yards of sand till he reached the shade of an awning in front of a tienda that had not yet opened for the day. The sun was not too high yet, but he was already burnt and had no hat.

Sitting against the building, he could focus on nothing more than how hungry he was, how tired he was, how plagued his mind was. How rotted his soul was. He might as well have died back there in Cuba with Willi and Pilar, that poor guajira. Maybe he would die too. Right here in this speck of earth in the Caribbean. It took too much effort to remain alive. To even sit up. He lay down against the wall.

But he wasn't dying. His mind had started racing again, blocking out the memory of what had happened the day before. Was that how long it had been? It seemed such a long time ago. But his mind raced on. When you're twenty years old, your body does not let you die, soul or no soul. So, how could he keep himself alive? He had nothing but his clothes, a t-shirt, army field pants, combat boots. And his knife in the sheath on his belt.

He had asked Gerry to meet him on Isla Mujeres. When was that? Just two days ago, when he had phoned her long distance from that cantina in la Bajada. She didn't exactly say yes, but she didn't say no, either. Maybe he could phone her again. Collect, like the last time. But it was doubtful this island even had a telephone. And he could not leave here; what if she did show up? He'd miss her and never find her again.

He could see down the dock to where Lerma was in the process of leaving with his boat. Maybe he should go back there and ask the man for the food he'd not been able to eat the night before. But just the thought of getting up off the ground and walking over there felt like it would take more energy than he had.

He must have fallen asleep again. The sun opened his eyes. It had moved to where he was no longer in shade. And two mosquitoes feasted on different parts of his flesh. He pulled himself to a sitting position and then crawled around to the front of the building to a narrow strip of shade. The town had come awake. People moved about. Cooking smells mingled with the salt smell of the ocean and the putrid odor of dead fish. He had to get up. He had to move, to do something for himself. If Gerry was coming, he had to keep himself alive until then.

He waited for her for three days. It was toward evening of the first day that he discovered that the people on the island spoke no Spanish, but some Indian language that sounded like it had no vowels, only glotal consonants. On the second day, with hand gestures, he sold his knife to a fisherman for a small percent of its actual value, but enough to buy himself a little food. He found the remains of a straw hat and spent two hours weaving palm fronds into it to rebuild its original structure. The next day he traded his boots. US Army combat boots were not much use to people in this climate, so they did not go for much. But he ate for two days. On the afternoon of the fourth day, when the ferry docked, bringing workers back home from Puerto Juarez, he saw her.

He had been scanning this boat, with its rusting hull and benches for passengers, every time it came in for three days now. A dozen passengers filed off, and a small blond boy that looked like Dan jumped off onto the wooden planking of the dock. And then there was Gerry, stepping off immediately behind him, grabbing for his hand. She carried a small suitcase in the other hand. Once she had the boy in tow she stood a moment, looking toward the town, as if unsure what to do next. Even the boy stopped his wriggling and quietly looked around him. A breeze off the water lightly flicked the hem of the simple aqua and pink frock she wore, her skin pale in the tropic sun, her dark hair pulled back and fastened behind her head. Dan had on blue short pants and a polo shirt. Both wore what looked like newly purchased huaraches on their feet.

From his spot in the shade of a store awning, Scheutz found himself merely taking them in with no reaction to what he was seeing. What was wrong with him? He was being presented with a sight he had longed for, the only salvation he could ever imagine for himself, and he stood there like an ox stunned with a pole ax. He had been imaging himself for days, seeing her at last and falling on his knees in some Biblical rapture, like Saul falling off his horse in epileptic awe. But nothing. He felt nothing. He might have been watching two shore birds alight upon the sand.

He was amazed at how young she looked. Even younger than twenty-one. A year older than himself, he had for some reason always thought of her as being much older than himself, more experienced, more knowledgeable about what went on in the world. But now, in this strange land, her face had taken on the demeanor of young girl, fearful, a little stunned even. Here eyes darted to the left and right and she pulled Dan in close beside her. She took a deep breath and, with a slight squaring of her shoulders, began a slow march toward the end of the dock.

Once on the land she stopped and looked around again. Her gaze passed over Scheutz but did not linger on him. Dan pulled himself from her grasp and headed across the sand, running in a zigzag pattern between the few fishing boats pulled up there. Gerry let out what sounded like an inadvertent little yelp and ran to take his hand again, afraid to let him loose in such a foreign place. The other people from the ferry had all made their way to the small town and disbursed. Three men stood outside a small cantina two doors down. Gerry directed herself toward them, but needed to pass within a few arm's length of where Scheutz stood against the wall.

"Gerry." He called to her from out of the flatness of his dead soul. She stopped and turned toward him, startled, her eyes wide with fear as she took in his bearded face under the half new-half old straw hat.

"Clem?"

"Gerry…." He groped, looking for something else to say. But nothing came. He could say, "I knew you'd come" but he hadn't known. Not until she stepped off that boat. He wanted to say, "I'm so happy to see you" but he didn't feel happy. He didn't feel anything.

Her face changed from curious to surprise, and then to fear. Dan's face didn't get beyond curious. He stood stock still, holding his mother's hand, and peered up at Scheutz. The sun, beginning to fall behind them, lengthened their shadows till Gerry's almost reached his own foot. The sea beyond the dock and the resting boats lay in a dead calm. Even the usual flock of shore birds visited elsewhere. Nothing moved. The fear froze on Gerry's face.

"I'm not doing very well," he finally offered. He could not blame her for being frightened of him. For the last three days, the people in this village had treated him as if he were a scourge God had dropped into their midst as a punishment for whatever sins they thought they were committing. The look on Gerry's face was not a whole lot different than the one he'd seen on the woman two days earlier who'd sold him the food he'd bought with the money from selling his knife. She had stretched her hand with the food parcel so as not to touch him or get too close. He had not seen his own reflection for longer than he could remember, but he was pretty sure that it would also show that stunned, wide-eyed look of fear.

"My God, what's happened to you?" She spoke at last.

He could only shake his head. What had happened to him? He could tell her the story of what had happened since he'd seen her last, the trip to Cuba, the mercenary project on the north shore, the flight across the island, his brother dying, but that was not what she asked. She asked what had happened to him, and he did not know himself. Whatever it was, it had left him stone dead.

Dan, apparently reaching the limit of interest in the apparition before him, turned his curiosity to whatever else might lie in new strange land. He pulled away from Gerry's hand and walked toward the cantina, his head tilted back, taking in everything he could. Gerry moved to grab him, but then decided to let him go and turn her attention back to Scheutz, keeping the boy in the corner of her eye. "I have to tell you, Clem, this is not what I was hoping to find down here."

"Can you help me?"

"Can I help you?" She shook her head, looked away toward Dan and then back. "I mean…I don't know…what's wrong with you?…I mean…I'll…yes, as far as I can help you. But, you're going to have to tell me what's wrong."

He opened his mouth, but nothing came out.

"Okay," she said. She went to get Dan and pull him back to where Scheutz stood. Then she looked around, taking in the town, the few people near the cantina, Scheutz again, his clothes, his bare feet. She sighed and bent her head in thought, finally exercising her little shoulder-squaring thing again. "Okay, let's start with the basics. Where can you get something to eat in the burg?"

And it was if someone had just broken through the wall of his crypt. A tiny light filtered in. Just maybe he could someday join the living. He felt his whole body relax its vigilance a smidgen, and felt he was seeing Gerry again for the first time. Damn. Now he knew why he loved that woman so much. He couldn't feel it right then, but at least he knew it was there. He motioned with his hand toward the cantina.

The bartender in the cantina spoke a very little Spanish and Gerry used what she remembered of her high school Spanish. She secured a table inside the cantina, ordered food, and made arrangements for them to spend a night in a room on the second floor of the building. The other patrons had all stopped talking when the three of them entered. Gerry, with difficulty, told the bartender that Scheutz was sick, but what he had was not contagious. Apparently, her obviously taking care of the weird gringo put the people at ease and they paid no more attention to them once they sat down. Scheutz's depressed appetite allowed him to only eat a few bites. Gerry was starved, she said, and ate everything on her own plate and everything he had left on his. Dan also did not eat much, but fiddled with his unfamiliar tasting food, and finally left the table to wander around talking at other patrons, not letting the fact that no one understood a word he said deter him in the least.

The rented room upstairs from the cantina was small, with a mosquito net over the one bed. Other than being also occupied by the ever-present tropical cucaraches, the room felt palatial compared to where Scheutz had been sleeping for the past few weeks. And no mosquitoes to bite him awake. Gerry carried a jar of water from kitchen below and wiped Dan's face, hands and feet. They put him on the bed and closed the mosquito net. The room, in the rear of the building so that it did not catch what breeze there was off the water, was stifling hot. Men singing in their alien tongue, with accompaniment of a few guitars, drifted up from the cantina below. Dan soon quit his fidgeting and dropped into a sound sleep.

Scheutz and Gerry each lay down under the mosquito net on either side of Dan. "You okay over there?" Gerry asked in the darkness.

"Yeah. Better."

"Better than what?"

"Better than I've been since I got on that plane in Cincinnati," she said. "It feels so good to finally lay down." She let out a long sigh. "This has been the longest day of my life."

"I still can't quite believe you're here."

"I can't believe I'm here either. I don't even know where here is. I thought this would be some fun adventure…the road to hell isn't paved with good intentions; it's paved with tropical heat, airplanes, and kids that can't sit still."

"Well, still…you have no idea what you're doing for me."

"I almost didn't come." She lay silent for a long time. He thought she had fallen asleep. "You should thank my mother for my being here at all."

"Really? I would've figured she'd see you dead first."

"Yeah, and that's what pushed me out of there. I told her what you said about my father."

"What did I say? I don't remember."

"You said that, if she had pushed him to come home, had really wanted him there, he probably would have come back. And I would have had a Dad."

"When did I say that? Back when we were in high school?"

"No. Just last week, when you called me from Cuba. You don't remember saying that?"

"Last week I would have said anything to get you down here. Are you sorry you came?"

"So far, yes. The trip was the worst thing I've been through in my life. And this is what I find at the end of it." Another long pause in the darkness. "You're very scary, Clem. I don't know how you got like this, and I don't really want to know. I can't bring myself to even touch you. It's like I don't know who you are."

"Don't leave me here, okay? I'm dead if you do."

"Let's see what happens in the morning. I'm so tired I can't think." She made rustling noises as she turned on her side and put her arm around Dan. "Are Dan and I okay here? I mean, do I have to worry about us being safe?"

"Yes, you are safe. I'd kill anyone who tried to harm you."

"That just scares me even more. Aside from the fact that you might have to kill someone, your willingness to do it means that I'm lying here, with my little boy, in a roach-filled room over a bar, in the same bed as a killer."

"No, that's not what I meant. I meant…you're fine. You're safe. Go to sleep. There is nothing to be afraid of from me. And this is a nice quiet little town. And with friendly people, as far I can tell."

She settled in and her breath deepened. He lay quiet for a while listening to the two of them breathing next to him. "I am really happy you came," he whispered in her direction. He did not know whether she heard him or not, but he did know, finally, that, yes, he was happy she came.

Chapter 26

The Long Journey Home

They awoke in the morning in barely enough time to catch the ferry to Puerto Juarez. If it had not been for Dan bouncing around, both Scheutz and Gerry would have slept on. Scheutz took Dan to the little outhouse behind the cantina and then waited for Gerry. He carried the boy as they rushed onto the dock and then onto the boat just as the crew were casting off lines. In the rush and a new breeze that came with the morning, his straw hat fell off and sailed out onto the water. Dan laughed and clapped to see it go.

"So where do we go from here?" he asked, once they had settled themselves on a bench under the boat's canopy.

"I'm hungry," Dan said.

"I know, honey." She kissed the top of his head. "We'll eat as soon as we get off this boat. Okay?"

Dan nodded and then reached up to touch Scheutz's beard. "You look funny."

"He talks a lot more now, doesn't he?" Scheutz said.

"Yeah. He's very smart. Aren't you, Mr. Wise-guy?" Dan smiled at her and then reached up to wiggle his fingers again in the hair under Scheutz's chin. Scheutz grinned at the boy. "You look a hell of a lot better this morning than you did yesterday," Gerry said to him. Her eyes had lost most of the fright he'd seen in them the night before.

"I feel a little better. That's the first night's sleep I've had in a long time." He could feel tears beginning behind his eyeballs and looked away. "I guess just having you two in the same room with me made a lot of difference."

She reached her hand to touch his shoulder but withdrew it and laid it on Dan's shoulder instead. "You're still pretty much of a mess, aren't you?"

He nodded, afraid that if he looked at her or spoke, he might burst into tears. He was a mess. And doubtful that he would never be anything but. He could not think about that now. What he needed to do was somehow to assure Gerry that she need not be afraid of him. Whatever happened from the time they got off this boat in Puerto Jaurez an hour from now would depend on her decision whether to stick with him. Maybe he was over-dramatizing it to himself but it felt like whatever happened to him for the rest of his life hung on Gerry's decision. If he could think of which switch to flip to tilt the decision in his favor, he would do it, but he had no idea what to do. "So where do we go from here?" he asked her again.

Gerry watched Dan as he climbed down off the bench and made his way among the other passengers to the prow of the boat. She shook her head. "I don't know, Clem. This is certainly not what I had imagined, coming down here."

"What had you imagined?"

"I don't know." She put her hand to her eyes that had filled with tears. "I don't know that I really imagined anything. I guess I had a fantasy of you and Dan and me rushing into each other's arms and promising each other that we would all have a long and happy life." She turned to look at him. "Well, I didn't imagine finding one of the Horsemen of the Apocalypse staring out at me. Jesus, you scared me"

"I'm sorry. I've been...."

"I don't want to hear about it. I'll bet it's gruesome." She sat silent, watching Dan, where he hung onto the railing and laughed as the sea water broke over the prow. "I remember what you told me back in Cincinnati about being a mercenary soldier in Cuba. You said you gave all that up. But you didn't, did you? You were going back in Cuba this time, too, right?" He nodded. "I don't want anything to do with that, Clem. Whatever happened to you over there, I can just imagine you doing worse to somebody else. I know that kind of shit goes on in this world, but I don't want to be around it."

"What if I promised you I would never, ever, have anything to do with that again?"

She looked at him for a long time and then looked away. "I'd have to think about that."

Fair enough. At least she was thinking about it. They both sat silently watching Dan up in the bow of the boat. Scheutz finally got up and went to sit next to the boy. Dan pointed at birds flying overhead and then at the water. "Fishies in there," he said. Scheutz repeated, "Yes, fishies in there." And pulled the boy onto his lap. They sat that way for a while until Dan couldn't stand it any longer and went to run up the aisle between the benches. Scheutz caught him and brought him back to sit with him on his lap next to Gerry.

"So, what did your mother have to say?" he asked her.

"What didn't she say? We had a hell of a fight." She shook her head in wonder. "I said a lot things I shouldn't have said. About her and my father. I doubt she'll ever forgive me."

"Did I set that off by saying what I did?"

"No. It's been coming for a long time. It was just a continuation of the fight we had when I left my husband. The only reason I gave in to her that time and agreed to go to counseling with him was to avoid this last argument. I should have gotten it over with then and saved us all a big hassle."

"Oh." The boat churned slowly along. Scheutz and Gerry fell into silence. And let the conversations in the strange Mayan language cushion them like packing material inside a carton, to keep them from mashing into each other like two pieces of delicate chinaware. In her own way, Gerry's mental state must be as precarious as his own. It took a ton of grit and daring for her get herself and Dan down here to meet him. Especially for a young girl who had never been anywhere else except Cincinnati. It obviously meant breaking with her mother, the only family she had. The break with her husband and that whole life she and Dan lived with him had happened before any consideration of running off to meet Scheutz. Still, it must have been hard to make the final decision to completely give up any chance of going back with him by running off like she did.

And even without all that, the journey from Cincinnati to Isla Mujeres must have been pure hell. She had related the trek over supper the night before, an entire day of flying to Atlanta, and then Miami, and then Mexico City, and then the little puddle-jumper plane to Merida on the Yucatan peninsula, and then the bus ride to Cancun, and then the ferry to Isla Mujeres. And all the while trying to—sometimes unsuccessfully—keep control of an over-active two-year-old. It rivaled his own and his brother's flight across the cordillera with the Cuban army chasing them.

So, here they were, both sent back to GO on the Monopoly board. And what did they have? A lot, actually, now that he thought about it. First of all, they had their son. That kid had enough life for all three of them. Gerry had left her husband to be with Scheutz because Dan was Scheutz's son. And also, as she had said back in Cincinnati, because she still loved Scheutz more than she could ever love her husband.

Dan had stopped in front of two middle-aged women sitting on the bench across from them. He pointed at what looked like a small parcel of food wrapped like a tamali one of the women was eating. He asked the woman something and pointed at the tamali.

The woman bent forward and held the tamali out for Dan to take a bite. With a mouthful of food, Dan made a face as if the food was something horrible. The two women laughed. "Dan, get over here," Gerry called to him. "Lo siento," she said to the two women. The woman with the tamali laughed again, showing her stained teeth, and gave Gerry a friendly wave. Dan turned and ran to where Gerry sat.

Scheutz grabbed the boy and pulled him up to his lap. "Why don't you sit here with us a few minutes?" he murmured into Dan's ear. Dan sat back, leaning against his chest, still chewing the tamali, and looking around as if the world had just too many things for him to take in in one lifetime. The pressure of the little body against his chest felt to Scheutz once again, by some strange osmosis, like he was sucking life back into his own body. As the life returned, so did the feeling. He tried to stop the tears that came to his eyes, but he could not. Dan turned and looked up at his face, watched his tears for a moment and then turned to his mother with a look of amazement. Gerry picked Dan up and moved the boy to her own lap. She put her arm around Scheutz's shoulder and said, "It's going to be okay."

All that did was cause the tears to flow in greater abundance. He could not stop now if he tried. He lowered his head and put his hand to his forehead in a vain attempt to hide his face from the other passengers who all watched him in silence.

"Did you fall down?" Dan asked.

Scheutz nodded his head. "Yeah. I fell down."

"Hurt his knee?" Dan asked Gerry.

"Yes, honey, he hurt his knee. But, he's a big boy, he'll be all right."

"Yeah. I'm a big boy," Scheutz said, barely able to fit the words in between the tears.

"Big Daddy," Dan said.

And Scheutz had to laugh. Rather than stop the tears, the laugh just made it worse. Just the presence of the boy, sitting there on Gerry's lap was almost more than he could stand. He was still trying to take in the fact that Gerry had actually gone to the extraordinary lengths of coming down there for him, and on top of that to have the boy, his own son, there with him also was almost overwhelming. He had for as long as he could remember taken comfort in emptiness. The dark spaces between the stars at night had been a source of strength. But Gerry's arm around his shoulder and this little ball of life sitting on her lap threatened the whole underpinning of his life up to that point.

From Puerto Juarez, they caught the bus, a crowded old school bus, the same overloaded bus Gerry and Dan had ridden from Merida on a highway still in the middle of construction. They traveled west on the road being cut through thick forest. After many delays, they reached the town of Valladolid, about half way across the peninsula, where during an hour long delay, Gerry bought new clothes, white cotton pants and a loose-fitting shirt. On the bus again, he fell asleep with head on Gerry's shoulder.

And he awoke screaming. He and Willi were setting off the explosive that blew up the sugar refinery in Mercedita. Black silhouettes of people ran frantically through the flames and then Willi himself joined them, pulling away from Scheutz's grasp and grinning his big wonderful, toothy grin as he hurled himself into the inferno. Scheutz fought his way to an upright sitting position to see the horrified looks on the faces of the people around him. Gerry had hold of his neck, restraining him from jumping up from the bus seat.

"Clem. Clem. Stop. It's okay. It's okay." She struggled to keep the horror out of her own voice. She squeezed his neck and pulled him toward herself. He looked into her eyes but had to look away. "You scared the shit out of me," she said quietly.

The Indians on the bus all looked away, but he could see them casting furtive little glances in his direction, just in case he went off again. Dan stared at him from Gerry's lap, his eyes wide, not knowing whether to be afraid or whether to laugh at his silly Big Daddy.

"You okay?" Gerry asked.

He hugged himself and nodded, afraid to look at her, keeping his eyes on the floor of the bus.

"You're going to have to get hold of yourself, Clem. You're really scaring us."

"I'm sorry. I don't exactly have nightmares on purpose to bother you."

In Merida, they were able to catch a flight to Mexico City.

Chapter 27

We Go Together

He fell asleep again during the hour-long flight to Mexico City in the plane that reminded him of an old C-47, the kind they used for parachute jumping on special missions in the army. He awoke as it bounced, landing at Aeropuerto Benito Juarez. When they descended the mobile stairway to the tarmac, Dan took off running. He'd been cramped too long. Scheutz ran after him. He caught him, but the run left him out of breath. Gerry touched his shoulder from behind and laughed. He shrugged off her hand.

"I guess I'm not used to running like this," he said.

"You're at about a mile and a half above sea level, you dope. Maybe that's why."

"Don't call me a dope. How the hell was I supposed to know that?"

"My, aren't we testy? You finally wake up after two days and right away you want to pick a fight."

"Sorry." She was right. It almost felt like whatever life that seemed to seep back into him since they'd met—when was it, yesterday, the day before?—just left him pissed off. At nothing and everything. Dan's running away from them, his own difficulty breathing, even her hand on his shoulder zapped him like a cattle prod. He turned away from her to watch an American Airlines flight reversing its engines as it touched down on a runway beyond the one they had just landed on. "I feel like I could sleep for another two days," he said to her.

"Well…" She took Dan's hand. "Listen," she said. "It's decision time. I have to figure out where I'm going from here."

"You mean we have to figure out where we are going from here."

"Well that too. That's the first thing to figure out." With Dan in tow, she began walking toward airport buildings at the side of the tarmac.

Scheutz fell in next to Dan and took his other hand. They passed through a shaded veranda where a breeze cooled the air and then into the terminal itself, cooler still. Almost too cool for Scheutz. Crowds of people moved back and forth, most of them Mexicans, but a few obvious foreigners, and a very few in indigenous Indian garb. They passed ticket counters for British Airways and Lufthansa to what looked to be a small cafeteria.

Scheutz sat with Dan and Gerry's bag while she went to the cafeteria line to get food for them. At the next table, facing them, a heavy-set man, obviously American, somewhere in his mid-forties, in a gray suit too warm for the climate, looked up from his lunch of tortillas and coffee, and nodded at Scheutz. "How ya doin', little fella?" he said to Dan around a mouthful of food. Dan giggled and said back, "How a doin', lifalla?" The man guffawed. "Damned cute little kid you got there, partner."

"He is, isn't he?"

"What's your name, boy?" He leaned his face in toward Dan.

Dan looked up at Scheutz and then at the man. "Dan," he said. Then he pointed at Scheutz and said, "Big Daddy."

The man laughed again. "What line are you in, Big Daddy?"

Scheutz shook his head. "I'm kind of between the lines right now. I just got in from Cuba. Did some work on a sugar refinery there."

"Construction?"

"More like deconstruction."

"Did some work in Cuba myself a couple of years ago. We were investing in a copper mine there."

"You're a miner?"

The man laughed. "No, no. I'm business man." He put down his coffee cup and reached into his pocket, bringing out a business card. Scheutz stood and leaned over to take the card. It read Latitude Mining Corporation, with the name Daniel Thompson, Vice President of Acquisition and Exploration. He went to hand the card back but the man waved his hand for Scheutz to keep it. "I'm just down here looking at a mine in Chihuahua we're thinking about sinking some money into, excuse the pun."

Gerry set down a tray loaded with food on the end of the table. She handed a Coke to Dan. "This is my wife," Scheutz said to the man named Thompson.

"Your wife?" Gerry said. She then turned to Thompson and said, "How do you do?"

"I was just admiring your little boy there. I've got two of my own. But I don't get to see them much, with all the traveling around I do."

Gerry nodded and continued setting plates from the tray onto the table. "He's in the mining business," Scheutz said and showed her the card.

"Oh, really." She brightened, looking at the card. "Do you happen to know a geologist named Gerald Rieker?"

"Rieker? No, I can't say as I do. Does he work in Mexico?"

"Yes. He has for years. He's my father."

"No kidding? What a small world, huh? So, we're both in the same business, so to speak. Where does he work?"

"I think in a place called Guerrero."

"Taxco?"

"Yes. How did you know?"

"Oh, I know 'em all. Your father must be in the silver end of the business if he's in Taxco."

"I'm surprised you've never heard of Gerald Rieker."

Thompson shrugged. "Sorry. Uh...wait a minute. I think I do remember a name something like that. And I think, yes, Taxco. Connected with that Spratling fellow."

Scheutz had finished eating and walked across the terminal with Dan to buy three Dixie cups of ice cream. By the time they returned to the table, Thompson was gone. His flight had been announced, Gerry said. She sat quietly, eating her ice cream with the little wooden spoon. Dan finished half of his and Scheutz ate the other half after his own.

"You know, I told you the other reason I wanted to come down here besides meeting you, was to find my father."

"I know. You think he might still be in Taxco?"

"His last two Christmas cards came from Taxco."

"Where's that?"

"Apparently, it's in Guerrero."

"Well, let's go. How we fixed for money?"

"Not so fast. Are we going to do this together?"

He paused, gazing at her. "You came all the way down here to get me. You can't leave me."

"It depends on you, Clem. I've got a lot going on here, you know. Just for openers, I've spent my whole life in Cincinnati. Mexico gives me the creeps. I can't make any sense of it. Flying down here was the first time I've ever been on an airplane. That alone scared the hell out of me."

"You didn't seem to mind the flight from Merida to here."

"You have no idea...And Dan is a handful."

"Well, I've certainly been trying to help out with Dan. You have to give me that."

"No, you're right. As screwed up as you seem to be, I have to admit, you are good with Dan."

"And I can be more helpful as soon as I get to feeling right again, myself."

"That's a major problem, Clem. I mean, I want to help you as much as I can, but all you seem to want to do is eat, sleep and take showers. It's like dragging around a rogue hippopotamus with a bad disposition."

"I'll be okay. I'll be fine. Give me a couple of days." He had progressed to the point where he could see his own symptoms. He knew what was wrong with him. During Ranger training in the army at Fort Benning, they had taught the trainees to recognize symptoms of a psychological breakdown, the symptoms of what, during World War II, had been called 'battle fatigue'. It came from lack of sleep, lack of food, and loads of stress. The cure was just the opposite, lots of sleep, hot food and hot showers. And, apparently, the more pressing a need a soldier felt to get himself together, the more it helped to cure him. Scheutz had his pressing need—he needed to keep Gerry from abandoning him. To this he'd add the effort of finding her father. He explained this to her and added, "Let's figure this thing out together. My helping you find your father down here is the kind of thing I need to help me pull myself together."

Gerry listened to him while wiping ice cream off Dan's face, hands, and the front of his shirt. "Okay. What you're saying makes sense. I mean, I want to believe it."

"I'm not really convinced either. I'm just telling you what I was told in the army. I don't know if that's what's wrong with me, but...but I got nothing else to go on."

"Okay." She held his hand in both of hers, and looked into his eyes, still unsure, but willing to give it a shot. "So, tell me. What's your idea?"

"How much money did you bring with you?"

"Enough. I've got the money you sent me from where ever that place was in Georgia, that training camp. I insisted that Jacob give me an advance on child support, or alimony, or whatever it's called. And, after that big fight with my mother before I left, I cleaned out her savings account. I've got a few thousand dollars in traveler's checks."

"Really? Wow. You really stole your mother's money?"

"No. It was a joint account, all the money my father sent for all those years. Remember, he used to send me a Christmas card every year with a hundred dollars in it?" Her mother had set up a savings account with both their names on it, to use in case of emergency. Even as late as this past Christmas, the money still came. With interest it came to over two thousand dollars. "That was only part of the big fight." Her mother declared that going to Mexico to find, not one, but two bums did not meet the criteria of what would be considered an emergency.

"Tough old lady."

"About eight hundred of the money is what you sent."

" You hang onto the money. Sounds like you're better with money than I am. Listen, unless you're in a big hurry, let's get a hotel and stay here in the city for a few days. Believe me, I'll be great in a couple of days. And then we'll go look for your father. Come on, what do you say?"

Dan made a move to eject himself from the chair, and she grabbed the back of his shirt, holding him in place. "No. Dan, sit still. I mean it. Goddammit." He reached for his ice cream cup and made as if to throw it, but she grabbed it from his hand. "Can you take him?" she asked Scheutz. Still holding the back of the boy's shirt, she steered him off his chair and around the table to where Scheutz lifted him onto his own lap. Gerry leaned across the table until he face was only a foot from his."One thing you have to promise me, Clem, if we are going on with this. No violence. I know in your world that kind of thing comes easy. But I just can't stand it. I won't live in that world. And I don't want Dan growing up in it."

"Okay."

"Okay what?"

"Okay, I promise. No violence. Toward anybody. Any time. No matter what. Is that enough for you?"

She stared into his eyes again for a long time. "You mean it?"

"I mean it."

They took a taxi to a hotel near the airport, on Avenida General Zaragoza, and booked a suite of two rooms with a marble-walled shower in the bathroom. Soaking in the hot shower, which seemed to have an unlimited supply of water, Scheutz could feel his body relax into a sense of well-being, the depth of which he could not remember ever having felt before. Muscles in the back of his neck and his shoulders seemed to let themselves fall into what must have been a natural state. Something else was missing also, and it took him a while to realize what it was—fear, a fear that had been with him since he could remember. As a child he had a recurring nightmare that a black macaque monkey sat on his shoulder while he slept. He must have been about ten years when he came across a picture of the monkey in a National Geographic magazine, staring at the camera, its lips pulled back away from its teeth, its eyes glaring in hatred and fear. That night he had the first of the recurring nightmares where he had to be very careful not to do anything that would provoke the monkey. Standing with his head bent under the cascade of steaming hot water, he could picture the monkey curling into itself, into a small furry ball, and going to sleep. So, he could relax his vigilance a little. He still could not do anything to wake the monkey, but at least it was not sitting there on his shoulder ready to pounce.

Gerry yelled into the bathroom, through the steam, that she was taking Dan out to a park she could see from the hotel room window. Let him run off some of the energy he had been storing up since they got on the plane that morning. When Scheutz finally left the shower, his body goose-pimpled in the air-conditioned bedroom of the suite. He put on the white cotton pants and a new t-shirt with a picture of Montezuma on the front that Gerry had bought for him at the hotel gift shop. And then he buried himself in the blankets on the bed and waited for sleep.

Movement in the room brought him slowly to consciousness. Gerry and Dan must be back from their romp in the park. He peeked out from the edge of the sheet intending to jump up and surprise Dan, but instead saw a man standing just inside the bedroom door looking through Gerry's purse, which she normally carried inside the small suitcase, but had left lying out on the bureau. Scheutz became alert, his entire body tingling with the danger he'd thought he'd left behind in Cuba. Instant reflex propelled him up from the bed, tossing aside the sheet and blanket. The man at the bureau looked up, grabbed the purse and bolted.

Scheutz ran after him, through the outer room of the suite and into the hallway. The man, shorter than Scheutz, with black, shaggily cut hair and a shirt sporting palm trees and native huts, moved quickly. Scheutz lunged and caught the tail of his shirt just as he pushed open a door to the stairwell. He grabbed the purse in one hand and then a hank of the man's hair in the other, slamming his head against the door jamb. The man, still with his back to Scheutz struggled against him as Scheutz brought him to the floor, dropping with the full force of both knees into the middle of the man's back. A moan of air escaped from the man's chest. The purse now came easily from his hand. The Mexican's chest heaved as he fought to get air back into his lungs.

The realization that the Mexican was subdued and the purse returned flitted through Scheutz's mind, but hard after it came a surge of rage. He lifted the man and turned him over, kicking him in the ribs and then dropping down again to smash his fist into the man's nose. He caught himself before hitting the Mexican a second time, and straightened to stand over him. A noise behind him caused him to turn and he saw Gerry, holding Dan's hand, just emerging from the elevator door to the left of the stairwell.

Color drained from Gerry's newly tanned face as she and Dan stared at the man writhing on the floor, trying to catch his breath, blood spurting from his nose onto the carpet. Heaving to get his own breath back, Scheutz smiled at her and held up her purse as if it were the head of Medusa. She stared at him in wide-eyed shock, and then, as if in a trance, reached out to take the purse he offered to her. She then turned and fled, with Dan in tow, back to the hotel room.

Scheutz lifted the bleeding man to his feet and, securing his arm in a wrist lock, escorted him onto the elevator and down to the lobby, where he presented him to the desk clerk. Three obviously gringo hotel patrons, waiting in lobby stared curiously at the scene in front of the desk as the clerk reached for the phone and called the security guards. Two guards in gray uniforms finally came and took custody of the still bleeding man. One guard handcuffed him and led him to the rear of the lobby. The other asked Scheutz to accompany him to their office in the back of the building to fill out a report of the incident. Not until the thief was actually out of Scheutz's sight did his body began to relax.

On his way back up the elevator, barefoot, still in the t-shirt and cotton pants, now spattered with the thief's blood, he felt a sense of elation. He had done something well. The lose of the purse and the traveler's check in it could have been at worst a catastrophe for them, and at best a major hassle replacing the checks and the other contents of the purse. Gerry had to see now that traveling around Mexico without him could be dangerous.

She did not answer his knock on the hotel room door. He waited, knocked, waited, knocked, and then took the elevator back down to the front desk. The clerk told him that, yes, she had gone out with the child. Something about that did not make sense. Schuetz took the room key and went back upstairs. Inside the suite, not only were they not there, but Gerry's little suitcase was gone. In the bedroom, on the bureau, lay a note to him beside a small stack of traveler's checks.

Clem,

I'm sorry. I can't live with this. Here is your $800.

You promised no violence. You broke it.

Goodbye

Chapter 28

Sons and Daughters

He was not able to get a bus out of Mexico City to Taxco until the next day. The last night in that hotel, with Gerry gone, had him right back in Cuba, jumping at every sound like he was on guard duty in a combat zone. He could not sleep with listening for her knock on the door, and then picturing it opening with her telling him she'd changed her mind.

Outside the bus window, the Sierra Madre spread out to the south as beautiful as anything he'd ever seen. Inside the bus made him want to scream. Tourists, heading for Acapulco, would be allowed to stop over in Taxco for two hours, the driver said in his fractured English, so that they could buy souveniers. People, gringos mostly from what he could tell, chatted and sang songs, inflicting their festive mood on everyone around them. God, they were infuriating. He sneered at one middle-aged woman who dared smile at him. He tried to sleep, leaning his head on the small ditty bag he'd bought for his few possessions. He'd placed it between him and the window he had closed to keep out the exhaust fumes. But sleep was impossible. The picture of Gerry standing there next to the elevator with that look of horror on her face would not leave him. For Chrissake, it was her purse he had been rescuing. Didn't that make a difference? True, the purse was already in his hand and the churrito who stolen it was thoroughly subdued before he broke the pendejo's nose, but...

The braying laugh of a woman directly in front of him on the bus pierced his brain. Another woman turned in her seat to carry on an inane exchange of views about one travel agency over another with the man in the seat next to Scheutz. He imagined again the delicious pleasure of smashing his fist into the thief's nose, and then pictured himself sauntering up and down the aisle of the bus, smashing noses left and right. He had to stop this. Getting pissed off at a bunch of touristas, as if their only reason for existing was to provide him with an adequate supply of punching bags, was as stupid as beating up that little hijo de puta back at the hotel. He placed the ditty bag on his lap, gripped it tight with his fists. As they bounced along, he pondered the similarity between the words 'travel' and 'travail'.

The bus stopped just inside the cobblestone cairn that marked the entrance to the town of Taxco. A whooshing sense of relief visited him as he stepped down and separated himself from the crowd rushing behind him. Like all good tourists everywhere, the people surged out onto the streets in search of buying something, anything they could take home to remind them that they had once endured an overcrowded, god-awful bus trip, crawling along a winding road in airless heat and gas fumes.

You'd think that at this altitude, you'd have some breath of wind. But no, the town felt as dry and parched as a desert. White buildings with red tiled roofs capped a small hill like snow on a mountain, topped off with the twin spires of the church the driver had referred to as the Catedral de Santo Prisco. The buildings glinted in the bright sunlight. Even through the sunglasses he'd bought in Mexico City, the town hurt his eyes. No one but the tourists seemed to be about in the streets. At that time of day, any Mexican in his right mind would be indulging in his siesta in the shade. Most of the shops were closed.

A tourista-looking place on the zocalo, called Paco's Bar and Restaurant, looked like a good place to get out the sun, but the thought of food nauseated him. Instead, he found a little cantina named El Alarcon, which, contrasting to the light in the plaza, looked almost like night inside. He asked for a cervesa fria and, when the bartender, a fat man in a dirty shirt, brought the beer, Scheutz asked him if he'd seen a tall gringa with dark hair accompanying a small child. The bartender merely shrugged and sauntered back to his chair at the end of the bar next to a small electric fan. Just one more turn of the screw that tightened the knot in his chest. The knot had started when he found Gerry's note inside the hotel suite. He'd run back down to the lobby and then out into the street. But she was gone. As if her and Dan had been vacuumed into some other world. Back in the suite, he read the note again and looked through the two rooms to see if she had left any hint of where she might be going. He went over the conversations of the last few days, the conversation with the mining engineer at the airport, and concluded the most likely place she would go would be Taxco. This was the address of the last Christmas card she'd had received from her father.

He sipped at the beer, which he did not really want, except that his throat was parched. The cantina, empty except for him and the bartender, was kind of a dump, now that his eyes had adjusted to the gloom. The thought of smashing everything in the place and punching out the bartender in the process gave him a pleasant moment. He had to get control over himself. Hitting that thief back at the hotel was not something he thought about before doing it. The movement of his arm, and his leg as he kicked him, seemed to be directed by some force other than his own.

Once, when he and Gerry were in high school, she had slapped him for laughing at her. His hand had actually moved to hit her back but he checked himself. The instinct to strike was merely a normal reaction to the world around him. This happened and then that happened, what could be more normal? If somebody threw a ball at you, you caught it. Somebody called you a name, you called him one back. Somebody hits you, you hit him back. Somebody steals from you, you beat the shit out them. Is that any reason for her to run off?

Before leaving the cantina, Scheutz stopped next to the bartender to ask him if he knew a man named Gerald Rieker, but got back the same minimal shrug. Outside he wandered the streets of what appeared to be a small city as opposed to the town he thought it was at first. In a silver craft shop named Los Castillo, he asked a counter man if there was an office for the mining company here in the city. Yes, in fact, there was an office for the Grupo Mexico mining company.

Four blocks further on, in the company's air conditioned office, a middle-aged secretary, with a round face and large eyes, looked up the name Rieker in file drawer for him. She open the file which looked like a payroll record. "El senor Rieker trabajia por esta compania en el pasado. No ahora."

"Hablas ingles?" he asked her.

She shrugged. "Un poco."

"He does not work here any longer?"

"No. Por muchos anos. Many years."

"Do you know him?"

She wagged her head slightly from side to side. "Si. Un poco. I know him a little. Estaba…he was un engeniero…engeneer? Si. Esta un amigo de El senor Spratling."

"El senor Spratling?"

"Si. The…first…como se dice?…owner… del mina por la plata en Taxco. Si. Senor Rieker was hees fren'."

"Was? Not now? No ahora?"

She shrugged again. "Yo no se, ahora."

"Where does he live now? A donde vive ahora?"

"Creo que…" She raised an index finger. "I theenk…el vive en Taxco el Viejo." She turned the payroll ledger so Scheutz could read the address on Calle de Delicias in the town Taxco el Viejo.

Twenty minutes later, a taxi deposited him at the address he had been given in Taxco el Viejo, a much smaller and apparently a much older community lower down and south of the small city on top of the hill. He stood for moment leaning against the wall on the shaded side of the street, catching his breath, wiping the sweat from his face, and contemplating how to handle meeting Gerry again. He was certain she and Dan were there. If old man Rieker had been that easy for him to find, it certainly would not have been any harder for her.

But what if she would not see him? She had to see him. He had run the scene over and over in his mind all the way down from Mexico City. He would apologize for letting himself go like that when he caught the thief in the hotel. How could she do that, leaving nothing more than a note on the bureau? He could feel himself getting pissed off all over again. And then checked himself. He didn't know whether Gerry was right or not. But it didn't matter. If he didn't stop himself from getting angry, that was it, there was no more Gerry. No more Dan. And then what else was there for him? He'd end up like his father, sitting in a room all night by himself, cursing and whining into his bottle of cheap wine about God taking away his wife and leaving him with nothing except having to raise those goddamned kids.

No, he had to do it. He could do it, the same way he'd checked his hand from slapping Gerry that time back in high school. He could make himself stop being so angry. He could make himself stop hitting people. When he weighed the momentary pleasure of breaking some guy's nose to a lifetime of loss, it was no more than a monkey pissing in the ocean. He wiped the sweat from his face, picked up his ditty bag and went to knock on the blue-painted wooden door that opened onto the street.

A tiny, elderly woman with what had once obviously been a handsome, high-cheekboned face, answered his knock. When Scheutz said Senor Rieker's name, the woman, without a word, nodded and turned away, leaving the door open for Scheutz to follow. They passed through a small courtyard, overgrown with uncared-for plants and vines that grew up the walls and had taken over a tree that stood dead in the middle of the yard. A shaded veranda led through a worn but ornate wooden door into the tile-floored hallway of the house. The interior felt immediately about ten degrees cooler. The woman, bent over slightly which made her smaller than she was already, gave a hand motion for him to stop where he was. She then disappeared into a door at the far end of the hallway.

Scheutz put down his bag and went through another effort of making himself look presentable for when Gerry opened the door in front of him. His impulse was to rush forward and hug her as soon as she appeared, but he then decided that would be all wrong. If her main problem with him was that she was afraid of him, rushing to hug her would only scare her more. No, he had to keep his cool. He had to do everything he could to impress her with his ability to at least act like a normal, civilized human being. He could not be seen as the impulsive person she witnessed the day before, beating up that thief in the hotel.

He waited. The hallway offered nothing to look at except for several paintings on the walls that were all done with such dark colors as to be difficult to see in the dim light that, like the cantina in Taxco, contrasted so starkly with the sunlight out in the courtyard. He opened the outside door to let in a little light in order to see the paintings better. It did not help much. Each of the paintings, done in deep shades of red-brown or purple and dark green, apparently done by the same person, gave the sense of looking into some dark cave, with only a few bright spots, like gems within. Here and there in each painting appeared to be faces of ghost children. He closed the door so as not to have to look at the paintings any longer. The last thing he needed right then was to be spooked by some nutty artist's bad spirits.

And he waited. The Spanish word came to him—tenebroso. Gloomy, that's what it was. Like standing in what, as a child in grade school he imagined to be purgatory, that place the nuns said people went to who were not really damned but not really saved either. It always seemed worse than hell, because at least in hell you knew where you stood. Being damned was surely no worse than not knowing whether you were damned or not. And that seemed to be the torment of the guy that painted the pictures that now oppressed him from the walls. He fixed his stare on the door at the end of the hall, not wanting to let himself give in to the mood of the hallway. But he could not ignore the paintings, the ghost children in them watching him, the tiny gems of hope in each of them taunting him.

He had decided to open the outside door and wait out under the veranda, when the inner door at the other end of the hall creaked open. He turned quickly, forcing a smile. But it was not Gerry. A tall, gaunt man in a white guayabera came to greet him, extending his hand and, with his head bent slightly to the side, said, "I'm Gerald Rieker. How can I help you?"

"Hello, I'm Clement Scheutz. I'm looking for your daughter."

"I'm afraid I don't understand."

"Your daughter, Gerry, is she here?"

"You're mistaken. I have no daughter."

"Oh. Well…um…I guess you must be the wrong Gerald Rieker. Did you never have a family in Cincinnati? A daughter named Gerry?"

The man looked at Scheutz for a long time in the dim light, as if trying to ascertain what species of animal had invaded his home. "Would you like to come in?" he said finally.

A narrow stone staircase led up off the inner hall to a wide, airy room that looked to be an artist studio on the second floor. The same style of paintings that hung in the first floor hallway inhabited this room, most of them leaning against walls or against other stretched canvases that leaned against walls. Two, obviously unfinished ones, were attached to large paint-spattered easels, facing each other. Every canvas that Scheutz could see displayed the same kind of images, a theme, reproduced over and over, of dark caverns in heavy, deep colors, each with their own tiny glittering spot--more than one spot on some--beckoning the viewer into its heart.

Rieker, with the long, thin fingers of one hand, motioned for Scheutz to have a seat in a canvas director's chair. Now that he could see the man in decent light, he looked even more emaciated than he appeared in gloom of the hallway. He stood almost as tall as Scheutz, slightly stooped, and so thin as to give the feeling that anything more than a gentle breeze might lift him off his feet. As he moved around the studio room, his wispy gray-white hair floated over the yellowing pallor of his face and skull.

"I thought you were a geologist," Scheutz said to him. "That's what Gerry told me."

"I am…was. But I am foremost an artist." He looked at the painting on the easel and then turned back to Scheutz, as if to say, 'see how wonderful it is'.

The total effect of all the paintings was exactly the same, depressing as hell. This guy obviously wanted Scheutz to like his paintings. He forced a grin and nodded at the old man. "Um…I wanted to ask you about Gerry."

"This Gerry you talk about—is she supposed to be my daughter?"

"Yes. And you're saying you don't have a family in Cincinnati?"

"No, I'm not saying that. I do…did…have a family in Cincinnati." He put the painting he was holding back in its original spot and turned, his eyes gazing in Scheutz's direction, but not connecting. After a long pause, his voice floated in as if drifting down from some unseen cloud in the upper regions of the studio room. "Would you like some coffee?" he asked. When Scheutz nodded, Rieker walked to the door, opened it and called, "Lourdes." And after a pause, "Traies dos cafes, por favor." He turned back to Scheutz. "That will take her a while." He came back to a stool next to one of the easels and perched lightly on the stool's edge. "So, tell me about Gerry. How do you know her?"

"We went to high school together. We have a son."

"You're married?"

"No." Rieker raised his eyebrows. Scheutz moved to explain. "I asked her to come to Mexico to meet me. I just arrived here a few days ago from Cuba. I told her I would help her find her father while she was here."

"And that would be me?"

"Am I wrong?"

"I suppose not." Long pause. "I have not seen her since she was three," Rieker said. Scheutz looked up at the ceiling. That was where the voice seemed to come from. "You get used to thinking of yourself in a certain way, you know. And I got used to thinking of myself as a man without earthly ties."

"You sent a present to her every Christmas. That's how she knew you were in Taxco."

What was the word he looked for to describe this man? Precious. He could picture himself reaching to throttle that scrawny chicken neck, but end up holding nothing more than a handful of smoke. The man would swirl outward and dissipate. Scheutz held the wooden chair arms and grinned at Rieker, feeling like a gargoyle perched at the gate to the real world.

"I sent only money," Rieker continued. "A present as abstract and ethereal as the little child I knew." He drifted off again. "Do you know the chubby little angels you see on Italian frescos? They're called 'putti'."

Scheutz found himself becoming inceasingly iritated as the man talked. It wasn't what he said, or even who he was. The problem lay in Scheutz himself; anyone would have irritated him right then. All he could think of was slapping this old guy. Willi might do something like that. But Willi had been like a big child. And so had he. What he needed to do was act like an adult. That was the only way to keep Gerry with him. He needed to practice this adult crap.

So all right, so this old guy was someone he could practice on, practice not slapping him, or not even thinking about slapping him. He had to find some other way to deal with the fact that Rieker kind of pissed him off with his precious little images and his fairy little hands. "So, you're telling me that your daughter has not contacted you, that she has not come here?" he asked the man.

Rieker shook his head. "I have not seen her since she was three. I really have my doubts that she could even find me."

"I found you easy enough. And she's smarter than I am."

"She was a bright little girl. I missed her. Then when I knew I couldn't go back, I had to make myself stop missing her. And it freed me."

"From what?"

"From the constant carping of a woman who feels her husband requires a daily introduction to the western value system of manners. You've heard the Latin expression 'Carpe Diem'? Well, with Cynthia, Gerry's mother, you know?" He gave a little nod of the head. "It was Carping Diem." He chuckled at his own joke.

Scheutz grinned, trying out his new gargoyle grimace. He tuned in again to what Rieker was saying. "...her mother. I am a coward, I suppose, but I couldn't take it."

Scheutz wanted to get up and run. The next best thing to slapping him. But this ashen-faced old man was the only possible link he had to Gerry. She was bound to show up here. In the meantime, he ought to settle himself into this man's good graces. That was sure to help if and when Gerry did show up here.

The door to the studio opened and the tiny old woman entered with a tray holding cups with steaming coffee, a bowl of sugar and a ceramic cruet filled with cream. She placed the tray on a paint-spattered table and stood looking up toward Rieker in an expectant mode. He smiled and nodded to her, at which signal she returned out through the door.

"Help yourself." Rieker motioned. "And so, is her daughter...my daughter...like her mother?"

"I don't know. We've not been together long enough to tell."

"Hmm. It's true, you do have to be in close quarters for a period of time before the glow wears off and the recriminations begin. But, I thought you said that you two had a child."

"Well, yes..." He told Rieker the story, how Gerry and he had met in high school, how she discovered she was pregnant only after Scheutz had left town, and then, upon her mother's urging, married a man several years her senior. Only after coming back to Cincinnati and finding her again, did he learn that the child was his. She left her husband for him, but then when realizing what kind of person Scheutz was, she went back.

"But you said she'd come to Mexico to find you."

"Yes. I phoned her at her mother's house, begged her to come. I told her that it was quite possible that if her mother had asked you to come back, she might have had a father all these years."

"Hngh. Well, that's certainly wrong. She did ask me. I would never go. That woman made me hate myself. Not that I didn't hate myself for not going back, but at least in Mexico I didn't have to feed on that self-loathing every day. I didn't have someone holding the up a mirror to show me how awful I was." As he said this, the fingers on his left hand flicked toward the painting on the easel next to him.

He fell silent and they both sipped their coffee. The coffee tasted good, better than any that Scheutz could remember drinking for a while.

"So, tell me, Mr…what was your name again?"

"Scheutz."

"Mr. Scheutz. You're saying that you and my daughter made an arrangement to meet here at my place in Taxco el Viejo? I find that hard to believe."

"That's not right. We did meet someplace else. But we got separated in Mexico City. And I came here thinking she would have found you…or will find you…and then I can find her again. I don't know where else to look."

"And tell me again how you got separated?"

"It was a misunderstanding. She asked me not to do something, and I did it…by mistake…not on purpose. And she left."

"Aha! I knew it. Just like her mother."

"Well, even if she is? So what? I don't know why people act like that but, Jesus, it's not the worst thing in the world, you know. If you can't take a little carping,...Maybe she's right. She is right. I don't need to go around punching people all the time."

"You punch people? You're not going to punch me, are you?"

"No. No, I'm not going to punch you."

"Well, then. Maybe you should sit down."

Scheutz did not realized he had gotten up from the canvas chair. He stood over the old man and had been waving his coffee cup around. He sat back down and drained the last of his coffee. Whew, that was close. He had almost lost control of himself. That would have really screwed things up.

"But you're right," the old man said. "Most people should find a way to deal with that kind of criticism. But I couldn't...can't. Just like going in the army during the war. Most people find a way to deal with it. And get themselves killed, or maimed, or something. But I couldn't...still can't."

"I'll deal with it when I find Gerry again. I have to."

"I hope you do." Rieker looked at him over the rim of his coffee cup. "I hope you do." He turned to set the cup down. "You seem to have a lot more strength that I do. A lot more than I had when I was your age."

Rieker suggested that Scheutz have Lourdes fix him some lunch. He himself had to get back to work on his paintings. Scheutz was welcome to stay at the house until Gerry showed up, sleep there if he wanted. He was, he said, afraid of meeting his grown daughter, especially since she sounded like her mother. For that reason he wanted very much for Scheutz to stay with him until she came.

"It's silly, I know, my being afraid to face a young girl of twenty-one, but, well...."

He kept an empty guest room with a bed at the back of house, on the ground floor, next to the one where Lourdes slept. Scheutz was free to use that room, but would he please not come to the studio until supper time.

Chapter 29

I Will Never Leave You

After lunch, Scheutz wandered the house and the front patio, going several times to open the front door to the street to peer up and down in hopes that he could see Gerry and Dan coming. He finally decided that it made no sense to keep prowling like a caged animal. He helped Lourdes heat water, which they poured into a tin tub in the kitchen, and into which Scheutz soaked his body until the water cooled. Then he laid down inside the mosquito netting, on the bed in the guest room and tried to sleep.

He needed to sleep more, but his mind raced, his body tingled. He made himself not think about Gerry by focusing on Dan. It was amazing how much Dan resembled his younger brother Willi. He'd noticed the likeness the first time he'd met Dan, back in Cincinnati. Willi was present in the room when Gerry brought the boy over to where Scheutz and Willi had been staying. And Willi was not the only member of Scheutz's family Dan resembled. The shape of his hands, the nape of his neck. Anger built up inside his chest at Gerry for taking the boy away like that. She had no right to do that. He could understand her marrying that Orenstein character back in Cincinnati to give Dan a good home. But that was when she did not know where Scheutz was. But now, to actually take his son away from him like that....dammit, she had no right.

No. He had to stop thinking like that. He'd scare her off again. And the next time she'd take off to where he could never find them. If she had not done so already. No, she was bound to show up here. He knew that about Gerry. If she had made up her mind to look for her father, she would do it. And she'd find him. All he had to do was hang in there and wait for her to come.

When he awoke, the sun had gone down. The door to the guest room led directly into the kitchen, and he found Rieker sitting at a table, eating. Lourdes, upon seeing Scheutz, got up from her place at the table and brought a plate of food from a pot that sat on an open hearth at the other side of the room. Rieker motioned him to a seat at the wooden table. Over supper, Rieker talked about his life there in Taxco. Scheutz ate and listened, the story not really interesting, but at least filling the air. Rieker talked of his friend, Bill Spratling, who owned a ranch down the road in the same town. The ranch, not really for the raising of cattle, formed a social nucleus, according to Rieker, that attracted famous people from all over the world. The old man ran off a few names that he obviously expected Scheutz to be impressed by, without knowing that none of the names meant anything to him. He watched Lourdes's face while Rieker ran off his list of famous names, and could tell that the names meant nothing to her either. She mashed the food in her bowl and then apparently gummed the mash, since Scheutz could see no evidence of teeth whenever she opened her mouth.

Rieker had plans, he said, for spending the evening over at Spratling's ranch, and would Scheutz like to go along? No, Scheutz would not like to. Gerry was very likely to show up that evening, and besides, Scheutz did not like that kind of thing. He could picture all those world celebrities he had never heard of, twirling around impressing each other. He'd stay here and watch out for Gerry.

"Well, yes, I suppose you are right," Rieker said. "For a young man, you certainly are focused. Myself, I've always had a problem with that."

Scheutz nodded and grinned around a mouthful of food. If the old man's obsession with his dark paintings was not focus, then what was it? He looked over at Lourdes again. What did she think of this guy she waited on hand and foot? Probably not much. And suddenly he felt his mood lighten. He stopped grinning and noticed that his food actually had a taste to it. And it was pretty good. The muscles in his shoulders and neck relaxed, his right hand no longer tingled, and he could not imagine why he wanted earlier to hit the old guy. Or anybody else for that matter. He stopped chewing and stared at the two people across the table from him. Lourdes gummed her food slowly. He thought he caught her looking up at him, but the glance was so quick he might have been wrong. She knew, though, didn't she? She knew what was going on. People like Lourdes always knew.

That evening, Lourdes helped him heat up another tub of hot water, which he fell asleep in. Afterwards, he sat up in the overgrown patio in front of the house, listening for sounds of someone knocking on the street door. Maybe he should have gone to the party with Rieker. Gerry just might show up in a place like that. But no, he was better off waiting here. Finally, he gave up and went to bed.

In the morning, still no Gerry. He went out to walk the town of Taxco el Viejo, a smaller, much older version of Taxco de Alarcon on top of the hill. Still nothing.

Back at casa Rieker, he explained as best he could to Lourdes that both he and Rieker were waiting for Rieker's daughter to show up. The old woman nodded her head without saying anything. Whatever the gringos did was of no importance to her. She walked away into the kitchen area and continued with what must have been her daily tasks. Later in the day, he came across her sitting in a wooden chair, her back to the wall on the other side of the hearth. Her gaze moved up slowly to him as he walked in and then lowered again, her eyes half-opened, like a domestic cat with no mouse to chase. It was almost as if, aside from her work in Rieker's house, she had no other interest. Scheutz tried to imagine what that would be like, not to care about anything other than the task you were performing at that moment. It must have been awfully peaceful.

But that wasn't him. He had something he had to do, and waiting around like this, hoping Gerry would show up was getting on his nerves. He wanted to go look for her. But where? The only place he knew for sure was back in Cincinnati. She had to show up there eventually. Yeah, like she had to show up here eventually. He went back to pace the street again.

The rain drove him back inside. Rieker finally made it out of bed by lunch time, and regaled Scheutz and Lourdes with stories of all the famous people he had met the night before at Spratling's house. He was well into a long, incomprehensible monologue on the similarities between his paintings and those by some woman named O'Keeffe when their lunch was interrupted by a knocking on the outer door to the street. Lourdes put down her spoon and rose to go answer the knock. Rieker continued on with hardly a pause for breath in the delivery of his oratory on the merits of both his own paintings and those of his colleague.

Scheutz heard Dan's voice before he saw them. He jumped up from the table and turned just as Lourdes came through the door with Dan running into the room behind her. Scheutz knelt and opened his arms, as the boy, yelling "Big Daddy" ran in to them. Scheutz hugged the boy as he might have hugged a life preserver thrown from a boat in a high sea. Dan squeezed his neck and squealed into his ear. Behind Dan, Gerry stood in the doorway, water dripping from her wet hair onto her face, which gaped in amazement at the sight of him.

Scheutz stood, holding Dan with his wet shirt to his chest. Gerry's eyes flipped back and forth like a tennis spectator's between him and Rieker who had stood up from the table. "I can't...Oh... Is this my father?" She asked Scheutz. Scheutz raised his eyebrows and shrugged. As far as he knew, yes. Gerry looked closer at the old man, putting her hand in front of her open mouth. She squinted, looking again at Scheutz and then back to her father's face. There was a resemblance between them, not much, but around the eyes and the way they both held their mouths. They were the same height, she almost as tall as Scheutz, and with a musculature similar to her father. The father's body resembled more that of a woman. Gerry stopped moving altogether, standing still between the old man and Scheutz, with only her eyes active, taking in everything, the two men, the old woman, the room. It seemed as if it was too much for her, and as if she did not want them, the men, to see her like that, stunned, at a loss.

Nothing moved for what felt like a long time. Even Dan ceased his interminable fidgeting, as if he also, along with Scheutz, knew that their life was about to change forever. Dan reached a hand toward his mother and wriggled to be free of Scheutz's arms. Scheutz put him down and he ran to Gerry, hugging her wet skirt. Tears had started down her cheeks as she lifted him up. Dan patted her hair, telling her not to cry. "There, there," he said.

"I'm Gerry," she said, turning to Rieker.

He nodded. "I gathered that." They both looked at each other in silence for another long pause, and then Rieker said, "You're just in time for lunch."

Behind them, Lourdes set plates and spoons on the table for Gerry and Dan. She raised her eyebrows at Dan, giving him a toothless grin, which seemed to frighten him a little. He turned his head into his mother's wet hair.

"We have much to talk about," Rieker said. "But let's eat first."

Gerry sat Dan on the chair that Lourdes had pulled from against the wall and placed at the table. She then turned back to Scheutz. "How did you get here?"

"Not that hard. I'm surprised it took you so long."

"I went back to the hotel to look for you. But you'd gone."

He took a step toward her, wanting only to put his arms around her. Her left foot stepped back as his right foot moved forward. The look in her eye showed she was startled by his move in her direction. Lourdes laid her hand on Gerry's arm and nodded for her to sit at the table next to Dan.

"Yes, why don't we all sit down," Rieker said. His eyes followed Gerry's face in wonderment, as if he'd just come across an apparition.

Gerry looked from Rieker to Lourdes and then back to Scheutz. She moved closer to Dan, but did not sit. The same look of a little girl Scheutz had seen when she stepped off the ferry in Isla Mujeres had come back to her face, even warier of what she'd walked into. She put her hands on Dan's shoulders. "I'm sorry," she said to Scheutz. "I shouldn't have left the way I did."

"Sienta se," Lourdes said.

They made love that night in the guest room of her father's house. This was nothing agreed on before hand, no lead-up to it, and nothing romantic about it. The love-making itself was as Scheutz imagined it must be for people who had lived together for the past twenty years or so. She took off the robe Lourdes had loaned her and parted the mosquito netting to climb into the side of the bed nearest where Dan lay sound asleep on a pallet on the floor under his own netting. She was exhausted, she said.

Scheutz undressed and laid next to her, careful not to do anything that might send her off again, escaping with her son into the night. No, that was not fair. She had run before, from the hotel in Mexico City, because he had frightened her. Well, hadn't he frightened a lot of people? He was physically a lot bigger than her. But then he was lot bigger than most people. And, yes, he'd frightened a few of them in his life. Some ran, some didn't. There was no blaming her. He just had to be more careful. She was not like a man. And he'd only ever lived with men. The year spent with his aunt, almost didn't count. His aunt had been like some distant church bell in a town on the other side of the hill, ding-donging its messages to its own parishioners.

Gerry lay on her back, her left leg, the one farthest away from him, cocked with her knee up, the arm on that same side raised with her hand under her head. He could not tell in the deep shadow of the room whether her eyes were open or not. Her right hand lay on her stomach. The pose invited him. And at the same time, warned him; whatever you do, be careful. He lay on his side facing her, his head in his hand propped onto his elbow. He pictured them making love, but the image seemed too foreign. When was the last time they had done that?

He laid his hand on the hand on her stomach, and so it began. But there were no words, and nothing felt familiar. Their love-making was not the warm, rhythmic, loss of self, that had been normal to them in high school. Gerry felt spastic, jangled, pushing herself to a quick relief. Even though it was over quickly, they both dripped with sweat. Afterwards, she wanted, needed, she said, to talk. They lay, entwined under the mosquito netting, their bodies slithering in the mingled sweat. She wanted to know, she said, she wanted some assurance of what it would be like, their living together and taking care of Dan.

Dan lay on the mat Lourdes had brought into the room for him, conked out from all the traipsing about he and his mother had been doing. Scheutz commented on the boy's ability to make himself comfortable in whatever foreign place he found himself.

"Kids ride on your back," Gerry said. "As long as he's with his mommy, there is no foreign place."

He had no problem, he told her, assuring her that a life together would be exactly what she wanted. The effort was easy to promise. It slid off his tongue. Whether he could do it, whether he had the control to stifle this seemingly primal urge of his, whether he could hold off smacking people for their own good, was something he could only work at one day at a time. He rested the side of his face on her sweaty chest and watched the dark form of Dan, listening to his son's sleeping breath. "I can do it," he told her. "I will do it."

"If you do," she whispered into his hair. "I'll never leave you.

Chapter 30

The Party's Over

They watched as Marty's car pulled onto the highway, followed by Dan's van, both headed away from the party. Gerry took another sip from the can of Heineken in her left hand. He looked into her eyes as she leveled her gaze at him. He had asked himself so many times in the last ten years whether or not she remembered saying that to him; that she would never leave him. He certainly had never hit anyone since making that promise to her, never lost his temper, never frightened her in any way. He had controlled his anger, wrapped it in something that felt like cotton batting, and tucked it away. He had lived up to his side of the deal. And for what it was worth, it meant something to him.

You left her first.

Oh, there you are. What is that supposed to mean?

She's told you. I've told you. Do we have to go through it again?

No. I know without you telling me.

Watching Gerry's face now, under the orange glow of the lanterns, he could see something different in her look, something he hadn't seen there in years. A fleeting acceptance in her eyes that he hadn't seen since before she left and took the kids to New York years ago. And just as quickly the look was gone. He smiled at her to let her know he'd seen it. The look was small, tentative, very quick and gone like a wisp, but it was there. Those tiny looks had probably been there often in the last ten years, but she'd never let him catch her at it before.

Now that Marty was graduated, officially a grown-up, now could they both allow themselves to feel what each one had hidden from the other all these years? Could she allow herself a smidgen of warmth toward him? And now could he allow himself to be pissed off at all the things he had not reacted to for twenty years? Like her affair with the Buttwad. Like her hauling the kids off to New York. Hauling herself off to New York. Maybe if he had been to got angry in a more civilized way she would have come back, found him interesting and exciting again. Truth was, he didn't know how to do it. People got angry all the time without getting violent. But, since he did not know how to do that, the only way he could handle the anger was to bury it. And it turned him into a lump. He couldn't blame her.

That's what I'm....

Shut up. Better still, go away. I don't need you anymore.

"Boy, with the kids gone, it sure leaves a big hole doesn't it?" Georgina appeared at Scheutz's elbow, talking across him to Gerry. Scheutz turned to look at the crowd still left at the party. If you'd call it a crowd. Most of the older people seemed to be drifting toward their cars. Over near the edge of the dance area Freddie Brockton's mother still chatted with two middle-aged couples. Freddie's father had left shortly after his son had taken off. Uppermann and his brother still stood at the edge of the lantern light, looking awkward and drinking steadily from their beer bottles. Samantha's father entertained a group of people like himself, his wife laughing loudest of them all. Only about a quarter of the original crowd remained. Olavi and his wife were gone, as were Pelletier and Nicole. That little knot of intrigue was sure to end with the two men beating the hell out of each other.

So this was it. Like the town itself, pretty and mostly empty. The kids all leave, the older folks drop off, and the rest are left to age in peace. He'd never be able to do it. He could not hide here for the rest of his life. If nothing else, the ennui would drive him mad. Technology was forcing him out of the woods, the same way that Dan's and now Marty's coming of age was forcing him to focus on his own life instead of theirs. And what was his own life? He couldn't say. He had done nothing for the past twenty years but focus it all on taking care of first Gerry and the kids and then just the kids. Not that it wasn't great, and not that he wouldn't give anything to have it all back again, but there it was. As of today, it was all gone.

Samantha had said, "God, I wish you'd take me away from this place." All those years she hung around, through high school and then beyond, imitating Gerry, keeping him company, helping him in small ways. Why had he never given her any thought before? He listened for Gerry's voice to pipe up and answer that question for him. But he could do it himself. The answer was...because....because ever since that day he had found Samantha and Dan screwing in the attic, he would not allow himself to think of her. The same way Gerry did not allow herself to have warm feelings toward him all these years. Because if the thoughts were allowed, they would leave the doors open.

He tuned back in to the conversation between Gerry and Georgina, both talking about how to handle the problem of losing their focus when the kids grew up and went away. Well, they didn't need to handle it, did they? Gerry had her life in New York with her advertising and design, and her boy toy. And Georgina had her restaurant. And what did other people do? He didn't know really, because he didn't know anyone else in town well enough to be able to ask them. From what little he could tell, most of them did things like get involved with town politics, run for selectman or the planning board. Others took classes or got real estate broker licenses or went to work down in Keene in a supermarket.

He'd have to leave. But go where? Up to Hanover to be a professor's spouse to Nanda? No, that was definitely out. Why had he even given it a moment's thought? Maybe he could go back to where all this started twenty years ago, back to Mexico. That was an idea worth thinking about. They had been happy in Mexico. They had all been happy, Gerry, Dan, even Gerry's father, once she and he got over their strangeness to each other. But then the sickness that finally killed the old man restricted him to his bed. For Scheutz, the time they spent in Taxco el Viejo stood out as being probably the happiest time of his life. It had been like an extended honeymoon for him and Gerry. And Dan had been like one of those little naked angels that go around shooting arrows at lovers. Who knows, maybe he could talk Gerry into going back to Mexico with him.

"Where did your friend take off to?" Georgina ask Gerry.

"Jerome?" She flicked her fingers in the direction of the highway. "Pfft. He went to the children's party. Apparently, he passed the age test."

"By a wide margin," Scheutz said.

"He's jealous," Gerry said.

"I am not..."

"Yes you are." She nudged his shoulder with the bottom of the beer bottle. "Oh, come on. I find it touching after all these years."

How could he consider going anywhere with Gerry? Everything she said irritated him.

Georgina grinned at him and then at Gerry. "Listen, you guys want to help me clean up here? My helper and her boyfriend have also gone off to the children's party and left me alone with all this mess. And I gotta tell you, I'm bushed."

Georgina and Gerry carried the left-over food inside while Scheutz put unopened beer bottles into their old cartons. He gathered empties and stacked them in cases at the side of the house. He and Gerry fell in the same pattern of wordless domestic motions, clearing the same tables, passing things in and out of

Georgina's kitchen the way they had performed the hundreds of mindless, menial daily tasks of housekeeping, side by side. How much of their life together had been consumed with that kind of thing, not talking much, each one knowing what the other was going to do. Apparently, without him realizing it, all that frictionless sharing of chores became stifling for her. And the kids certainly chafed against it. But the minutia of the two of them making a home for their children had held such a fascination.

More townsfolk drifted away toward their cars, waving goodnight to Scheutz and to Georgina. No one, it seemed, remembered Gerry enough to say hello or goodbye. It had been over ten years since she had lived in their town, and even then was only here for a short time. When the last cars left and the food and trash had been brought inside, Georgina clicked off the strings of paper lanterns, throwing the outside area into darkness. Gerry and Scheutz scraped the plates and stacked the dishes, bowls, pots, and utensils in the deep sinks. Georgina went out to close and cover up the sound system. They should just leave everything else until morning, she said, coming back into the large kitchen. She was just too tired to even think about it. "If the damned raccoons find food on the ground, more power to them."

With the leftovers and condiments put away in the two restaurant-sized refrigerators, Gerry opened another Heineken and settled herself at the table. Georgina said she was going to bed. "You know where the towels are," she said to Gerry. "And you know where the guest room is. Make yourself at home. Clem, stay as long as you want. I'll see you folks in the morning." She paused in the kitchen doorway, looking back and forth from Scheutz to Gerry, on the verge of saying something. And finally just shook her head and left the room.

He slumped with his back against the counter. His own tiredness tugged his shoulders down. This was the first time he could remember being alone in the same room with Gerry since she had left for New York. For ten years, there had always been at least one other person present. He had noticed this before, but only now realized that she had always engineered her visits that way.

"It's not even ten," Gerry said looking up at the clock over the refrigerator. "In the city, the evening is just getting going. Out here, it's like the middle of the night. How do you stand it?"

"This is the middle of the night for me. I'm usually asleep long before this." The day had been long, and the short nap after work had helped a little but he could feel the sap in his body seeping.

"You want another beer?" Gerry opened the refrigertor.

He shook his head. Oh, God, here he was being the lump of sod she had left him for being. Well, he couldn't help it. But, at least, he shouldn't be hanging around letting her see how bad it got. "I ought to be going. I'm falling asleep standing here."

"Stick around. You're my last hope." The uncertain movements of her hand around the beer bottle gave away her mood. Something bothered her. The self-possessed façade she maintained with him ever since he knew her in high school was showing its seams. Was Gerry having the same qualms at the ending of their twenty-year effort to raise their children? It was better not to read too much into it. "I mean," she said. "That you're my last hope of getting through a long boring night in the country."

She took a sip of beer and then waited again for some response from him, resting her eyes on his. Being here alone with her stirred something vaguely unsettling in him. Had he also been a partner in making sure they were never alone in a room together? He hoped the voice in his head would stay quiet. He tried to think of something to say to her.

"I have to tell you, Clem," she said. "That's one thing that's always bugged me the most about you…." Oh? So, finally, after all these years she was going to tell him what really lurked under that façade, what it was that drove her away from him. "It's the way you, ever since I first met you, the way you act like you're so much more…what's the word?…self-possessed than everybody else."

"Wha?"

"Like right now. You stand there with that look on your face like you're Miles Davis or somebody. That's the same look you carried around when you first transferred into Mariemont High School your junior year."

"What did you expect, I was fresh out of reform school. I was scared shit of all you cheery-faced, American Bandstand types."

"And now?"

"And now.... I think you're reading it all wrong. Besides, if there's anyone who walks around acting they're above all this, it's you, not me."

She lifted the Heineken bottle and drank without taking her eyes off him. When she put the bottle back on the table, she looked away to another corner of the room, leaning her elbow on the oilcloth cover of the table. "That's because I am. I don't mean above it all, I mean so different than all this." She waved her hand to take in the town, the countryside. "It bores the shit out of me."

"And me, too, huh?"

She looked at him without saying anything, her eyes slowly drifting away. "Yeah, I guess so. You, too." She cupped her chin in her hands, rubbing her eyes with her fingers, then moved her hands down so the fingers covered only her nose and mouth, while she stared at the oilcloth. "That's an awful thing to say, isn't it? But it's true." Her eyes looked up at him without her head moving, a look of pity on her face. "It wasn't always true, though."

"Oh, whoopy. That cheers me right up."

She smiled. "I'm sorry." She rubbed her eyes again as if they itched, the way she always did when she did not want to let herself cry. "There was a time when you were the most exciting thing I could think of. In high school I latched onto you like a fast train out of town. You took me away from...." She waved her hand in the air. "We screwed on top of a moving boxcar, for Christ's sake. Who was ever as romantic as that?" She looked up at him again and they both laughed. "That was the night Dan was conceived, you know that?"

"How could you know that? We did it so much in those days."

"I know that because I want it to be true. Because that was the greatest fuck I ever had in my life, and because Dan was the most beautiful thing I'd ever seen."

"More beautiful than Marty?"

She shook her head, looking away. "No. But by the time Marty came, the boxcar-Dan connection was etched in stone. Marty is just Marty. God love him, I sure do. But Dan was always part of something else. Maybe because he was first. He was my first love."

"Before me?"

She nodded, never taking her eyes away from his. "Before you. It's different, you know? I did not fall in love with you. But I fell in love with Dan. You were....how do I say it? You were a kick, exciting, different."

"A kick? That was it?"

"No. More. When you went away I missed you. But not like if Dan had been taken away. I would have died. And when you came back....yes, I did love you. A lot. I left my husband for you."

"But still, I've been competing with my own son."

"Two sons. You didn't stand a chance, buster." She picked up the beer bottle and wagged it, smiling at him.

He smiled back. That was always something he'd suspected. It was the children that she loved, and him only relative to the them. Yes, she had left her husband for him, but he remembered her telling him at the time that her allegiance had shifted from Orenstein to himself when she saw the depth of his feeling for Dan. It was always about the kids. Here the one great love of his life was not even about him.

Well no shit, dummy. I could've told you that.

"But...." He started to answer the voice but stopped himself. He did not need to answer the voice any longer. It would take him a while to get over it, but the only way he could was to just not answer it. Anyhow it was not even her voice, it was his own, telling him what to do. He knew that. He probably knew it all along, just didn't want to cop to it, like not allowing himself to think about Samantha as being the lovely woman he actually did enjoy having around his house.

"But what?" Gerry said.

"But....I guess I could've told you that years ago."

"Maybe you should have. But you were so busy being Mr. Cool, acting like you didn't care what I did."

"That's not true."

"No, it isn't. I'm not being fair. But I had to guess at it. Buying carpentry tools for my birthday isn't exactly the way to a girl's heart, you know."

"Why not? You bought me tools for my birthday."

"Come on, Clem. Even you are not that obtuse. And a little passion now and then might have made a big difference. A little passion goes a long way, you know."

"Passion? I thought we always did okay in bed. What're you talking about?"

"I'm not talking about sex. I'm talking about love…romance…you know? Christ, maybe I've had too many beers. What the hell am I doing talking to you about romance? Your idea of romance is hanging around in a forest by yourself."

Gerogina's voice came from the stairway in the hall. "Hey. You guys want to pipe down a little? What the hell are you yelling about, anyway?"

"We're not yelling," Gerry yelled.

"Your voice was rising a little there," Scheutz said to her.

"Well, shit." Gerry took another sip of beer. "I forgot what it's like living in small-town New England. "Everyone, please, modulate. Modulate your voices. Modulate your lives.' One decibel over a whisper is what goes for passion up here."

"What about all those times I read to you while you were painting? I thought that was pretty romantic."

"Yeah. I guess. What the hell. And, you know, sometimes I miss that. That nice modulated tone, with your Cincinnati accent that reminds of my home growing up. My mother ran our home the same way she ran the library at school. Everything very dispassionate, very modulated, controlled, organized. A body can only take so much of that, you know." She stared down at the wet rings the beer bottle had made on the oilcloth, then lifted the bottle to repeat the pattern. "Somebody—I forget who it was—said something I read once about creativity, that you can only make art out of the mess of your life. That all art is, how did he say it, 'creating a little island of order in your own sea of chaos'. But, if your life is too organized and modulated, there's not enough mess to create anything out of."

How odd to hear her go on this way. During their whole time together, it seemed to him that they had spent their days trying to clean up the mess of their life. In Mexico, then in Santa Fe, then the short time in Cincinnati, and then the first two years in New Hampshire. Thinking back on it now, he realized that they had come close to a nice stable life in Santa Fe before having to pull up what roots they had out of the sandy New Mexican soil and migrate back to the mid-west. And then, of course, when it seemed they had finally gotten everything under control here in New Hampshire, she ran off to New York.

Hearing her voice in his head all these years had always been when he needed her to help him keep from messing things up, help him modulate life for himself and the kids. How weird was that? Up here he had Gerry's voice helping him keep a lid on things while Gerry herself was down in New York letting all the snakes out of the basket. He'd always thought of her as his civilizing influence, and she wasn't that at all. He could see the pattern now. When she was with him, his life had always seemed fresh in spite of himself. Since she had gone, he had fallen so easily into comfortable routines that kept his life exactly where it was, hidden away from the rest of the world that he had always had such a difficult time dealing with.

Chapter 31

The Rings on the Tree

"Come on," she said. "Let's go for a walk." She plunked the beer bottle down on the oilcloth and stood.

"A walk?"

"Yeah, something. Anything. Let's just get out of here."

He shrugged. "Okay." He felt too tired to go walking, but if that's what she wanted to do, he'd do it with her.

Once outside, assaulted by mosquitoes, she changed her mind. "You know, if we were in the city, we could…"

"We're not in the city."

"Your truck is here, right?"

"No, I came in Samantha's car. It's still parked here, though. She went off to the party with Dan and Livia."

"Well, let's take Samantha's car and…"

"Go where?"

"I don't know, anywhere. Los Angeles? Dusseldorf? Someplace we've never been. God, I just want to do something. Can you believe my own son, my forever-lovable Marty telling me I'm too old to go to his goddamned graduation party?"

"These kids today, huh?"

"Don't make fun of me. I'm feeling particularly old tonight. I can feel my life being pulled out from under me. Like sand on the beach when the surf is rolling out. I'm not on stable ground here."

"You look a little drunk to me."

"Oh Jesus, you're as bad as the mosquitoes. Come on, let's get in the car."

Inside the Saab, Scheutz sat and stared out the windshield into the night. Gerry sat quietly beside him, waiting, he could feel, for him to do something, take her somewhere. An odd sensation, her waiting for him to do something. She was the same person, but not the same person, he'd been so close to all those years. Tonight, just the last half hour, he'd found someone more mercurial than he'd ever know her to be. She may not be drunk, but she was definitely a little tipsy. Any other time, she would be giving orders by now, telling him where to drive. The few times he could remember when they had not both been motivated in the same direction at the same time, he had been content to go along with wherever she wanted to go or whatever she wanted to do.

Her silence in the seat next to him was a little unnerving. He did not want to be the one responsible for saying where they went. Even for an evening's drive to kill a few hours before bed time. It occurred to him now that her willingness to take the lead and his to follow had always been predominant between them. Yes, they had always pulled together, but he felt himself to be the off-horse, the secondary power wheel in the differential of their relationship. And he liked it that way. She was like his older brother, Hank, when they were kids. Hank ran the show, leaving Scheutz and his brother Willi free to relax and enjoy things any way they came. Gerry did that for him in high school, and then later from Mexico on. Until she ran off to New York.

He had never realized that before. But that had always been there between them, so close and so natural to him that it was almost like breathing. Maybe that was why he had never seen it before. Of course it made sense for him to depend on her that way. Look what happened when he did things on his own—that was how he ended up in Cuba, and getting his brother killed. And look what had happened since she'd left him—he ended up working in the woods for ten years.

But he couldn't beat himself up for that. The work in the woods had allowed him what he needed to raise the kids. Now that he did not need it any longer, he could move on.

"Do you have the keys?" Gerry's voice came from her shadow in the passenger seat. It sounded so much like the one in his head.

"Yeah, they're in the ignition."

"Oh, that's right. I forgot. Nobody ever takes their keys out of their ignition up here. That's one of the few things I liked about this place when I lived here."

"So, where do you want to go?"

"You pick."

"I…can't," he said.

"And that is another one of the many things I did not like about living here."

"Boy, you're really slamming me tonight, aren't you?"

"I'm sorry, I don't mean to." They sat in silence again for what seemed like the longest time yet. A whole herd of angels passing through. Finally, she said in almost a whisper, "It's just…I don't know. I'm having a really hard time with all this. Marty growing up. I'm not handling it well. I brought Jerome with me as a diversion from all this. No, not from all this, from myself. And he is not a twit like you said; he's just young, and nervous with you around. Stands to reason he'd measure himself against you. Isn't that what all you guys do?

"I'm glad he ran off to the kids' party. If he was sitting in the seat where you are, I'd be blaming him for all this. That's the one great function people like him serve in this world." Another long silence. "You're seeing an ugly side of me, Clem."

"Well, you're a little drunk. Maybe you say things like that when you're drunk. That's also a side I've never seen. You drink much in New York?"

"No. I don't drink at all. This is a first, that's how bad it is."

A car came down the highway behind them, its headlights flicking, illuminating them both as it pulled into the parking lot. Goncharov. She pointed the high beams directly at them, parked the car nose to nose with the Saab and got out. Like a she-bear prowling a campsite, she walked around to the driver's side window, bending and peering in at them. Scheutz left the windows up. He had no interest in talking with Goncharov, and had no intention of even being polite to the woman. He kept his face forward and slid his eyes to meet hers as she put her face almost against the window. He had expected to see fury in the Russian's face, but all it showed was pain.

She turned and walked around the back of the Saab, appearing on the passenger side. If anything, the pain had deepened on her trip around the car. Bending down to where she needed to look up to scrutinize Gerry's face, she looked reminded Scheutz of Marty's yowls of pain the time he had pulled a splinter out of his son's palm. Inconsolable agony. He had a fleeting urge to take the Russian bear on his lap and let her cry until the poison had all been drained from her system.

"Wow," Gerry said as Goncharov, apparently satisfied that Nanda was not in the car, lumbered back to her own. "Wow. That's about the ugliest woman I've ever seen."

"Kinda spooky, huh? How does that country western song go? 'Lookin' for love in all the wrong places'."

"Can we get out of here?"

"Yeah, okay." He started the car. Goncharov had backed up and turned onto the highway in the same direction she came.

"You sure you want to go out somewhere?" he asked her. "I know you say you want to distract yourself, but you don't look capable of amusing yourself right now."

"Help me out here, will you, Clem? Don't make fun of me. Let's just go."

"Where?"

"Anywhere, I don't care. Where would you like to go?"

"Home."

"Home? Okay, let's go home. Your home."

"Dan and Marty's home."

She began to cry. Her body shook suddenly. She put her face in her hands and sobbed through her fingers. "Yes, Dan and Marty's home." When she was able to control herself again, she dropped her hands. "All these years, I've always told myself that I would someday—soon—make a good home for them again, and they would come and live with me, and...and now it's too late. I will never...be able to...never be able to be a real mother to my children...ever again." Her sobs increased, her head and shoulders bobbing as the tears fell into her lap. "What did I do, Clem?"

He reached across the seat and laid a hand on her shoulder. "You did just fine, babe. Those guys are wonderful. They could not have turned out better than they did. Really."

"Thanks." She leaned her head to the side and squeezed his hand between her head and shoulder. "But I missed so much. It use to kill me going back to the city after visiting here. And when they came for the summer, or Christmas, or whatever, it tore me up to put them on the train. I know they're wonderful, but I missed so much."

"You have Dan in the city."

"It's not the same. Yeah, it's great, but...he was my baby. And I know this is crazy, but I wish he still was." She fell quiet again, snuffling. What she was saying was not crazy. He had had the same thoughts. Whenever Dan came into his dreams at night, Dan was always about four years old. And Marty, too. If they were in one of his dreams together, which they often were, they were both the same age, about four. That was the age when they were still part of you, just before they became separate identities.

"That time before you came back," Gerry continued in a soft, nose-clogged voice. "That time when I was first married to Orenstein, when it was Dan and I against everybody? Against Orenstein, against my mother, just the two of us. God, that was great. That time was the closest I've come to living in the state of grace. And then you showed up, you bum."

"You looked like you were in the state of grace in those days. I'll never forget you coming down that staircase. And I could do nothing but stand in awe."

She laughed. "Yeah, I remember. Your mouth hanging open like an unclogged sewer drain. Dan wasn't the only reason I left Orenstein and came to find you. Nobody has ever, in my whole life, looked at me like that."

He laughed with her. "I would have ridden my gaunt nag into battle for just so much as a nod of your head."

"And look at me now."

"You're still holding up. I mean for an old drunk."

"Can we get out of here?"

"Where?"

"Just go."

He drove onto the highway, turning off on Route 123, and then in the center of town, up the hill to home. Coming up the long driveway, the house and barn loomed like dark two-dimensional shadows on the crest of the hill. He parked next to his pick-up truck and they walked silently through the dark to the kitchen door. A gentle summer breeze blew up over the hay field, bringing with it the scent of the first mowing.

"Got any beer in the fridge?" she asked as he turned on the kitchen light.

"Not for you. You want some coffee?"

She sighed. "Yeah, I suppose." While he put the coffee on, she sat in his chair by the now cold wood stove and picked up Nanda's book on Zoroastrian religion he had been reading the night before. "Still reading all this religious stuff, huh?"

"Yeah. I find it interesting." He put milk from the refrigerator in her coffee and handed her the cup.

"Thanks," she said. "You're not having any?"

"I'm going to have a cup of tea."

"So, what's so interesting about these religions?"

"This one's one of the oldest religions around. Goes back before the Bible. In fact, the Jews, at least the Bible guys, copied a lot of their stuff from these folks. Things like the Garden of Eden and Noah and the flood, all those stories. That kind of stuff is interesting to me."

The way he had let Gerry into his head was kind of like a religion. In the early years, when they lived together, he had let her make the decisions. In the latter years, he continued to ask her voice to lead him. Just the way people let a prophet lead them. In ancient times, before the bibles, before the Pharoahs, before Ahura Mazda, people followed the decisions of their leader and when the leader died, the people made him divine, and hallucinated his voice so he could continue to lead them. That's what Scheutz had done, like some devoted acolyte in the aerial temple of Gerry Rieker. *Notre Dame des Bois.*

He brought his tea cup to his lips, leaning with his back against the counter, watching her as she sipped her coffee and thumbed through the book. She had always been what he needed. Even when she was gone. Even though their relationship had been so unbalanced—he was orbital to her, as she was central to him—she had kept him on the right path in the pathless woods. And he loved her for that.

She stopped flipping pages and read a short paragraph, then looked up at him and smiled. It was not a particularly big smile, not like something in the book had struck her funny. He had to smile back. They both lingered there for an extra beat longer than they would normally have. And that one beat gave him everything he needed from her.

Everything. Did that mean it was over? Was there nothing else he would ever need from her? He could feel the anger rise up behind his eyes. The tea he sipped turned bitter in his mouth. He watched her with her head bent, reading the book. The anger had nothing to with her. It was not her he was angry at. Gerry was just Gerry. She had never done anything to harm him. Her leaving him was something she needed to do for herself, not something she did against him.

He did not have to not be angry for her sake anymore. He could just be as pissed off as he pleased. What a glorious feeling that was. He didn't have to hit anyone or break anything, he could just be angry and leave it at that. Like Orpheus, he suddenly ascended into the land of the living. He no longer needed Gerry's acceptance of him. He did not need her to tell him how to live his life, or raise the children, or how he should feel about something, whether he could be angry or not. He could do all that himself.

The opening of the outside door startled him. And there was Samantha. "Oh, I'm sorry," she said, looking back and forth from him to Gerry. "I thought you were staying over with Sharna's mom," she said to Gerry.

"I am. I'm just not sleepy yet."

Samantha turned to look at Scheutz. "That state cop, what's his name?"

"Johnstone."

"Johnstone. He dropped me off. We went to Georgina's Café to get my car, but it wasn't there, so I figured it would be here. You wouldn't believe what happened."

"What happened?"

"Freddie. He's in the hospital. I'm still kind of shook up."

She did look a little pale and shaky. He felt the urge to put his arms around her again, as he had at the party. Was this going to be his new obsession? "What happened to Freddie?"

"He smashed his truck. I could've been killed. But the truck hit the tree on the driver's side and I was thrown out into the ditch."

He held his stance at the counter. Gerry closed the book and asked if Dan or Marty had been in the truck.

"No. Just me. God, I hate him. That's it, I'm never going to talk to the prick again."

"You hate him for wrecking his truck?" Gerry asked.

"No, I hate him for why his truck got wrecked in the first place." She looked away from Gerry and said to Scheutz, "He's just such a shit. He was saying all this stuff about you, about how you were crazy and all, and we got into this big fight again, and he said how he was going to come over here and beat the shit out of you. And I tried to stop him and jumped into his truck before he could drive away. And then he was screaming at me and went off the road and smashed into that big oak tree, you know, down at the bottom of the hill in South Acworth."

"Will he be all right?"

"I guess. You know how drunk people are, they never get hurt much. I'm really lucky he hit the tree on his side. The ambulance guy said he probably had a broken leg and a few broken ribs." She went to sit at the table, put face in her hands and began to cry.

"I'm glad you weren't hurt," Gerry said. "But I've been telling you for years now, Samantha, you have to get away from that guy."

Samantha looked up at Scheutz through her tears. Turning back to Gerry, she nodded her head in resolution. "You're right."

Gerry laid the book on the floor next to the chair and stood. She walked across the room and stood in front of Scheutz. She looked into his eyes and then held out her arms for him to hug her. He put down his teacup and stood straight, and without a word put his arms around her. She squeezed him and held him there. "I'm going to go," she said. "I guess I'm not the fun party girl I like to think I am. All that beer doesn't make me drunk; it just makes me sleepy."

He let her go.

She stepped back and turned to Samantha. "Are you okay to drive?" Samantha nodded. "Could you drop me off at Georgina's on your way home?"

Samantha's head bobbed. She wiped her eyes and stood.

"Or do you want to sit and talk for a while till you feel better?'

"No, I'm okay. I'm just....I'm just so mad. I really mean it about Freddie. I'm getting out of here." She stopped. Gerry and Scheutz waited, watching her. She looked up at first Gerry and then Scheutz and began crying harder. "My brother Joe is going off to college. And Dan and Marty will be gone. And I'll be..."

"And you'll have the whole world. Whatever you wanto do." Gerry put arms around Samantha, who buried head into Gerry's shoulder. Gerry raised her eyes to the ceiling the way Marty often did, with alook that said she felt bad for Samantha and at the same time wishing she would just get on with it, already.

Samantha finally stopped sobbing and pulled away toward the door. "Goodnight, Mister. Scheutz," she said.

"Goodnight, Samantha. Maybe tomorrow we can talk about where you might go. You know, to start a new life. I've got to start doing the same thing. Maybe we could help each other out."

Samantha nodded and walked to the door. Gerry followed, but turned to him before stepping out.

"You going to be all right?" Gerry asked Scheutz.

He nodded. And then smiled at her. "Maybe I'll show up in New York again come Christmas."

"And maybe this time I'll look forward to it."

When the door closed he put the cups in the sink, turned out the lights, except for the one over the sink he always left on for Marty. Then he made his way upstairs, brushed his teeth in the bathroom, and used the toilet. In his bedroom, he undressed and, before getting into bed closed the window. The night had gotten chilly just like the previous night. He got into bed and lay listening to the silence. He was tired, very tired, but his mind raced. Today was like a tree ring that made you notice the growth and the passage of time. He floated in the quiet of the house, and of the countryside surrounding it. If he left here, the one thing he would miss would be the quiet.

And the woods. Back before the Christians, the people who lived in the woods believed that the gods lived in the trees, in the rings of the trees. He could feel himself drifting down into sleep. Tomorrow would be the start of a new ring, a new life. He could do anything he wanted. That thought was a little scary. Since he had no idea what he wanted. And especially since he did not have Gerry's voice or Gerry herself to tell him what he wanted. Maybe he would leave Acworth. Give the house to Gerry and the kids so they could come back here whenever they liked. He'd like to go back to the Carribean, or to Mexico. And, what the hell, maybe he'd take Samantha with him. Why not?